P
The Library of Lost I

"A straitlaced San Francisco li
of characters in Hooper's latest, which jumps from modern day to Belle Époque Paris before taking off like a rocket through the twentieth century."

—Fiona Davis, *New York Times* bestselling author
of *The Stolen Queen*

"*The Library of Lost Dollhouses* is impressively shape-shifting. It's a story that ranges over a century and continents, but it's also a portrait of the artist as a young—and not so young— woman. It's a coming-of-age tale—two, in fact—but it's also a beguiling mystery. And in every incarnation, it's as inspiring and extravagantly detailed as the miniatures at its heart."

—Laurie Frankel, *New York Times* bestselling author
of *Family Family*

"Who would have guessed the transformative secrets a long-forgotten dollhouse could hold? In Elise Hooper's wonderful *The Library of Lost Dollhouses*, librarian Tildy Barrows discovers two mysterious miniature realms. As Tildy solves the dollhouses' mysteries, she also answers long-standing questions about herself in this compelling tale."

—Marie Benedict, *New York Times* bestselling author
of *The Queens of Crime*

"Elise Hooper's latest marvel takes readers on an enchanting journey from San Francisco to Paris, love to war, deception to redemption, as her main character—a little-known artist—moves out of the shadows into the limelight."

—Janet Skeslien Charles, *New York Times* bestselling author
of *The Paris Library*

"Elise Hooper's latest heartwarming novel, *The Library of Lost Dollhouses*, is as intricately detailed as a dollhouse itself and full of remarkable heroines, from twentieth-century ones who bravely made history happen to modern ones drawing inspiration from their efforts."

—Natalie Jenner, internationally bestselling author
of *The Jane Austen Society*

Also by Elise Hooper

Angels of the Pacific

Fast Girls

Learning to See

The Other Alcott

The Library of Lost Dollhouses

A Novel

ELISE HOOPER

WILLIAM MORROW
An Imprint of HarperCollins*Publishers*

HarperCollins books may be purchased for educational, business, or sales promotional use. For information, please email the Special Markets Department at SPsales@harpercollins.com.

FIRST EDITION

Interior text design by Diahann Sturge-Campbell
House illustration © anna42f/Stock.Adobe.com

Library of Congress Cataloging-in-Publication Data has been applied for.

ISBN 978-0-06-338214-5
ISBN 978-0-06-342757-0 (hardcover)
ISBN 978-0-06-343621-3 (international edition)

25 26 27 28 29 LBC 5 4 3 2 1

For Becky Gannon,
my good friend and fellow miniac

Prologue

New Hampshire, 1950

The woman steps back from her workbench, surveying the completed boxy wooden structure. It's a shell, not yet a doll-house. Tomorrow, piece by piece, clapboard siding and roofing will be applied. After that, windows, shutters, doors, and a chimney will be installed. Then the dollhouse maker will turn to the interior. She'll wire the place for electricity. Then she'll carve and cut baseboards, millwork, tiling, trim, and flooring. But before she installs any of these pieces, she'll place sheets of wallpaper in every room, making sure to use the right amount of paste. Too much and the paper will grow soggy and wrinkle. Too little will cause peeling. Each sheet has been designed for a specific wall within the dollhouse. Their placement is important, because the patterns tell a secret story.

The miniaturist stretches her arms overhead and exhales. Late-afternoon sunshine spills across the plank floor of her workshop like maple syrup sliding from a spoon, making the air warm and languorous. The sweetened scent of the forest rises from freshly milled pine. When she lowers her arms, a nearby stack of mail in a basket catches her gaze. Letters from prospective clients. How do these women find her? Word of her dollhouses and their secrets travels on whispers over the rims of teacups, the steps of front porches, and across kitchen tables and market counters. Until the dollhouse maker delved into the world of keeping other women's secrets, she had no idea there were so many possibilities: women write books and articles and publish them under men's names; they print and distribute subversive newspapers anonymously; they covertly offer illicit medical services to those in need; they bear children they cannot claim as their own; they spend years developing inventions, only to have them stolen by men.

The dollhouse maker documents all this—accomplishments, betrayals, and forbidden passions—in her miniatures.

Her clients' stories are sometimes haunting, often heartbreaking, but always powerful and inspiring. The dollhouse maker feels solidarity with these perfectly lovely women and their imperfect lives, because she hides her own secret, one not recorded in any dollhouse. She's learned to push away her own shame. Her penance comes in the form of unburdening other women of the truths they hide.

At this moment, the dollhouse maker exists solely in the service of her client from Arlington, Virginia, a seemingly ordinary woman. The wife of a newspaper reporter. A mother of three.

Eventually, when the miniaturist reveals the finished product to her client, the woman will peer inside its six rooms. The miniaturist will hand her a magnifying glass and point to the parlor.

At first glance, the woman will only see swaths of flowers running along walls. When her vision adjusts to the magnification, she'll see how the dollhouse maker has taken her encrypted story and used its tiny collection of letters and numbers. From a distance, the small points blur together to create the wallpaper print.

This client has been deciphering messages since the early '40s. Except for the dollhouse maker and the officials who oversee her work, no one knows about her secret vocation. Her husband believes she takes in typing assignments and thinks the couriers who come and go from their house are from a law office in Washington, D.C., not from the US government.

During their initial meeting, when the client worried someone would spot the strange pattern hidden in the wallpaper, the dollhouse maker reassured her: no one will notice. Secrets can exist in plain sight because people only see what they expect. Sad, but true.

The dollhouse maker has employed a variety of techniques to conceal her clients' stories in the dollhouses. Secret compartments, fake walls, tiny books, furniture with camouflaged panels, but never before has she designed a pattern with code. She's particularly proud of this deception and is already eager to show her client the finished product.

But that will have to wait.

For now, with the miniature's carcass complete, the dollhouse maker is done working for the day. She sweeps up shavings, splinters, and dust, then reaches behind her to untie the heavy canvas apron she wears.

As she's switching off lights, preparing to leave for the evening, the shrill ring of the telephone startles her. When she reaches for its receiver, she has no idea how her life is about to change. She'll journey to a new place. Unload her secrets. And rediscover her first love.

1
Tildy

2024

No one knew a secret room existed in the library until Tildy Barrows found it.

The discovery occurred on Monday, February 26, at 8:21 a.m., a time when Tildy would have normally been sitting at her desk in her office, cup of coffee in hand, reviewing her day's schedule and fretting over how to dig the Belva Curtis LeFarge Library out of the deep financial hole it currently found itself in.

Instead, Tildy was inside a storage closet on the library's top floor, preoccupied with organizing several vintage gowns and accessories once owned by the place's founder, Belva Curtis LeFarge. As Tildy slid a fox stole onto a hanger, a glimmer of something metallic flashing behind swirls of tulle crinolines and taffeta ball gowns caught her attention. Intrigued, she pushed the garments aside, squinting into the dim light.

A latch.

Alongside the latch, a crack in the wall appeared. *What in the world?* Tildy reached out, tracing her index finger along the crack, and when she stepped closer for a better look she realized the crack was actually a doorway.

As head curator, she was supposed to know every square inch of the Belva Curtis LeFarge Library and she took her job seriously. To call her *hands-on* was an understatement. Tildy managed all aspects of running the small historic institution. She gave tours. Oversaw acquisitions. Called a repairman when there was a problem with the furnace or air-conditioning system. In fact, atop her desk, Tildy kept a bullet journal outlining every task of her day. By the time she left the library each evening, she made it her mission to cross off every item on that to-do list. For Tildy, no task at the library was too small, too lowly.

So how could she have missed this door? Books, paintings, periodicals, journals, films, ephemera, vintage clothes, music, maps, manuscripts, even an old bear claw necklace from the Lewis and Clark expedition could be found at the library. But a hidden door? This was a first.

Tildy rubbed her eyes. She really needed coffee.

THE MORNING had started normally enough. Tildy was a big believer in the stabilizing power of routines. During the years of her father's illness, she'd learned the best way to mitigate his cognitive deterioration was through a carefully followed daily schedule, so she now applied the same practice to her own life. That Monday she'd arrived at the library at her usual time—7:30 a.m. sharp—and started the coffee machine behind the circulation counter, but when she got to her desk and prepared to settle in, she heard a strange sound. A distant rumble, deep and low like thunder. The noise quickly intensified, groaning and grinding, and then ended in a long, exhausted hiss. Tildy twisted to look out the nearest window and there in the middle of the street, a bright yellow school bus had stopped crookedly, its front bumper enveloped in smoke. The vehicle's positioning was obviously worrisome, but when Tildy looked closer and spotted wide-eyed little faces filling the bus's windows, she leapt from her desk chair and raced outside. The pungent stink of burning rubber hovered over the library's courtyard. Though it was a chilly morning in late February, Tildy didn't even feel the cold. As she neared the bus, its door folded open, revealing the driver's weary face.

"What happened?" Tildy asked, pulling her phone from her pocket, ready to call 911.

"Might be something to do with the fuel filter," the driver grumbled.

From the front seat a small girl raised her hand. "I need to use the bathroom."

"You'll have to hold it, Saffron," the driver said.

Tildy looked beyond the small girl, assessing the rest of the worried little faces watching her expectantly. Tending to a school bus breakdown had definitely not been on her to-do list for the day and that quick burst of adrenaline she'd felt only moments earlier was already wearing off. She needed coffee. But these were elementary school kids. Twenty-four of them, to be precise.

An older girl in the second row turned her head to look through the smudged window at the library. "Whoa, fancy."

"That building looks like a wedding cake," the girl sitting next to her added. The other kids turned, intrigued by the mention of dessert. The girl was right. In the crisp winter sunlight, the white limestone of the three-story rectangular library gleamed like vanilla buttercream, carefully smoothed with a pastry spatula and sprinkled with cane sugar. To the imaginative eye, the decorative garlands, classical pilasters, and Corinthian columns festooning the facade could have been piped into place by a skilled baker.

Set amid the gleaming, newly renovated, seismically reinforced mansions of Pacific Heights, the Belva Curtis LeFarge Library clung to a ridge, overlooking Cow Hollow and the Marina. Its picturesque placement and grande old dame charm made it popular with tourists as a top spot to snap an iconic shot of the San Francisco Bay. Many people admired the lovely old Beaux-Arts building, but for those types who preferred sleek industrial design and minimalism—and San Francisco teemed with those types—they considered the library unfashionable and long in the tooth.

The sounds of children chattering brought Tildy's attention back to the bus.

She turned to the driver. "I'm Mathilda Barrows, the head curator at the Belva Curtis LeFarge Library. How about the kids come inside with me so you can sort things out? I'm used to having school field trips, and they'll love having the place to themselves before it opens to the public. It'll be just like *From the Mixed-up Files of Mrs. Basil E. Frankweiler.*" She smiled.

The reference to one of Tildy's all-time favorite books went nowhere with the bus driver, but there was no time to be disappointed because the little girl named Saffron piped up again.

"Hello! I *really* need to pee."

The bus driver hauled herself to her feet, placed her hands on her hips, and faced out toward her young passengers. "Kids, here's the deal: while I figure out what's up with this bus, you're all going inside this library with Ms.—" The driver looked at Tildy expectantly.

"Barrows. Ms. Barrows," Tildy filled in.

"Go with Ms. Barrows and if I get any reports of disrespectful behavior, and I'm talking about *anything*—I promise you, there will be consequences. Everyone got it?"

The students nodded and filed off the bus as Tildy recounted them—still twenty-four in total.

"Welcome to the Belva Curtis LeFarge Library," she announced, walking backward in full tour guide mode.

"The Bella *what*?" asked one boy, pulling a goofy face that made the other kids giggle.

"I know, it's a mouthful, right? But here's a little tip: most of us just call it the Bel." Tildy propped open the heavy oak front door. "Go ahead and leave your coats and backpacks in the foyer. And guess what? Since we have the place to ourselves, you don't have to use your quiet library voices."

She expected to see immediate excitement, but the kids just shuffled past, yawning. Tildy frowned. Tough crowd.

All was quiet in the library except the rustling of jackets and the occasional squeak of sneakers. As the kids took in the shiny marble floors and paintings lining the walls—a glorious abstract seascape by Valadon and minimalist desert landscape by O'Keeffe—they straightened from their slouches and stopped rubbing their drippy noses and picking their wedgies. Tildy had seen this before, the Bel's effect on its visitors. Say what you want about old buildings and the headache of maintaining them, but the fact remains: they make an impression.

While Saffron and three others skittered to the bathroom, the rest of the kids milled around the foyer.

"Hey, a dog!" a boy called. The other students quickly gathered to see what the commotion was about.

"You found Gruffy," Tildy said, joining them and pointing at the brass statue. "See that golden patch on his snout? If you pat Gruffy right there, it's good luck."

"Why's he here?" one of the kids asked.

"The library's founder had a beloved French bulldog for many years. When Gruffy died, she had a statue made of him to stand guard over the place."

"He's cute," a girl said, patting the worn spot. "For such a little dog, his ears were pretty big."

Tildy agreed. "If you keep your eyes peeled, you might find statues of more animals."

"More? How many pets did this Belva lady have?"

"Gruffwood was the only one," Tildy said. "But she liked animals."

"Even in her library?"

"Belva was an unusual lady. She liked to do things her own way," Tildy explained, launching into her usual tour guide spiel. "Her grandfather was one of the principal investors in the transcontinental railroad, so she was very wealthy and grew up in a big house, not far from here on Nob Hill. During the 1906 earthquake, that house burned down, but Belva wasn't there because she'd moved to Europe. While traveling through Paris, she met the man of her dreams—a handsome aristocrat, Comte LeFarge—and she married him. It was just like a fairy tale."

The kids had stopped patting the dog and were watching Tildy, intrigued.

"Belva and her husband lived in a big, beautiful house in Paris and had a baby boy, but then tragedy struck. Her beloved husband died, so she and her son moved back here to channel their grief into helping the community by building this library. It was finished in 1926, and she lived here until she died."

"Wait, she lived here *and* it was a library? Could anyone just walk in?" a boy asked.

"During the library's open hours, sure."

"She lived here surrounded by books? Are you for real?" another boy asked.

"I am. Her private apartment was on the top floor."

"Hold up." An older girl placed a hand on her hip. "If she had enough money to build this place, why didn't she build a separate house too?"

Tildy shrugged, smiling. "Don't you think this would be a cool place to live?"

The kids considered this.

"Do you live here?" one girl asked.

"I wish."

"You should. You'd be just like Belle from *Beauty and the Beast*. She lived in a big fancy old house filled with books and art. And you kinda look like her," the girl said, smiling, pleased with her own logic.

The others agreed, nodding excitedly.

Tildy ran her fingers self-consciously through her ordinary shoulder-length brown hair, embarrassed by how delighted the girl's compliment made her feel. Clad in her usual basic black pants and navy button-up shirt, she was about as far as you could get from resembling a Disney princess, but she'd imagined herself living in the Bel many times.

She leaned closer to the kids and, in a conspiratorial tone, whispered, "Well, if I did live here, *this* is where I'd spend all my time."

And with that, Tildy stepped backward into the Main Reading Room, swooping her hands like a magician letting a hidden dove take flight. The kids reacted exactly as she'd hoped: they let out a collective gasp and took a few steps closer to her, turning in circles, gaping at the triple-tiered, intricately carved dark cherry bookshelves filling the west wall; the arcade-styled balconies on the east and north side of the space; and the rows and rows of classic study desks on the ground floor. Slowly their gazes traveled three stories upward to the brilliant stained glass overhead.

"Magical, isn't it?" Tildy was not normally someone prone to hyperbole, but in the case of the stained-glass ceiling, "magical" was entirely appropriate.

Of the Bel's many charms, certainly one of its most notable was the Main Reading Room's art nouveau–style stained-glass ceiling. At that time of morning, dazzling fingers of pale sunlight flexed through the ceiling's intricate pattern of colorful flowers, leaves, and birds, bathing the room below in a rainbow of gold, emerald, coral, cobalt, rose, cerulean, and salmon.

Mesmerized, the kids fell silent, but an impatient throat clearing soon broke the spell. "Uh, Ms. Barrows?"

Tildy turned to find the bus driver, hand on hip, standing in the library's foyer. "The bus is running again. I gotta get these kids to school."

"Okay." Tildy was gratified to hear disappointed grumbles from the kids. "Saffron and a few others went to the bathroom, so let me hurry them along."

As Tildy jogged across the Main Reading Room to the front hallway, the sound of laughter reached her, but it seemed to be coming from overhead, not from the closest ground-floor bathroom. Where had the kids gone? Tildy hurried up a flight of stairs, and then another, following the giggles and whispers to the Map Room on the top floor, a space that once served as Belva's private apartment.

There, she found little Saffron and three of her classmates gathered around an open storage closet. One boy crouched over a fox stole lying on the ground, assessing it warily, while another girl held up a peach-colored 1950s satin ball gown, admiring it. At the sight of Tildy, their youthful smiles collapsed into guilty expressions.

"This door was open, I swear it was!" the girl holding the vintage dress whimpered. The other kids backed away from the closet, leaving its contents strewn on the floor.

Tildy took the dress and gently placed it on a nearby bench. She could scarcely blame them for being curious. After all, what was the point of a library if not to encourage curiosity? Also, she admired their daring. At their age, she would never have broken away from the group. With her little *Harriet the Spy* notebook in hand, young Tildy would have clung close to the tour guide, eagerly taking notes as if preparing for a quiz.

Despite the kids' protests, she guided them back to the library's foyer, where they reconvened with the rest of the group. Tildy waved goodbye, suddenly sad. She liked having the energy of children in the library, even if they hadn't exactly followed her directions. But there was no time to dwell. It was already 8:15 a.m., and Tildy was terribly behind on her morning routine.

She hastened back to the Map Room planning to clean up the mess before getting down to the day's business.

AND THAT was how she'd ended up in the top-floor storage closet, staring at a mysterious door. It looked like a pocket door, the kind that slides into the wall. Also, the doorway was big, far wider than the traditional size.

This was no utilitarian entry to a crawl space. For one thing, a detailed geometric pattern of lines and swirls embellished the door's latch, giving it a gothic aura of consequence and mystery. (Tildy would learn, in fact, it was a Windsor pattern, a Victorian classic.) Tildy paused, intuiting this represented a momentous juncture, a threshold that would always demark a *before* and *after* in her life. Deep in her bones, even at 8:20 a.m., she knew the hidden door was significant—extraordinary even.

She took a breath and tamping down the nerves humming inside her, she reached for the brass latch and threw her weight behind it, sliding the door back to reveal a dark opening. She expected to feel the pressing heat of a sun-warmed attic, but the air was cool, surprisingly fresh. Before stepping inside, she ran her palm along the wall in search of a light switch: once located, she flipped it on. A line of overhead recessed bulbs illuminated the space.

Tildy crossed the threshold and found a small narrow room with a lone shuttered window at the distant end. Two large objects encased in canvas coverings stood between Tildy and the far window.

She approached the first large covered object, noting it was atop a sturdy, well-crafted mahogany cabinet. Cautiously, Tildy lifted the edge of the canvas and found herself peering into a window.

A miniature window.

Like Alice in Wonderland, Tildy felt a dizzying sense of shifting perspective, as if she'd drunk an unlabeled potion and grown to a tremendous size. Gingerly, she eased the canvas cover off and stepped backward, inhaling sharply as she surveyed her discovery.

It was a dollhouse. A *magnificent* dollhouse.

The neoclassical dollhouse exterior was designed to look like stone. Recognition flickered through Tildy. She knew this building from old photos. It was a re-creation of Hôtel LeFarge, the Paris mansion where Belva had once lived during her marriage in the early 1900s. Tildy circled the miniature and found an open backside revealing interior rooms—thirteen of them. She gasped in delight. Tiny paintings dotted the dollhouse's walls. Bejeweled chandeliers resembling finely crafted jewelry hung from the ceilings. And the millwork! Elegant wainscoting panels with crisp corners, carved mantels and ceiling canopies, and crown molding daintier than babies' teeth decorated the rooms.

On the dollhouse's bottom floor, Tildy spotted a kitchen, its walls covered in tiny white hexagonal tiles. Shelves were filled with copper pots and pans, thimble-size porcelain storage canisters, and jars of pickled vegetables and fruits that looked amazingly real despite being minute in size. Extraordinary. In the other rooms, Tildy recognized several paintings that now hung in the Bel, here in miniature. The dollhouse had a library on its second floor. Rows and rows of miniature books lined its shelves, and a model of a schooner, its rigging as delicate as spiderweb filament, was displayed on a table. Nearby was an elaborately decorated floor globe smaller than a golf ball. The details were incredible, the craftsmanship mind-boggling. *Why was this hidden away?*

A wave of nostalgia crested over Tildy. She must have been six or seven years old when her mother surprised her at Christmas with a kit for a dollhouse resembling one of San Francisco's Victorian Painted Ladies. Tildy had spent many hours snuggled up beside her mother in an alcove off the kitchen, building the four-room dollhouse and furnishing it. Later, during Tildy's first year in college, her mother had died, so working on the dollhouse that dark, rainy Bay Area winter represented nothing but happy memories.

Heart pounding with excitement, Tildy turned to the second dollhouse. It was colossal: four stories high. To remove the cover, she had to rise to the tips of her toes. Once revealed, it reminded Tildy of the type of grand country estate she'd seen on *Downton Abbey* or in a Jane Austen movie adaptation. Unlike Belva's Hôtel LeFarge, Tildy couldn't identify whether the second enormous dollhouse was a replica of a real house or simply a flight of Belva's imagination.

Latches held the larger dollhouse's facade panels in place, and Tildy opened them one by one, peering into the structure from different sides. Thirty rooms! She had no idea a dollhouse could be so big and elaborate.

In the grand dollhouse's main entrance, past a line of tiny tarnished suits of armor standing guard, a grand staircase swept up to a second-floor gallery, where old master–style miniature portraits and landscapes in baroque gilt frames covered the walls. An enfilade of sumptuous staterooms led from one to the next with grandiose furniture small enough to fit on Tildy's palm. The precision of the artistry staggered her.

The excitement of discovery was as intoxicating as swilling an entire bottle of champagne.

These weren't children's toys.

They were works of art.

Tildy felt light-headed with excitement as she surveyed her findings.

But why were these dollhouses hidden?

Tildy's fingers worried the buttons of her shirt as she stepped back to take in the two dollhouses together. Only then did she notice the drawers in the cabinet below the Hôtel LeFarge dollhouse. In the top, she found more miniatures organized into tiny wooden compartments. Paintings, textiles, chairs, dishes—all kinds of additional miniatures, including Christmas decorations like a tree, wreaths, and wrapped presents. To think of the dollhouse decorated for the holidays made Tildy smile. When she opened the second drawer, another organizer became visible, each of its compartments filled with more dollhouse furnishings. Belva had been quite the collector.

Tildy pushed the drawers back in, straightening, and that's when one miniature in particular caught her eye. On the dollhouse's top floor, she recognized a familiar chair in Belva's bedroom. The Bel still possessed the original full-size art nouveau–styled bergère, upholstered in salmon velvet, down one flight of stairs in the library's Conservatory. The chair had reportedly been Belva's favorite spot to read and there were photos in the library's collection of their patron seated in the chair, her nose buried in a book. Tildy's gaze continued to roam the miniature room. Over the bed hung another item Tildy recognized: a stylized studio portrait of Jack, Belva's son, photographed by Dorothea Lange in the late '20s. The full-size print hung behind the circulation desk on the library's first floor. Tildy squinted, admiring how it had been scaled down and re-created so effectively in black-and-white pen-and-ink to resemble a photograph.

Tildy's gaze traveled to another small framed picture next to Belva's bed. As Tildy stared at the familiar piece, she felt the blood drain from her face. The hair on the back of her neck stood on end. In a room filled with surprises, nothing had prepared her for this discovery. Her legs suddenly went rubbery.

The girl in the picture was Tildy's dead mother.

2
Tildy

2024

Tildy gaped at the miniaturized sketch of her late mother, searching the heart-shaped face for answers. Over the course of her thirty-four years, Tildy had only seen one childhood image of her mother, and now, unexpectedly it had turned up in Belva's dollhouse. *Why? What was it doing here?*

The original portrait was an eight-by-ten-inch pastel sketch of Tildy's late mother, Meg Leigh Barrows, from when she'd been twelve years old. As the one item to survive a house fire during Meg's girlhood, it was now Tildy's prized possession and rested on a bookshelf back at her apartment.

Tildy stared at the miniaturized sketch. Even in small form, her mother's dark wide-set eyes appeared large and lifelike and lent her a surprised and curious expression. Tildy recognized her own pointy chin and the same shy mannerism of tucking it down when she smiled.

Every cord, every muscle, *everything* seemed to be tightening in Tildy. She didn't know how to feel, what to think. Why wasn't she more excited? Tildy had never liked surprises very much. Slowly, she stepped away from the dollhouse and took a deep breath, willing her brain to connect all these unexpected discoveries into a cohesive narrative—the hidden room, the dollhouses, and now this miniature of her mother.

Coffee. She stifled a yawn. Coffee would help.

With trembling fingers, Tildy gently removed the miniature

from the dollhouse and slipped it into the breast pocket of her button-up shirt. She then hurried from the hidden room and took the stairs to the ground floor, where she beelined to the coffee maker in the kitchenette behind the circulation desk, poured herself a generous helping, and topped it all off with cream from the nearby fridge. Mindful of the heat, she took a careful sip, swallowed, and sighed with relief. *Finally.* Order felt restored, at least for a minute or two.

Tildy was exiting the kitchenette when she ran into a trio of librarians wearing their work clothes with running shoes and carrying paper coffee cups from a nearby roastery. When the first one spotted Tildy, she yanked her phone from her pocket in alarm.

"What time is it? Are we late?" the woman asked.

"No, no, it's not even nine yet," Tildy answered.

"What's wrong then? Are you sick?" one of the other librarians asked, taking a step away from Tildy.

"I'm fine." Tildy almost told them about the schoolchildren and the secret room, but she shook her head instead, deciding to keep the news quiet at least for a little longer while she tried to figure out exactly what she'd found. "Just a little off schedule."

The librarians laughed, relieved.

"Well, it happens," one said.

"We can set the clocks in this place by you and your routines, you know," said the second.

"And calendars." The third nodded at Tildy's coffee cup. "Monday, is it?"

Tildy glanced at her bumblebee-yellow mug, smiling at the familiar ribbing. *Bookmarks Are for Quitters* was written in big rainbow letters across it. Everyone at the Bel knew this was Tildy's "Monday mug." They all viewed Tildy's predictability as an entertaining quirk, but they had no idea that this daily rotation of colorful mugs with their jokey sayings represented quite a wild streak for Tildy. Back at her apartment, her decor was white—the bedding, towels, upholstery, dishes, throw pillows—*everything* matched and was clean and bright and . . . well, white.

Tildy raised her mug to the librarians in a *cheers* motion and dashed toward her office, keen to avoid more chitchat.

A staff of twenty worked at the Bel, mostly librarians, but also people who specialized in public relations, marketing, membership, facilities maintenance, and security. Within the small group, a tight-knit community had developed. After work, her colleagues often ran or biked together. Others went out for happy hour. When the traveling Broadway production of *Hamilton* came to town, a group bought tickets together for the show. There were also office showers for weddings and babies, and Tildy always chipped in on these gifts, but she never went out of her way to stop by the celebrations. She felt awkward trying to get into the different friend circles. Small talk was not her thing. It was easier not to get involved. She was their boss, after all, and who really wants their boss around when they're trying to unwind?

TILDY CLOSED her office door and leaned against it.

Since she'd first spotted the secret room's hidden door the morning had taken on a dreamy quality. Finding the room and then the dollhouses had been dazzling, puzzling, and wonderfully mysterious. But unearthing the miniature of her mother in the hidden chamber of the Bel? It made no sense. What did it all mean? Tildy experienced a profoundly eerie sense of dislocation.

And then, like an underwater bubble rising to the surface, a memory came to her.

During a field trip in fifth grade, Tildy had first visited the Bel. In the Main Reading Room, she had been transfixed by the quiet—not the usual quiet you experience in a library, but a quiet *within* her. All too often her young mind felt jumbled and busy, like she was trying to make sense of the garbled static coming from a location with spotty reception. But at the Bel, she finally calmed. Surrounded by books and art, she suspected she could unravel life's mysteries, especially how others seemed to effortlessly understand how to function in the world's chaos. If Tildy hung out long enough in a library, she decided, she'd figure out the things other people seemed to understand by instinct. Maybe not that day, that week, or even that year—but someday.

Tildy had returned home to Mill Valley that afternoon, eager to tell her mother all about the Bel. Since her father had signed the field trip's permission slip, her mother knew nothing of her adventure (a rarity), and Tildy sat at the kitchen table, eager to surprise her. As her mother placed a plate of Mint Milanos in front of her, Tildy said, "Guess where my class went today?"

"Where?"

"Into the city."

Her mother poured two glasses of iced tea and turned toward Tildy, drinks in hand. "Oh? Why?"

"We went to a beautiful place. A library called the Bel."

At mention of the Bel, her mother's face drained of color and the glasses slipped from her hands, shattering on the floor.

"Mom, is everything okay?"

Her mother nodded, color rising on her cheeks. "I'm . . . just surprised. I haven't heard the Bel mentioned in a long time."

Cleaning up the mess distracted them from any more discussion of the field trip, but after the floor was dried and vacuumed, Meg left the kitchen, claiming the laundry needed folding, and Tildy was left alone, munching on a cookie, aware that she had said something deeply distressing to her mother.

The subject of the Bel was dropped, but Tildy couldn't stop

thinking about it. One day during college when she called home to announce she wanted to pursue a career as a librarian, her mother surprised her.

"You know, the Bel is a fantastic place. You could consider working there."

Tildy was baffled. Had she misheard her mother?

"They'd be lucky to have you. At least consider it, Til!"

Tildy gripped the smooth plastic case of her phone more tightly. She had so many questions. Like why had her mother acted so strangely after Tildy's fifth-grade field trip? Why did she suggest the Bel now? But after an entire lifetime together of not asking questions, Tildy found herself tongue-tied. Meg Barrows had always been mysterious.

The details Tildy knew about her mother were scant. For all of Meg's quiet warmth, creativity, and humor, when pushed to certain boundaries—like Tildy asking too many questions about her past—a rigid, unyielding side emerged, and Tildy knew to tread no further.

Her mother's childhood had been sad, that much Tildy understood. Of the few facts she gathered, this is what she knew:

1. Meg Leigh Barrows had been born somewhere in California in 1953.
2. Within a week of Meg's birth, a fever stole her mother away, leaving her father to raise her on his own.
3. Then, at fourteen years old, a house fire killed Meg's beloved father, and she was sent to Allston, an all-girls boarding school in New Hampshire.

Beyond that, specifics were hard to come by, but what had always fascinated Tildy was imagining her mother as a solitary teenager crossing the country to attend a distant boarding school in

New England. Such bravery, such independence was beyond the scope of anything Tildy could dream of doing, especially as a young girl.

Information about her mother's college years was eminently more forthcoming because that's where she'd met Tildy's father, Cliff Barrows, a loquacious storyteller.

"Back in 1971, Yale had only been coed for a couple years and there weren't many women yet, so you can bet I always tried to sit next to one whenever I could," Cliff told Tildy, a playful twinkle in his eyes. "Your mom and I had a freshman English class together, and I sat down next to her on the first day. Boy, was I lucky."

Whenever he told that story Tildy's mother rolled her eyes and laughed. "He found me in a moment of weakness. I'd just sprained my ankle while moving in and lugging my bags up my dorm's stairs. I was a captive audience."

Cliff winked at Tildy. "Thank god for Yale's steep stairs."

After college, Tildy's parents married and moved to a small town north of San Francisco. Her father commuted into the city each day to work at an architecture firm and her mother took a job as a high school English teacher not far from their home in Mill Valley.

Tildy's father was the opposite of his wife in almost every way. For one thing, he came from a huge Boston family. Every summer, he and Tildy flew east for the Barrows family reunion on Cape Cod. For two weeks, while her father, aunts, and uncles swam in the ocean, drank beer, fished, played bridge, traded recipes, and debated the best grilling techniques, Tildy would be thrown into the scrum of her countless cousins, a peripatetic world where children fended for themselves. Despite a low hum of exhaustion brought on by going to bed whenever she felt like it, scavenging breakfast off remnants of cheese and cracker plates from the night before, enduring the scraping of ever-present sand in her bedsheets, and suffering the occasional jellyfish sting, she survived. The chaos of those fourteen days thrilled and stressed Tildy in equal measure.

Tildy's mother always demurred on the summer trip, explaining she'd use the time at home alone to plan her classes for the following year. Cliff never argued and urged Tildy not to nag her mother about joining them. "Your mom's not used to having a big family, and let's face it, the Barrowses are a lot to handle."

This was true. A visit to the Barrows reunion meant surrendering to disorder and noise, but Tildy suspected her mother's reluctance to spend time with her husband's family had more to do with how she'd carefully walled off her past from the present, because time spent with the Barrowses centered around reminiscing and telling stories, and this was an activity Tildy's mother avoided as much as possible.

On the few occasions when Tildy asked her mother about visiting the place where she'd grown up, Meg would shoot down the idea swiftly. "It's probably blown away in the dusty heat. There was barely anything there to begin with. Just a handful of buildings. Not even a real town."

"But what was it called?"

Meg grimaced. "Nothingsville. Tildy, the place was miserable. Please don't make me think about it."

Now, looking at the miniature of her mother, Tildy felt a deep yearning. Was this the call of family? Of blood? The force was as real as gravity. Tildy wasn't imagining it. At least, she *hoped* she wasn't imagining it. That she worked at the Bel wasn't coincidence. She'd followed her mother's cryptic advice. Could this miniature explain her mother's past? Perhaps it could help to answer many of Tildy's questions, like where had Meg Leigh Barrows *really* come from? Who were the people who'd shaped her? And why had Meg ended up at a boarding school in New Hampshire, of all places?

As Tildy grew older, she wished she'd pressed harder for answers when she'd had the chance, but now her mother was dead. Meg had died at night, hit by a drunk driver while navigating her way home along Mill Valley's dark, narrow, curving mountainside roads after attending a play at the school where she taught.

And Cliff Barrows could no longer provide any information about his wife either. Two years after Meg's death, when Tildy was at graduate school in Berkeley, Cliff received his diagnosis: early-onset dementia. Unlike the shock of her mother's accident, her father's decline was a slow-motion free fall into a choppy ocean of uncertainty and sadness. As the end of her graduate program neared, Tildy turned down job offers from the Smithsonian and London's Victoria and Albert, deciding to remain close to home, caring for her deteriorating father. The Bel had been hiring and Tildy, remembering her mother's advice, leapt at the chance to work there.

For three years, Tildy juggled work and caring for Cliff while living in her childhood home north of the city, a move that marked her retreat from her college and graduate school friends. Or they retreated from her—she could never be quite sure. All she knew was that while her friends moved through their twenties, traveling, getting engaged, and experiencing the other usual rites of passage into adulthood, Tildy remained stuck in the Bay Area, single, grief-stricken over her mother's death, and anxious about her dad's illness. Tired of watching everyone else move on with life, Tildy had shut down her social media accounts, a move that only widened her disconnect.

At her father's memorial service, the Barrows relatives descended upon the Bay Area and tried to convince Tildy to relocate to Boston.

"One of my good friends runs the Isabella Stewart Gardner Museum. We can get you a job there," Tildy's aunt Barbara insisted. "Come back with us. We'll have you settled in no time."

The lure of being brought into the insular world of the Barrowses was hard to resist. Tildy had always loved spending time with them, but they exhausted her. A visit was one thing, but seeing them all the time? She was tired just thinking about it. And was she really ready to leave everything and make a move across the country to a city she barely knew? Highly, *highly* unlikely.

"Let me think about it," Tildy said.

"You bet, hon. Whenever you're ready, we'll be there," Aunt Barbara said, squeezing Tildy's shoulders. "But I know you. You think too much. Sometimes you just need to leap and trust that things will work out."

Tildy nodded, hiding her irritation. Easy for Aunt Barbara to say. Her life hadn't been turned upside down by losing the two people who mattered most before she turned twenty-five. Tildy didn't share her aunt's confidence that *things will work out.* Not at all. Tildy stuck with San Francisco and the job she loved. By choosing to work in libraries and museums, she'd unwittingly taken a safe path: surrounded by the detritus of events and people from the past, she needn't fear losing anyone else. They were already gone.

TILDY DRIFTED from the door to her desk, where she put her mug down and dropped into her chair. From her pocket, she removed the miniature and stared at it. Her grief over losing her parents still felt raw, spiky, and painful. Only after her mother was gone did Tildy realize the enormity of what she'd lost. Tildy had always viewed her mother in relation to her own needs as a daughter. She'd never stopped to consider her mother as an individual.

The miniature offered possibility. An opening. For the first time in her life, perhaps her questions about her mother could be answered.

Tildy stood. She needed to return to her apartment immediately to remove the full-size portrait from its frame, look for a signature, date, *anything*. She was sliding into her coat when her phone pinged with a notification. On its screen, a text message appeared.

Dale: I need you in my office ASAP

Tildy groaned in frustration at the interruption. She wriggled out of her coat and hung it back on the hook next to her door. Before leaving her office to see what her boss needed, she placed the miniature in the top drawer of her desk. A slippery feeling slithered through her as she crossed the room. Regret. She didn't like to think she was hiding the miniature, but until she knew more, she planned to keep its existence to herself.

3
Tildy

2024

Tildy crossed the hallway to the office of Dale Anderson, the Bel's executive director, and knocked.

When he opened the door, he beckoned her inside impatiently. "Ah, good, here you are."

Tildy was on the verge of telling him about the secret room, but she realized they weren't alone. The Bel's board president, Lauren Kitterell, and an unknown man stood several feet away, gathered around something. Not until they turned to greet Tildy did she spot the object of their attention: propped upon a wooden display easel was *Young Woman in Hat*, the Bel's most valuable painting.

Dale, smoothing back his neatly coiffed gray hair, launched into introductions. "Tildy, you know Lauren, of course, and this is Sean Finneman, the founder of Dataspot."

Tildy recognized the tech innovator, who had recently graced the cover of *Time* magazine. In that photo, he'd squinted through his black horn-rimmed glasses. His arms, folded across his chest, had looked strong and surprisingly muscular, giving the impression of a nerdy but handsome scientist who saves the planet from alien destruction in a blockbuster film. In real life he appeared harried, thin, wiry, and irritable. Not for the first time, Tildy cursed Photoshop's treachery.

"I was hoping you could tell Sean why this portrait's so important to us," Dale said to Tildy.

"Oh, okay." But Tildy frowned, unsure why Dale had moved the painting from its usual display spot in the Main Reading Room. And why did Finneman need a private viewing?

When she turned to the portrait, preparing to launch into her usual spiel about it, seeing it so up close left her momentarily mute. *Young Woman in Hat* was glorious. Its attraction lay not in its size—the young woman in the portrait had been rendered only slightly larger in scale than real life—but in her beguiling, enigmatic expression and the intimacy of the composition. The model was posed leaning slightly toward her viewers, a wide-brimmed Gainsborough perched atop her head. The hat, an extravagant showstopper of an accessory, was covered with a riot of colorful silk flowers, while ostrich feathers streamed from its band, framing the model's face. Aside from the hat, nothing else adorned her. No jewelry or clothing. Her décolletage, bare shoulders, neck, and face gleamed, pale and smooth as the inside of a conch shell. The portrait's pinks, indigo, greens, tangerine, and sunshine yellow glowed with such force that Tildy felt the colors in her molars, the same way sugary desserts sometimes made her teeth ache. As Tildy soaked up the painting's intensity, the secret room upstairs and its mysterious contents faded to the background of her mind.

"*Young Woman in Hat* was painted in 1863 by a Frenchman named Gustave Blanchet," Tildy said. "Are you familiar with him?"

Sean nodded. "Yeah, after Dale invited me to check the painting out, I did a deep dive on Blanchet and how his work paved the way for the impressionists, guys like Monet, Degas, and Van Gogh. I always respect a market disrupter, and that's exactly what Blanchet was, right?"

Tildy nodded, casting a curious look at Dale. When he wouldn't meet her gaze, she turned back to Sean. "Correct. Blanchet is widely acknowledged as the father of modern art for many reasons, but one is because he didn't stick to the usual subjects of that era, like historical and biblical scenes, or stiff, formal portraits of well-known wealthy figures. Instead he painted ordinary people engaged in modern, urban activities."

In the 1860s, the portrait's vivid palette alone would have startled viewers, but there was more to its charm than just the unmixed colors. The portrait also showed an extraordinary range in technique rarely employed before the impressionists crashed onto Paris's art scene. Vigorous, loose, sketchy brushstrokes gave the hat and its frothy ostrich feathers a sense of movement, vitality, and spontaneity, and this style contrasted with the detailed, labor-intensive layers of thinly applied paint depicting the model's milky, warm skin. The pads of Tildy's fingers practically itched with the desire to check for a pulse beneath the surface of the woman's neck—that's how lifelike she looked. But more than the vibrant colors or the artist's technical range, it was the woman's animated expression that always knocked the wind out of Tildy. From underneath the brim of her hat, the model gazed out from the canvas with bright lively eyes that gleamed with intelligence, but also a tinge of sorrow. A whole story played out in her expression. It was as if she was considering telling her viewer a juicy secret, but one that would come with a cost.

Sean took a few steps to the right and then a few more. "It's like she's watching me, no matter where I go."

Dale chuckled. "That's just one of her charms."

"Is she . . . nude?" Sean asked.

"The composition of this portrait is very clever, isn't it?" Tildy said. "We see the woman's bare shoulders and enough of the swell of her breasts to suspect she's not wearing a dress, but we can't quite be sure. It's one of several tensions Blanchet created in this composition. In 1863, this daring cropping of the image would have been quite modern, more like a photograph than a painting."

"Did LeFarge acquire this in Paris?" Sean asked.

"No, it was part of the Met's collection in New York, but Belva saw the portrait on a trip to the East Coast in 1954 and declared it the most beautiful painting she'd ever seen. On the spot, she offered to buy it, but the museum's director declined, explaining the portrait was one of the institution's most beloved pieces. What the man didn't understand was that Belva never took no for an answer. She increased her offer until the director realized he could buy several masterpieces with the amount she was willing to spend, and in the end, Belva prevailed. The jaw-dropping $55,000 price tag sent the art world into a frenzy."

"Historians point to that sale as the modern-day beginning of the art market's high prices," Dale added, lifting a glossy black Montblanc from his desk to fidget through his fingers, one by one. "Interestingly enough, I just got off the phone with our agent at Christie's. According to her, Blanchet's work has become *très populaire*. Four years ago, his huge canvas *Adele en Été* went for $165 million at a Christie's auction."

Sean whistled.

"Right? Just imagine what this one would sell for." Dale shot a wolfish grin toward Sean. "But of course, if the right person came along, we would consider a private sale, which would probably be a better deal for the buyer."

"Hmm," Sean said, rubbing at his chin.

"Have you done much in the way of art collecting?"

"Not really. I've got a few NFTs." Sean shrugged, checking his phone. "I've got to go so let me cut to the chase: I'm more of a big ideas guy than an art collector, and it's the Bel that interests me, not the painting. This place is old-fashioned for sure, but with a little updating and out-of-the-box-type of thinking, it could be very cool."

Dale frowned. "Out-of-the-box, huh? What are you suggesting exactly?"

"Well, for one thing, the collection really needs to be completely digitized. If you eliminate the books, think of the possibilities. A spot like this in the center of San Francisco? It has potential to be an awesome thought leadership space." He then raised his phone to record a voice memo. "Circle back with location team on current Pacific Heights real estate prices."

Eliminate the books? Tildy stiffened. What was going on? Beneath his year-round suntan, Dale suddenly looked pale.

Lauren frowned. "As president of the board, I'm a steward of this collection, and upon her death, our founder, Belva Curtis LeFarge, left very strict provisions for how this library was to be managed. We can't just change our operations overnight to match the latest fads."

"With all due respect, going digital is hardly a fad," Sean scoffed. "Belva Curtis LeFarge could never have imagined all the recent technological advances we now enjoy. Libraries are no longer mothballed places filled with old, dusty books. You've got to embrace innovation. If you ask me, it's time to bring in a team of new lawyers who can rework Belva's old plan. The Bel could serve a global audience, not just your little community here in San Francisco."

Before Lauren could respond, Dale cleared his throat, took Sean's elbow, and steered him toward the door. "We hear you, man. Sometimes you've got to evolve with the times, am I right? This is a lot to think about. Thanks for stopping by."

As soon as Dale closed the door behind Sean, Lauren snorted. "What the hell was that? I thought he was here so you could gauge his interest in *Young Woman in Hat*?"

"Wait, what? Are we selling the Blanchet?" Tildy asked, looking back and forth between them.

Dale let out a long sigh. "You know we're on pretty thin ice at this point. Our balance sheet is not good. Not at all."

A sinking feeling took hold in Tildy's chest. Of course, she knew the Bel was in trouble, but until now, she hadn't realized how vulnerable it truly was.

In 2014, before she had started working at the Bel, a man named Gil Foyle, the library's comptroller, had been caught embezzling millions of dollars from the library's endowment. A sensational trial ensued. Foyle was sent to jail. The library's previous director, a bespectacled old man who'd been at the Bel's helm for twenty years, was also sent packing, collateral damage from the scandal. As the dust settled, the board hired Dale to take over, and eventually Dale hired Tildy.

On her first day at the Bel, seven years earlier, Dale called her into his office and admitted the library's situation was far worse than had been reported publicly. "The library's been on a slippery slope since the recession in 2008. The endowment wasn't being particularly well managed and it took a big hit from some irresponsible investments. We've been limping along ever since, but several of our big sponsors chickened out when Gil Foyle went to prison. It's been rough trying to attract new ones. I need you to help me bring this place back to life."

And they had. They'd instituted a number of new programs—an ongoing concert series, classes, even summer camps for kids—and as a result, the Bel's membership numbers increased steadily. Several corporate sponsors signed back on. Things were looking up. Until the pandemic. When the library had to close its doors for a year, all the staff's hard work had been reversed.

Lauren's face burned red with anger. "You can't just invite someone in to take us over."

Dale raised his hands in surrender. "Honestly, I didn't realize how different his vision was from ours."

"Before we talk partnerships with anyone, we need to be crystal clear about what we can offer and what we can't. Transparency is important," Lauren said. "You know as well as I do that the Bel is bound by strict rules. Belva's endowment is contingent upon very clear operating procedures. I'm not even sure we can sell the Blanchet."

Dale nodded. "I get it, Lauren, I do. But the problem is that we're not very attractive to a lot of today's potential partners. For decades the Bel has gotten away with being all over the place. We're a research institution, a historical site, an art museum, even a community center, but today's big companies don't see versatility as a strength. They spend millions on crafting mission statements and value propositions to package into pithy thirty-second Super Bowl ads. They want a clear, easy-to-understand purpose. They want new, shiny, streamlined operations. No matter how I spin it, we're none of those things."

Lauren pursed her lips. "We'll have to talk to our lawyers, but Finneman's not the right fit for us. Not at all."

Dale looked back and forth at Lauren and Tildy, a pained expression on his face. "Look, things are going to have to change around here, that's just the way it is. But think about the big picture. If it's a choice between the library closing and it staying open and evolving, I think we'd opt for the latter, right?"

Tildy swallowed hard. So this was it. Closing the Bel was a real possibility. From her time poring over the library's operating budget since the pandemic, she'd known the situation was dire, but she had hoped the board had a rainy day fund tucked somewhere in the organization's endowment. Was that wishful thinking? Of course, but the Bel had always survived difficult times. The Great Depression. Belva's death. The embezzlement scandal. For Tildy, it felt impossible to consider the Bel closing. Until now. Though she dreaded the answer, she asked, "How much longer can we stay open?"

Dale wilted. "Under our current operating plan, we run out of cash by September."

September? Tildy gasped, stunned that Dale and the board had kept this from her.

Lauren nodded glumly, avoiding Tildy's gaze. She slid her handbag onto her shoulder and headed for the door. "I have an appointment down in the financial district, but keep me posted if Finneman gets back in touch, okay?"

"And I need to check in with—" Dale muttered something unintelligible as he followed Lauren, leaving Tildy alone in his office, blinking in shock.

4
Tildy

2024

In a daze, Tildy wandered out of Dale's office, trying to absorb the news about the Bel's possible closure. Instead of sneaking home to check out the pastel sketch of her mother, she scrambled back to the secret room. Her heart ached at the prospect of losing the Bel. She'd put so much time and effort into keeping the beloved place afloat.

During the most anxious months of the pandemic, when no one knew exactly what was happening and everything was shut down, Tildy crept out of her Lafayette Square apartment, walked the short distance to the library, let herself in, and cataloged the Bel's contents. Wearing a mask and plastic gloves, she'd spent hours and hours alone, combing through the various rooms, writing up entries for her findings. It was how she'd coped with uncertainty when the world turned upside down. Some people watched Netflix; others baked sourdough bread; she inventoried the Bel.

"Good morning, Tildy," Harvey, the library's security guard, said in his familiar melodious deep voice as she passed him on the stairs. "Everything okay?"

No, she wanted to shriek. *We're in danger of losing everything!* Instead she forced a smile and answered brightly. "Yep, great!"

Tildy glanced over her shoulder, taking in Harvey's straight posture and shiny polished black shoes as he receded from view. She hated to think of her colleagues, these people she enjoyed seeing every day, being spread far and wide in new jobs.

The Bel had brought her so much consistency during difficult times, and she took enormous comfort in the security she felt within its book-lined walls. Every time she walked through the Main Reading Room and admired the stained-glass ceiling, she found solace in the magical effect of the colored lights gently refracting through the space. The Bel's beauty and history provided much-needed ballast; the library had endured hard times and she would too.

As Tildy reached the top floor and paused a moment, catching her breath, she decided something important. Her list of devastating losses was too long; she refused to add the Bel to it. She would do whatever it took to keep the library open.

With this newfound resolve, she slipped into the Map Room unnoticed. The Bel didn't open until ten o'clock, so the top floor of the place was still quiet and empty. After crossing the large, airy room, she opened the storage closet and slipped through the secret door again.

Slowly, she circled the dollhouses, unsure of what exactly she wished to find, but hoping to discover clues that might shed more information on their origins. Who made them? And where did they came from? In the bigger dollhouse, she paused to examine a dressing room on the third floor, adjacent to a grand Edwardian–styled lady's bedroom. She inhaled sharply, admiring the dressing room's miniaturized clothing and accessories, outfits for every occasion. A green walking suit embellished with geometric-patterned trim. An evening gown with silver beads that sparkled enticingly and could have fit on the tip of Tildy's index finger. Ball gown slippers, heeled shoes, and boots—each smaller than a jellybean—lined a shelf, alongside handbags the size of thimbles and hats no bigger than buttons in a variety of styles from cloches to straw boaters to fascinators. A glass display case filled with minuscule necklaces and bracelets shimmered under the lights.

These dollhouses really were marvelous, their details staggering.

Was it possible one person had made them and each of the amazing miniatures inside? The scope of such a project felt impossible. Painting, sculpture, sewing, metal work, engineering, woodcrafting . . . could one person be capable of so many skills?

People would want to see these, Tildy realized. The dollhouses were extraordinary works of art.

She turned to the Hôtel LeFarge. Many of the paintings covering the dollhouse's walls were miniaturized versions of art that now hung in the Bel, but one caught her attention. In a small cobalt-blue room on the top floor, she spotted a portrait she'd never seen before, though its familiarity struck her. Despite the painting's diminutive size, there was no mistaking it was a rendering of Belva LeFarge when she'd been a young woman. Tildy leaned in a little closer, admiring it. The vivid colors, the brushwork—the portrait reminded her of *Young Woman in Hat*, especially its composition. Tildy smiled at Belva's risqué posing. The library's founder had always been a woman with an unconventional streak. If she'd wanted to be painted in a style like the iconic Blanchet, of course, she'd made it happen. No wonder Belva had been so eager to acquire the original masterpiece when she came across it in person years later.

And that's when a new idea struck Tildy: perhaps the dollhouses could help the Bel.

Tildy yanked her phone from her pocket, tapped out a quick text, and stared at the screen, awaiting a reply.

LATER THAT afternoon, when Dale and Lauren entered the secret room, both fell silent.

"Does this one look familiar?" Tildy asked them, pointing at the smaller dollhouse. When both appeared mystified, she answered. "It's the Hôtel LeFarge, where Belva lived in Paris during her marriage."

"These are exquisite! Why would Belva have hidden them away?"

Dale asked, chewing a piece of Nicorette gum and mopping at his forehead with a lime-green pocket square. Now that Tildy knew the precariousness of the Bel's situation, she could see the toll the stress was taking on her boss. He looked older, haggard even.

"I have no idea. I don't know why this room existed." Tildy didn't mention her mother's miniature. Until she understood more, she'd say nothing about it. "Don't you think people should see these?"

"I do, but it feels irresponsible to exhibit them until we know more, doesn't it?" Lauren asked.

Tildy nodded. "Normally I'd say yes, but perhaps we need to throw out our usual playbook and be more creative."

"Creative? What do you mean by that?" Lauren asked.

"Well, what if we put the dollhouses on display and encourage the public to help us solve this mystery?" Tildy gestured at their surroundings. "Someone out there might know who built these dollhouses and why they're hidden in here."

Lauren straightened her thick tortoiseshell glasses. "I suppose everyone loves a good mystery."

"And people love miniatures. While I was waiting for you two to arrive, I was just reading that the Art Institute of Chicago's Thorne Rooms, a collection of sixty-eight tiny dioramas, are one of its most popular exhibits." Tildy held up her phone.

"Oh, I saw those a few years ago, all decorated for Christmas. They're wonderful," Lauren agreed.

"Exactly. I can already picture our headlines." Tildy moved her hands as if framing her words. "*Two mysterious dollhouses discovered in a secret room at the Bel.* Don't you think the public would love this?"

Dale brightened. "And maybe some potential sponsors will take note and want to get involved."

"What if we invite one of our favorite reporters to see this space and the dollhouses?" Tildy suggested. "We could pitch the story as a quirky mystery, a change from the usual depressing headlines about political divisions, war, and natural disasters. Getting the Bel into the news could generate more interest in our collection and bring in visitors."

After a few more minutes of discussion, they agreed to issue a press release. Dale and Lauren didn't need much convincing. After all, what did they have to lose?

Dale and Lauren hustled out of the secret room to catch up with their respective schedules, leaving Tildy alone with the dollhouses. Tildy moved around to inspect the exterior of the miniature Hôtel LaFarge. Next to the front door was a sign the size of a thumbnail. Tildy crouched forward, squinting to read whatever had been stamped or carved into the square.

In slightly larger print, a date: 1914. Above the year, a monogram. Tildy studied the tangled letters: CH.

Immediately, she turned to the bigger dollhouse's facade. Sure enough, the same monogram: CH. But this one displayed a new date: 1918.

Tildy studied the CH monogram, knowing it was the dollhouse maker's mark. She fished her phone from her pocket and googled "CH and dollhouses," but nothing relevant came back in the results.

Again, Tildy circled the two dollhouses. Why were they here, hidden in the Bel? And why was Meg's portrait in Belva's dollhouse?

Belva had built this library, so she must have known about this secret room and the dollhouses. Whoever made these miniatures might be the connection between Tildy's mother, Belva, and the library. The library's staff always joked that the Bel was haunted by Belva and this idea brought a strange comfort, one they all enjoyed. Now, in this small hidden room, Tildy felt Belva's ghostly presence, circling her, nudging, trying to tell her something.

Given the old age of the dollhouses, Tildy understood her

mother hadn't played a role in building them, but she was obviously connected somehow.

For what felt like the hundredth time that day, Tildy flew downstairs, grabbed her coat and her mother's miniature. When she dashed outside into the Bel's courtyard, the bright sun blinded her. Tildy rarely left work in the middle of the day. She marched home. Once in her apartment, she headed straight for the bookshelf in her living room, without even stopping to take off her shoes. This was no time to stress about tracking dirt inside. With her heart in her throat, she lifted the full-size sketch of Meg, and carefully withdrew the delicate paper from the silver frame. She placed both images, large and small, on her couch. Side by side, they were identical.

When Tildy turned the full-size sketch over to inspect its back, she inhaled sharply.

There, on the bottom right corner of the sketch, was an inscription:

To Daisy
CH, 1965

Stunned, Tildy lifted the sketch closer to study the handwriting. *Daisy*? Had her mother once gone by a different name? And there was CH again, so whoever made the dollhouse had also sketched this portrait.

"Who are you, CH?" Tildy asked aloud. "And how did you know my mother?"

5
The Confession of Cora Hale

1910

I arrived at Gare Saint-Lazare clad in a lightweight wool suit too hot for the steamy August day, but I could not have cared less. I was seventeen years old and in *Paris*. Of course, you know—*everyone* knows—how this marvelous city sparkles, especially for the first-time visitor, but for my wounded spirit, it was just the tonic I needed.

Amid the trolleys, pedestrians, horses, and automobiles, I turned in a full circle taking in my new surroundings. The gleaming plate glass shop windows, the balconies, mansard roofs—every detail appeared choreographed to sing a perfect melody.

And this was just the plaza surrounding the train station.

Outside the Gare Saint-Lazare, I hailed a motor cab, informed the driver of my destination, and motioned for the station's porters to load my luggage and crates filled with my late father's most-prized woodworking tools. From the open air of the conveyance's back seat, I was determined not to miss a single sight. I wanted to immerse myself in this city and forget about the series of disasters that had befallen me back at home in New York. Despite the damp blouse clinging to my back and the grit of travel covering my skin, for the first time in months I felt awash in excitement.

Here, in Paris, I'd find my footing and forge my way. I just knew it.

The driver merged us into the city's wide boulevards, and because I was leaning so far out of the window, I practically tumbled out and fell flat onto my face, but fortunately I regained my balance and withdrew into my seat, reminding myself I hadn't endured a miserable Atlantic crossing only to perish within minutes of arriving in the City of Lights. By the time we reached the Place de la Concorde, my driver was playing me for a fool, but I cared little about spending a few more francs on a circuitous route if it meant marveling at the gilt Fames guarding the garlanded Pont Alexandre III. How they glittered in the sunshine! That a bridge commanded such artistry boggled my mind. Nothing comparable existed in New York. From the quaint cobalt-blue and white street signs and grand candelabra lamps dotting the city's avenues, everywhere I looked, beauty and sophistication ruled the day. Here, in Paris, art didn't simply hang on the walls of museums. Parisians *lived* amid their art.

En route to France, when I'd studied maps of Paris and consulted the trusty pages of my *Baedeker*, I understood the appeal of my destination in the sixth arrondissement. Its location was nothing if not ideal. A mere three-blocks' stroll would land me inside the city's only remaining Renaissance garden—the Jardin du Luxembourg—and furthermore, the École des Beaux-Arts and teaching studios belonging to both William-Adolphe Bouguereau and James McNeill Whistler lay not much farther away, indicating the area's healthy demand for art instruction.

Years ago, around the turn of the century, American magazines and newspapers, like *Collier's* and *Ladies' Home Journal*, dedicated considerable coverage bemoaning how the vulgar Bohemian excesses of young female American art students abroad reflected poorly on the nation's reputation and character, citing—and I'm using language from the times—the women's *loud voices, cocksure attitudes, swaggering, immoderate use of slang,* and *careless wantonness*. I should point out this hand-wringing was all part of a concerted effort to rein in the boundaries being pushed by the era's New Woman feminist ideals and keep young women at home under the watchful eyes of their parents—and it backfired. From what I observed, many continued crossing the pond, and fortunately for us, several benevolent organizations stepped in to provide subsidized housing intended to promote safe, wholesome, and enriching places for these new arrivals, who were serious about their studies in art, literature, science, and other high-minded pursuits.

Ephraim Curtis, an American industrialist who'd built the transcontinental railroad, was one of these virtuous benefactors. He established Curtis House, only a few blocks from Jardin du Luxembourg, as a haven against the dark forces threatening to tug America's feminine innocence asunder. Before leaving New York City, the director of my art school wrote a letter of recommendation on my behalf to this boardinghouse.

When we passed through Curtis House's wrought-iron gates, I dismounted from my motor cab as if in a trance. Spread before me was a charming three-story parchment-colored château. Never had I pictured myself living somewhere so elegant. Sunlight filtered through the surrounding plane trees and elms, creating a dappled pattern along the gravel driveway. If I'd painted the scene, it would have been blurry, thick brushstrokes of rich indigos, verdigris, vibrant mustard, absinthe, and ultramarine. Near the front door, ivy threaded upward through the lacy design of wrought-iron balconettes gracing the second floor of the facade. I inhaled the cool scent of damp soil. After months of struggle and grief, I could never have imagined a place more lovely. Honestly, I wasn't sure I deserved it.

Two months earlier, my father had died. Since my mother had perished shortly after my birth, I was now orphaned and clearly an obvious candidate for corruption by Bohemian depravity, but here was the rub: I'd already been ruined in my native land, and Paris offered me a path for escape.

My saving grace was the decent inheritance my father had bestowed upon me, but if I squandered it on fancy accommodations and too many evenings smoking, drinking, and dancing the illicit turkey trot at the Chat Noir on the rue Odessa, it would not last long. I may have been a young fool, but I knew enough to understand that. I needed Curtis House.

I climbed the steps and entered the foyer. A matronly-looking woman perched behind a desk, poring over a sheaf of papers, a pencil held aloft ready to make notes. Her dowdy appearance seemed a purposeful contrast designed to highlight the refinement of our surroundings. When she spotted me, she snapped to attention, placing the horse racing report from Longchamps down in front of her.

"Mrs. Winnington, house matron at your service," she said.

I introduced myself and slid my reference letter toward her, feeling on top of the world. "This is from the director of the New York College of Art. He suggested that Curtis House would be a good spot for me."

To my surprise, she lifted my letter of introduction between her thumb and index finger like it was no better than a soiled stocking.

"My dear, I wish we could help you, but our rooms are accounted for. As I'm sure you're aware, Curtis House is one of the most desirable places to live in Paris. Typically Comtesse LeFarge likes three letters of recommendation and a sample of your work." She made a tutting sound. "We don't allow women to simply walk in off the street and ask for a room. Why, if that was the case, we'd be no better than Rue Pigalle. Surely your benefactor must have known that. He did you few favors by not writing ahead to secure you a spot."

My breath stuttered. My journey from America had taken almost two long weeks and I'd been seasick the entire time. By the point of my arrival at Curtis House, I would have killed for a bath and hearty meal, so with every passing minute, I was growing more and more short-tempered, and Mrs. Winnington's lofty tone wasn't helping matters. Right then and there I decided I would not leave the place without securing a room, no matter what it cost me.

I leaned over Mrs. Winnington's desk, clasping its edge so tightly I was certain my fingers would leave indentations. "Madame, I've traveled long and far and I simply must stay here. Please," I implored through gritted teeth.

Mrs. Winnington looked thoroughly horrified, but I couldn't hide my desperation. I was wrung out, weary, and famished.

"Eustice, what's happening here?"

At the sound of a new voice, I cringed, mortified. *Perfect*, I thought, *please, let's invite more people to witness me at my lowest.*

But then the newcomer surprised me. "Surely there's a bed in here somewhere for this woman?"

An ember of hope flickered inside me.

Backlit as she was against the afternoon light pouring through the château's front door, my first impression was of an angel's arrival—a very stylish angel. As my eyes adjusted, I made out her dramatic silhouette, starting with the hem of her ivory-and-salmon-striped silk chiffon walking suit, moving upward to the distinctive kimono-styled jacket. And finally, her hat. Black velvet sculptural swirls rose into the air like the long narrow leaves of a fiddlehead fern. On anyone else it might have looked outlandish, but on her it was spectacular. That hat should have hung on the walls of the Louvre. I gaped, fully enchanted.

Mrs. Winnington folded her arms. "Madame, unless you want this young woman to sleep on the Music Room's davenport, there's no space. We're absolutely packed to the gills. Not a single spare bed is available."

The elegant angel of mercy glided past me and lifted my recommendation letter to read it. The lighting shifted, and I could finally see her calm smile.

"I'm Madame LeFarge," she said to me.

"The comtesse is our benefactor," Mrs. Winnington announced, giving me a pointed look as if to say *pull yourself together.*

"Oh, Eustice, you know I'm not a stickler for the honorific," Madame said, batting her hand into the air dismissively. "Now, according to this letter, Miss Hale represents one of New York's most promising painting students." Madame LeFarge looked me up and down. "Miss Hale, where do you plan to study while you're here?"

"I'll be working as a private art instructor."

"And do you have clients already in place?"

"Yes, I have several appointments lined up for next week." This was a bald-faced lie, and my palms itched with anxiety, but I couldn't let up now. Keeping my voice steady, I rattled off several fabricated names and addresses I conjured from the map I'd studied during my travels. "My clients include Mrs. Bentley on the rue de Grenelle. And Mrs. Moffat on the rue de Bac and Mrs. Hughes by Parc Monceau. They're all expecting me."

Madame considered this information, and I held my breath, bracing for her to decide against me. If she called my bluff, the jig would be up. Instead, she turned to Mrs. Winnington. "Really, we have nothing available? What about Bronwyn Thorpe's room? Doesn't she leave soon for Berlin?" Madame could see how closely I was following this conversation, so she added proudly: "Miss Thorpe has been accepted into a prestigious music school in Berlin to study violin."

Berlin? Impressive. I straightened, hoping Madame could not sniff out the scandal I feared clung to me like an unfortunate case of body odor.

Frowning in concentration, Mrs. Winnington opened a large leather-bound ledger book that looked as worn and intimidating as a witch's book of spells. She flipped through the tome's pages carefully and then stopped, running her knobby index finger along a column until she found a particular spot and nodded.

"Yes, she's given her notice, but I'm not exactly sure when she's leaving," Mrs. Winnington conceded.

"Well then, can't Miss Hale take her room?"

Mrs. Winnington pursed her lips to one side. "At dinner this evening, I'll consult with Bronwyn. I'll know more tomorrow."

"Very well. If we can store Miss Hale's items overnight, I'll take her back to my house for the evening. Tomorrow, she'll come back and you can make room for her."

"As you wish, Madame," Mrs. Winnington said, but her compliance didn't fool me, not for one minute. My hope for the woman's cooperation guttered like a candle in a sharp wind.

"Thank you for being so flexible, Eustice. I know I ask a lot of you. Now, is Sophie Welk in? I just picked up several copies of her latest poem in *Vers* and wanted to drop a few issues off."

I tried to catch a glimpse of the stack of pamphlets Madame placed on Mrs. Winnington's desk. I had little experience with poetry, but knew publication to be a notable accomplishment. And another resident was a world-class violinist? Suddenly I wondered if I was in over my head.

"She's not here at the moment, but if you leave them with me, I'll make sure they're delivered to her."

"Perfect." Madame moved past us, saying over her shoulder, "While I visit the kitchen to share a recipe with Cook, could you please tell Miss Hale everything she needs to know to live here?"

"*If* she ends up living here. No guarantees."

"Right, *if*. Could you please tell Miss Hale what she needs to know *if* you're able to secure a room for her."

Mrs. Winnington appeared slightly appeased. "Madame, please leave the recipe with me, I shall have it squared away in no time."

"I know you think it's the height of irregularity for me to go back there, but honestly, I don't mind. If I'm lucky, Cook's made some of that delicious lemon cake and I can sneak a slice. But thank you."

Mrs. Winnington surrendered and refocused her attention on me, launching into a lecture about Curtis House: meals were served in the dining room; the library contained over six hundred volumes; male visitors were permitted as long as their presence was limited to the Music Room; the house's front doors locked at ten o'clock at night; and if I was interested, a lively lectures series was hosted in the parlor every Wednesday evening.

Sighing after she completed her speech, Mrs. Winnington gave my rumpled and sweat-stained traveling suit a dubious once-over, causing me to reposition my hat self-consciously.

"Oh heavens, look at that blazing head of red hair. There's certainly no losing you in a crowd," she cried.

Nothing galled me more than people making comments about the striking color of my ginger-hued hair, but fortunately, before I could fire off an indignant retort and get myself in trouble, she leaned in, whispering, "If anything goes wrong tonight, don't expect a room here to materialize." She tapped a leather folder lying on the corner of her desk. "This entire file's filled with qualified young women who would kill—*kill*—to take our next vacant room at a moment's notice." Then, as if washing her hands of my almost-certain imminent humiliation, she shrugged, pushing a hank of frizzled gray hair off her forehead. "Well, good luck, my dear."

I nodded, understanding I'd been dismissed. Gathering every ounce of dignity I could assemble, I marched out of that foyer, my chin held high. If I played my cards right, by the following evening, I would be surrounded by this collection of bright, energetic, and daring women.

Before departing New York City, I'd been warned to leave my

scandal behind by not drawing attention to myself. I'd been instructed to keep myself small, yet nothing about living in Curtis House appeared in line with timidity or anonymity. It was no place for wallflowers. If I was going to thrive, or even just survive, I'd need to guard my past carefully. Of all people, you, my dear, know exactly what it feels like to keep this kind of secret.

When Madame LeFarge and I left Curtis House, her driver steered the motorcar through Faubourg Saint-Germain, where elegant homes peered out from behind crumbling stone walls and golden leaves, like beautiful women sneaking glances past their lace and ivory fans. After driving a little over a mile, we pulled up to Hôtel LeFarge, and I could see why Mrs. Winnington didn't think me worthy of Madame's invitation. The Hôtel LeFarge's neoclassical facade was sublime, far grander than any residence I'd ever stepped foot in. At the door, a valet let us inside a marble entryway and we climbed a swooping grand staircase to the second floor.

Madame directed a maid to fix me a bed for the night and then led me into a room with cobalt-blue walls set off by crisp white wainscoting and exquisite millwork, a space that felt both feminine and bold at the same time.

A black-and-white French bulldog bounded toward us, huffing indignantly at my unexpected appearance.

"Good day, sir," I said to the dog.

A low growl rumbled deep in his tiny chest.

"Oh, Gruffwood! Don't be such a terrible grump," Madame said, lifting the squirming dog into her arms to kiss him between his ears.

Since Mrs. Winnington's warning to be on my best behavior, something had been nagging at me.

"Madame, may I please ask, why are you going out of your way to help me?"

She placed the wriggling dog back on the floor and looked toward the window as if wishing to be outdoors, walking the paths of the estate's garden. For a moment I didn't think she'd heard me and was about to repeat the question, but then she spoke quietly, a tinge of longing coloring her voice.

"When I arrived in Paris eight years ago, I was eighteen and traveling with my mother. The trip was a thinly disguised excuse to introduce me to as many eligible men as possible. Of course, my mother hoped I would marry one of them. I fulfilled that goal, but—" A brief cloud darkened her face, a face that was lovely, but definitely sad. "Well, I've always admired you girls who land at Curtis House, determined to make names for yourselves. To arrive in a foreign city alone while holding such lofty professional ambitions is something I feel compelled to support. When I walked into Curtis House today, I'm not sure why, but I knew you belonged there."

"Thank you. What good fortune *someone* believed in me!"

A smile quirked at Madame's lips. "You'll come to find that Mrs. Winnington comes across as unfailingly set in her ways, but she'll do anything to protect the girls at Curtis House. Once she's on your side, she's staunchly loyal."

She then gestured to a tea cart set with Limoges china and a tiered plate loaded with patisserie, each a masterpiece of its own. Tartelettes heaped with glistening blueberries, strawberries, and raspberries; mille-feuilles with sharply distinguished layers of chocolate and pastel-tinted creams—my mouth watered at the sight of such bounty.

"Have a refreshment," Madame said airily, removing her hat and handing it to a nearby attendant. "I can see that you're practically hungry enough to eat Gruffwood."

On cue, a maid handed me a small plate with a fruit tartelette, just as the word *refreshment* caused Gruffwood to stop snuffling around my hemline and circle back to his mistress. As he neared, she bent over and fed the dog a strawberry-and-pistachio eclair directly from her fingers. The dog must have sensed my envy because he radiated a smug look of triumph and trotted away.

Madame chuckled and popped a large chocolate into her mouth. Seeing my surprise, she laughed. "Come on now. Don't be shy. I hate the idea of such marvelous creations going to waste."

Who was I to protest? Not wanting to be a bad guest, I slid my fork into my tart. Despite my attempt at restraint, the pastry disappeared. I simply inhaled it.

"Clearly that was terrible, wasn't it?" Madame gestured at a maid to serve me more pastries. "Let's find something that you like better."

"I've never been known as a quitter."

"That's the spirit."

For several minutes, we sat in silence, trying one delicious morsel after another. Through the French doors on the other side of the room came the whisper of rustling leaves. Eventually I laid my fork down, feeling my stomach strain delightfully against my skirt's waistband. Sated, I studied my surroundings in more detail. Covering the walls were shelf after shelf of leather-bound books and colorful paintings, many of them quite modern. Madame's taste in design was exceptional, and I pointed at a nearby desk, admiring its graceful lines and leafy motifs.

"That Gaillard is beautiful. If I could sit at it every day, perhaps I'd be a writer," I said with a laugh.

She looked at me, curiously. "You know your furniture."

I accepted a cup of tea from a maid, weighing how much to divulge. "My father was a cabinetmaker and owned a woodworking studio."

"And now you're a painter? I'd love to see your work," she said, feeding Gruffwood the final pastry.

I placed my teacup next to my now-empty plate, hoping to hide the furious trembling that came over my hands whenever I thought about my unfortunate exile from New York City. "I didn't bring any of my old work with me. I want to start anew."

Even to my own ears, my voice sounded sharp and tight. I glanced at Madame to see if she'd registered my discomfort, but to my relief she was watching her dog, who now snuffled around the edges of her hem in search of crumbs until she shooed him away. "It looks like you've finished your tea. What do you say, would you like a tour of the place?"

"Yes, please." I rose eagerly.

"This house was a wedding gift from my in-laws, but it was in rather rough shape, so I completely renovated and modernized it."

"I can't even imagine the house in a state of neglect. It's so perfect now."

At the doorway, Madame hesitated. "Nothing's perfect."

Before I could answer, she shrugged. With her back facing me, her expression was hidden.

MADAME LED me to the nearby nursery, where we found Jack, her boy of five. He sat on the floor, his chin tucked in toward his chest, a headful of dark ringlets spilling forward as he held a book. When introduced to me, he raised a small pale hand politely and I shook it.

"What are you reading?" I asked.

He held out a small volume of *Alice's Adventures in Wonderland*.

"I'm impressed by your reading skills, young man."

He considered my compliment, riffling through a few pages before nodding.

"It's the *One Syllable* version, but I am quite good at reading." His English contained a faint trace of French accent, and from beneath long dark lashes, big Delft-blue eyes gazed up at me.

"He's modest too," Madame said, patting his head.

When we took our leave of the nursery, young Jack nodded solemnly as if granting us permission to go.

"What an old soul," I said, as we walked along the hallway away from the nursery.

Madame smiled proudly and we proceeded to the library, and then she led me to the ground floor and through the kitchen and its preparation and storage rooms. The modern facilities of the service quarters impressed me terribly. The latest stoves and refrigeration units. The water heater. The shining white tiles lining the floors and walls.

Our final stop was the ballroom on the main floor.

"It's large enough for a chamber orchestra and two hundred guests," Madame said. Fully awed, I took in the floor-to-ceiling windows, mirrors lining the walls, two magnificent Venetian chandeliers, and frescoed ceiling, but before I could ask how often they entertained, the door opened. A man strode into our midst with the self-possession of someone who believes the world's been built to fit his exact specifications.

"*Qu'est-ce qui se passe ici?*" he asked, his expression impassive. When his gaze glided over me, I sensed a flicker of interest akin to when a drowsy cat grows alert after spotting a mouse.

"*Mon cher*, this is one of the new Curtis House girls." Little warmth existed in Madame's use of *mon cher*. If anything, the endearment sounded like a warning. "Her room isn't quite ready, so she'll be spending tonight here."

With wavy dark hair and the same light blue eyes as his son, Madame's husband was more beautiful than handsome. A sly smile played at his lips as he made note of the color of my hair and said in a low voice, "*La renarde*." From the way he rolled the accents around on his lips, the word held the same danger and menace as a blade being sharpened.

Madame wrapped an arm around my shoulders. "Cora, you must be exhausted. Let's get you settled for the evening. I'll have Cook send dinner to your room," she said, pushing me toward the door.

When a kitchen girl showed me to my quarters, I felt nothing but relief at the sight of the spare accommodations. The single cot. Washstand. A basic cabinet with drawers. Madame apologized that the only room available to me was in the servants' hall, but I assured her its location and simplicity appealed to me. After the relentless rocking of sea travel, I would have slept on the cook's cutting board without complaint as long as it remained stationary.

When I shut the door behind the maid, I noted the loose screws on the sliding lock. Any pressure on the door would probably make the entire device pop right off. For reasons I couldn't fully understand, the uneasiness I'd felt under the comte's gaze returned, so I mustered the last of my energy to lean against the nearby cabinet and push it into place against the door. Though I felt foolish for such extreme measures, as soon as I sank onto my small single bed, I fell into a deep sleep, forgetting my worries.

In the morning, after I'd risen, washed my face, and dressed, I summoned my strength to push the cabinet back to its original spot. Only then did I notice the lock had indeed fallen off the door and lay in several broken pieces on the floor. My empty stomach seized. I told myself I must have knocked the lock off the previous evening, but still, my fingers trembled as I placed the broken pieces atop the windowsill. I forced myself to quell any darker theories from surfacing in my mind. Nothing good would come from such imaginings.

6

Tildy

2024

The day after Tildy found the secret room and dollhouses, she arrived at the Bel, foggy-headed thanks to a restless night of little sleep. In the tote she carried she'd tucked her mother's miniature. She dropped into her desk chair, already exhausted though the day hadn't even really begun.

Emiko Woods, the Bel's head of marketing and press relations, burst into the office, startling Tildy. Tildy quickly nudged the tote bag under her desk with her foot, out of sight, before Emiko could see what had preoccupied her.

"Good morning," Emiko said, her brows raised. "You okay?"

"I'm fine, just didn't sleep well last night."

"Well, this good news should perk you up: I've managed to snag Kitty Kim of KTVU for you and Dale today. She'll be here at noon with her crew to see the secret room!"

"Well done." Tildy nodded and took a deep breath. Once Kitty Kim and her crew saw the hidden room and its dollhouses, there'd be no turning back. Of course, Tildy hoped someone would see Kitty's broadcast and come forward with information about the dollhouses. Maybe this person would even know how Tildy's mother connected to the dollhouses and the secret room. But it was *exactly* this possibility that both thrilled and worried Tildy in equal measure. She had no idea what to expect, and that didn't sit well.

Tildy and the Bel's facility manager spent the rest of the morning preparing the secret room and dollhouses for their television debut by rearranging them so they were positioned side by side, their front facades facing the same direction. Tildy then opened the window shutters, vacuumed, dusted, and added more lighting. Thanks to their protective cloths, the dollhouses were in remarkably good shape. They needed some conservation work, but that could wait until after the day's news coverage.

Of the Bay Area's on-air news personalities, Kitty Kim was the best known by far and had been broadcasting since Tildy had been a high schooler. For Tildy, Kitty Kim's voice conjured the smell of morning coffee, the sticky feeling of maple syrup on her fingers, and the sweet, crunchy taste of Eggo waffles, not to mention the flutter of anxiety she felt before leaving the house to navigate the complicated social networks that filled her day of classes. Over the years Kitty moved back and forth between morning and evening news slots, and her shows consistently snagged the highest ratings.

When Kitty and her cameraman arrived, Tildy led them to the secret room.

"Whoaaaa," Kitty said, taking in the Hôtel LeFarge. "You really have no idea why these are in here or why Belva created this room?"

"We don't even know if Belva was the one to create this room, although it seems reasonable to guess that she did," Tildy said.

"These are fabulous," Kitty said, admiring the bigger dollhouse. "And you're going to display them?"

"Yes. They need a little cleaning up and minor repairs, but we're planning to exhibit them within the next two months," Tildy said, explaining how she hoped the public might be able to help the Bel figure a few things out about the dollhouses.

"Love it. Our viewers will eat this story right up." Kitty turned to her cameraman. "Danny, can you get some B-roll of the entrance? And then let's get a bunch of close-ups of the different dollhouse rooms."

Just then Dale walked in, centering his tie on his chest, followed by Emiko. He sported a navy blue suit, chartreuse bow tie, and coordinating pocket square, but despite his debonair appearance, Tildy saw the tight set of his jaw.

Dale smiled widely before air-kissing Kitty on both cheeks.

"Everyone ready?" Emiko asked.

"Let's do this." Dale rubbed his palms together as Kitty explained how she wanted to structure the interview.

Once Kitty and Dale were standing in front of the dollhouses with the camera rolling, Kitty beamed. "I had a beloved dollhouse when I was a kid, but what you've got here is totally different. These aren't toys, are they?"

"You're right, Kitty, these are definitely not toys. In fact, dollhouses didn't really become considered toys until after World War II when mass manufacturing made them affordable to produce. Before that, upper-class women were known to commission dollhouses to show off their wealth as status symbols."

"So like before *Architectural Digest* or *Lifestyles of the Rich and Famous* came along, women used miniatures to brag about how grand their houses were?"

"Exactly. Amsterdam's Rijksmuseum has several examples of dollhouses owned by wealthy women that date back to Holland's seventeenth-century Golden Age. Dollhouses were also popular in England. The most famous is Queen Mary's Dolls' House. It's a five-story structure, complete with elevator, electrical lights, and running water." He paused to chuckle at Kitty Kim's flabbergasted expression. "I know, amazing, right? Queen Mary commissioned it after World War I to raise the nation's spirits after such a difficult period. She enlisted a top English architect to build it and document how the royal family lived. She also invited the country's businesses, artists, and craftsmen to produce miniatures to furnish the dollhouse."

"No kidding. Why did she think a dollhouse would raise people's spirits?"

"She believed putting creativity and beauty on display would cheer people up. And interestingly enough, she was onto something. There's actually a psychological rationale to explain our affinity for small things: dollhouses offer us a sense of control and imagination. They can provide a feeling of agency. Miniatures allow us to create the world as we'd like to see it."

"Huh, that's fascinating. So did the Queen's plan work? Were people cheered up by her dollhouse?"

"When it was put on display in 1924, a million and a half people turned out to see it, so yeah, I'd say her plan worked."

Kitty shook her head in amazement and turned toward the larger dollhouse. "Wow, well, the range of craftsmanship in these is extraordinary. Painting, textile design, woodworking, sculpture, ceramics, printmaking—it's all here. So, what can you tell us about these two dollhouses?

"Honestly, Kitty, not much."

"Seriously?"

Dale nodded. "These dollhouses are quite mysterious to us at the moment, but let me show you the few clues we've figured out." As Dale pointed to the signs with the CH monogram and dates and explained their significance, Tildy's heart rate accelerated into a gallop. Someone out there had to know more about the dollhouses, she was sure of it.

"We're hoping your viewers might be able to help us figure out why this secret room existed and why the dollhouses were hidden in it. We assume Belva commissioned this one"—he gestured to the Hôtel LeFarge—"because we've identified it as the house she lived in during her Paris years, but we don't know if this other dollhouse is based on a real house or not. We have no idea who commissioned it. And most importantly, we don't know *who* made the dollhouses. Was it an individual? A group of artists? We're planning to display these miniatures to the public within the next couple of months, so we'd love more information. Anything, really!"

While Dale recited an email address the public could ping with any leads, Tildy found herself clasping her hands to her chest as if she was praying. She wanted, no, she *needed* someone to help her understand her own past.

WHEN DALE and Kitty finished recording the segment, the group headed downstairs, pausing in the Main Reading Room so the photographer could take more video.

"That ceiling!" Kitty whistled, looking upward. "It's really something. I'd forgotten how beautiful this place is." She frowned. "But what's up with that crack?"

Confused, Tildy squinted against the sunlight filtering through the room. And that's when she saw it: a dark crack, maybe five to six feet long, spread across the ceiling's center like an ugly varicose vein.

Beside her, she felt Dale stiffen, but he waved a hand as if brushing away a fly and said in a blasé tone, "Oh, every now and then we have to undertake some minor restoration work on the ceiling. There's nothing to be concerned about."

But Tildy's stomach dropped. Dale wasn't telling the truth. Aside from its semiannual cleaning, no one at the Bel had restored any part of the stained-glass ceiling.

The crack was a problem. A *big* problem.

7
Cora

1910–1911

Much to my relief, Mrs. Winnington found a room for me at Curtis House after only one night. While I had high hopes for my new home, little did I know how utterly life-changing the experience would be. This dignified old château housed thirty writers, musicians, scientists, designers, and academics; women who drank too much coffee and stayed up too late reading and talking, who skipped meals and forgot to brush their hair if an important deadline loomed. If a housemate passed by without saying hello, rather than interpreting the silence as rudeness, I quickly learned it was because she was preoccupied with thinking.

This preoccupation also extended to housekeeping issues. Thank goodness for Mrs. Winnington and her obsession with tidiness. Without her, newspapers would have covered the parlor, along with egg-smeared dishes and bowls crusted with hardened oatmeal; cobwebs would have hung from the ceilings like lace curtains; and stacks of books would have towered in every room, especially next to the bathtubs. Anyone who believed women to naturally be the more orderly sex had never met the inhabitants of Curtis House.

What my neighbors sometimes lacked in style, they made up for in substance. Never before had I encountered such an eclectic assortment of women. While my artistic training was thorough, the gaps in my formal academic education made me self-conscious among such accomplished cerebral types, yet no one ever tried to make me feel inferior. Because many of my housemates were educators, they welcomed the opportunity to gently inform me about political, social, and scientific topics. Curtis House was my type of place.

Once I'd settled my meager possessions into my new home, I hunted for clients. It didn't take long. Paris was a city filled with women eager for art instruction so I soon had a roster of students, who filled my days with teaching. For months I didn't pick up a single sketching pencil or paintbrush, except to guide my students during sessions.

My desire to paint itched, vibrated, and ached like a phantom limb, but I was too distracted, worrying about my past, to focus on producing anything new. The only way to quiet my mind was to physically exhaust myself, so I walked everywhere, all over the city, no matter the weather. On blustery days, I strolled under the birch and poplars along the Seine, patting the dogs tied up, waiting to be washed and groomed. I'd cross the little bridge behind Notre Dame to Île Saint-Louis, wander the charming old seventeenth-century neighborhood, and then return to the Left Bank on the Pont de la Tournelle to browse the shelves of the Bouquinistes. In the colder winter months, I sidled through the Louvre, rambled along the straightaways of the Jardin des Tuileries, and then circled the Place de la Concorde's fountain. There, I'd stop for a few minutes to admire the frolicking mermaids impervious to their icy conditions. I kept up this routine during that first winter, and as the months passed, my fears about my scandal catching up with me began to fade.

Maybe no one was coming for me, after all.

Spring always embodies a certain magic, a feeling of redemption and possibility. The thrill of crocuses poking through soil and green buds sprouting on tree boughs, the relief of longer days after months of dreary skies and darkness—although these changes occur in many places, Paris has a special claim on springtime magic. Pale pink cherry blossoms brightened the Trocadero Gardens. Spears of asparagus, big spiky heads of artichoke, and crisp stalks of rhubarb filled the baskets of the market's stalls. Café terraces suddenly overflowed with Parisians eager to sip a cappuccino or a glass of wine while tilting their faces to warm in the sun. After months of being cooped up inside, my housemates and I eagerly spilled into Curtis House's gardens to read, write, and socialize.

I WAS heading out for my daily constitutional one spring day when Madame LeFarge intercepted me on the château's steps. "Come to the Palais Garnier's museum with me! I recently finished reading *Phantom of the Opera* and am now dying to visit. What do you say?"

During my city walks, I'd passed the grandiose theater many times, but never entered.

"I know nothing about opera or ballet."

"Don't worry, as the resident artist here, you'll be the perfect guide."

Always game to explore more of the city, I climbed inside her motorcar.

"This morning I finally bid farewell to the crew overseeing my renovation of Hôtel LeFarge," Madame announced happily, settling into her seat.

"So your house is complete?" I asked, only half listening to her describe the last stage of work being done. In the months I'd spent at Curtis House, I gleaned certain facts about Madame LeFarge from my housemates, who were absolutely besotted with our patron. Everyone viewed her as a magical figure akin to a fairy godmother.

During a winter's evening spent in the château's library, one of my housemates, Peggy, informed me candidly about Madame and the family she'd married into. "The LeFarges may be able to trace their lineage back to Charlemagne, but they don't have two francs to rub together and they resent our Madame for her largesse," Peggy explained, swirling a glass of red wine and clearly relishing her role as informant. "To an old woman like the dowager comtesse, nothing breeds resentment quite like watching your young handsome son announce he plans to marry the daughter of an American industrialist of questionable ancestry. In her mind, it's an unnatural upset of the social order." She lowered her voice to a conspiratorial tone. "They say the old comtesse calls our Madame 'the shopgirl.'"

Even with my rather rudimentary grasp of how upper-class Parisian society functioned, I understood the cruelty of that dig. For most of us, to acquire a position as a shopgirl would be perfectly acceptable and desirable, but for someone like the dowager comtesse, a snob who'd never worked a day in her life, any form of employment was akin to prostitution. I shook my head in annoyance with such antiquated thinking. "But the old lady doesn't even have her facts straight," I huffed. "Doesn't the Curtis money come from railroads?"

"Mostly, yes, but it started with a shop in California," Peggy said. "Madame's grandfather kitted out the fools who arrived in gold rush country hoping to strike it big. Shovels, picks, bull's-eye lanterns, waxed-canvas slickers, coffee, bacon, and beans—that's how he built his fortune."

"So he parlayed that money into the Transcontinental Railroad?"

"Did he ever! Let's just say the dowager comtesse's opposition *softened* to her son's marriage once she figured out that Mr. Curtis could practically buy all of Paris if he wanted. Still, the old bat gets her barbs in. When she gave the young couple the Hôtel LeFarge as a wedding present, it was barely habitable, but our intrepid young American bride took one look at it and decided right then and there that she and her crisp green dollars would get the last laugh."

Madame may have built herself a beautiful house, but when I remembered the cold eyes of her husband and the chilliness between them, I wondered if it was worth it.

When Madame and I entered the Palais Garnier's museum, I wandered away on my own, exploring the collection. To be honest, little about old musical scores interested me, so my mind drifted. I was paying little attention to the displays. Only when I entered a strange, dark hallway lined with windows did I finally snap to attention. What was this?

When I peered inside the nearest window, I gasped at the view of sea and cerulean sky. The scene's deep, liquid colors glittered like sapphires, peridots, and emeralds, their facets catching in the sun. The label affixed to the front of the display: *Salammbô.*

It was a miniature of an opera set.

In the next window, graceful boughs of deciduous trees filled the foreground. Behind them, the ruins of an old castle loomed. The set's details captivated me. The outline of each leaf. The variety of shades of green. The rough texture of the castle's stonework. I could sense romance, secrets, a mysterious world. This set's label: *Tristan et Isolde.*

In the third window—another labeled as *Tristan et Isolde*—the prow of an elaborately rigged ship appeared. Everything whispered *adventure*, *enchantment*, and *excitement.*

I inched along the corridor absorbing each magical miniature scene, one by one, amazed at what could be rendered with a little paint, paper, wood, and silk. Mundane materials could create remarkable textures and brilliant colors.

And just like that I was whisked back in time to my father's cabinetry studio. As a young girl, I spent hours nestled on the floor below his workbench, watching cracked brown leather boots stomp between lathes, saws, and milling machines. I could still smell the sun-warmed pine, the tang of wood stain. I could feel velvety paper-thin curled alder and birch shavings in my hands.

My eyes blurred with tears as I remembered how beautifully constructed cabinets, and sometimes even chairs, tables, and shelves, took shape under my father's strong hands, each piece a work of art. He was a man with vision and commitment to his craft. I'd learned so much simply by watching. How I missed him!

Entranced, I made another circuit of those miniature sets. I was on my third tour through them when Madame joined me. "What have we here?" she asked, pointing to the miniature *Salammbô* set.

"Look at these wonders," I gushed. Those sets had stirred something in me. Inspiration.

I remained in that hallway, watching Madame. What if I offered to make a portrait of her in a form far different from anything I'd ever tried before? I knew little about opera, but I understood the concept of theater. We all have roles to play. For most women, the home is their stage. What if I produced a portrait of a woman, not by creating a likeness of her, but by showing the stage that defined her role in life? I'd always hoped to produce portraits that hinted at the interiority of my subjects—what would happen if I took a very literal approach to such a piece?

This idea would change everything for me.

8
Cora

1911

For the first time since leaving home, I possessed not only a unique vision for what to make, but motivation. While at art school in New York City, I'd been trained as a portrait painter, but if I resumed my former career in Paris, I feared my past would sniff me out like a bloodhound. I'd barely survived my first encounter with the snapping jaws of scandal and stood no chance against a second. I needed to break with my origins completely, and seeing the miniature sets at the Palais Garnier had sparked a new idea within me.

I envisioned a new type of portrait, one that would employ the full range of my skills. Woodworking, painting, sculpture, and textiles. It would be something different. Rare. Challenging.

I didn't just want this project. I needed it. I felt confident Madame understood this. Like me, she didn't view ambition as an affliction, but a strength to cultivate and nourish.

Two memories help explain the impatience and prickliness of my striving.

The first: My father's client, Mr. Transome, built house after house in New York City, each one grander then the last, and he always hired my father to handle his special carpentry projects. One day—I must have been about thirteen years old—Transome dropped by my father's studio, and after spotting several woodworking pieces I'd fashioned, he complimented my talent for creative endeavor.

"It's a pity there's no future for her here running my workshop," my father said to him. "Men would never take orders from a woman."

"Send her to art school. Have her learn a trade," Transome said, his long, pale thumbs hooked behind his mustard-colored suspenders. "With my recommendation, she can get into any school."

And just like that my fate was sealed. Two men decided it.

The second: Several years later in art school I overheard two male students complaining about how I garnered so much attention because of my sex. "Everyone likes novelty," one said. "She's like a dancing dog, but there's only so long she can remain on those hind legs. Soon she'll be on all four, begging for scraps like the rest of us." My initial indignation at their criticism gave way to worry. What if they were right? That one bitter conversation barbed its way under my skin like a splinter, leaving a wound that remained raw, even years later.

From our first encounter in the lobby of Curtis House, Madame LeFarge recognized that I contained enough boiling ambition to fill gallon buckets, not just teacups, and she wanted to make sure that not a single drop was wasted.

In the back seat of her car, with the museum fading into the background, I clutched one of her gloved hands in my own. Madame turned to me, her eyes wide with surprise, but rather than feeling embarrassed and letting go, I squeezed her fingers tightly. "May I create a portrait for you?"

Her shoulders rose excitedly. "I've been wanting one, but you've seemed so reluctant to paint on commission."

"This won't be a painting." I pointed over my shoulder toward the Palais Garnier. "It will be like one of those tiny sets we just viewed. *A dollhouse.*"

"A dollhouse," she repeated, puzzled.

"I will re-create *your* masterpiece: the Hôtel LeFarge, but in miniature, its exterior and interior. We will show off your vision, how you transformed the house. I can't think of a more striking subject." Already it was taking shape in my mind. The thrilling rush of creative anticipation filled me, and I imagined myself to be a great ship, its sails full of a powerful wind, racing across the North Atlantic. I was breathless. "Just think how magnificent it will be. Original. No one will have anything like it."

Madame nodded, eyes glittering, buoyed by my enthusiasm.

From my reticule, I extracted a tiny pencil and notebook and quickly sketched the Hôtel LeFarge's silhouette. "Remind me of your floor plan. I'm picturing three stories. What rooms would you like re-created?"

So IT was decided in the back seat of Madame's motorcar: I would build a grand dollhouse for her, a piece of art unlike any other.

Although this dollhouse would be miniature, there would be nothing humble about it. It would capture the elegance and modern benefits of the LeFarges' grand home in tiny, exquisite scale. In fact, given the materials we'd need and the amount of time I'd spend on making the dollhouse, the project would cost more than most Parisians could afford to spend on the full-size houses they actually lived in. Madame worried about none of this. She assured me a handsome salary and waved off any concerns about money. I was learning how the lives of the wealthy are big in scale, even when they're trying to be small.

We decided the Petite Hôtel LeFarge would have a facade resembling its namesake's real appearance and an open back to enable easy viewing of the rooms and their contents. To ensure a consistent and realistic rendering of our miniaturized version of the house, the scale would be simple; one inch would equal one foot. The dollhouse would only include rooms we decided would be interesting to re-create in miniature. On the first floor: the primary kitchen, wine cellar, servants' hall, and a small maid's bedroom. The main floor: the ballroom, dining room, parlor, and grand entryway. On the third story, I'd place Madame's bedroom and washroom, the comte's bedroom, the library, and the nursery.

"But what of this lovely spot?" I asked Madame one afternoon while we sat in her beautiful Blue Salon.

"The dollhouse doesn't need to be an exact replica of the house, does it? I can fill it with whatever I want, right?"

"Of course. It's yours, no one else's."

She smiled slyly. "Then I don't need my Blue Salon. I can use the entire dollhouse to collect the type of art and books that interest me and put them wherever I want. The Petite Hôtel LeFarge will reflect who I truly am."

AFTER REVIEWING the dollhouse's plans again and checking its measurements, Madame and I discovered a problem. The Petite Hôtel LeFarge would be too big to fit through the door of my room at Curtis House. I couldn't build it there.

Madame was unfazed. "We can convert one of the château's outbuildings for you to use as a studio, and you can continue to live in the main house."

Behind Curtis House lay a building once used for stabling horses and livestock, but since no animals had resided on the premises in fifteen years, the structure had been converted into a garage and general workshop. The groundskeeper took no issue with allowing me a portion of the space to work, so after a few modifications were made, I moved in. The other women regarded my comings and goings from the château to the outbuilding, my arms filled with crates of tools, as a peculiarity, but no one asked questions. Apparently artists were considered to be figures prone to strange, experimental interests, and a general attitude of open-minded bonhomie and self-sufficiency reigned at Curtis House, so I was given ample latitude for my creative pursuits.

To find the tools and wood I needed, I visited the winding cobbled alleys of the city's Faubourg Saint-Antoine district, where the woodworkers, cabinetmakers, and carpenters kept their workshops. There, I studied timber—ebony, beech, and tulipwood—searching the grains and whorls until I found what I wanted. After purchasing several planks of rosewood and padauk, I cajoled one of the cabinetmakers into allowing me to mill the timber on his premises before returning to my studio with the wood ready to be put to work. With each tool I unpacked, I felt close to my father. Finally I'd formed my own vision for a new project, one my father would have been proud of, I told myself.

Over the next several months, I was in my new workshop focused on finishing the carcass of the dollhouse before Madame returned from her summer coastal sojourn in Deauville. Many of my wealthy clients fled the city during July and August, leaving me more time to focus my attention on my new project. Curtis House also emptied as my housemates jumped at any opportunity to vacation in the countryside, but except for a few brief escapes to the ocean, I remained behind, working on the Petite Hôtel LeFarge.

One morning in early September I visited Hôtel LeFarge to finalize a few designs. Madame was still in Normandy, but before she'd left, she'd given me permission to stop by the house anytime to review my plans, so after a servant let me inside, I headed upstairs to the library. It was quiet, and much of the household appeared to be out on social calls or tending to errands. After I completed my sketches and plans for the wall shelves, I gathered my papers and pencils to head downstairs to the servants' hall to take final notes on the kitchen. As I approached the library's door, low voices drifted toward me, but when I exited, no one was to be found.

Farther down the hallway, the door to the comte's bedroom was open. I recognized the lilting high voice belonging to Madame's lady's maid. Then silence. I proceeded toward the bedroom to ask her a question about access to the first floor's china room, but when I reached the open doorway, I froze.

I found the comte draped across his enormous four-poster bed with the maid on her knees folded over his lower half. It only took a moment for me to figure out what was happening, but in that brief beat of time, from where he lay, my patron's husband locked eyes with me and his lips quirked into a triumphant smile. The woman continued servicing him, unaware of my presence. He gave no sign of shame or embarrassment. He said nothing. He made no move to bring the deed to an end.

I backed away from the doorway, not daring to breathe.

In the years following this incident, I've imagined many ways I *wish* I'd reacted. I wish I'd rushed into that bedroom, pulled the girl off the comte, and berated the man for his infidelity.

Instead I skittered away from the bedroom like a frightened mouse. I fled down two flights of stairs, my head pounding. Unnoticed amid the bustling kitchen, I leaned against the wall, holding my hand to my thundering heart. In that moment, I'd have given anything to forget what I'd just seen. *Anything.*

One of the maids hurried past me with a tray of unbaked pastries. "*Puis-je vous aider, mademoiselle?*"

"*Non, non,*" I said, waving away her offer of help.

I slunk into the empty servants' hall and collapsed onto one of the long dining table's benches, debating what step to take next. Should I tell Madame the truth? The very idea of such an awkward, dreadful conversation defied my imagination, no small feat. Even if I could get the words out, I feared what wheels would be set in motion by my revelation.

Let's not forget I had no real functional knowledge of how

a marriage worked. Given that my father had never remarried, I hadn't seen the expectations of a husband and wife up close. Could it actually be possible this type of behavior was commonplace?

Perhaps Madame already knew of his indiscretions. From my painting clients, I'd learned how the Parisian upper class was famous for the creativity of its extramarital romantic entanglements. Maybe such an arrangement existed between the LeFarges. It was possible she knew exactly what he was doing, but didn't care.

But really, I knew the truth: Madame was faithful and thoughtful. She would not see the comte's actions as anything other than a betrayal. Fury heated me. I felt a fierce protectiveness toward my patron. She'd been nothing but generous to me, and for that she had my loyalty, but now I possessed the awful knowledge of her husband's perfidy—and under her very own roof, no less. This knowledge would devastate her, so I made a decision.

I would say nothing.

Though I wanted to tell her what had happened, this would satisfy only my need to unburden myself of a secret. Nothing good would come of her knowing. Only heartbreak. I needed to spare her the pain of this secret.

What I couldn't forget was the dirty little grin on the comte's face when he saw me. He had enmeshed me in his sordid dalliance and enjoyed it. The bastard. I would bide my time, waiting for a moment when I could make him pay for his recklessness.

A WEEK after my dreadful encounter with the comte at Hôtel LeFarge, I was applying tiles to the dollhouse's roof when Madame arrived in my doorway, trailing the autumn scent of dry leaves and damp wool. She had never paid me an unannounced visit, and I stiffened, fearing she knew what I'd witnessed at her house. I stayed silent. Fortunately for me, Madame was focused on the dollhouse. As she circled the miniature, her nostrils flared.

"I apologize for that smell," I said, relieved for the distraction as I pointed to a small pot atop the stove in the corner. "I've heated up glue because I'm applying tiles to the roof today."

"How industrious."

I nodded, busying myself with tidying the workspace, anything to keep from looking in her eyes, but she was preoccupied with unsnapping the clasp of her slim black handbag and withdrawing a package. "You must see this. Go on, open it!"

She handed me a small package wrapped in brown felt, and I gently pulled back the fabric to reveal a tiny painting. A seascape. Simple linear horizontal brushstrokes of violet and indigo with a few dashes of crimson composed the ocean, but the sky—the sky!—even in miniature it was radiant. Gold and violet paint swirled above the ocean, creating an evocative contrast of soft rounded shapes and textures. "It's lovely."

"Isn't it? A Dutch artist painted it for me. He arrived fairly recently here in Paris, but already he's taken up with Mr. Picasso and Mr. Braque. Won't this seascape be perfect for the dollhouse?"

"It will."

Madame's face mirrored the excitement I felt. "We make quite a pair, don't we?"

We looked at each other in silence for several beats, smiling. I hated keeping a secret from this woman but remained convinced the truth about her husband would only bring pain.

"I view the world differently now. Everything I see makes me wonder how I could miniaturize it," I confessed.

"Well, I hope you're not living in this workshop. The heat was ghastly this summer. Did you manage to get away at all during August?"

"I went to Honfleur with a few of the girls for a week."

A flicker of distress shadowed Madame's face. "Only a week? Are you spending all your time out here alone?"

"I'm still teaching too."

Madame placed her handbag on one of the chairs, peeled off her gloves, and then unpinned her hat and removed it from her head. "Where can I put these?"

"What are you doing?" I asked, taking the hat and gloves warily.

"I'm going to help you apply roof tiles. It looks like a fairly mindless task. Should be perfect for me," she answered with a wink.

"Madame, the glue is messy. You'll ruin your suit." Her skirt and jacket alone probably cost enough to feed an entire arrondissement.

"Then give me a smock. Show me what to do."

I handed her one of my heavy canvas aprons, which she slipped over her head before turning her back for me to tie it. As I stepped forward to fasten the sash around her waist, I noted the tendrils of hair loosened from her hairpins, the way they glistened gold, vining against the threads of blue veins under the delicate skin of her neck. I felt an unexpected urge to unpin the rest of her hair and run my fingers through it.

I stepped away to busy myself with stirring the glue, and as I did, my hand hit against the hot rim of the pot. When I yanked it away, the flare of the burn reddening my skin was a relief. I needed a reminder that close intimacy would only bring pain.

9
Tildy

2024

As soon as the Bel's front door had closed behind Kitty Kim and her KTVU photographer, Dale spun around to face Tildy and Emiko in the foyer. "How did we not know about that goddamn crack?"

The two women traded cautious looks. Seeing the cracked stained glass had rattled Tildy to her core. How *had* she missed it? Even if it had developed in the last week or so, she should have noticed it. It was her job to know everything about the Bel, and that crack was in plain sight. She pulled up her phone, quickly scrolling through her emails to find a specific one. "The stained glass had its semiannual cleaning three weeks ago. I have the report right here, and"—she paused, scanning the email—"there's no mention of the crack."

"So it formed that quickly?" Emiko glanced toward the Main Reading Room. "Is it safe for us to be in there?"

The air crackled with tension.

"Shit, shit, shit, I'm too old for this," Dale muttered. "Do you think I managed to convince Kitty it wasn't a big deal?"

Emiko nodded. "Yes, you seemed completely unconcerned. Kitty was much more focused on the dollhouses, and since they didn't take any pictures or video of the ceiling, I think we'll be fine."

But the quickly developing crack *was* worrisome. Tildy hoped it was simply cosmetic, a sign that the ceiling needed minor repairs.

But it was also entirely possible the crack indicated much more serious structural problems. *Stay calm*, Tildy thought. It made no sense to freak out until an expert weighed in.

"Let me do a little research," she said. "I'll check back with you in an hour."

At the appointed time, Tildy found Dale pacing around his office.

"I've already called Rogers and Delaney, the top engineering firm in the city, and they can get an inspection team over here next Thursday afternoon," she said.

"Other than cleaning, has there been any other work done on the ceiling in recent years?"

Tildy wielded a rather tattered manila folder. "According to these old records, some minor repairs and seismic retrofitting were done after the Loma Prieta Quake of 1989, but that's it."

Dale huffed a sigh. "The last thing we can afford is a big infrastructure project."

"Let's not get ahead of ourselves. Rogers said if there are no other signs of cracking, we should hold tight until he sends an inspection crew over next week."

At five o'clock that evening, Tildy and Emiko gathered in Dale's office to watch Kitty Kim on the news. Her segment on the Bel was the second one into the show. As Tildy watched, she realized she was holding her breath. She forced an exhale, telling herself there was no need to be so nervous. Kitty's story on the Bel's secret room and the dollhouses was terrific. Wisely, the cameraman always included Kitty's finger pointing at the miniatures to give a sense of scale within the dollhouses, so the exquisite craftsmanship came across, even on television. No mention was made of the crack in the ceiling.

When the segment ended, they all heaved relieved sighs.

"There's no way someone could watch that and not want to visit the Bel immediately, right?" Emiko asked, laughing.

"Let's hope," Tildy said over her shoulder, dashing back to her office to take care of a few more tasks before leaving for the evening.

A little over an hour later, Tildy's head jerked up from her laptop at the sound of Dale shouting. She hopped from her desk and found him in his office, still watching the television and pointing at the screen. "Look!"

Tildy turned and watched as Kitty's segment on the Bel played again, but this time it was repackaged with a different news logo and chyron.

"Our story's the feel-good finale on the national news!" Dale cheered.

Open-mouthed, Tildy gaped at the television screen, watching as the story ended and Pilar Holt, the famous news anchor, reappeared on-screen.

"I've actually lived in apartments smaller than those dollhouses," Pilar joked. "Well, folks, if you know anything that can help the Belva Curtis LeFarge Library solve their mystery, please email them using the address at the bottom of your screen. That's all for this evening. Good night. See you tomorrow."

Dale clicked the television off with his remote. "Well? Have you checked the special email to see if anything helpful has come through?"

"I'll look!" Tildy beelined back to her office and logged into the email they'd set up for leads. Her eyes widened. Over a hundred emails. She smiled, opening the most recent and scrolled, only to find a rambling message about fond memories of a woman's childhood dollhouse. Tildy clicked to the next one. Spam about a nutritional supplement smoothie. The third was a plea to consider adopting a rescue shelter dog.

Tildy groaned, as Dale appeared in her doorway, expectant.

"This is going to take a while," she muttered.

TILDY SPENT another hour scanning the inbox. Only a handful of the emails were actually about dollhouses, and they weren't relevant to the Bel. Later, when Tildy crawled into bed that evening, strange voices from the emails echoed throughout her sleep, creating weird, unsettling dreams about skin care systems, weight loss programs, and requests for money.

The next morning, Tildy returned to her desk, dreading what she'd find in the inbox, but her spiraling doubts were interrupted when the distinct FaceTime trill lit up her phone. She accepted the call, and an out-of-focus blur filled Tildy's phone screen. The blur quickly refocused into what appeared to be the sleeve of an oatmeal-colored cabled sweater.

A voice asked, "Hello, is this Mathilda Barrows?"

"Yes, it is," Tildy said slowly, trying to make sense of the sweater close-up.

"Drats, am I using that Facephone thingie? For Pete's sake, what the heck is going on? Hello? Hello?" An old woman, her face haloed by white hair, popped up on Tildy's screen. "Goodness, there you are. And I look like a fright! How did I end up on the Facephone?"

Tildy suppressed a smile, unsure how to answer.

"My dear, do you work at the Belva Curtis LeFarge Library in San Francisco? I called the number on the library's website and was redirected to you, I think."

"Yes, I'm the Bel's head curator."

"Excellent, I've ended up with the right person. My name's Phyllis Mason. Joy Wolfe was my mother."

Joy Wolfe . . . Tildy frowned, trying to place the name.

Seeing her confusion, Phyllis Mason helped. "You know, Joy Wolfe, from *It's a Beautiful World*?"

Immediately Tildy got it. Joy Wolfe was a legend. Her memoir *It's a Beautiful World* had been adapted into a beloved musical and movie of the same title. Tildy thought of her favorite holiday tradition: every year at Christmastime, for as long as she could remember, she and her mother had curled up together on the family room couch to stay up late watching *It's a Beautiful World* and singing along with the musical numbers.

"Oh my gosh, yes! She was your mother?"

"She was."

Tildy stared at the woman's face on her phone screen. *Why on earth was Joy Wolfe's daughter calling her?* Tildy almost dropped the phone before steadying herself. "Wow, this is such a . . ." She didn't know where to start, but luckily Phyllis jumped right back in.

"Last night I was watching the evening news and saw a story about your library's discovery of a pair of old dollhouses in a secret room. When I spotted the little sign with Cora Hale's signature, I knew I had to get in touch with you immediately."

"Cora Hale?" Tildy repeated slowly, not understanding.

"Yes, Cora Hale the dollhouse maker. I have another one of her masterpieces! My mother commissioned it back in the thirties."

Tildy's mind began whirring like a helicopter blade coming to life. She pictured the CH monogram marking both dollhouses and her mother's sketch. Cora Hale was CH . . . yes! But *Cora*. Cora was also Tildy's middle name. That connection couldn't be written off as coincidence, she was sure of it.

Tildy's first name came from her paternal grandmother, Mathilda Grace Barrows, a rather stern matriarch Tildy had met several times during visits to her father's family. But whenever she had asked about the inspiration for her middle name—Cora—her mother would say little more than "I named you after a good friend."

A prickle of goose bumps rose on Tildy's arms. *A good friend.*

How had Cora met her mother? A sizable age gap existed between the dollhouse maker and Tildy's mother—about sixty years.

With her free hand, Tildy reached for her laptop and googled *Cora Hale*. Nothing. She then typed in Phyllis's mother, *Joy Wolfe*. Up came a lengthy Wikipedia page, and Tildy skimmed its introductory paragraph.

> **Joy Wolfe** (née Patchly, 1902–1939) was an aviatrix, explorer, naturalist, photographer, filmmaker, public speaker, and author. When many of the young men of her small Kansas town left to fight in World War I, sixteen-year-old Joy learned to fly a crop-dusting plane to help support her family. In 1919, she met Charlie Wolfe while he was touring Kansas with the artifacts and photographs he collected during a 1907–1909 around-the-world sail with the great naturalist Edmund Paris. After Joy and Charlie married, the photogenic couple captured the public's imagination with their adventures to then-far-flung lands in East and Central Africa, the Middle East and South Pacific, China, and Alaska. The Wolfes disappeared in their famous airplane *The Ray*, a Sikorsky S-39, off the coast of North Borneo in 1939 and their deaths were confirmed after the US Navy discovered the crash site in 1944. Joy's memoir, *It's a Beautiful World*, describing her globetrotting was published posthumously in 1940. After becoming a bestseller, the book was adapted into a musical (1956), and then again into an Oscar-winning film (1964).

Flustered, and fearing she was repeating herself, Tildy asked, "So . . . your mom commissioned a dollhouse from Cora Hale?"

"Yes, in the thirties. Sawhill, our family home, was almost like a natural history museum filled as it was with all the artifacts and specimens my parents collected during their travels. Unfortunately Sawhill burned down in 1940, but the dollhouse survived. It was in Cora's workshop at the time of the fire."

"And you have it now?"

"I do. After I married, Cora gave it to me."

"Oh, so you remained in touch with the dollhouse maker over the years?"

"Goodness, yes! She was a great source of personal inspiration for me. Such an extraordinary artist, she was. All the remarkable things she re-created in miniature, well, it was just marvelous, I tell you. I suppose if you have two of her dollhouses, you know exactly how special she was, don't you?"

Tildy couldn't believe this lucky break.

"Yes, yes, the houses are remarkable. Can I ask, where did Cora Hale live?"

"New Hampshire."

Tildy nodded at the connection between the location of Cora's workshop and where Meg had attended boarding school. Sure, New Hampshire was a small state, but how exactly would they have crossed paths?

"My mother had a favorite story about the dollhouse," Phyllis was saying. "Apparently Cora couldn't achieve the aged affect she wanted on her miniature replicas of fossils, so she wandered the woods around her home at night, listening for owls. Whenever she heard one, she'd search for their droppings and use the mouse bones in those scat pellets for her fossils. Those tiny things doubled as the skeletons of larger animals that my parents had on display in Sawhill. I'll say, Cora was nothing if not resourceful."

Tildy nodded, amazed.

"Her whole family was so dear to me," Phyllis continued.

Frantic, Tildy searched her desk for a pen and paper to take notes. "When's the last time you saw Cora?"

"I remained in touch with her over the years. We wrote letters and she even came to New York City a couple times to see a few of my own art shows."

"You're an artist too?"

"I am. A textile artist. Cora always supported my art, although when I announced I was going to school for it, she did everything she could to dissuade me. She worried it would steal the joy from my work."

"But it didn't?"

Phyllis chuckled. "No, I've remained an artist through it all." She leaned in very close to the phone screen, squinting. "The last time I saw Cora must have been in the early seventies, shortly before she passed away. Perhaps 1973?"

"Where was that?

"New York City. After art school, I never returned to New Hampshire. Eventually I married, had my own children, and kept making art." A pause. "But I haven't just called to reminisce. I'd like my mother's dollhouse to be included in your upcoming exhibit. It's time the world learns about Cora Hale and her marvelous creations."

Tildy nodded, thinking quickly. Joy Wolfe was an adored American historical figure. A household name. *It's a Beautiful World* had been a bestselling book and the theatrical productions won multiple Tonys and Oscars. She'd been honored at countless institutions like the Smithsonian and New York City's Natural History Museum. To add a dollhouse version of Sawhill to the Bel's two other dollhouses would raise the library's profile considerably. It practically offered a guarantee that people would visit. And with three dollhouses, Tildy could stage this as an actual exhibit, not just two new interesting pieces to be displayed.

"Wow, thank you so much for offering it. We'd be honored to exhibit your dollhouse. I'm more than happy to arrange for its transportation."

"Actually I'll need to travel with it."

"I'll ensure it will be treated very carefully, but if you really want to keep a close eye on it, of course I can arrange for your travel too."

Phyllis's face twisted into an expression Tildy couldn't fully decipher. Annoyance? Anxiety? Indignation? Before Tildy could think more about it, Phyllis sat straighter, looking serious. "The dollhouse contains important information about my mother and while I have no doubt you'll take excellent care of it, I'd feel best if I can show it to you myself. The dollhouse reveals some surprises."

"What kind of surprises?"

Phyllis waved an impatient hand at the screen to halt more questions. "It's just easier if I show you in person."

"Okay, I understand." The last thing Tildy wanted was to somehow lose this important connection to Sawhill.

Phyllis's expression softened and she nodded, placated.

"I'll look into flights," Tildy said.

"Oh no, I don't want to fly. My daughter and I are thinking about taking a road trip across the country and bringing you the dollhouse. A great adventure!"

Phyllis had to be at least ninety years old. How would she manage a cross-country drive?

"I imagine we'll arrive in about two weeks or so. How does that sound?"

Two whole weeks? Tildy forced herself to keep a smile plastered on her face. She needed conservation work to begin with the dollhouses immediately if she was going to exhibit them anytime soon. In addition to a handful of minor repairs, the dollhouses needed their contents inventoried, as well as thoroughly dusted, cleaned, and polished.

"Terrific. But if you change your mind, again, I'm happy to make any travel arrangements you like."

"As soon as I have a more concrete timeline, I'll send you the details. May I text you at this number?"

"Sure."

"Wonderful. Toodle-oo, my dear."

Tildy lowered her phone to her desk, still shocked.

Any of the dollhouses—the Hôtel LeFarge, the thirty-room grand home, or Sawhill—would be wonderful to exhibit individually, but the three of them together? Tildy knew this exhibit would be special. Unique. No one would have ever seen anything like this. Just imagining it made her sweat with excitement.

From a professional standpoint, Tildy knew designing an exhibit by this previously unknown woman artist—Cora Hale—was the opportunity of a lifetime. If Tildy could learn more about Cora Hale and her extraordinary work, she could design an exhibit that could put the Bel in an important spot of uncovering the legacy of a significant woman artist. This would be sure to draw interest from sponsors, wouldn't it?

The personal implications offered by this opportunity were even more thrilling: Tildy would learn more about her mother. Answers, that's all she wanted.

Cora Hale. Cora Hale. Cora Hale.

The name ran on a loop through Tildy's mind as she slowly rose from her desk and headed for the circulation desk in search of Iris Feng, the Bel's genealogy specialist.

Tildy found Iris perched in front of her computer, her spine straight, eyes focused on her monitor. Tildy described her call with Phyllis and before she'd even finished, Iris's fingers were dancing over her keyboard.

While Tildy waited for Iris to find more information about Cora Hale, she googled Phyllis Mason. Judging by the number of search results, Phyllis had downplayed her own significance as an artist.

Reviews popped up from *Artforum*, the *New York Times*, *ARTnews*, as well as notifications about her exhibits, many at acclaimed museums and galleries. Tildy scrolled through the results, admiring the images of Phyllis's art. From what she could see, Phyllis created mobiles and installations of clouds using a variety of materials ranging from silk to wool to glass. They were striking, haunting, and beautiful.

Minutes later, the printer hummed to life and the genealogy specialist handed over several pages of notes. Iris had run Cora's name through the digitized library records and found several old photos of Cora attending Belva's parties between 1955 and 1965. She also appeared in old accounting records for being paid to create several statues around the Bel—the bronze one of Gruffwood standing sentry in the foyer, a bronze owl in the Main Reading Room, and the mice and baby elephant in the Children's Room. Tildy pondered these findings. Cora and Belva had worked together quite extensively. How had her young mother known these women?

"I can't believe you found all this in less than ten minutes!"

Iris nodded, shrugging. "You'd be amazed what's possible to uncover about someone with only a few details. There are several comprehensive genealogy databases, but my favorite is YourStory.com. It has everything."

Tildy traced her finger down the page. "It looks like Cora's great-grandson is alive and lives in the same house she once did."

"Yep. Did you see he teaches science at the local high school? His school contact information is there."

Cora Hale's great-grandson could be the key.

As if reading her mind, Iris cracked her knuckles. "Well, what are you waiting for? Aren't you going to call him?"

10
Cora

1911–1914

That fall Madame LeFarge started visiting my workshop several times a week, eager for a task to complete. Not only did she prove to be helpful working on the dollhouse, but her presence drew my housemates out to help us. Several of the women stitched window treatments and while others embroidered rugs, the rest applied tiles and wooden planks to the dollhouse's floor and walls, allowing me time to put my painting skills to use by re-creating the Hôtel LeFarge's frescoes and works of art in miniature.

One afternoon, Madame arrived and from her handbag, she tugged out a small leather-bound book. "I'm in the mood to read aloud. Who's ready for *Jane Eyre*?"

My housemates cheered, but I said nothing.

"Cora, is this book disagreeable to you?"

"I've never read it," I answered.

Everyone's mouths dropped open in incredulity. "What?" Peggy asked.

But Madame gave no time for discussion of the limitations of my experience with reading. "Well, then, allow me the honor of introducing you to one of my favorites, a classic." She flipped through the first few pages and began reading. "*There was no possibility of taking a walk that day . . .*"

I returned to painting the nursery's furniture. Time flew as Madame read, and before I knew it, lavender-colored shadows laddered the floor.

"Goodness, the hour's gotten late. Winny won't be pleased if I keep you all from dinner," Madame said, snapping the book shut. Groans of disappointment erupted from each corner of the workshop, but Madame locked eyes with me.

"You're enjoying the story, Cora?"

"Those dreadful Reeds. Jane's expectations are so low. When she says she'll let a horse dash at her chest for a chance at love, it breaks my heart."

Madame rose, looking thoughtful. "Sometimes we don't realize how harmful love can feel until it's too late."

CHARLOTTE BRONTË was the first novelist Madame introduced to me, but not the last. Jane Austen, Jack London, Edith Wharton, and Upton Sinclair soon followed, but we didn't limit our entertainment to fiction. On another afternoon, one of my housemates arrived with her cello and proceeded to regale us with an improvised concert. I soon became familiar with music from the moderns, Debussy and Ravel, while enjoying traditionalists like Chopin and Liszt too.

The best part of my busy workshop wasn't the swift progress on the dollhouse—it was the education I received. While installing parquet flooring, painting surfaces to resemble marble, and creating tiny millwork for the walls, windows, and doors, my friends introduced me to thought-provoking ideas and we discussed the news of the day. We celebrated Mrs. Curie's Nobel Prize award for her discovery of new elements. I learned how a Manhattan shirtwaist fire tragedy was inspiring a number of different labor regulations, including a law to limit the workweek to fifty-four hours.

Never before had I experienced such full, rewarding days. I was learning not only about topics as wide-ranging as geography and literature, but about friendship. How had I led nineteen years of such a solitary existence? When news of the *Titanic*'s sinking reached us, we were in my workshop listening to Madame read *Twenty Years at Hull House*. As the scope of the tragedy was revealed, we absorbed the grim news together, weeping on one another's shoulders.

And we had fun too. When the tango craze swept through Paris during the spring of 1913, we parked a gramophone in my workshop and took to our feet. One evening, when I stood at my workbench watching the other women pair up and dance, Madame leaned in close to my ear. A tendril of her hair grazed my temple, tickling me. "Be my partner?"

"I really don't know how to do it."

"You won't learn by watching. Come on, I'll lead."

She clasped my hand and I surrendered to the tidal pull of her. Without wasting a moment, she started humming. Soon we were whirling around the room, swinging our hips from side to side.

"The steps are small, but fast," Madame instructed. We danced a path along the periphery of the room. "See, that's not so hard, is it?"

"You make it easy."

Our faces were very close together and with her breath on my neck, I couldn't help but lean in closer. During one of our laps around the workshop, she tightened her grip around my waist and tucked her face into my neck. A moment later, when we pulled apart to turn, I stole a glance and saw how her long pale lashes flickered downward as if she'd been caught looking at me. Unlike so many of Paris's fine ladies, Madame wore her face bare of lipstick and rouge. Her only adornment was the confetti toss of freckles smattering her cheeks and the bridge of her nose. Our dancing—and maybe our proximity—raised a flush to her face, giving her a girlish air, and I could imagine how young, bright-eyed Belva Curtis would have looked upon arriving in France, a daisy among hothouse roses.

Our bodies warmed from dancing, causing a sweet lily of the valley powdery scent to rise from Madame's exposed skin, her neck and maybe her hair too. With every breath I took, I grew increasingly light-headed. The beating of my own heart thundered in my ears. In the distance, the music rose and fell. It took every bit of my willpower to resist leaning in close enough to graze her with my lips.

As the gramophone wound down, her gaze locked with mine. Slowly, our hands fell apart, but heat still scorched my skin where her fingers brushed the bare, tender section of my forearm below the cuff of my sleeves. On the spot of my lower back where her hand had once rested, the blood below my skin pulsed wildly.

Around us, the air was full and alive. I imagined this was what it would feel like to be surrounded by a shimmer of hummingbirds and the frantic whirring of their tiny wings. Belva and I stepped back from each other, but I steeled myself to look straight at her, my eyes intent with a single question: *Am I imagining this attraction between us?* Anticipation rose so high in my chest, in my throat, I could scarcely breathe.

Nearby church bells chimed the hour. Mrs. Winnington, or Winny as I'd come to call her, suddenly stood in the entrance watching. She was the one woman from Curtis House who rarely stepped foot in my workshop. Judging by her stony gaze, it was clear she believed the dollhouse to be an appalling example of excess and frivolity.

"Ladies, it's time to wash up for dinner."

"Is it six o'clock already?" Madame asked, her voice high and fast. She looked away and moved swiftly to where she'd hung her jacket on a peg, giving me no opportunity to answer. "I must be getting home, my dears, but I'll be sure to come by later this week."

In the wake of her departure, I told myself not to read too much into her attention. She was in search of friendship. If Madame

LeFarge was spending time in my workshop, it was because she felt lonely. If she was preoccupied with collecting pieces for the dollhouse, it was because she needed a project. If she leaned toward books with romance, it was because she was filling the void in her marriage. I examined these explanations the way an orchestra conductor studies their musicians, searching for timing, meter, dynamics, and artistry. I desperately wanted a cue that she returned my feelings, but I would not initiate an overture myself. After my debacle in New York City, I would never act impulsively for romance again.

DURING THE spring of 1914, as the Petite Hôtel LeFarge neared completion, Madame planned to unveil the dollhouse at a grand party. Though I should have been delighted for my work to be exhibited, I found myself growing increasingly anxious. The dollhouse had been the center of my life for three years. Miniatures had changed me. I viewed the world differently now. Everything I saw, no matter if it was a building or a hairbrush, I studied, wondering how I could miniaturize it. My skills stretched and expanded. The amount of problem solving that went into building the Petite Hôtel LeFarge lit up my mind like no other endeavor, and I relished the consuming burn of creativity it required. Much like falling in love, making miniatures became my obsession. I was building a new world, one I controlled; but one part of myself that I could not control was my growing attraction to Madame LeFarge. Once I finished the dollhouse, I feared I'd barely see her. Desperate to distract myself from these concerns, I immersed myself in the project's final details.

When Madame arrived in my workshop one day in early July, I removed my latest creation from the dollhouse and placed it on the workbench.

"What's this?" she asked, coming closer.

A miniature Queen Anne secretary. After realizing I couldn't find small enough cuts of high-quality wood for such a tiny piece in Faubourg Saint-Antoine, I had visited a luthier. There, in his guitar studio, he had laid several samples atop a piece of velvet. I selected the oak and veneered burled walnut.

The piece represented my finest craftsmanship to date. I'd spent weeks creating a holly starburst design inlay on its front.

I drew on one of the tiny brass pulls to remove a drawer and reveal its dovetails. The desk functioned exactly as it would in full-size. I'd visited both a jeweler and clockmaker to acquire tools small enough to produce such detailed work.

"There are nineteen secret compartments inside. Just think, you can hide something in it," I said proudly, envisioning placing a pearl in one of the drawers. I started removing each one to prove my point.

But when I glanced at Madame, expecting to see delight, tears streaked her face.

I faltered. "I'm sorry, I thought . . ."

"The miniature is exquisite," she said, sniffling. She buried her face in her gloved hands. "My secrets are too big to fit in a miniature."

I took a seat next to her and rested my hand on her shoulder, pondering what to say next. Of course, I could guess at the problem. My fury over the comte's betrayal still clung to me, vivid and sticky as a fresh coat of paint.

"It's my husband."

I kept my face blank.

"When I met him, he was different from everyone else who had tried to win me. Obviously he was handsome and young, but he was also sophisticated and aloof. My parents were skeptical of his intentions, insisting he believed himself too good for me, but with the overconfidence only the young possess, I took their opposition as an invitation to pursue him with every means at my disposal. In no time we were married, and almost immediately trouble began. I spotted signs of his late-night carousing and infidelities, but I was already expecting his child, so what was I to do?" She rubbed at her eyes. "I've made the best of the situation. My son is my treasure. I've built a beautiful home and used my days to help others, but now my husband's pushed me too far. Last night he brought one of his women into our house and bedded her under the very roof I paid to have redone."

I blanched at the heartbreak in Madame's shuddering voice. I hated to see her distress.

"For the last few years, you and this dollhouse have brought me such joy during difficult times, but you're almost done. You'll soon move on. After I unveil the dollhouse to my friends, your skills will be in high demand."

I shrugged. "Madame, I can scarcely think of moving on. With everyone else unsettled by politics these days, I'm more than happy to be absorbed with finishing this."

Somewhere in a distant city I'd barely heard of, a young man assassinated the heir to the Austro-Hungarian throne, and this incident was setting off wave after wave of conflict and tension between the various governments of Europe. How such a faraway event could cause such a violent reaction in Paris was beyond me, but the drumbeat of war had grown unmistakable. Suddenly the tricolor flickered in the breeze on every city block, even the residential ones. Talk of seizing back the Alsace-Lorraine filled the streets, shops, and cafés of Paris. Even I, absorbed with my work, couldn't miss the chatter.

But Madame shrugged off my mention of political affairs and reached out to smooth my hair, letting her fingers trail along my cheek until she cupped my chin. "You must call me Belva now." She leaned closer, whispering, "What will I do without you?"

Her touch felt like flames along my skin, but even as my heart galloped, my mind was occupied with the dollhouse. Since my earliest days of contemplating this project, an idea had been forming—this was my opportunity to use it. For my portrait of Belva to be honest, I needed to reveal the truth. To the outside world, her life appeared perfect, but it was not. It was complicated. I wanted to hint at the reality. To do so, I needed to place clues in the dollhouse. Few people might notice them, but the comte would.

"Take off your blouse," I said.

Belva recoiled. "Excuse me?"

"I'm going to paint your likeness right into the dollhouse."

"But why do I need to—"

"I want your terrible husband to see what he's been missing."

Belva's hand went to the lacy collar of her blouse. "I can't do that."

"Of course you can. You're Belva Curtis LeFarge. You can do whatever you want."

The stunned look on Belva's face gave way to something more nuanced. Though her eyes darted around my studio nervously, she sat taller, her chin tilted upward. With steady fingers, she started to unbutton her blouse.

I rushed around the workshop, angling my hand to test the light from different places. By the time Belva peeled back her blouse, I was about to direct her to a spot by one of the windows, but when I looked at her, words died on my lips.

"What?" she whispered, folding her arms across her breasts.

"Don't do that." I gestured for her to drop her hands.

Reluctantly, she stood before me, her chest uncovered.

"You're beautiful."

She started to protest, but I cut her off.

"Stop. Listen to me: you're beautiful."

I circled Belva, admiring the delicacy of her clavicle, the wings of her scapula, the long, graceful lines of her humerus. Forget woodcarving, joinery, turning, intarsia and marquetry, there's no finer example of craftsmanship than the human body. Clasping her hand, I ran my index finger along the nobs of her wrist as she smiled at me, shivering.

Bit by bit, Belva unfurled the way a flower's petals slowly loosen and open when brought into a warm interior. She shed her shyness and soon stood tall.

I gestured for her to sit in the chair I'd placed by the window. Once she was seated, I studied the streaks of light, the planes they created across her face, neck, and chest. I reached out to move her chin and when my fingers grazed her skin, I savored the moment, absorbing the current passing between us with a steady hum.

I shifted her shoulders and leaned close, our faces only inches apart. But I didn't dare look into her eyes for fear of risking everything. I couldn't afford to be banished from Paris the same way I had from New York.

I sat across from her and sketched, adjusting her positioning a few more times so I could make several studies.

The entire time—Was it thirty minutes? An hour? Two hours? I couldn't tell—we didn't speak. It took all my willpower to focus on the work. The lines. The shading. With my pastels, I crosshatched and stippled to get the lighting right, the textures. As I drew her cheeks and nose, I tried not to imagine how smooth and soft her skin would feel under my fingers. When I sketched her hair and the tendrils curling around her temples and neck, I didn't permit myself to think about how I could wrap my hands in those pale strands and bind myself to her.

And then—Winny pushed through the door.

She didn't cross the threshold, just stood motionless, backlit by the afternoon sun. The lemony smell of the nearby crepe myrtle wafted over us, and behind her, long thin leaves of oleander and rounded blooms of common gorse appeared gilded and still in the heat, giving the scene a honeyed glow.

I couldn't see Winny's expression, but Belva remained stock-still.

Finally, Winny coughed. The spell was broken.

"Excuse me, Madame, I apologize for the interruption, but we have an emergency. The American consulate is urging we evacuate. War appears imminent."

11
Tildy

2024

Tildy paced a few laps around her desk, trying to settle her thoughts. Finally, she picked up her phone and tapped the number for Cora Hale's great-grandson, Ben. After two rings, a man answered, sounding irritated. Voices in the background made it hard to hear but Tildy did her best to explain who she was and that she was trying to put together an exhibit of his great-grandmother's work. Before she could mention the dollhouses, he cut her off.

"I know nothing about my great-grandmother. Now if you'll excuse me, I must return to my students."

Tildy scowled. *Rude.* When she opened her mouth to say good-bye, he spoke again over the loudness, this time a little more gently.

"Sorry, things are a little crazy here right now, but I can put you in touch with my mom. She's always talking about organizing my great-grandmother's workshop."

The background noise had faded, making it easier to hear him.

"Your great-grandmother's workshop still exists?"

"Yeah, it's still here. I live in her old house, and the barn is still filled with decades' worth of her things. I think she used to make furniture. Is that what's going in your exhibit? Her furniture?"

"No, we have a collection of her dollhouses."

"Dollhouses? I don't know anything about those. As far as I can tell, the workshop's full of dusty old tools. I always assumed she made furniture, but that would have been unusual for a woman back then, wouldn't it? All I know is that no one's touched the workshop in ages except to use it as a storage unit. A lot of junk has piled up. I guess if I was smart, I'd contact *Antiques Roadshow* to see if there's anything of value."

Antiques Roadshow—*or me*, Tildy thought. Important papers, old photographs, sketches, artifacts, who knew what she might find? Tildy bit her lip. She was getting closer to answers. She didn't need to rely on junky emails sent to the Bel. She could figure out her mother's story on her own.

"I'm really excited to be putting together this exhibit. Her work is amazing. From what I can tell, she did it all—woodworking, painting, ceramics and sculpture, metalwork, and textiles. Her versatility is truly astounding. What if I came out there to look through the workshop? I'd like to find more content for our exhibit. Her old tools, photographs, notes, sketchbooks . . . anything, really."

"You'd come all this way? These dollhouses must be special."

The surprise in his voice gave her pause. Her idea sounded far-fetched. Perhaps she'd only find a mess of spiders, mice, and old Christmas cards. And who was this Ben? Why had she rushed into suggesting she meet a complete stranger at his rural, isolated farmhouse? This had all the makings of a bad *America's Most Wanted* episode. Tildy chewed her lip. Then again, teachers underwent criminal background checks as part of their licensing process, didn't they? Ben would be fine. A geeky old science teacher. What could really go wrong?

After all, this trip was about more than the dollhouses.

Belva, Cora, the library, the dollhouses—Tildy was tired of being alone, grieving, and missing her parents, especially her mother. For years, Tildy had felt slow and logy, like glue ran through her veins. Not an industrial-strength brand glue that you knew to handle with caution, but the white, watery, innocuous kind used in elementary schools. The kind that needed to set for a long time to work properly, but once dried, it was fused solidly. In Tildy's case, this was exactly the problem—she'd stayed in one place too long and now she was stuck, glued into place.

That changed with finding Belva's secret room and its mysterious contents.

This exhibit was no longer just her job. It offered Tildy a possible connection to her mother, a connection she was desperate to tighten. Trying to unravel the story of Cora and her mother was giving Tildy the sense of agency and power she'd been missing. It was an opportunity to push herself out of her small life, to go places, to meet people, to discover new feelings. By putting questions about the past to rest, she could get back to living. She needed to take a few risks, and this trip to New Hampshire to meet a stranger was one of them.

"I know it sounds nuts, but I need to come out there."

"Well, my mom's been living in England for a while."

Tildy's shoulders caved. "Oh."

"But I guess I could show you the workshop. Maybe we can find something that would help."

She perked up. "I . . . I don't want to get in the way, but that would be amazing."

"You wouldn't be getting in my way at all. Like I said, I don't know anything about my great-grandmother and now you've made me curious."

They discussed travel logistics for a few minutes and then Tildy said, "Okay, I'll look into flights and get back to you."

When Tildy ended the call, she didn't immediately start searching travel sites. Years had passed since she'd last been on a plane. Normally, she hated flying, not because it was dangerous—she trusted the statistics that flying was safer than driving—but it could be so unpredictable. Argumentative passengers, cramped seats, storms, staffing shortages, mechanical problems, overbooked flights. Too many things could go wrong, especially in winter.

But none of that mattered, not this time.

Tildy took a deep breath, trying to settle the whirl of excited nerves zipping around her stomach. No doubt about it: Cora Hale represented a groundbreaking artist for her era. Designing a show about her felt important. But also, if there was a chance Tildy could learn more about her mother, she needed to go.

12
Cora

1914

Overnight Curtis House emptied of boarders. With the American consulate urging its citizens to return home, my housemates prepared to comply and insisted I leave with them, but where was I to go? I had no home in New York City anymore. I needed to finish the dollhouse—and I couldn't leave Belva. I sent my friends away, wishing them safe travels, but Winny was not put off so easily. She arrived in my workshop, her hands balled onto fists, itching for a fight. "If you wait too long, you'll be trapped here," she scolded. "You should see the lines wrapping around the banks and travel ticketing offices. Trains are packed, ships are sold out. There's not a minute to waste."

"When are you going?" I asked.

"I'm staying. I work for Madame."

"Well, so do I."

"But your dollhouse can be left behind whereas I manage this entire property and have no plans to hand it over to any invading Huns."

I considered this. It wasn't hard to imagine Winny cutting the kaiser down to size. If I was going to hedge my bets on who would survive this war, my money was squarely on Winny. "I'm staying here with you."

"Why must you be so stubborn?" she huffed, turning to storm back to the château, but before she left, I swear a grudging respect gleamed in her eyes. On the other hand, it's entirely possible her eyes were irritated and tearing from the dust kicked up by my housemates as they fled.

Despite the mass exodus of people leaving Paris, plenty stayed. Spirits were high in the city. National pride was at stake, especially among the upper class. Many Parisians refused to concede any sign of weakness to the Huns. Belva had no intention of canceling her upcoming party, and not even a potential war would alter her plans. If anything, it caused her to double down on the festivities.

"Dearest Cora, if the worst really is on its way, we might as well enjoy ourselves in the meantime," she wrote in a note to me in mid-July. I wondered if she really believed that, or if her husband was behind the insistence that all would be well. Either way, my orders were clear. I had a dollhouse to finish.

For two weeks, I rarely left my workshop. Though I'd quit portrait painting when I left New York City, I would allow myself one more for Belva. A miniature.

I worked and worked until the portrait was complete, perfect. On the morning of Belva's party, two older groundsmen from the Hôtel LeFarge met me on the doorsteps of Curtis House. Behind them, a horse and cart awaited. They loaded the dollhouse for transport and the cart departed, its wheels creaking like arthritic knee joints. I stood in the yard. Alone. I'd been so focused on finishing the dollhouse that I hadn't considered how Belva would react to the recent changes I'd made. Suddenly my stomach seized with nerves. The dollhouse would impress the party attendees, and I would have more miniature commissions coming my way—of that I felt confident—but none of it mattered if Belva was unhappy with my work and with me. I needed to get to Hôtel LeFarge as quickly as possible to meet with her in private before the party to show her the ways I'd altered the dollhouse. I prayed she'd be pleased.

After hurrying from Curtis House in search of a taxicab, I'd made it no farther than rounding the corner of Boulevard Raspail when the steady click of hobnailed boots marching on cobblestone and the opening bars of "La Marseillaise" washed over me.

Aux armes, citoyens!
Formez vos bataillons!
Marchons! Marchons!

Throngs of men in dark blue overcoats and scarlet trousers and kepis filled the avenue. Women followed, pushing carts filled with pots and pans, bundles of bedding, a caged cochin or two. Everyone flowed toward Gare de l'Est. Vehicles had vanished. Not a single cab, taxi, or motor-omnibus rumbled along the streets. It seemed I'd be walking to Hôtel LeFarge.

I fell into the crowd. The men appeared serious and focused. Sheens of sweat glazed everyone's faces, but even if the sun hadn't blazed down on us, the city's mood felt feverish and hot. Elbows jostled. Suddenly the horde felt like a river, and I was a mere twig in a strong current heading for the German border. For the first time, I questioned my plan to remain in Paris, but by that point, what else was I supposed to do? I had no options.

I arrived at Belva's only minutes after the dollhouse was delivered. Once it was settled into one of the ballroom's alcoves, I removed the protective canvas cover I'd sewn for its transport.

Belva's eyes grew as large as dinner plates when she realized the changes I'd made.

"Where's the comte's bedroom?" she whispered.

"Gone." I smiled. After Belva told me of his indiscretion, I'd stripped his bedroom of all furnishings and decor and remade it as her little Blue Salon.

She raised her hand to her mouth. "Everyone will wonder why there's no sign of him . . ."

"Didn't you say everyone knew what he'd done?"

"Well, yes, but . . . now he'll see he's been erased."

"Exactly."

She leaned in to inspect her little Blue Salon, pointing to an empty spot at the center of the back wall. "Is something missing?"

From my pocket, I withdrew a rectangular parcel wrapped in black velvet and placed it on her palm, where it was no larger than a square of chocolate. Once she'd unwrapped it, she gasped.

Even rendered in miniature, Belva's likeness in the portrait was striking. A faint smile played at her lips. Her eyes contained a knowing glint. Her hair fell around her face and shoulders in long waves, bright and golden, especially striking against the cobalt-blue walls of the room. Aside from a dusting of the freckles covering her shoulders and décolletage, her skin was bare. As a final touch, atop her head I'd added a cerise-hued hat, festooned with lacy ostrich feathers that dipped and swirled, adding movement and even a small dose of levity. Though I'd cropped the portrait's borders to hide her breasts, the painting implied an unmistakable intimacy. The composition was daring. Her husband would dislike it, of that I was certain.

When I stole a glimpse of Belva from the corner of my eyes, a mixture of delight and shock spread across her face.

"Oh, Cora, the comte's not going to be happy with this. Not one bit."

But she was smiling.

IN THE ballroom later that evening, the orchestra was playing "California and You" in homage to the party's host. In her raspberry-hued velvet gown, a cluster of silk peonies at her breast, Belva stood out from the crowd. The draping silhouette favored her height and curves. Her cheeks reflected the high color of her dress and ringlets of hair fell about her face, unpinned. She wasn't alone. Blame it on the heat or the manic energy accompanying the city's heightened anticipation of war, but *le gratin*, the city's high society, all seemed slightly undone. Voices boomed, gestures grew more expansive, collars and gowns appeared askew. Everyone knew life was about to change, but no one understood exactly what was coming.

The ballroom quickly filled. Several army officers in full decorative uniform pulled their glittering silver bayonets from their scabbards and pretended to duel. Women laughed, falling over themselves to get out of the way of the roughhousing. The frosty detachment that typically characterized Parisians had washed away with an overabundance of champagne.

When darkness fell, the air remained hot, both inside and out. Crushed in the sweaty, sticky press of bodies in the ballroom, I'd never been so happy my loose beaded and satin tunic didn't require a corset.

At one point, through the crowd, I spotted the comte at the same time his dark gaze found me. We stared at each other. Gone was the smug expression he'd worn when I interrupted his tryst with the maid nearly three years ago. His eyes, blank and cold, told me everything. In that instant, I knew he'd broken the lock on my door that one night I stayed at Hôtel LeFarge. I felt it with certainty.

With the dollhouse, I'd struck back. Perhaps few would notice the significance of his missing bedroom and the portrait of his wife, but he understood it. He knew a connection existed between Belva and me and he hated it.

Hours passed in a dizzying blur. As the crowd thinned, Belva kept me close to her side, and soon we were bidding farewell to the final guests. When I made to leave, she held me back. "Come to my Blue Salon. We have much to celebrate."

I climbed the stairs, following Belva. The backs of my heels stung where my slippers had rubbed. Hunger squeezed at my belly. I was exhausted, yet knew sleep would not come for me anytime soon.

When we entered the Blue Salon, she crossed straight to the French doors, threw them open, and leaned out onto the balconette. I joined her, resting my elbows on the wrought-iron railing, breathing in the quiet. Cool evening air drifted over us, making the skin on my chest and arms rise into tiny goose pimples. Beyond us, oaks and lindens rustled in the breeze, reminding me of the swish of gowns filling the ballroom only moments ago. Overhead, a waxing gibbous moon was stamped against the black sky like a chalky smudged fingerprint. A maid delivered a cart of refreshments to the room and left swiftly. Belva peeled off her long white gloves, tossed them behind her, and stretched.

"We must make a toast," she said, hurrying back inside, but I stayed in place, staring at the night sky. She returned moments later to hand me a coupe. Bubbles of champagne sloshed over its side, making her giggle. "Your hair is a disaster."

I laughed, raking my fingers through my long, loose tangles of hair. "I think my combs are still in here somewhere. I feel them. It's just that this humidity makes my hair thicker than ever."

Belva reached up with her free hand and combed her fingers toward the crown of my head. Her touch against my scalp set off a flurry of electricity, running along my neck and shoulders. I closed my eyes.

"This magnificent mane of yours. Some girls get all the luck," she murmured. Gently, she extracted one of my haircombs. "Look what I found."

When I took it, her fingers lingered against mine for an extra beat, before I swept the comb back into my hair.

We then lifted the rims of our glasses together and clinked. She sipped and placed the coupe on the smooth edge of the railing's top, but when I raised mine, I couldn't get enough of the bubbles, the sharp crispness of flavor, and the cold against my tongue. I drank the champagne down, emptying my glass as if it held water, but Belva didn't notice. Her eyes were locked on mine.

"The Petite Hôtel LeFarge is *magnifique*." She stepped closer to place her palm against my burning cheek. Her own hair curled like waves on a choppy sea, the strands plastering themselves to her damp cheek and neck. "What I would give to have such talent as yours. Such vision," she whispered, and she leaned forward, placing her lips on mine. They were soft and tasted of champagne and salt. Muggy and sticky, we clung together.

"Come away from the window," she breathed, pulling me into the room and onto one of the long settees, where she folded her arms around my shoulders, studying me like I was a gift wrapped with a bow.

"You must leave with me," I said raggedly.

"Shhh," Belva whispered.

"Let's take Jack and go back to the United States," I said. "War's coming. We can't stay."

Belva buried her face in the hollow of my neck. Her lips blazed a path toward my ear and I closed my eyes, my head spinning with champagne, the heat, and the swoony feeling of exhilaration that accompanies not getting enough sleep. I pulled her face toward me, eager to kiss those freckles that sprayed across her cheeks like a sprinkling of brown sugar. For months those freckles had enticed me. When, moments later, Belva's lips found mine, I could have floated straight up to the ceiling.

Then a clatter at the door sent us leaping apart, my heart in my throat.

"Madame, does Mademoiselle Hale require the driver's services?" a maid asked, venturing a step inside, and peering around into the dark indigo shadows painting the room.

Belva and I turned to each other, both flustered. "Yes, yes," I stammered.

"The driver's outside the front door when you're ready," she said quietly, moving to leave.

"Thank you," Belva called, before turning to me to whisper, "Come back in the morning."

It felt as though a cool wind had swept through the room. I wrapped my arms across my chest.

"You'll leave Paris with me?" I asked.

"I want to."

"Then do it. The war will—"

"Yes, yes, I know. Come back tomorrow. We'll hatch a plan," she said.

13
Tildy

2024

The evening before Tildy was scheduled to fly to New Hampshire, she visited the secret room one more time to review her plans. While she was away, Emiko would serve as the point person for exhibit planning and one of the librarians would manage Tildy's daily tasks and oversee the small conservation team that would be moving into the space to prepare the miniatures for display. Tildy circled the dollhouses, savoring her final time of having them to herself. When she returned, the room would be busier and filled with additional tables, lighting, equipment, and people.

Despite a week of passing in and out of the hidden space over and over, it hadn't lost its sense of thrill and mystery. Every time Tildy looked at the dollhouses, she found new things to admire. Clocks, cocktail shakers, candlesticks, cabinets, cutlery, blankets, baskets, billiard tables, bottles of wine and spirits, books, beds, brooms, pianos, paintings, pillows, plants, and playing cards—each dollhouse contained an extraordinary universe of tiny things.

Even after a century, the intensity of the blue used to paint a small room on the smaller dollhouse's top floor was eye-catching. Again, Tildy admired the portrait of Belva positioned on the room's far wall, but a flash of reflected light on the glass doors of a small cabinet caught her attention. Once she'd managed to dodge the glare, Tildy removed a magnifying glass from her pocket and studied the cabinet more closely. On its shelves, she could see an arrangement of tiny framed photos. With tweezers, Tildy opened the cabinet doors for a better look.

She never tired of looking at old images of Belva. Tildy loved that generation's salon-styled hairdos; the ubiquitous strings of pearls; white gloves and dark and glossy lipsticks; fitted frocks, tailored suits, pencil skirts, and polished pumps. No one would ever have described Tildy as any sort of fashion icon—day after day, she wore the same boring basic uniform of black slacks or dark wash jeans, denim button-up shirts, and black sweaters and T-shirts. Still, she appreciated Belva's elegance.

Tildy ran the magnifying glass over the assortment of photos, seeing one of Jack LeFarge in uniform and several of his baby pictures. A candid snapshot of Belva snagged Tildy's attention. It was the type of imperfect picture long gone from the carefully curated photos clogging everyone's social media feeds nowadays. Next to Belva was an unknown woman. She was laughing, her face upturned, eyes shut, mouth open. Really, the shot was an unflattering angle of the unfamiliar woman, yet her expression was so authentic, so unguarded, that it was very endearing. From where she sat next to the woman, Belva smiled widely, clearly delighted. Even in the slightly out-of-focus, grainy black-and-white image, Belva's eyes radiated a hungry and intense longing as she looked at the woman beside her.

Tildy swallowed past a lump in her throat.

Belva's expression caused an ache to pulse deep in Tildy's chest, somewhere behind her solar plexus. This ache seeped through her the way an ice cream cone dropped onto a hot sidewalk will melt and spread well beyond its initial point of impact.

Tildy had never looked at someone that way.

Only then did she notice a shape in the image's background: a dollhouse, one Tildy didn't recognize. The dollhouse was barely visible behind Belva and the woman, but it was there.

Aha! Tildy leaned closer, blinking her eyes, willing the background to clarify. Could this woman be Cora, the dollhouse maker? It would make sense. The women had been very close, that much was obvious from the photo. How had they met? What exactly was happening here?

To the right of the frames on the shelf were five books resembling leather-bound photo albums. Tildy nudged the magnifying glass closer. On the spines of the books, an embossed name glittered in gold lettering.

Meg

Tildy reared back in surprise. She stuffed the magnifying glass into her shirt's breast pocket, slid a white curatorial glove onto her left hand, and using the tweezers with her right hand, she removed the photo albums from the cabinet and placed them on the rim of the dollhouse room.

With her breath held, she transferred one of the albums to her gloved palm and opened it slowly, fearful of cracking the old leather spine. Fortunately, the cover fell to the side without incident, giving Tildy a look at a tiny black-and-white photo of Belva standing in the Main Reading Room next to an unfamiliar young man with a baby in his arms. Tildy held up the magnifying glass again. Underneath the miniaturized snapshot, a caption was written in neat block letters: *Belva with Eddie and Daisy Hart, March 1953*.

The next page showed a toddler standing in the Children's Room. Tildy's pulse quickened. Plump cheeks, distinctive pointy chin, big dark eyes—Tildy's left hand shook slightly as she read the caption: *Daisy, 1955*.

Tildy was nearly positive Daisy Hart and Meg Leigh Barrows were the same person, although she didn't understand the reason for the name change. At some point, her mother had decided to go from being called Daisy to Meg. Tildy told herself it was no big deal. Nicknames changed over time. But then there was the changed surname. Despite Tildy's attempts at reassuring herself, she had a bad feeling about the name changes. Her mother's reluctance to talk about her past raised a lot of red flags.

Page by page, Tildy continued examining the tiny album, hoping for answers.

She paused on one of Belva wearing the custom suit she'd had made for Forty-Niners games, back when the team played in Golden Gate Park's Kezar Stadium. The library still had the striped red-and-gold suit in its collection, sometimes displaying it during football season. Smiling alongside Belva were two of her dear friends, Jane and Josie Morabito, the first women to own a professional football team.

In front of Belva and the Morabitos stood Tildy's mother in braids, beaming, arms raised victoriously. A knee sock had slipped down one of her long thin legs, giving her a puckish look. The lengthy caption covered the other side of the page: *Belva, Jane and Josie Morabito, and Daisy Hart. October 8, 1961. Niners beat Los Angeles Rams, 35–0.*

After several more pages of photos, Tildy found a miniaturized clipping of a *San Francisco Times* newspaper article. Even with the magnifying glass trained on the tiny newsprint, she could only read the date of April 7, 1967, and the headline: "Two Killed in Pacific Heights Fire: Fourteen-Year-Old Girl Accused of Arson, Murder."

Tildy's stomach dropped.

With a growing sense of dread and trembling fingers, she traded the magnifying glass and tiny albums for her phone. On her web browser, she accessed the archives for the *San Francisco Times*, using the library's account, and copied the headline and date from the miniaturized article. Instantly, results filled her screen. She clicked on the first one and started reading.

**Two Killed in Pacific Heights Fire:
Fourteen-Year-Old Girl Accused of Arson, Murder**

San Francisco—In the late hours of April 7th, fire raced through a small cottage behind Pacific Heights' Belva Curtis LeFarge Library (2687 Pacific Ave), resulting in the deaths of Mr. Edward Hart, 44, and his son, Henry Hart, three months old, who had been sleeping in the upstairs bedroom. Mr. Hart, a US Navy veteran who survived the World War II sinking of the USS *Juneau*, has served as the caretaker for the Bel and resided in the cottage since 1945. Three of Mr. Hart's family members, his wife and two daughters, managed to survive.

Fire Chief William Murray said the three-alarm blaze caused total destruction of the building. The fire is believed to have started around 11:25 PM in the kitchen. By the time fire crews arrived, flames were already shooting through the roof of the cottage. Despite efforts by firemen to reach the second floor, Mr. Hart and his son were unable to be saved.

Accusations of Arson, Murder

Firemen found Mrs. Hart unconscious in the two-story building's downstairs parlor. After she was revived in the Bel's courtyard, she informed the authorities she had fallen asleep while reading. Controversy erupted on the scene when the widow learned of the death of her husband and infant and she immediately turned on her fourteen-year-old daughter, accusing her of setting the fire and murdering her father. Mrs. Hart was taken to Van Ness Emergency Hospital to be sedated and treated for her injuries.

Surviving Children

> The two Hart daughters, aged fourteen and seven, managed to escape by crawling out the ground-floor window of their shared bedroom and alerting the neighbors for help. Arson Inspector Gerry Stone is investigating the claims of arson and promising swift answers.

Gripped by a cold horror, Tildy read another article, then another. Soon she'd torn through nearly a dozen.

Long before seeing these stories, she'd known that a fire had once destroyed the caretaker's house behind the Bel, but the back lot of the library's property had been sold off in the early 1980s and developed into more residential housing. Tildy had never paid much attention to the fire. Had never known there were casualties.

Never once had she heard about arson or murder.

Though newspaper accounts of the fire varied, several details were painfully consistent: Eddie Hart had died, along with his infant son, and although the stories never named Daisy, Mrs. Hart accused their fourteen-year-old daughter of setting the fire. In a few of the stories, Mrs. Hart was described as Daisy's mother, in others, her stepmother. These types of inconsistencies, sketchy details, and speculation were not unusual within old newspapers, but still, they raised more questions than answers.

Tildy put her phone down and cradled her face in her hands, feeling sick to her stomach. A dead baby brother? A hysterical widow? Accusations of arson and murder? These newspaper accounts differed vastly from anything Meg had ever told Tildy. Meg had been very clear that her mother died shortly after childbirth, and she'd been alone with her father. But this awful new version of events would explain why Meg—or Daisy—had never readily spoken of her childhood.

Tildy skimmed the articles on her phone again. For about ten days, the news of the fire and possible teenaged arsonist had convulsed the city, but then the stories vanished. Tildy tried several more searches on the fire, but the results of the arson investigation were never reported. No further mention of the Harts could be found anywhere. The Bel didn't appear in the news again until Belva's death on April 28, 1967.

Tildy reviewed the implications of what she'd just learned. What exactly had happened to her mother? Tildy couldn't fathom the trauma of surviving a fire, only to be accused of starting it. And the worst part? The terrible allegations came from the girl's own mother, or stepmother. Tildy tried to imagine the set of complicated dynamics that could lead to such a tragic situation.

But could Tildy's mother really have been guilty of arson? Of murder? And if so, what circumstances led the young girl to commit such a terrible act? An anguished sense of disloyalty washed over Tildy. How could she consider such dreadful possibilities? But also, how could she not? She had no idea what had happened.

Tildy knew only one thing for sure: her mother had obscured major parts of her past.

And as far as the public knew, Daisy Hart had disappeared.

Except she hadn't.

She'd started a new life by moving to New Hampshire as Meg Leigh and later married to become Meg Leigh Barrows.

Tildy shivered. She was trapped by a cage of her own making. For over a week, she'd done everything she could to shine a light onto the existence of this secret room, its contents, and Cora Hale, but what if people figured out the connection of Tildy's mother to the Bel? If this past tragedy and scandal became widely known, what would it mean for the Bel? Or for Tildy and her reputation?

Tildy looked through the window into the veil of dusk. Were members of her mother's family still alive? According to these newspaper articles, Tildy could have a surviving grandmother and aunt. Tildy's unfocused gaze lingered on the darkening sky. Somewhere out there was a woman—maybe two of them—with their own version of what happened in April of 1967. After having been alone for so long, the prospect of discovering more family members tugged at Tildy.

She continued looking through the albums, spotting Cora Hale in many of the photos from the '50s and '60s. In some of them, Cora posed with young Daisy Hart at the Bel and other locations around San Francisco.

Exhausted by the questions swirling through her head, Tildy carefully slid the albums into an unused curatorial glove, closed the doors on the miniature cabinet, and checked to ensure the little blue room appeared undisturbed. After that, she carried the stash of tiny albums downstairs to her office, removed her mother's miniature from her desk, and placed the contraband in her tote bag. For someone who'd always followed rules and never even had an overdue library book, this deception terrified Tildy, but she didn't dare risk anyone else finding the tiny photos, not until she could explain them. Just thinking about the accusations against her mother made Tildy feel sick. She needed to hide the miniatures in her apartment until she returned from New Hampshire.

Hopefully by then she'd have answers to her growing list of questions.

14
Cora

1914

When I arrived back at Curtis House, I fumbled through my tools in the dark, packing what I needed. My lack of sleep had left me emotional and restive. I could scarcely wait to return to Belva, but how I'd miss Paris! I hated the idea of this city being swept into the storm of war, but Belva would get us out of harm's way. She knew important people and could arrange the logistics, visas, and tickets necessary for our departure.

I blissfully believed that Belva, young Jack, and I would soon be standing in the shadows of the SS *France*'s four smokestacks, waving farewell to the crowds lining the port at Le Havre. I was sure of it.

By midmorning the next day I was ready to leave Paris. Though I couldn't find Winny anywhere on the premises, I knew she'd be pleased by my decision. I left my stack of belongings next to the front door, ready for one of Belva's porters, and headed off to find Belva and Jack.

When I returned to Hôtel LeFarge, a maid led me to the Blue Salon, where I waited for Belva. The door opened moments later, but it wasn't her. Instead, the comte charged into the room aiming straight for me, fury stamped all over his face. I jumped up, and we moved as if in a strange dance. He reached for me and I stepped back, back, back until I was against the wall. His fingers clasped my throat. I couldn't breathe. A vein at his temple pulsed with the fervor of a boiling kettle.

"You want my wife all to yourself?" he seethed.

Panic made my vision swim. Instinctively, I squirmed. Tried to peel his fingers from my neck.

His face darkened into a startlingly violent shade of purple. His hands tightened even more sharply around my throat. The edges of my vision dimmed.

But then, a face from New York City that I'd tried to forget flashed through my mind's eye. I was not going to allow another man to take advantage of me, not that day, not ever. Strength surged within my chest. Scrabbling for a piece of the comte, my fingernails raked along his cheeks. Every part of me burned with energy, with the desire to survive, and I kicked and kicked, using every ounce of resistance I could find within me.

Finally I landed one particularly potent strike right between his legs. He cried out and staggered backward, releasing me.

I blinked, trying desperately to restore my speckled vision as I glowered at him. "I'm leaving and taking Belva with me," I finally spat.

He reared back and struck the side of my face with his fist, causing my head to knock against the wall behind me. *Crack!* Stars exploded across my vision. A nearby painting fell from the wall, landing face down on the floor, but I barely registered it. Unable to fight more, I collapsed. No matter how much I wanted to resist him, to put him in his place, he was stronger. Much stronger. I didn't stand a chance.

He wanted to kill me.

I could vanish, I realized. No one would know what happened.

Just as he raised his fist for another blow, a sharp voice cut through the room.

"Stop."

Through my blurry vision, I could see the comte stiffen.

Behind him stood Belva. Fury had twisted her face into someone almost unrecognizable.

My eyes closed. I heard raised voices and footsteps, but I couldn't make out what was happening. My brain felt sluggish, my head heavy. I must have lost consciousness, at least for a minute or so, because when I came to, I found Belva crouched beside me, her lovely face furrowed with concern. She helped me to sit. The right side of my face throbbed and burned. "Cora, Cora, my dear, Cora," she fussed. "Are you all right? I'm so sorry!"

"Where is he?" I spluttered.

Belva's jaw clenched, her expression hardening. "Gone."

"He's a monster," I said weakly. "We must leave."

"You're not going anywhere until you look a little steadier."

"This is no place for you and Jack."

She vanished and then returned, holding a glass of water. She crouched, lifting its rim to my lips. After a few sips, I pushed it away. "We have to go now."

"No, you have to go, but I'm staying. This is my home." The steeliness in her voice surprised me.

I shook my head in disbelief and immediately regretted it as a sharp pain flashed behind my eyes. I groaned. "How can you stay here? You're unsafe. Not only from him, but a war is coming!"

"I can't leave my husband. He'll never let me take Jack, and I won't leave my son behind."

"But what if we—"

Belva raised a hand. "Stop. There's nothing to discuss. I won't go."

Desperate, I searched her face for a sign of agreement, but she wore an expression of impassivity, even coldness. I needed to chip away at this new icy veneer, but I was struggling. It was too much. My entire body ached. My brain was so slow. "Bring Jack with us."

"You don't understand. I'm bound to the comte. But you"—she

put the glass of water down and moved to help me to my feet—"*you're free*. Go home. Get out now."

Why was she suddenly so cold? We'd grown close, certainly closer than anything she shared with her husband. I lurched to my feet, holding on to her arm. We teetered precariously.

"If you're not leaving, I'll stay here too. I'll—"

"Don't be such a child!" she snapped. "The two of us could never be together! I've been caught up in the nonsense of a girlish whim. I admire you, but that's all. There was never anything real between us."

The weight of her dismissal shattered me, like a brick through glass. I swallowed, appalled she could utter such hurtful words. As much as I wanted to argue, I knew that glint in her eye. She had dug into her position deeper than any soldier's trench. But I was no child. And I wasn't going to beg. Without another word, I jerked my arm from her grip and struggled to balance on my own. Placing one foot in front of the other took all my concentration, but I did it. I left. I was done with Hôtel LeFarge.

Once I reached the street, I was startled by the clang of church bells. Their import sank in.

War! War! War!

It was happening. The reverberations ran through me.

Somehow I needed to get out of Paris immediately.

15
Tildy

2024

The day after Tildy learned about the fatal fire at the Bel, she flew to Boston, rented a car, and drove north to New Hampshire to spend two days searching Cora Hale's old workshop for tools, sketches, diaries, photographs, anything. Tildy had told Ben, Dale, and her colleagues that she hoped to find materials to help the exhibit, but what she really wanted to uncover was the connection between Cora, the Bel, and her mother. The blurring of scenery at the sides of the highway as the miles ticked away was a relief. Tildy was in motion. Until this moment, she hadn't realized how much she needed a break from the Bel. She'd been reluctant to delegate overseeing the conservation of the dollhouses and the ceiling inspection to her staff, but now the library and its problems felt distant. Away from San Francisco, she could finally breathe a little deeper.

Since discovering her mother had once been named Daisy Hart an incontrollable restlessness had plagued Tildy. She recognized the familiar staticky feeling crackling inside her head. Her mind was stuck. Tildy's thoughts were taking on lives of their own. Like fireflies in a jar, they circled, knocking against the glass, whirling from spot to spot, refusing to settle down. Tildy was prone to this single-mindedness. Obsession, that's really what it was. Her focus and drive could be a strength, but also exhausting.

She was consumed by the secret room, the dollhouses, her mother's past, and the questions she'd been dredging up through Belva's trail of miniatures.

Tildy wanted answers and needed to find them in Cora's workshop.

It was late in the afternoon when she took an exit and found herself driving through Hopkins, a picturesque town center complete with a general store, two steepled churches, and a bunch of classical colonial houses, all nestled close to the main road. Not a single traffic light could be seen. Few cars passed her. Even fewer people walked along the town square's sidewalks. At the empty main intersection, she turned onto Ridge Hill Road and soon came to a gravel driveway.

When a stately old white clapboard house came into view, she took in its steeply pitched roof and wraparound porch. Subtle Italianate details like the post on pedestal columns hinted at the house's mid-nineteenth-century roots. It was two full stories with a smaller third-story cupola, complete with arched windows. A pair of enormous elms on either side of the house provided picturesque framing. Even leafless, they appeared imposing and elegant. The house and property came off far more impressive than it had in photos.

Tildy parked and hopped out, eager to stretch her legs, but as soon as her running shoes hit a thin patch of snow freckling the driveway, her footing slid. Carefully, she inched away from the car, climbed the front porch steps, and knocked on the door. Inside, a dog barked. Tildy waited, but there was no sign of Ben.

Shivering, she retreated from the front porch and carefully followed a path around the back corner of the house, figuring she'd get a lay of the land while she waited for her host.

The house was set on a ridge, overlooking a pond, and, in the distance, the sun was setting over the rolling mountains. Tildy shielded her gaze from the sky set aflame, then turned back to the house, making a small sound of appreciation as reflections of pinks, peach, and shades of violet streaked across its exterior, reminding her of an impressionist painting.

After taking in the striking views, Tildy focused her attention on figuring out the layout of the property. To the left of the house, closer to the pond, a small cottage was barely visible through a copse of evergreens. Closer to the house, to its right, was a barn. Tildy guessed this building housed the workshop, so she headed toward it. Upon reaching the old structure, she peered in the windows, but boxes blocked her view. Lots and lots of boxes. She tried the workshop's door and found it unlocked.

After gently prodding the creaky door open, she flicked a light switch on. Overhead bulbs dangling from cords came to life, giving off a harsh brightness to the space. Tildy stepped inside, inhaling the familiar scent that's particular to unused spaces—warm, dry, still air, peppered with old paper and dust.

Cardboard boxes, crates, Tupperware bins, and old furniture covered in sheets surrounded her. On the walls hung tools. Hoes, rakes, hammers, a sander, a leaf blower. Several coils of hoses lay in a tangle on the ground. None of the tools looked very small, nor old. The workshop was big and, as far as she could tell, it was packed to the rafters. The two days she'd allotted for this trip might not be enough. The exhaustion of traveling across the country slammed into Tildy and she rubbed at her aching lower back, sore from the long hours of sitting.

Her phone rang, and she answered it, grateful for a distraction.

"Hey, Emiko."

"Hi! How's your trip so far?"

"Fine. I've made it to New Hampshire and am in Cora Hale's workshop now."

"What's it like?"

"There's a lot of stuff. My work's cut out for me, that's for sure."

Emiko laughed. "If anyone can find a needle in a haystack, it's you."

"Thanks for the pep talk."

"Anytime. Listen, I've been keeping an eye on the tips emails, and one just came through saying that the larger dollhouse looks like a place in England."

"Really? Something helpful finally came through?"

"I think so. Google Roughmore Park. To my eye, it matches the dollhouse. What do you think?"

"England, huh?" Tildy put Emiko on speakerphone, googled Roughmore Park, and scrolled through the image results, nodding. "You're right. This looks like a match."

"Did your dollhouse maker have any connection to an American heiress named Ursuline Maine?"

"Not that I know of," Tildy said, clicking on a Wikipedia page about Roughmore Park and skimming through its history section. When she landed on the part about the twentieth century and the estate's heir, the Duke of Lennox, marrying Ursuline Maine, Tildy chuckled. "Ah, so Ursuline was a dollar princess."

"A what?"

"During the Gilded Age, when having millions of dollars wasn't enough, American heiresses would raise their social status by marrying English and European aristocrats."

"Lucky lads."

"Well, actually they were. Most of them had fancy titles, but no cash, so taking an American bride provided much-needed American dollars."

"So, a win-win for everyone."

"Right. Belva fulfilled the same role propping up a French aristocrat. Totally possible she and Ursuline ran in the same circles."

As Tildy spoke, she heard voices in the background, talking to Emiko.

"Tildy? I've got to run." Emiko sounded distracted. "Hope the Roughmore Park tip helps."

"It does."

Tildy ended the call and clicked on the Duchess of Lennox's hyperlinked name.

> **Ursuline Newcomb, Duchess of Lennox** (née Maine, 1890–1960) was an American-born heiress, best known for her adventurous exploits as a motorcar racer and athlete. While residing in London with her father, Leland Maine, the industrial thread manufacturing capitalist, who served as the US diplomat to England from 1902 to 1909, young Ursuline cultivated an interest in alpine sports. Over four winter seasons in Chamonix, France, Ursuline won several titles in downhill skiing and bobsled racing. The young woman then pursued motorcar racing and flying. Not only did Ursuline set a record for top motorcar speed at the 1909 Brighton Speed Trials, she was one of the first female pilots offered membership to the Royal Aero Club. Eventually the debutante married Archibald Newcomb, the 9th Duke of Lennox, and settled into domestic life . . .

Tildy's reading was interrupted by the workshop's door opening. She looked up and saw a figure backlit by day's final light. She shielded her face, blinking furiously. When her eyes adjusted and she got a better look at Ben, she stared. He wasn't what she expected at all.

16

Cora

1914

After leaving Belva, I dragged myself back to Curtis House drenched in a cold sweat, despite the afternoon's blazing heat. My head throbbed. On my way toward the front door, I stopped to catch my breath. I leaned against a motorcar parked crookedly in the driveway, staring at my reflection in the vehicle's shiny black paint.

How had I let myself be taken in by romance again? Had I learned nothing in New York? I was a fool. Such a fool. On top of this humiliation, the reality of my situation was becoming increasing clear with each clang of the city's church bells announcing the onset of war. I'd been too absorbed with my fantasies about Belva and finishing the dollhouse to bother myself with the practicality of making a plan. My friends had left. I was on my own in a place on the verge of war. As I berated my shortsightedness, it didn't occur to me to wonder at the presence of the beautiful motorcar beside me, despite the fact that all vehicles in the city had been recalled for the war mobilization.

When I entered the château's foyer, voices drifted toward me. I staggered to the sitting room and found Winny with two other women sitting around a liquor bottle, exhaling long plumes of smoke. Never before had I seen Winny with a cigarette in hand.

"Well, well, is this who we're whisking out of harm's way?" a small dark-haired woman asked, tilting her head curiously. "Looks like harm's already found her."

Winny placed her cigarette on the edge of a crystal ashtray and leapt to her feet to lead me to the closest settee. "I have a good guess as to what happened."

The dark-haired woman handed me a glass. "Here, knock this back."

From its smell, I knew it to be whiskey, which I never normally drank, but that day would prove the exception. Desperate times and all that. I tossed it straight down my throat, gasping as it burned. My shaking finally eased.

"That's the ticket. Let's do another for good measure." The woman gestured at her companion to pour me a second. I downed that one too before pausing to appraise these two newcomers.

On the table in front of the dark-haired woman lay a camel-colored leather helmet, goggles, and driving gloves, prompting me to remember the fancy motorcar out front. I'd personally never met a woman who drove, although I knew such a thing was possible. The newcomer's hair gleamed so black, it had a blue sheen when the light fell a certain way. Her hair was short, cut bluntly right below her ears in a style I'd never seen before. One by one the clues of the woman's identity fell into place. The car. The haircut. More than anything, it was the scarlet silk scarf around her neck that cinched it. I'd read all about her in the newspapers. Only one woman cut such a singular figure on England's and France's roads: Ursuline Newcomb, the Duchess of Lennox.

Reporters on both sides of the Atlantic couldn't get enough of her. Even before her whirlwind romance and sudden wedding to England's Duke of Lennox, a man seventeen years her senior, young American Ursuline Maine had been beguiling everyone with her adventures as a "scorcher," one of the rare breed of women who not only drove, but drove recklessly, often attracting the attention of the police. And her love of speed wasn't limited to motorcars. Reporters had also breathlessly described her daring approach to horse racing, her domination during the winter ski racing season at Chamonix, her bobsledding trophies, and her aviation expertise as a licensed pilot under the Royal Aero Club. Initially these interests were financed by her wealthy widowed father, the industrial thread manufacturer Leland Maine, who traveled with his young daughter to London so he could serve as the American diplomat to England, but then later, when she met Archie Newcomb, the Duke of Lennox, her new husband was all too delighted to support his bride's unconventional interests. The fact that she'd promptly bestowed twins upon her husband helped her cause considerably. Photos of her draped along the wing of a biplane sporting a glamorous grin and daring hairdo would have been enough to send everyone in London and Paris into paroxysms of fascination, but it was the two cherubic babies nestled into her arms that had all but guaranteed the newspapers sold out within minutes. Rich, beautiful, intrepid, and apparently fertile, the young duchess appeared to have Europe right where she wanted it—under her well-manicured thumb.

Though my brain was slow, it managed to form a single question: Why was a woman of such notoriety sitting in Curtis House smoking and drinking with Winny in the middle of the afternoon?

"So you're Cora Hale?" the duchess asked, holding her cigarette at a lazy angle and exhaling a ring of smoke from her cherry red lips.

While I rubbed at the back of my aching head, I glared at her.

The duchess let out a braying laugh. She had a surprisingly deep, throaty voice for a woman of such girlish appearance. "Winny warned me you'd be prickly."

In no mood for jest, I put my hands on my hips and turned to Winny. "What's going on?"

"This is my friend, the Duchess of Lennox, and Her Grace's lady's maid, Davis," she said calmly.

The duchess was Winny's friend? This was a baffling statement.

The duchess took another quick drag on her ciggie, exhaled, and waved away the smoke impatiently.

"We met at Longchamps. Winny has a real knack for knowing which horses to bet on. She's got a good eye, this one."

I turned to Winny, who gave an unapologetic shrug. "The duchess can get you to England. She's on her way out of the city and has offered you a spot in her car."

"Actually I'd like to get back to America."

The duchess laughed as if I'd told the funniest joke in the world. "My dear, that's quite impossible. For weeks now the American Embassy has been swamped with people willing to do anything to get out of here. Furthermore, I've heard both the Red Star Lines and White Star Lines are now canceling bookings. And no matter which direction you head, the trains are packed as tightly as a tin of sardines. Even if you end up crammed onto one, forget bringing any luggage. It's a real mess out there," she said cheerfully.

I pictured my belongings in the foyer. My precious tools. I couldn't leave those behind. I tried to think quickly. Fortunately I'd kept my teaching earnings and Belva's payments in cash under my bed, so I had money on hand.

The duchess stubbed out her cigarette and stood, shouldering her way into a stylish powder blue dustcoat. "Hitch a ride with us. If we leave straightaway, we can make it to the Channel by nightfall."

"Nightfall? Isn't that optimistic?"

The duchess smirked. "I'll have you know I was one of the top finishers in last year's Hereford 1,000-Mile Light Car Trial and I even served as my own mechanic. If you think I can't manage a simple drive from here to the Channel, you've got another thing coming."

"What makes you sure we'll get a spot on one of the crossings tonight?"

"Leave that to me. Not only do I have a winning personality, but I have two forms of insurance." She slapped one of her dustcoat's pockets and removed a thick stack of English pound notes, and then she reached into the other and held a Colt automatic pistol aloft. "This little gem's fully loaded. One way or another, I'll get us out of here." She winked at me. "By cock's crow tomorrow, I promise we'll be in England."

"What will I do there?"

"Head on to Southampton and try to catch passage to New York. Or you can be my guest at Roughmore Park. This little war won't last long. It'll be over by Christmas, tops."

I'll admit, my curiosity was piqued. "What about my luggage? I can't leave my tools behind."

"Have a little faith, won't you? My husband's family keeps an apartment in the eighth arrondissement, and I came over to bring a few valuable pieces back to England, just in case the Huns end up here. There's a truck out front. My fellas can put whatever you've got in it. They'll meet us in England tomorrow. So what do you say?"

Sweat prickled my skin. I needed to leave. I could still hear the echo of Belva insisting I was a child. My jaw tightened. Nothing was left for me in Paris. Though I had no idea what might come next, throwing my lot in with the duchess certainly offered the prospect of adventure. I had nothing to lose.

To emphasize the duchess's point, she pulled up her sleeve to check her diamond-encrusted wristwatch. "Shake a tail feather. The clock's running."

As I hastened to prepare for departure, I turned to Winny. "You're staying?"

She nodded. "More girls will be coming, even if there's a war."

"But you knew I'd need to leave?"

"I had a feeling."

Weary and humiliated, I only nodded, but Winny patted my shoulder. "Stick with the duchess. She's like a cat—always lands on her feet. Now off you go."

So I left.

All I can say is the duchess's reputation as a scorcher was well-earned. Using an elaborate web of small streets, free of the traffic clogging the main thoroughfares, her Bugatti, truly a beautiful piece of machinery, even to my untrained eyes, roared out of the city as if the kaiser himself was hot on our tail.

17
Tildy

2024

When Cora Hale's great-grandson Ben strolled into the old workshop, Tildy forgot all about Roughmore Park and the Duchess of Lennox. She hadn't expected Ben to be so close to her age. And not only was he young, he was cute. Tall and broad shouldered, his solid figure took up much of the doorway.

"I see you've found my great-grandmother's workshop. Welcome."

Tildy blinked, tongue-tied. "Uh . . . yeah, I did. I hope it's all right I got started. You're Ben?"

"In the flesh."

"You don't sound like the same guy that I spoke to last week."

"Eh, I had a cold and was feeling terrible." Ben grinned roguishly, revealing straight white teeth and twinkling pale blue eyes.

Wow, Tildy thought, smiling back, a little dazed. Ben's dangerous smile reminded her of a young Paul Newman from *The Hustler* and *Cool Hand Luke*, films she'd watched a million times with her parents over the years. Of course, there had to be more recent movie stars to compare Ben to, but she was completely flustered, so a young Paul Newman would have to do.

"Well, glad you look better now. I mean, *feel* better now," Tildy fumbled, annoyed. She'd turned into such a cliché: cute guy appears, girl loses her mind.

He laughed. "Just when I wanted to be done that day, my students showed up after the final bell, complaining about a recent test they claimed was unnecessarily difficult. But let the record show, they didn't study hard enough."

"Hmm." Tildy nodded, suspecting the kids may not have been quite as miffed as he believed. If Ben had been her science teacher, she certainly would have found lots of reasons to stop by his classroom. To distract herself from the dangerously unprofessional direction of her thoughts, Tildy thrust her hand toward him. "I'm Mathilda Barrows, head curator at the Belva Curtis LeFarge Library in San Francisco."

Something nudged against her knee. She looked down. A white-muzzled black lab circled, wagging its tail.

Ben gestured at the dog. "Meet Zelly."

Tildy reached down to stroke one of the lab's silky ears. "This place." Tildy waved her free hand toward the open door, eager to get Ben's twinkling eyes off her. "The photos you sent don't do it justice. The house, the property—it's really gorgeous."

Ben thanked her. "Sorry I'm late. I coach the school's boys' basketball team and practice ran long. We've got a big game this weekend." He jammed his hands deep into his coat pockets and bounced on the balls of his feet. "Want to go inside and warm up?"

"Go inside your . . . house?"

"Yeah. You're shivering."

"I underestimated the cold."

"Not exactly California, huh?"

Tildy followed him outside, not quite believing her luck. Cora Hale's great-grandson was the kind of guy who never normally paid attention to someone like her. He possessed that laid-back charm that belonged to people who'd always been popular and good at stuff. Life had probably always come pretty easily to Ben. She envied him.

A few minutes later, they reached the door to the screened-in porch. Ben held it open for Tildy but she didn't move from the step below.

"You okay?" he asked.

"I'm gathering myself."

"You're what?"

"I'm *gathering* myself. You know, taking a breath, trying to get it together before I enter the house where Cora Hale once lived."

"Ah. So you're fangirling over my great-grandmother?" His eyes were twinkling like crazy.

Tildy looked away, studied the house's clapboard siding. All that twinkling was killing her. "I am. You know I've spent the last ten days thinking about her nonstop, so this visit is kind of big for me."

"Well, I hope the house lives up to your expectations."

Nodding, she climbed the remaining stairs and passed through the screened-in porch to a back door. As she stepped into the large farmhouse-style kitchen with butter-yellow walls and exposed oak beams running across the ceiling, she covered her mouth.

Cora Hale's house!

She'd spent so much time imagining this woman and now she was standing in the exact spot Cora Hale had once stood. Tildy exhaled, lowering her gaze from the cabinets to survey the rest of the room, but as she took in her surroundings, her initial delight faltered.

A tower of plastic planters leaned against the wall, trailed by spilled potting soil on the floor. Gardening gloves and a trowel lay abandoned next to the pots. Gingerly, Tildy stepped across the floor, dodging scattered muddy running shoes, cleats, and work boots. How could one man own so much footwear? When she reached the long soapstone countertop, she recoiled. Old yellowing *Concord Monitors* and mountains of mail, circulars, and catalogs spilled over its surface. Food stains splattered the antique blue-

and-white-porcelain-tiled backsplash. Piles of dishes sat in the sink. Greasy pans cluttered the stovetop.

The house was a mess.

The vibe was less *Antiques Roadshow* and more *Hoarders*. It took every ounce of Tildy's willpower not to start sorting and cleaning.

She glanced at Ben, unable to hide her surprise. How could he tolerate such disorder, such dirt? Didn't this kind of chaos go against his scientific training? How could he let such a beautiful, historic home fall into such disarray?

She struggled to say something that didn't sound critical. "Umm, has this kitchen ever been remodeled?"

"Sort of, we've updated the appliances and repainted several times, but it's pretty much exactly the same as when my great-grandmother lived here," Ben said, picking Zelly's dishes off the floor to refill them.

Tildy highly doubted Cora Hale would have lived in such mayhem.

After placing Zelly's dishes back on the floor, Ben straightened, pointing through a doorway to a room with cherry paneling and a long dining room table, barely visible below the boxes and clothing strewn across it. "I rarely eat in there except for the occasional poker night, fantasy football draft party, or when my family comes here for the holidays."

"Where do they live?"

"My parents have a place in Rye, on the coast, but they're currently visiting my sister and her family in London. My sister just learned she's having twins and was put on bed rest, so my parents are trying to help out by watching my niece and nephew."

While Zelly inhaled the food in her dish, Ben led Tildy into another room filled with comfortable-looking chairs and a couch, all upholstered in a casual denim-blue ticking stripe pattern, but clumps of dog hair flitted across the floor like tumbleweeds blowing through the set of an old western. An overturned basket of mangy tennis balls made crossing the room a hazard. From the way playing cards and poker chips covered every surface, it looked like a tornado had blown in straight from Vegas. Dog-eared copies of *Sports Illustrated* slid off a chair. A whiteboard with a basketball court sketched on it leaned against one of the chairs. Heaps of laundry—clean or dirty, Tildy couldn't tell—were strewn across the couch.

Tildy's enthusiasm for the house was cooling rapidly. She eyed the door. How quickly could she leave without being rude?

"Hey, I made a huge pan of lasagna yesterday. Want some? You're going to need serious fueling for a project like sorting through the workshop."

Hell no, Tildy thought. "Oh, please don't worry about me, but thanks. I'll just head to my hotel."

"Where are you staying?"

"Let me check." Tildy pulled her phone from her jacket pocket. "The Elm Motel in Concord," she read from her email, wrinkling her nose. The motel's guest review rating was abysmal: one and a half stars. *Yikes*. How had she missed this? Tildy cringed, skimming the customer reviews. Water stains on the walls and ceilings? Dirty towels being passed off as clean? Bedbugs? Tildy shook her head, regretting her haste to make plans without doing the due diligence of reading reviews.

"That motel's at least thirty minutes away," Ben said. "And I hate to break it to you, but by the time you'll have gotten there and checked in, you'll be hard-pressed to find something decent to eat at this hour. Everything will be closed. Come on, I insist on feeding you."

Tildy weighed her options. A very good-looking man was inviting her to dinner, and that in itself was thrilling. Also, she was starving and loved lasagna, but was food made in that filthy kitchen even safe to eat? It turned her stomach to think about those stacks of food-encrusted plates in the kitchen sink. Could a granola bar or bag of chips from a motel vending machine get her through the night? Unfortunately she knew the answer.

"Lasagna sounds great," she said weakly.

WHEN THEY returned to the kitchen, Tildy could no longer contain herself. "You really need to do some cleaning," she said, sweeping a bunch of old newspapers into a pile.

Sheepish, Ben nodded. "You're right."

He opened a cabinet under the sink, causing several brown paper and plastic shopping bags to tumble out. After retrieving one of the brown bags, he held it up and Tildy dumped the pile of newspapers into it.

She then pointed to a stack of nearby boxes, each labeled *Christmas ornaments*. "Doesn't having all this stuff around drive you nuts?"

He ran a hand through his thick head of hair, looking suddenly both embarrassed and weary. "Yeah, it does." He sighed, deflated. "Recently I've run into a bit of a rough patch."

Tildy nodded, her annoyance fading. If there was one thing she understood, it was rough patches. She tapped on her smartwatch, checking her step count. "I've been stuck sitting on a plane all day and need to move around, so how about I help with this mess while you get dinner going?"

"I accept that offer! As long as you fill me in about my great-grandmother while we work."

While Tildy retrieved a few more shopping bags and tackled the detritus on Ben's kitchen table, she let the whole story spill out about finding the secret room and the dollhouses, although she withheld admitting to the Bel's financial problems and the crack in the ceiling. She wanted him to feel confident that the Bel was equipped to handle an exhibit on Cora, not worry that the place was falling apart. She also said nothing about her mother's miniature. No need to get too personal.

Ben listened carefully while he microwaved two generous pieces of lasagna and began making a salad. When he ducked his head into the fridge, Tildy caught a view inside and was relieved it looked surprisingly clean compared to the rest of the place. As she finished her story, she burrowed into her purse, brought out a binder, and carried it over to where Ben stood at a clearing on the counter, slicing vegetables.

"Here. See the dollhouses yourself. I've included photographs."

Ben dumped the vegetables from the cutting board into a wooden bowl and took the binder. As he flipped through its pages, his eyes widened and Tildy felt a familiar tinge of embarrassment at how much effort she'd put into the binder. She always had to go overboard. The color-coded sections, labeled tabs, and precise layout of images suddenly felt like too much, especially in comparison to Ben's sloppy approach to life.

"I know, it's a lot, but . . ."

"Are you kidding? This is great. Thank you. I had no idea my great-grandmother made such beautiful things." He nudged the salad bowl toward her. "Here, help yourself."

She nodded gratefully at his kindness and lifted the silver tongs from the salad bowl, no longer feeling quite so intimidated by Ben. There was something about seeing a man's dirty socks strewn along his kitchen floor that made him look less golden. Once she'd scooped enough greens onto her plate, she raised her fork to dig in, but he stopped her.

"I know you're in a hurry, but really, would you please humor me and sit?" Ben moved quickly to the table and pulled a chair out for Tildy.

"Oh."

"I mean, you put effort into cleaning the table. Let's use it."

Tildy sat and when the microwave beeped, Ben removed the lasagna. "Buon appetito," he said, handing her a plate.

When she took her first bite, she closed her eyes, savoring the creaminess of the cheeses, the kick of garlic, and the woodsy flavor of mushrooms.

She nodded, impressed. "This is good. What's in it?"

"I'm vegetarian so it's got spinach, kale, and mushrooms, along with a bunch of cheese. I made the noodles myself."

For several minutes no more words were exchanged, but it wasn't awkward. It was nice. And the lasagna's blend of flavors and textures was just right.

"How long have you been vegetarian?"

"For about six years. Vegetarianism can sort of come with the territory of teaching environmental science. Reports on animal cruelty in the food industry are a perennial favorite for my students. And I don't want to bore you with a lecture about how we're killing our planet, but seriously, as I learn more and more about best practices in environmental sustainability, a plant-based diet just makes sense."

Tildy repressed a smile. The last thing she'd expected from Ben was an earnestly delivered lecture on the environment. "Do your students turn vegetarian when they learn all this stuff?"

"Sometimes. I've definitely gotten annoyed emails from parents, blaming me for making their dinners more complicated."

"They've really chewed you out, huh?"

Ben gave her a pitying shake of his head. "Wow, okay."

Tildy giggled. "Not much of a pun guy?"

He skewered a mushroom and wiggled it. "Eh, more of a fun guy."

They laughed.

"I've also gotten into sourcing my own ingredients. Not to flex, but in the summer, my garden's insane. I've also taken up foraging so I can harvest foods directly from wild spaces."

"What if you make a mistake and eat something poisonous?"

"There's certainly a risk of that, but back in 2015, I spent a couple weeks in Idaho, apprenticing myself to an herbalist expert. Since then I've studied under a few other master foragers, so now I feel pretty confident I know what I'm doing."

"Sounds like you're a legit foodie."

"Having my summers off allows me to try stuff. I've gotten committed to learning how to live on this planet in ways that are less exploitative than relying on slaughterhouses and mass-produced, chemically treated foods."

"Good for you. I can definitely see the benefits of vegetarianism, but I don't know about the foraging part."

"I hear you. It takes practice."

They smiled at each other. Tildy was realizing that Ben was actually a nerd who happened to have the good fortune of being trapped in cute packaging. Tildy couldn't remember the last time she'd enjoyed a meal so much. At home she usually stood at her apartment's kitchen counter, reading emails on her phone while she ate. Meals had simply become rote, one more item on her to-do list, not an opportunity for fun and discovery.

Over Ben's shoulder, Tildy spotted the time on the microwave and groaned. "Ugh, I should get back on the road, but this has been really great." Reluctantly, she got to her feet and carried her plate over to the sink. Ben followed her.

With the small of his back against the counter he stretched overhead, and she admired his long, ropy arm musculature visible beneath the short sleeves of his T-shirt. Tildy tried not to look at his arms. How solid and strong they were.

She tried not to imagine those arms tossing a basketball or working a shovel in a garden.

She tried not to wonder how it would feel to touch those arms.

She needed to stop thinking about his arms.

"Sorry, I lost track of time. I can get carried away talking about food, gardening, and foraging," Ben was saying, resting his hands on the counter behind him. Tildy shifted her gaze to the ground. She definitively didn't want to start thinking about those hands.

"Not at all. This was fun. Your students must love having such an energetic teacher."

"Hey, so this may be weird, but I really hate the idea of you driving in the dark in an unfamiliar place. No pressure or anything, but as you can see, I've got this huge place all to myself. There's a guesthouse just across the yard, and I promise it's mess-free because it's where my mom stays when she visits. It has its own bathroom and kitchenette, and you can lock the door. It would be totally private for you." He checked Tildy's expression carefully. "Did I just turn this into a weird episode of a new show called *Homicidal Hoarders*?"

"I don't know," she said, her expression wary.

"Well, think about it—if you stay here, you can just get up in the morning and start working. Trust me, you're going to need every minute you can get in that workshop. I leave for school superearly, so you won't even see me."

The window over the sink revealed nothing but a very dark night. The prospect of driving half an hour on icy roads and getting settled in a strange motel held little appeal. But Tildy was acutely aware that her current situation had all the ingredients of a horror movie. A very isolated rural Victorian mansion? Check. Agreeing to spend the night with a stranger? Check.

But then she remembered the Elm Motel's lousy star rating.

"You're not worried about having a stranger on the premises?"

"Nope. Zelly may look like a lazy old dog, but she's actually part of an elite canine unit. She'll keep me safe."

A few feet away, Zelly was snoring loudly on her blue gingham dog bed.

Tildy raised a brow. "She doesn't look very fierce."

"It's her fart attacks. Silent but deadly."

Tildy laughed. "Noted. Okay, I'll stay. I'm actually about to fall over from exhaustion."

"Well, let's get you settled in. How about I go out to the cottage, turn up the heat, and make sure everything's okay? If you toss me your car keys, I'll take your bags over too." Ben headed for the mudroom, adding, "It's nice to have you here, Tildy. Since we talked on the phone and you told me about Cora, I've been realizing how little I know about my own family. It's embarrassing, really. I live in this beautiful old house surrounded by history, but I've never asked questions. It's definitely time for me to learn more."

A pang of doubt clanged through Tildy. On top of hoping she'd learn more about her family, now Ben's expectations weighed on her. She thought of those endless stacks of boxes in the workshop. How would she find anything in there?

Tildy forced a smile. "No problem."

18

Cora

1914–1916

True to her word, the duchess got us out of France. After a choppy nighttime Channel crossing to England that left me hanging over the boat's railing sicker than I'd ever been, the thought of heading back onto a ship to cross the Atlantic made me green. I accepted my host's offer to visit her country estate. Where else was I to go?

From the coast, the duchess drove us north of London, following a river through rolling green and tawny fields. When Roughmore Park grew visible in the valley ahead, the late-afternoon light imbued the landscape with a burnished glow. The great house reflected the lowering sun, golden and glimmering like the eyes of a cat. I admired its balanced baroque facade—three stories, nine wide bays, the central three windows offset by four Corinthian columns and pilasters. Its carved stonework gave the place a stately bearing.

"Welcome to Roughmore Park. It's been through many stages of renovation over the centuries, but the original structure was built in the eleven hundreds." The duchess stole a mischievous glance at Davis, her lady's maid, in the back seat. Both women giggled. "Right. That's the *twelfth* century. Even the late Mrs. Astor can't compete with that kind of pedigree."

By the time the duchess pulled the hand brake and stopped her automobile in front of the house, an impressive collection of house staff had formed in a precise line to welcome us. Out in front of the servants, a large pram was parked alongside a sturdy, sensible-looking woman wearing a nurse's uniform. When we climbed from the car, the duchess rushed to her twins, hovering over where they lay, dozing.

I crossed the threshold to the great hall, then froze, dumbstruck by my surroundings. None of my visits to the finest houses in Paris could compete with this. The detailed woodwork adorning the walls and the grand staircase must have required an army of craftsmen. In the hall leading to the staircase, brightly polished suits of armor stood sentry lined against the walls. Upstairs, paintings by old masters covered nearly every inch of the gallery. Roughmore Park exuded an unmistakable sense of longevity, stability, security—and money.

"Miss Hale, I'm sure you're exhausted from our long trip. Supper will be delivered to your room shortly and tomorrow I'll plan to meet with you in the Morning Room after breakfast. I'd like to discuss a commission. I've heard about the dollhouse you created for the comtesse LeFarge and want one of my own. Are you interested?"

My gaze returned to the nearest suit of armor. I was already imagining how I would re-create it in miniature. If Hôtel LeFarge had offered me my first taste of dollhouses, with Roughmore Park, a feast lay ahead.

"Yes. I'd be honored," I answered.

"Excellent. See you tomorrow," the duchess said, sauntering away. Davis motioned that I was to follow her upstairs. Fortunately I had a small valise filled with necessaries for an overnight. I hoped my tools and trunk would be arriving soon in the truck.

The trip to my room lasted nearly ten minutes and involved a multitude of stairways, hallways, and entryways, but once I was there, I dropped to the edge of the bed, suddenly utterly overwhelmed and exhausted. How would I make a dollhouse of such a sprawling, complicated place? A project like this could take ten years, and its embellishments lay beyond my skill set. What was I getting myself into? At the same time, a new, consuming, challenging project sounded just right. The last thing I needed was to dwell on my disastrously abrupt parting with Belva.

I sank onto the soft duvet covers, staring at the stylish coffered ceiling. Belva's betrayal still stung. When I remembered her calm expression as she'd told me how foolish I'd been, a visceral sense of humiliation washed over me, turning my stomach. Thank god Paris lay in the past.

I was furious, yet missed her so much it pained me.

After two weeks at Roughmore Park, I moved into one of the estate's empty tenant cottages, about half a mile away from the main house and far from the topic dominating all conversations: war. Englishmen were signing up to fight in droves. A small recruiting office had opened in a nearby village and had been so overwhelmed it was forced to turn men away, telling them to come back a different day.

My new cottage was rustic, its ceilings low, and consisted merely of two rooms: a kitchen and bedroom. In the adjacent barn, I set up my dollhouse workshop, after cleaning it thoroughly. Under the duchess's supervision, Roughmore House had only recently installed modern plumbing, but her mission to modernize the estate hadn't yet made it as far as the cottages, so I had to rely on a cramped, dark outhouse for my personal business, which was not ideal, but I was simply grateful to be safe from war.

August stretched into September, and the Germans surprised France by not attacking from the east. Instead they marched through Belgium, amassing on France's northern border. Hopes for a swift Allied victory over the Central Powers faded with every passing day, but after stopping the Germans in the battle of the Marne, the French and British Expeditionary Forces dug in. Still, any sense of optimism dimmed at the sight of September's staggering casualty numbers. I couldn't help wonder what had become of Belva and Winny. How were they making do in Paris? Although the city had managed to stay beyond the reach of the invading Huns, I feared that security wouldn't last.

To keep my worries at bay, I immersed myself in designing the duchess's dollhouse. My plans called for thirty rooms divided between four stories, and though the prospect for such an elaborate structure kept me up at night, the challenge also excited me. Both the front and back facades would open on hidden hinges so the miniature could be more than one room deep in places. The top floor would be made up of servant quarters and a luggage room while the bottom floor would consist of the scullery, wine cellar, kitchen, household offices, china room, and various storage cellars. Staterooms, bedrooms, the library, morning room, armory, portrait gallery, dining room, and others would be located on the second and third floors. In addition to this collection of rooms, I'd build eight passages, five of which would be considered "secret" servants' hallways. The grand staircase alone would require over a hundred tiny pieces of wood. As the duchess and I surveyed my initial sketches, she tapped her finger on the one showing the entire dollhouse from its rear view.

"Cora, this project must remain our little secret."

"The dollhouse?"

"Yes. With the war underway, the duke's requested I keep a low profile. No racing, no extravagant shopping expeditions. Anytime the press mentions his family name, he wants it to be in support of the war effort."

From her flat tone, it was clear this pronouncement disappointed her, but I understood the duke's point. He spent most of his time in London working for the War Office. Of the few times he'd visited his family at Roughmore Park, he'd come across as affable and quiet, a man who was utterly enthralled with his spitfire wife. Given his sad history, he was clearly in awe of his good fortune. During his youth, he'd been betrothed to one of London's most coveted debutantes, but the week before his wedding, his fiancée died of a sudden fever. Three years later, he was engaged a second time, but his bride died unexpectedly of a heart attack. And then two years after that, again tragedy: the third fiancée choked to death on a strawberry during her wedding morning breakfast. After that, he appeared cursed. People took to calling him the Duke of Despair. No woman in her right mind wanted to risk marrying him—except for young and lovely Ursuline Maine. Always a believer in the unshakable power of her own good luck, she ignored the duke's reputation and took a shine to him. No wonder he proposed to her in the blink of an eye. And then, not even a year later, when the duchess delivered twins, a boy and a girl, the duke possessed the very thing he'd been longing for: a family.

Nevertheless, despite his wholehearted adoration of his wife and family, the duke wasn't completely blinded by love. This dollhouse was a massive undertaking and would cost a mint. During lean times, it could come off as an unnecessary vanity project. The duke understood the importance of appearances, especially while a war raged nearby.

"What should I tell people if they ask what I'm doing?" I asked.

"Simply say you're a historian working on an account of the estate. You're cataloging the great house's contents, researching its architecture and renovations, that kind of thing."

I nodded. To be fair, it wasn't much of a stretch.

Alone in my cottage, I missed the bustle and camaraderie of Curtis House. My small cottage was picturesque, resembling something from a fairy tale, but remote. As the elms, oaks, chestnuts, and ashes surrounding my cottage lost their leaves, a crisp chill knifed its way under my skin, despite my constant tending to the cottage's and barn's stoves. In the long, gloomy months ahead, I feared I'd be lonely. Far from Paris's shops, cafés, and museums, I missed my former life. Never before had I felt so solitary. Entire days could pass without me seeing another person.

More than anything, I missed Belva. My hurt still felt raw. Why hadn't she chosen to leave with me? I would have taken care of her and Jack, whereas her husband offered nothing but heartbreak. Of course now, decades later, I see how terribly naive I was, but at the time, I was completely blind to how little power a married woman wields over her own life.

Isolated in the countryside, still wounded by Belva's dismissal, my dislocation, despondency, and disquiet grew. I'd never wanted to marry. I wanted a life filled with art and adventure. And now with a war happening, I wanted to go to the front. Granted, part of this desire was driven by my longing to return to Paris to see Belva, but also, with the men assuming their roles as soldiers, women were filling the empty spaces left behind as agricultural workers for the Land Army, police officers, ticket collectors for the railways, clerical workers, and radio operators. Several of Roughmore Park's housemaids moved to London to take on munitions factory jobs, and though I had no illusions about the tedious nature of that type of work, I envied their move to the busy city.

My only method of coping with my anguish was to work and to immerse myself in plans for the Roughmore Park dollhouse. Since I'd first seen those small-scale sets at the Palace Garnier, building and creating the furnishings for the Petite Hôtel LeFarge had brought me immense satisfaction. Every day when I'd arrived in my workshop behind Curtis House, I'd pause and study my progress. Pride filled me. With my own hands, my own ingenuity, I'd designed and built something lasting and beautiful out of the roughest of supplies—wood, paper, paint, metal, fabric, and other humble items—and my muse had been my love, Belva. What could be more fulfilling? Even though our relationship had ended poorly, I could still appreciate the feelings that had fueled that project. As both an artist and a woman, those years in Paris had energized me.

But now, in the hinterlands of the English countryside, this new dollhouse brought a different type of satisfaction. In a world upended by war and uncertainty, miniatures brought me a sense of security. I could control the world I was constructing. The level of concentration for such precise work required a steady hand and clear mind. While I fixated on whatever tiny project was in front of me, anything bothering me about what was happening across the Channel felt far away. Just as the world seemed to be falling apart, I was creating and building, trying to be productive.

DURING THAT spring of 1915 the Germans shocked us by employing poison gas during the Second Battle of Ypres. According to the newspapers, the effects had been ghastly. And to make matters worse, in early May, German U-boats torpedoed the British liner *Lusitania*, ending over twelve hundred unfortunate lives as it sank in less than eighteen minutes. Rather than dampening my conviction to go to the front, the grim war news cemented my commitment.

That summer I would go, I decided. Surely, I figured, my talents could be put to good use somewhere in France. And if I survived the war, I told myself I'd return to Roughmore Park to finish the dollhouse.

One afternoon in early July as I was layering thin pieces of wood to create a special ceiling effect for the dollhouse's main dining room, I smelled cigarette smoke and turned to find the duchess in the doorway. She exhaled, dropped her cigarette to the ground, and stubbed it out with her heel, before stepping into my workshop. “Hello! A walk, some sunshine, and a smoke—this is exactly what I needed. I already feel like a new woman.” She squinted at me through the columns of sunbeams slanting through the nearby window. “I told Davis I’d go mad if I didn’t get out of the house by myself. It’s a lovely day and I’ve been feeling terribly cooped up.” She circled the dollhouse slowly, her smile widening. Eleven months into the project, the structure had been built, much of the exterior looked complete, and the kitchen and the other downstairs rooms had flooring, doors, and windows. “It’s coming together.”

“It is.” I paused. This was my opportunity to tell her I wanted to leave for the front, but she spoke over me.

“I need to let you know about some changes afoot here at Roughmore Park.”

Surprised, I set down my measuring tape and leaned against my workbench to hear her out.

“I’ve just been made colonel-in-chief of the Women’s Volunteer Reserve.” At my confused expression, she continued. “Now that so many men are leaving for the front, this volunteer group was established to fill the gaps in our labor force with women. Because of my role as a founding member of the Ladies Automobile Club, I’m charged with training a group of women motorcyclists to transport messages around the country.”

A tinge of envy struck me at the duchess’s participation in the war effort, but I tried to tamp it down, thinking this new job might make her amenable to my plan of returning to France. “What a perfect way to put your skills and experience to good use.”

“I hope so, but I’m taking it a little further. I’m opening a driving school for ladies.”

“Doesn’t the British army forbid women from serving as drivers on the front?”

“Just because the British army won’t allow women to drive

ambulances doesn't mean the Belgians and French forces won't. They're more than happy to accept us."

"I see. So you're supporting the war effort by undermining the government?"

"Exactly! Potato, patahto. Those fellows in London don't understand the big picture the way I do, but they'll figure it out soon enough."

I chuckled. "And then they'll be thanking you, right?"

"They'd better. From the way I see it, Roughmore Park has plenty of space a few miles away from here at the estate's old hunting lodge, deep in the woods. I'm converting the place into a garage and dormitory for the women to bunk. There's enough acreage for my students to practice driving cars instead of simply sticking to motorcycles, so I'll teach driving and mechanical repair to any women who want to learn, no vehicle necessary. When they've completed my course, there's plenty of work in the cities as bus, truck, and ambulance drivers, messengers, all sorts of jobs, really. If women want to serve on the front, they can."

"And the duke has signed off on this school of yours?"

A daring glint came into the duchess's eyes, one I hadn't seen since she swore to get us across the Channel a year earlier. "Roughmore Park is to become a hospital."

"For the war effort? Troops will be coming here?"

"It seems the War Office vastly underestimated the number of wounded and hospitals are overwhelmed so I suggested we offer up Roughmore Park for service." Her hand clutched the gold locket around her neck, where she kept locks of hair from her twins. "English mothers are sacrificing their sons and we must do something to honor them."

"So you struck a deal with the duke: If Roughmore Park is to become a hospital, you'll get your driving school? Is that it?"

She laughed. "You really understand me, Cora, don't you? Yes, this is the bargain I struck. I'll serve the war effort publicly with a hospital, if he'll let me privately run this driving school."

"Your school's meant to be a secret?"

"Well, the War Office thinks I'm training motorcyclists, not drivers, so I need to keep things a bit quiet. The duke's convinced teaching women from all walks of life to drive will stir up trouble. Here's something that Englishmen of all classes tend to agree upon: their wives and daughters don't belong behind the wheel. God forbid what will happen next if women are given a taste of independence.

"And they're right. Once we women have proven ourselves and we've won the war, they'll no longer be able to deny us the vote."

The duchess's optimism was undeniably contagious. "When's all this happening here at Roughmore?"

"Preparations for the hospital are already underway. Of course, Mrs. Matthews, the housekeeper, thinks it's a dreadful idea. She's certain the troops will arrive, seduce all the housemaids, and then burn the place down with a misplaced cigarette, but she's not in charge." Her expression turned even more wicked. "I am. And that reminds me, if you need another look at the house for your work here, I recommend you do so immediately because we'll be rolling up carpets soon and putting quite a lot of furniture and art in storage until the war ends." The duchess dropped into a nearby chair, pleased. She crossed her legs and proceeded to jiggle her top foot distractedly as she told me more about the plan for the hospital. "The house will serve as a convalescent home, meaning the men who arrive here will be in need of some quiet so they can recover, both physically and spiritually. Many suffer from a condition called 'shell shock.' The stresses of war—the noise, the violence, the constant tension of being alert—it's taking an unimaginable toll on many of the servicemen. The War Office warns that our new arrivals may experience nervous episodes and nightmares and other . . . complexities of the mind."

"Goodness, that sounds grim," I said. "What about the driving school? When are you opening to students?"

The duchess rubbed her hands together, excitedly. "Soon. What would you say to being my first student driver?"

I remembered the exhilaration I'd felt when we sped out of Paris at the start of the war. I needed a good dose of that again. "Yes, please, I'll do anything you need."

"That's the stuff." Nodding, she pulled a booklet from her pocket. "I've written a draft of my instructional text. Read it and tell me what you think."

And with that, she handed over a thick pamphlet titled *Women at the Wheel: A Chatty Little Handbook for the Lady Driver* and I flipped through the pages. "When do we start?"

"First things first. If you want to drive, you must know the mechanics. As we ladies know, if you really want to make your engine purr, it's important to know how things work under the hood."

A WEEK later, I met the duchess at the hunting lodge to embark upon my first driving lesson. Adrenaline coursed through me, knowing I was close to taking my spot at the wheel.

Nowadays it's nearly impossible to imagine a life without driving, but back in 1915, such a skill was a novelty. For women used to being reliant on men, learning to drive served as an invitation to adventure and independence, a way to discover new interests and jobs and connect with friends. In anticipation of my inaugural drive, I'd barely slept the previous night, yet I felt wide awake.

After we checked that the petrol, oil, and water tanks were full, the duchess grimaced at the collection of pedals and levers in the driver's seat. "Don't worry about knowing what each of those does. I'll walk you through them."

"But I already know." And I did. Over and over, I'd read her pamphlet, committing each part of the car to memory.

"Always check the brakes," the duchess warned, pointing to a small handle. Once we'd checked the brake's tension, we turned on the battery's electrical current in preparation for starting the engine.

"Grasp the handle with all five fingers below. If your thumb's on top, you could break it." She demonstrated the motion before stepping aside so I could try it. With two decisive cranks, I felt the handle catch. The motor roared to life. We hurried around the bonnet to take our positions in the front seat.

For someone like me, a woman used to tools and building with my hands, clambering into the driver's seat of a car, much less holding a steering wheel in my hand, introduced me to a whole new sensation of control. As the car rolled forward, jostling along the dirt road, it swiftly gained momentum, prompting me to shift into second gear. With each of my adjustments to the wheel and the pedals, the car responded. This enormous machine accepted my control. I was in charge. My chest expanded, my shoulders and arms loosened. This was power. What a feeling!

"Woo-hoo!" I yelled, leaning into a turn in the road.

"When we get to a straightaway, shift again. We can get this going up to twenty-eight miles an hour!" the duchess shouted over the din.

Though the car made a fearsome racket, the experience was wholly intoxicating! Trees and shrubs passed in a blur as I steered us along the road, the wind whipping at our hats and collars. I was familiar with the sense of strength and agency that came from building, but driving was an entirely different sort of authority and force. The speed, the movement, my mastery over such a large machine that shook and quaked with a life of its own—such domination! I never wanted that first drive to end.

OVER THAT summer, the transformation of Roughmore Park from a sleepy house echoing with ghosts to a bustling rehabilitation hospital put a spring in everyone's step. My impatience to leave Roughmore Park waned. Each time I visited the main house, maids scurried past carrying feather dusters and pails filled with suds. Footmen scooted up and down the stairs, carrying everything from candlesticks to card tables to large framed oil paintings. The estate no longer felt like a backwater. New energy suffused the place. It didn't take long for the trucks and ambulances to start delivering the veterans. Rail-thin, white as milk, and drifting like wraiths, the new arrivals made it painfully clear how tough life on the front lines must be. Even from a distance, I could see the damage wrought on their bodies and minds. Their fragility made my own hale heartiness feel embarrassing, an affront to the men who'd already sacrificed so much.

At the same time, but with less fanfare, students started to arrive at the duchess's school. From her years of racing, the duchess had connections to people who could pass along word of her endeavor to women who might be interested in such a radical undertaking. These women came from all walks of life. A few were restless aristocratic daughters in search of adventure, others were university students who wanted to play a role in the war effort, and one was a chambermaid sent by her employer, an older marchioness who believed in occasionally advancing the cause of a clever, promising girl of lower birth. What the women all had in common was that none knew the difference between a carburetor and a crankshaft, but within a week they were sporting oil-stained overalls and repairing truck engines. Most of the duchess's students stayed for about two to three weeks honing their driving and learning the basics of mechanics before they left to apply their skills. At any given time, six or seven students were on the premises.

I loved spending time at the driving school, where sounds of machines humming and engines revving rose over the laughter and chatter of the women. An unmistakable sense of conviviality clung to the grounds the way the aroma of butter and sugar trails a freshly baked pie. My longing to go to the front faded. I was busy, not only preoccupied with driving, but as soon as I climbed out of the driver's seat after that first lesson, I understood I needed to document the duchess's efforts to support the war: I'd re-create the driving school in miniature. After making a few adjustments, I built a base for the dollhouse and made space to include the driving school's garage, bunk room, and kitchenette in miniature, all hidden by a panel.

One morning in late fall of 1915, I arrived at the school and found the duchess making an announcement: she would be sending ten volunteers to Paris to learn how to use the radiological cars Marie Curie had developed to deliver mobile x-ray machines to the front lines. "Once you arrive in France, you'll be trained in basic anatomy, photographic processing, and the elemental application of electricity and x-rays so you'll be able to operate one of these special ambulances."

Several days later, a proud band of recent graduates from the duchess's school left to be trained under Mrs. Curie herself.

It wasn't long before all the women at Roughmore Park—from the nurses to the kitchen girls and housemaids—knew the fundamentals of how to repair a flat tire and drive. By 1916, when the British army opened its ranks to women drivers and mechanics, many of the duchess's graduates headed off to the front in France to serve with the Women's Auxiliary Army Corps and a great many headed to the city to be among the forty-six hundred women employed by the London General Omnibus Company to work as conductors. With the role of women drivers made official by the government, opportunities for learning to drive throughout the country broadened, so the duchess closed her driving school, but her role in contributing to the war effort only grew. She left on frequent tours throughout the country, promoting and recruiting for the Women's Emergency Corps and advising many of her aristocratic friends on converting their great houses into hospitals. Unfortunately the need to care for wounded veterans showed no signs of abating.

I finished the hidden driving school scene in the dollhouse's base and returned to working on the main rooms. Everyone seemed to be playing a vital role in supporting the war effort, except for me, but I'd soon discover my own unique way of helping the troops.

19

Tildy

2024

On Tildy's first full day in New Hampshire, she arrived at the workshop dressed in woolly layers scavenged from Ben's mudroom. Outside, brilliant sunshine reflected off the thin crust of snow and gushed through the dusty panes of the workshop's windows, sharpening the contrast between the bright patches of light on the floor and the room's dark shadows. Somewhere, Tildy hoped, she'd find a stash of Cora's photos, journals, tools, sketches, or *anything* that had once belonged to her.

"So where should I start?" Tildy asked Zelly.

The dog wagged her tail and leaned against Tildy's knee before moving off to lie down in a patch of sunshine a few feet away. Brushing the dark dog hair off her leggings, Tildy moved in Zelly's direction, wending a narrow path between the stacks of boxes. When she reached the middle of the room, she started opening the dusty cartons.

Tildy rummaged through piles of yearbooks, *Star Wars* figures, cassette tapes, stiff terrycloth-footed baby pajamas, spools of tangled thread, cracked Christmas decorations, records from bands she'd never heard of, sheaves of grammar worksheets, and other items long past their prime.

The hours passed and Tildy's fingers began to ache from the cold. She had found nothing but junk. Frustration chafed.

Tildy rubbed her hand across her forehead just as Zelly lumbered over, nuzzling her leg.

"Right, Zel, I haven't forgotten about you," Tildy said, glancing at the disappointing number of steps displayed on her smartwatch. "Let's go for a walk. And then I should probably eat something."

At the mention of a walk, Zelly galloped around her in circles and Tildy couldn't help but laugh. The dog had the right idea.

LATER THAT afternoon, Tildy had made it through a large section of the workshop but found nothing relevant to Cora. She was peering into a box filled with photo albums when Zelly suddenly lifted her head, then nudged open the door and trotted outside. From the closest window, Tildy heard the crunch of tires on gravel. She followed the dog out of the workshop and found Ben, crouched over, greeting Zelly.

"Any luck in there?" Ben asked Tildy, nodding his chin at the workshop.

She shook her head.

Ben gave her a sympathetic look. "Well, I'm thinking of heating up some Moroccan lentil soup I made a couple weeks ago and froze. How does that sound?"

"Delicious. Thank you!"

Ben opened the trunk of his car and pulled out a canvas tote. "I stopped by the store to pick up a few things." From the bag, he held up a set of rubber dishwashing gloves. "Before you join me for dinner, I'm going to do some cleaning."

AS TILDY approached the house's back door to join Ben about an hour later, she noted the stacks of garbage bags outside on the screened-in porch and entered the warm kitchen to find the counters empty of debris and the dirty dishes and pans cleaned and put away. She applauded. "Hey, it looks much better in here. Good job."

Ben waved his dish towel with a flourish and took a bow. "Thanks for the gentle reminder to get my shit together."

Tildy slid onto a kitchen chair and was about to tell him about finding a collection of 1980s Jazzercise video cassettes in the workshop, but Ben kept talking. "About eighteen months ago, I was engaged, but my fiancée dumped me shortly before the wedding. After that, I just stopped caring about how this place looked. I figured I had no one to make it nice for anymore, you know?" He forced a laugh, but Tildy could see how his eyes looked sad.

"I'm sorry that happened to you."

"Yeah, we'd been together for ages." He slid a frozen block of soup from a Tupperware container into a pot and turned on the stove. "Like since high school. After we both graduated from UNH, she went on to a PhD program in biology and tried to talk me into a similar one for chemistry, but I was happy with teaching high school science and coaching. The whole time she was in graduate school, she urged me to apply to PhD programs, but I ignored the pressure. Then we got engaged, and a month before our wedding, she was offered a fellowship in London. I didn't want to move, but encouraged her to do the program if she wanted. I promised I would visit a lot, especially because my sister lives there. So she decided to go, but then two weeks before the wedding, she called off our engagement, saying we had nothing in common anymore. Before I knew it, she was gone."

"Oh man, that's coldhearted. I'm sorry, Ben."

He sighed, stirring the soup. "Yeah, she called me *unadventurous*."

"She called *you* unadventurous? You're a guy who eats stuff he finds in the woods! If that's not adventurous, what is?"

He chuckled, then shrugged. "It was humiliating and turned life upside down for me. This is a small town. Everyone knew exactly what happened."

Tildy winced. She shook her head, disgusted with this woman she'd never met. Just as Tildy was contemplating how generous, charming, and handsome Ben was, he pulled a loaf of rustic-looking bread out of a cabinet and set it on a cutting board.

Tildy's eyes widened. "Did you bake that?"

"Yep." He took a serrated knife from the butcher's block, cut off a slice, and offered it to her. "I know carbs are out of fashion, but—"

"Not for me!" Tildy held the bread up to inhale its fresh scent.

"Well, June—that was my ex's name—didn't eat bread."

"For what it's worth, I think you're better off without her."

He shrugged, nudging a ramekin and knife toward her. "Try this salted butter."

Tildy didn't need to be told twice. She slathered butter on the bread and took a big bite. As she chewed, enjoying the bread's perfect balance of crusty exterior and fluffy sourdough interior, her frustration over not finding anything related to Cora seemed to melt away. The bread really was delicious. Next to her, Ben cut his own slice, but when he glanced over at her, he laughed, put down the knife, and lifted his hand to brush her cheek gently.

Tildy froze, her face suddenly on fire.

"Sorry, you had a big hunk of butter on the side of your mouth." He tilted his head, studying her. "I like how you eat with such gusto. It's nice to have my meals appreciated. June barely ate anything I cooked."

Tildy scrunched up her nose, trying to imagine this woman. June might have been book smart, but in every other sense, she sounded like a fool.

"Does she ever come home?"

"Thankfully, no. As far as I know, she's stayed in London."

"Good." Tildy eyed the pot on the stovetop and inhaled the rich aromas of coriander, paprika, and ginger rising off the bubbling soup. "Now, when do we get to dig into that?"

20
Cora

1916–1918

During the spring of 1916, the dollhouse's main stairwell took up most of my time. It was a complicated piece. Progress was slow. One afternoon, I stopped my lathe after realizing I'd let the wood get too thin on a baluster. Over the sudden silence of my workshop came the sound of a man cursing. Annoyed with the disruption, I crossed the room to peer out my door.

There, in the clearing in front of me, lay a man face down, sprawled on the ground, yelling a steady stream of oaths as he writhed in an effort to rise. Was he drunk? As my eyes adjusted to the sunshine and I spotted his hospital blues, the flannel uniform worn by the servicemen able to get out of bed, my concern grew. My workshop was located a half mile away from the great house. How had an unsupervised hospital patient made it this far? What kind of loose operation were they running up there?

I stepped from the workshop, wiping the sawdust from my hands on my apron. "What on earth's happening out here?" I asked, my tone curt.

The man froze.

"Do you need help?"

Without raising his face to meet mine, the man said, "Just a bit of an accident. If you could push my wheelchair closer to me, I can manage."

At the mention of a wheelchair, I instantly regretted my sharp tone. I searched the clearing. Sure enough, a wheelchair lay overturned in the shadows of a nearby tree. I walked toward it, muttering, “Sorry, I didn’t—”

“It’s fine.” Now his tone was clipped.

“Well, let me help.”

“No, thank you.” The tendons of his neck strained as he spoke.

When I reached the wheelchair, I spotted the reason he’d been upended. One of the wheels had fallen off the rear axle, probably the result of a loose lug nut. I bent over for a closer look, and after seeing my suspicions confirmed, I searched the surrounding area and located the small missing piece, lying several feet away, nearly obscured by a thicket of grass.

“I’ve found the problem, sir, but some minor repair work will be needed.”

“Bollocks,” he muttered, working himself up to sitting. Until that point, he’d been avoiding meeting my eyes, but now he took a look at me and his face reddened with embarrassment.

“I can fix this. Give me a moment.” Without another word, I returned to my workshop and grabbed two different wrenches to complete the job.

When I reemerged, his eyes widened at the sight of the tools in my hands. “If you’re planning to put me out of my agony by clubbing me over the head with those, I urge you to make the blows hard and quick.”

Chuckling, I got to work, placing the wheel back onto the axle, being careful not to break anything else. Within minutes, the wheelchair was fixed, no worse for wear. When I set it back upright, I looked over at him. With a high forehead, sharp cheekbones, wavy hair the color of whiskey, and glowering eyes, he was handsome. Very handsome. For a moment, neither of us spoke.

“Did you wheel yourself all the way here?”

He grimaced and grumbled, “Bloody stupid idea, it was.”

I pushed the wheelchair over to where he sat on the ground. "Can I help you up into this?"

"If you could just hold it in place, that would be grand." His sullen expression told me that nothing about this was grand. His pride was at stake. Quickly, I grabbed a nearby fallen branch to serve as a wheel stop, and before he could argue, I helped hoist him into his wheelchair. While he settled himself, I occupied myself with retrieving my tools.

When I turned back to him, the high flush of his complexion had faded. He cleared his throat. "Miss, I apologize for acting in a most uncivilized manner. I'm restored now." He held out a hand. "Corporal Hugh Havilland, Royal Engineers."

I introduced myself.

"What in the dickens are you doing out here?" he asked, eyeing my tools.

"I'm . . . working on a history of Roughmore Park."

"And this history requires wrenches?"

"Some days, yes."

He scoffed. "What are you really doing out here? Is this some sort of secret operation for the War Office?"

I laughed, wishing it was true. Tired of my deception, I decided to tell this stranger the truth. "If you must know, I'm building a dollhouse for the duchess."

I expected the corporal to laugh, but instead, he mulled over my answer.

"Why a dollhouse?"

"It's a form of portraiture."

"And you're building the whole thing yourself?"

I bristled. "I can manage it."

"I'm not implying you can't. If anything, I'm impressed. Recreating Roughmore Park is no small feat, I should think."

Slightly mollified, I considered inviting him in to see my work, but feared he'd tell me how to do it since what I was doing was widely considered a job befitting men, not women. "Do you have much experience in woodworking?"

"I do. Funny story, actually. My father was a magician and made his own props. Disappearing boxes, platforms with hidden doors, that sort of thing."

"A magician? Really?"

"Indeed he was. Eventually I took over the prop making, not only for him, but for some of the other performers."

"This was a show?"

"Yes, a vaudevillian show—a group of acrobats, animal trainers, you know the lot."

I stared at him. "Actually I don't. Are you pulling my leg? Did this really happen?"

"It was as real as rain."

"What about your mother? Was she part of this enterprise?"

"Oh yes. She could conduct optical illusions, disappear, predict the future, and other marvelous feats of daring. Heaven help the poor fool who unwittingly referred to her as my father's assistant. Sadly I inherited no special entertaining skills. Instead, from an early age, I made myself useful by being the troupe's handyman, and then most recently, I was assembling bridges for the army." As he spoke, his eyes brightened. A curl had fallen over his forehead, and he looked so boyish and charming that I found myself softening toward him.

"Would you like to come in and see what I'm working on?"

"Why, thank you. I'm honored to be invited to see the object of such secrecy, but I've got good news and bad news. Good news first: last I checked, my dance card's empty. I've got all the time in the world to tour your illustrious dollhouse-making endeavor. But now for the bad news: I can't get up those stairs, not in this blasted wheelchair."

He was right. Three stone steps led to my workshop's doorway.

I raised my index finger. "Give me a minute."

He nodded, extracting matches and a pack of cigarettes from inside his jacket pocket to occupy himself.

When I'd first arrived at the cottage, I'd removed a door from the kitchen's small pantry and placed it in storage in my workshop. After locating the door, I carried it back to the entrance where Corporal Havilland waited patiently for my return. "This could be a ramp. It'll be a little wobbly, but don't you think this is our best option for right now?"

"Rather quick thinking, I'd say. Well done." He took a final deep drag, exhaled, and flicked the remainder of the cigarette to the ground while I lowered the door onto the steps.

"I'll need a shove."

I nodded, positioning myself behind the wheelchair. "Ready?"

Havilland adjusted the jaunty red tie that completed his hospital uniform. "Fire away."

To get his wheelchair up over the lip of the ramp, I gave it an unceremonious jolt, causing him to groan, and I immediately froze in regret. "Oh no, did I hurt you?"

He looked over his shoulder at me. "The only thing I've hurt today is my dignity."

My improvised ramp was a bit bumpy, but it worked. Once Havilland was inside, his gaze roved over the room quickly as he pushed himself forward. His countenance was alert and curious, a sharp contrast to the wan souls inhabiting Roughmore Park. Havilland was different. He was lively. And funny. He'd said he'd inherited no special skills as an entertainer, but I disagreed. He radiated an enviable sense of confidence and ease that would have made him a natural onstage. As he rolled along the plank floor of the workshop, he moved gracefully. Under the felt of his flannel uniform jacket, the muscles of his back rolled much like a ripple travels across the smooth surface of a lake.

Approaching the dollhouse, he let out a low whistle. "So this is it, eh?"

"It is." I watched his expression carefully. He appeared genuinely interested as he leaned in to study the rooms from different angles.

He pointed to the small pieces of wood I'd scattered in frustration. "What's all this?"

"The grand staircase. It's causing me nothing but problems."

"Staircases of any size are never simple tasks. My father once told me that to be accepted into their craft guild, French woodworkers must demonstrate mastery by building a self-supporting staircase in one-twelfth scale."

"So my chagrin is understandable."

"Completely. I'm impressed you haven't been driven to drink already."

"Who says I haven't? You have no idea what's in my teacup."

"Ah, I see. Well then, please share. At this point, I could use some liquid fortification."

That's when an idea struck me. I'd wanted to put myself to use on the front, but what if I could assist the war effort here in my own workshop? The duchess had said the veterans needed peaceful ways to occupy themselves while they recovered. Didn't working with one's hands offer a productive, quiet, even therapeutic way to pass the time? Perhaps my workshop could help. "Please feel free to say no, but would you like to assist with this project? I could use as many able hands as possible."

"My dear girl, it's taken every ounce of my restraint not to beg for a job! I can only play so many rounds of ruddy cards at Roughmore. When may I start?"

"Now. I need your help with this staircase. Your engineering background makes you the perfect man for the task."

He leaned in to study the notebooks on my workbench. "Sure, I'll take a crack at it."

"Please do."

He flipped through my sketches, studying them closely. "I probably won't be any faster than you."

"That's fine. There's no rush."

Havilland continued to pepper me with questions about the dollhouse, so we kept talking, and it grew late. I checked the clock hanging over the door. "You should be back at Roughmore Park by now. In fact, you were probably due back ages ago."

Havilland pulled an indignant face. "I'll try not to take it personally that no one seems worried enough to send out a search party for me."

Despite his sense of humor, he looked tired and pale. I thought about the effort he'd need to make it back to the main house. "I need to stretch my legs. Mind if I walk with you?"

"Just can't get enough of me, is that right, Miss Hale?"

"Exactly."

"If we leave now, we can probably make it back in time for tea."

"Here, let me push," I said, gently grasping the handles of his wheelchair, and the fact that he didn't protest showed me how tired he really was. "Tell me more about your parents. Do they still tour with their show?"

"Sadly, no. They'd been touring in the United States and were traveling home aboard the *Lusitania* last spring."

I gasped, wincing. "I'm so sorry. You've lost a lot in a short amount of time."

"My parents actually had quite a romantic story. My mother grew up wealthy and educated, but when my father's act came to town, she spotted him onstage, and according to her, it was love at first sight. She gave up everything to spend the rest of her life with him—her inheritance, her parents' approval—everything."

"Was running away worth it? Were your parents happy together?" I asked.

"Very. My parents, may they rest in peace, enjoyed an enviable romance. They were a perfect match. Tell me, Miss Hale, do you believe there's one true love out there for each of us?"

As we strolled toward the great house, for an instant I pictured Belva sitting in the stables at Curtis House, reading aloud. I'd loved her. If I was honest with myself, I knew I still loved her. Had I lost my one shot at romance? I pondered this question, savoring the sunshine warming my shoulders, and the whir of insects rising from the woods around us. I pictured my father, how he never remarried. He had always been so sad. He had never gotten over losing my mother, his one true love. Instead of courting and remarrying, he immersed himself in his cabinetry business. For a long time I'd viewed his sacrifices as selflessness, but now I was starting to wonder if fear had driven him to remain alone—fear of disappointment and loss. When I remembered back on all the women who'd stopped by our house, hoping for an encounter with him, it was hard not to wonder if he'd missed his shot at finding a second chance at love.

"No, I don't believe so," I finally said. "Think of the pressure that would put on the fates. Call me optimistic, but I choose to believe that multiple opportunities come along, if we're brave enough to seize them. After all, it takes a lot of courage to fall in love."

Hugh glanced over his shoulder at me, nodding in approval. "It does. You're right. When I think of the risks my young mother took to marry my father, I see nothing but bravery."

We ambled along the road in silence, until eventually he cleared his throat. "So tell me how a girl like you ended up hammering nails in exchange for dinner."

"Don't you think a better question is how I ended up making dollhouses? They're a fine example of butter on bacon wouldn't you say?"

"I grew up making disappearing boxes, remember? I'm rather partial to whimsy."

I started at the beginning, telling him about my father and his cabinetry shop, my years in art school, and then my arrival at Curtis House, meeting Belva, and how we landed on the idea of making Le Petite Hôtel LeFarge. Of course, I mentioned nothing about my debacle in New York City. By the time we arrived at Roughmore Park, one of the Voluntary Aid Detachment nurses met us at the front door, smoothing down her white nurse's uniform. Her pretty face crinkled into delight at the sight of Corporal Havilland. I realized he hadn't said anything for at least ten minutes, and that's when I noticed the downward angle of his head. Slowly, I brought the wheelchair to a stop and stepped around for a better view of him. The man had fallen asleep. The fringe of his long dark lashes rested against his high cheekbones. For a flicker of a moment, I could see past his movie star good looks and picture him as a young boy.

"He's a bonny one, isn't he?" the VAD whispered, motioning to take over pushing the wheelchair. "He's been having an awful time lately. Terrible nightmares, poor fellow. To see him asleep is a wonder! Good on you."

I nodded, certain he'd eventually give me an earful about how my life's story put him to sleep, but I didn't mind. I was eager to see him again.

Corporal Havilland returned the following day and brought others. First, Lieutenants Shaw and Graves arrived. When I rose from the table to greet them, my chair's legs scraped across the floor, making a screeching sound, and Shaw fell to his knees, his arms covering his head.

"I'm so sorry," I said, silently cursing my thoughtlessness. After that, I learned to move slowly and quietly around the workshop. The men were like a school of minnows, easily startled and sent veering into different directions.

Graves's left arm hung in a sling and Shaw had suffered a head injury that left half his face bandaged. I set them on basic jobs like placing miniature tiles on floors and walls, but soon they'd cultivated interests in wood turning, and after several months, they'd become skilled at creating miniature pieces to be used for tables, chairs, bedposts, and a variety of other furniture pieces.

I met with Dr. Tabor, the supervising medical officer at Roughmore Park, and he sent me more patients suited to the type of occupational therapy that making miniatures could provide. After one captain informed me he'd studied painting at the Slade, I tasked him with creating miniatures of Roughmore's Main Gallery masterpieces. A lieutenant who rarely spoke took over re-creating the house's various wallpaper prints in miniature with ink, paint, stamps, and stencils. A number of the men proved to be adroit with needlework so I set them upon the task of reproducing Roughmore's carpets and other textiles.

"If my mother could see me now," one of the embroiderers chuckled one day, his needle held aloft over the carpet he was stitching, "I daresay she'd burst her buttons."

Over the coming months, more men trickled into the workshop, and progress on the dollhouse sped up considerably, but even more rewarding to me than the advances in our work was how the men shed their skittishness and settled into a close-knit community. Life on the front had built an unshakable sense of loyalty between them, and I witnessed these bonds firsthand in the workshop. They cared for one another with a tenderness that often brought a lump to my throat. Of course, woodworking, sculpting with clay, painting, and needlework had proven to be restorative to their damaged psyches, but it was in the small acts of kindness between them that I saw their shattered minds mending together. Without the attention of the nurses at Roughmore Park, the men settled into quiet routines of tending to one another.

One morning I observed how Shaw watched one of the new arrivals attempting to thread a needle. Each try left the newcomer increasingly frazzled and trembling until, without a word, Shaw slid on the bench next to him, gingerly took the needle and thread from the man's shaky hands, and fixed the problem. With a reassuring pat on the man's shoulder, Shaw slipped away as calmly as he'd arrived.

Back in my workshop in Paris, when my housemates gathered to work on the dollhouse, Belva had supplied the oxygen. She had been the center of Curtis House's solar system, the sun. Though it was subtle, a competitive undercurrent had powered the place. We strove to reflect Belva's brightness, to dazzle her, to show her we were special. Certainly I did. I wanted her to love me. At my Roughmore Park workshop, a different dynamic emerged. We were gentle with one another. Nurturing. Quiet. Although I missed the sisterhood and excitement of Curtis House, I was thriving with the war veterans. I was useful. I served a larger cause. We weren't just building a dollhouse, we were building each other back to health and soundness of mind.

The years I spent at Roughmore Park's workshop surrounded by veterans of the Great War represent one of the happiest and most interesting periods of my life. My father would never have imagined I could oversee a workshop filled with men, but there I was. Our days making miniatures were not only productive, but harmonious. When I thought of Belva, the pain of our parting softened into a sense of nostalgia. I grew capable of looking back on my time in Paris with affection. After all, Belva's patronage had been the gateway to discovering miniatures and reclaiming my career as an artist. How could I remain angry with her?

WHILE EACH of the veterans grew dear to me, most of all I appreciated Havilland's presence in the workshop. When he completed the grand staircase after several months, I joined him at his workbench, leaning close to admire the details: the fine acanthus carving on each newel at the staircase's base; the turning on the balusters; the perfect angles of the stringers. In a remarkable feat of engineering, the staircase stood on its own, but also could be slid into its space in the grand entry effortlessly. When I was done complimenting his work, I moved to straighten, but my scalp suddenly stung painfully. Quickly, I realized a hank of my hair had caught on one of the buttons of the corporal's jacket.

"Uh, Havilland?" I ventured. "I'm stuck."

Behind me, I could feel his chest bounce as he laughed. "Looks like I've got you right where I want you. All right, not to worry, sit tight. Let me work this out."

While I waited, contorted in a half-standing, half-crouching position, his fingers deftly unsnarled my hair in a way that almost massaged my scalp.

"Sorry if this hurts," he said.

"You have a good touch. I barely feel a thing."

"The gloriously bright color of your hair makes it easy for me to see what I'm doing."

Soon my thighs and calves burned from my awkward stance, but as I waited for him to free me, I realized my predicament wasn't all that bad. In fact, it was almost pleasurable. By the time I could feel my hair slipping from its entanglement, I realized I'd unconsciously settled right into sitting on his lap.

"My girl, much as I'd like to keep you snuggled up against me, you're free."

But he made no move to help me to my feet.

I confess it was with no small amount of disappointment that I stood and turned to face him, feeling my cheeks flush. His eyes fairly danced with merriment.

"Thank you," I said, softly.

"No, thank you," he said with a wink. "Those five minutes constitute the highlight of my last two years."

I swatted at his shoulder. "If I didn't know better, I'd think you tangled my hair on purpose."

"What can I say, I'm not afraid to make my own luck," he said, turning back to his workbench.

THE STAIRCASE was just the beginning for Havilland. He possessed his own remarkable brand of magic: that of a consummate tinkerer. His inveterate curiosity led him to constantly take items apart—clocks, radios, toasters—and put them back together, often in an improved state. When making miniatures, Havilland always knew when to push for realism and make objects function as they would if they were full-size and when to rely on illusion. The corporal was an improviser and let intuition guide him. I admired his talents and easygoing attitude.

His workbench soon filled with all manner of miniatures: a card table made from walnut veneers; a gramophone no larger than a spool of thread; a puppet theater complete with four marionettes whose strings looked as fine as spiderweb silk. His precision, artistry, and attention to detail inspired me to improve my own skills and be more daring with what I set out to create.

Havilland was not only a talented miniaturist, but I enjoyed his company. When I think back and try to pinpoint when I first fell in love with him, I'm unable to identify the exact moment, but I'd be lying if I didn't acknowledge it might have been when he first glided through my workshop in his wheelchair, moving the way I imagine a salmon carves through water. Havilland always exuded that kind of athletic grace despite the nature of his grave injuries. My affection grew quickly. Still, I dared not reveal my true feelings. I'd been hurt before.

Unlike many of my peers, I never felt the pull of a clock ticking toward my wedding day. For as long as I could remember, I'd pictured myself an artist, and even as a young girl, I knew creating art and tending to a household and husband did not go hand in hand. Perhaps because I grew up motherless, I had no one in my life urging me toward mastering domestic tasks. I simply envisioned a life like my widowed father's. I'd take care of myself. That was the familiar example available to me. If I fell in love, well, wonderful, but without feeling the need to rush along society's well-trod path to the marriage altar, I felt little pressure to act upon my feelings for Havilland. With no interest in taking romantic risks, I would wait, see what happened.

My wariness seemed well-placed because while Havilland was always bantering with me, he acted familiar with everyone, men and women. I had no reason to think his gentle flirting with me was anything but blowing off steam. I'd seen the way the men made eyes at the nurses mercilessly. It's how everyone coped with the stress of injury, war, and being cooped up with the same people day after day.

One afternoon early in 1917, late in the day, as the men cleaned their workspaces and readied to leave, Havilland continued to hunch over his project: a canary within a birdcage. This was nothing unusual. He often stayed late to work. After he finished whatever project had absorbed him, I'd walk him back to Roughmore Park, helping him navigate his wheelchair over the road's rough surface. These walks were my favorite part of the day.

So, on this particular afternoon as the workshop emptied, I was unwrapping a tiny set of Spode china the duchess had commissioned from the manufacturer. While we made most of the dollhouse's pieces in the workshop, occasionally the duchess liked to use her influence and order bespoke pieces from companies she knew would be amenable to special projects. The dollhouse's glassware, dishes, and pots and pans had all been produced this way.

"How are you getting on?" I asked him. "Want some tea? I can put the kettle on. Cook sent me a tin of biscuits yesterday."

"You're a good egg to let me linger around for so long," he said. "I suppose having the slowest recovery in the British army has its advantages. All the lads are impatient to ogle the VADs, but they're missing out on the prettiest lass in England."

I threw a handful of packing straw toward him. Dr. Tabor had told me that Havilland's surgery report from Sidcup, the hospital that first received him, warned he would most likely never regain the ability to walk. He'd been ambushed while constructing a bridge with the Royal Corps of Engineers and taken a heavy load of shrapnel to the spine and legs. Despite his grim prognosis, Havilland never failed to attend his physical therapy appointments.

"You, my friend, have a way of making the best of things. I know your slow recuperation has frustrated you, but you're always so upbeat. And the men look up to you for it."

"Thank you, Miss Hale. My mother was an incorrigible optimist. She always believed in happy endings." His gaze settled on a spot somewhere in the distance and he smiled to himself. "And nothing seemed impossible to my father. It must have been in his performer's blood. He was always looking for the magic in everyday life, always willing to experiment and try something new for the sake of adventure. You remind me of him in many ways. Bravo on how the main kitchen's come together, by the way. It's first-rate."

"Thank you. To be honest, the stove's very delicate. It requires a very gentle touch."

"How will you judge who has a touch gentle enough to try it?"

I saw he was barely suppressing a devilish grin. "Oh, stop with your teasing. None of you blokes will be allowed near it."

"What's this? *Blokes?* You're using English slang now?"

"I didn't realize I needed permission. I like blokes."

He snorted with laughter. "You don't say."

"You know what I mean. I like the *word.* You're a dreadful flirt, Havilland."

"I think it's time you start calling me Hugh. At least when it's just the two of us."

"We've got the right energy now. I don't want to change a thing."

"But what if I do?"

I looked up, surprised by his sudden serious tone. "What do you mean?"

Havilland ducked his head toward his birdcage. "I mean I have a surprise for you. Didn't you mention Cook sent us some biscuits?"

I pointed to my workbench. "Yes, the tin's over there."

"Perfect. We need something celebratory."

"Really? What are we celebrating?" I asked, crossing the room to where he sat, working on his birdcage.

"Wait! Stop there," he said as I neared him. Confused, I paused. Before I could ask any questions, Hugh rose slowly from his wheelchair. I held my breath as he began to take one hesitant step after another in my direction. When he reached me, I let out a small cry of joy and wrapped my arms around him.

"This is a surprise, a *wonderful* surprise!" I cried, my voice muffled from where I tucked my face into his neck. I breathed in the scent of soap and tobacco clinging to him and didn't move away. For over a year, we had been working so closely—literally inches away from each other—and with the exception of when my hair had tangled with his uniform, we'd never allowed ourselves an intimacy like this. I hadn't dared. I didn't want to disrupt the magic I felt in the workshop. My father's warning that men would never take orders from me was like a nettle stuck deep in my thumb, a constant reminder of how precarious my situation felt. Surely a romance would disrupt everything. It always did. A memory of dancing cheek to cheek with Belva in my old workshop flashed through my mind, but I pushed it away. I didn't want to think of her, not when Hugh was near. He brought me such joy, whereas thinking of Belva always left me yearning for the past.

Despite my grip, I felt Hugh slipping away from me. He slid into a nearby chair wearing a sheepish expression. "Apparently you make me a bit weak in the knees. I suppose I must work on my endurance now."

"Right, endurance." I bit my lip, feeling foolish for having hung on to him for far longer than was necessary. If I wanted an opportunity to tell him how I felt, this was it, yet I could barely string together two words, much less a complete sentence.

He smoothed back his hair. "Well, that little adventure's wiped me out. What do you say we head back to Roughmore?"

"Of course."

"I still fancy a biscuit though. Shall we split one?"

"You've earned the entire thing," I said, relieved to face away from him while I fetched the tin.

"You're too good to me, Miss Hale. Too good."

HUGH AND I continued working together for another year, but I didn't permit myself to indulge in any romantic daydreaming. I'd played a fool before and had no intention of repeating that folly.

The United States finally entered the war, creating an unmistakable shift in momentum. Finally we dared to think maybe the war wouldn't last much longer. Still, men came and went from the workshop. Some deemed healthy returned to the front while others left to become instructors at various military training schools. Several retired with honors and headed back to civilian life. Through it all, we continued making the dollhouse, and the workshop became quite popular with the house staff and villagers.

The miniature Roughmore Park never failed to bring a smile of delight and wonder to people's faces. If a villager had been fortunate enough to visit Roughmore, they'd probably only caught a glimpse of the kitchen or the great hall, but the dollhouse put parts of the building on view that would be out of sight for most people. Suddenly the staterooms, the bedrooms, and the downstairs quarters were visible, and I watched how the villagers stood tall and proud as they inspected the history, art, and craftsmanship on display in the dollhouse. It reminded them why England was special, why it was worth sacrificing and fighting for.

Shortly after the start of 1918, German bomber planes attacked Paris, killing twenty-six people and wounding over two hundred others. The aerial assault's brazenness stunned us out of our newfound sense of confidence in the war winding down.

Later that month, the duchess and Dr. Tabor showed up in the workshop with an announcement.

"I've just received good news. Princess Marie Louise, the Queen's cousin, is planning to visit us," the duchess said. "Apparently Doctor Tabor's paper for *The Lancet* about the therapeutic benefits of working on miniatures has caught the royal family's attention. As a result, Princess Marie Louise is planning to come and see the dollhouse next Wednesday."

The men and I beamed at one another as Dr. Tabor held up a copy of *The Lancet* and saluted. Looking at the excited smiles lighting up the men's faces, I felt so proud of them. We needed the good news. Although not every man had exhibited a talent for miniatures, they'd improved their health during their time in the workshop, and that was more important than anything. I thought back to Evans, a lieutenant from Bath, whose hands had trembled like jelly when he first arrived. After several weeks of making tiny books for the dollhouse library, not only had his hands steadied, but his eyes no longer looked haunted. There had also been Wilson, who didn't speak, but after months of sitting in the corner transforming bits of paper, silk, wire, and felt into plants for the dollhouse's conservatory, he quietly told me the Latin name and the historical symbolism for every bit of greenery he'd created.

"Apparently Queen Mary's quite the enthusiast of miniatures

and she'd like to see what you've been making. Perhaps you can spare the princess a few of your creations so she may return to the Queen with a gift or two for her collection."

Everyone nodded enthusiastically, and the men returned to their work with renewed vigor. For the next week, the workshop buzzed with activity in preparation of the royal visit.

On the morning of Princess Marie Louise's arrival, I awoke early. Though the men had tidied their workstations the previous evening, I swept again and wandered around the room, dusting and organizing tools and supplies. When I could detect no stray items that needed straightening, I stopped in front of the dollhouse to admire our work. Though I'd never publicly acknowledge any favorite items, I had a few: for the Music Room, Lieutenant Graves built a piano with black and white keys no larger than a comb's tines; Lieutenant Webb, who exuded a gruff demeanor, had hand painted a surprisingly sweet series of Beatrix Potter–inspired murals in the nursery; Hugh had produced a set of hunting rifles leaning against the wall in the library; and then there was a dollhouse within a dollhouse that I'd made—oh, I had fun with that. Of course, the miniature dollhouse in 1/144 scale didn't have anywhere near the level of detail of the one we'd been making in 1/12 scale, but whenever I looked at it in the miniature Morning Room, it was like opening a beautiful oyster shell, only to discover a small pearl resting on the inside.

When the men began arriving, Hugh didn't stop to talk with me as he usually did. Instead he headed straight for his workstation. He'd regained functionality of his legs and no longer needed his wheelchair, though he would use a cane for the rest of his life. For the last few weeks, he'd been helping me create a set of wicker furniture for the conservatory by weaving a fine-gauge wire in place of willow, and he settled into the project, not saying anything to anyone. His reticence was uncharacteristic, but there was no time for a private word. We tried to immerse ourselves in our projects, and though we pretended it was just another day in the workshop, we listened for the sound of motorcars outside.

When the duchess arrived with her royal guest, she introduced Princess Marie Louise to everyone.

"Isn't this marvelous?" the princess said, taking in the dollhouse before addressing me directly. "And you're in charge of these men, is that right?"

I hesitated for a moment, unsure how the men would react to me overtly being described as their supervisor, but for the first time since he'd arrived that morning, Hugh caught my eye and nodded emphatically.

"I am."

"Isn't that something?" The princess turned to Hugh. "Tell me, did you ever imagine yourself making miniatures?"

"I reckon I didn't, but then again, these last few years have really defied all imagination, haven't they?"

The princess nodded solemnly. "Indeed." She stepped forward to inspect the miniature lathe. "My, this is quite a curious contraption. Would one of you show me how it's used?"

I nodded at Hugh and he stepped forward, handing me his cane. "We're going to turn a table leg, how does that sound?"

"We?"

"Yes, Your Grace. We'd be honored for you to join us."

"I thought you'd never ask!" The princess promptly held out her wrists to the duchess, shaking off her stack of gleaming diamond-and-gold bracelets. "My dear, could you unclip my jewelry and help me out of these gloves?"

Once unadorned, the princess wiggled her bare fingers, looking delighted. "Goodness, this feels rather wild."

Hugh lifted a bulky pair of safety glasses and held them toward her. "Before we start, though, I'm afraid I must recommend you wear a pair of these." For a moment, my breath caught as I thought the princess would balk at donning such an ugly accessory, but she slid them on, giggling.

"I imagine I must look quite fetching in these."

We laughed along with her. If anyone could get the elegant princess to wear the most atrocious glasses in the world, it would be Hugh.

He lifted a roughing gauge, switched on the machine, and demonstrated for a moment before stopping it, stepping away, and gesturing for the princess to take over. "Maple is a harder wood, so you'll have to be steady. Don't be afraid to give it a little muscle."

When the wood turning demonstration ended, the princess brandished a miniature table leg for everyone to see. "Righto. Making miniatures is wonderfully satisfying, though I daresay my amateur participation would slow your progress woefully."

"Hardly. We'd be honored."

The princess flashed a smile at the group before her gaze landed affectionately on Hugh for a beat. She then raised a triumphant chin. "I think the Queen needs a dollhouse for herself."

"And I just happen to know a talented group of war veterans who would be proud to serve their queen by building her one," I said.

"What about you?" she asked me.

"Though I'm honored to be asked, I think these brave heroes would be best suited for such a patriotic endeavor."

The princess beamed at the men. "Thank you for your service. You'll be hearing from the Crown soon."

Eventually the princess left amid a flurry of excitement and thank-yous, but not before we bestowed several miniatures upon her: an embroidered rug, a dresser, and a painting. After the royal entourage departed, three girls from the kitchen arrived with a special celebratory lunch for us. While the houseboys set up a table and the kitchen girls scrambled to lay out sandwiches and several cakes, I approached Hugh.

"I had no idea what to expect from a member of the royal family. She was lovely," I said.

"She was." He barely lifted his gaze to me. "That was good of you to recommend the lads to serve the Queen."

"I know they're worried about what they'll do for work when they leave here. The princess's offer felt like the perfect opportunity."

He nodded.

"Is something wrong?" I asked. "You've been unusually quiet this morning."

His eyes darted around the workshop, and when he was assured the rest of the men were occupied with lunch, he said, "I've gotten word I'm to return to active service."

My gaze traveled to his cane. Hugh was lively and healthy, but certainly not ready for military duty. There had to be a mistake. This man had already sacrificed so much. He couldn't be sent back to war. Though I knew it was selfish, my heart sank at the idea of his departure. Without Hugh, there was nothing for me at Roughmore Park.

"Trust me, the last thing I want to do is leave," he said quietly.

I willed myself to speak, to tell him how I couldn't bear to see him go, but words failed me. I feared embarrassment and pain. After all, my track record with romance was abysmal. Finally I mustered a few questions in a ragged voice.

"Where are they sending you? What will you do?"

He looked at me sadly, brushing a patch of sawdust off my sleeve. "I'm afraid I can't say. This mission is top secret."

I should have been honest about my feelings for him, but instead I turned and fled the workshop.

21
Cora

1918–1919

Less than a week after the princess's visit, almost everyone from Roughmore House attended a bazaar at the village's primary school to benefit Paris's victims of the recent German aerial raid. I hitched a ride into town with the men from the workshop. As our wagon rattled along the road, Havilland and I sat across from each other. Since I'd learned of his departure we'd barely spoken. He was scheduled to depart Roughmore Park on Monday, only two days away. If I wanted to confess my true feelings about him, time was running out.

Our convoy stopped in front of the village's honey-colored limestone church, and as soon as we unloaded, I found Hugh beside me.

"Shall we find some cream tea?" he asked, pointing to the school's entrance.

I nodded, and he took my arm, guiding me into the school's auditorium, where villagers had set up tables for selling garlands of dried flowers, jars of jam and honey, and other assorted sundry items. From the corner of my eye, I watched Hugh, weighing my decision to tell him about how I felt. Really, what did I have to lose? If he didn't return my affection, he'd be leaving, sparing me a prolonged period of embarrassment. I'd never have to see him again. So why not risk it? In my head, this logic made perfect sense. But whenever Hugh looked at me to smile or point something out, words died in my throat.

"Try your luck in the raffle, miss?" a man called to me, giving the tombola in front of him a lazy spin. "It's all for the lads in uniform, of course." He pointed at his Red Cross armband, nodding respectfully at Hugh.

I dropped my coins into a jar, reached into the tombola rim, and plucked out a red ticket.

The man squinted at the number printed on it. "Lucky seven. A good pick. Hold on to it, enjoy the fete, and we'll announce the raffle winners after the final best in show for desserts award is handed out later."

Hugh and I took seats at a cluster of tables set underneath bunting streamers. One of the villagers wearing an apron stitched with decorative oak leaves set a teapot, jam, cream, and a plate of scones in front of us.

"Why have you been avoiding me?" he asked.

I put a scone on my plate, screwing up the courage to say something, while pouring us cups of tea. Finally I spoke. "I don't understand why they're sending you back."

"Don't worry. I won't be heading to the front."

"But then where are you going?"

Hugh slathered a layer of strawberry jam across his scone. "If you put jam on first and then a dollop of cream, it's known as the 'Cornish split.' That's how I like it. How about you?"

I didn't even bother to look at my scone. "Hugh, I'm worried about your return to action." This was a vast understatement. Worried? No, I was utterly devastated, but considering how much trouble I was having getting the words out, it was a start.

Hugh chewed his scone and shifted his gaze from me to the vendor tables, where a collection of Victoria sponges awaited judging. Finally he swallowed and leaned forward, moving his hand to cover mine where it rested on the white tablecloth. I quickly glanced around to see if anyone was watching, but he held my hand firmly in place. “I’ll be fine. I’m not being sent back into battle. The army wants my engineering skills for a different type of war project. I wish I could tell you more, but I’ve been sworn to confidentiality.”

A different type of project. Hugh always downplayed his skills. I worried about what exactly he was getting himself into.

Suddenly my cup of tea sounded good. Though it tasted more bitter than I expected, even filled with cream and sugar, I relished its warm comfort. “How long will you be gone?”

“You know as well as I do that there’s just no telling.”

I felt furious. Not at him, of course, but at the mysterious powers in London who pulled all the strings. Why did they have to take him from me? I glanced at his cane leaning against the back of his chair. Hugh had already sacrificed so much.

“You should stay here,” I said sullenly.

As soon as the words came out of my mouth, a pang of shame echoed through me. I was thinking selfishly. Judging by the ever-lengthening casualty lists posted on the vicarage wall in the square, it didn’t take any advanced math skills to know not many men would be returning from the war.

But I was tired of sacrifice. We all were.

Around us, the bazaar was in full swing. Nearby at the Crockery Smash stand, a young boy hurled a heavy ball at shelves teeming with plates and mugs. When his throw made contact with three plates, they broke into pieces with a satisfying crash. The young children clustered around him, cheering with excitement as the game’s barker, an old man sporting orange polka-dot suspenders, made a show of sweeping away the wreckage. Aside from the hospital patients milling around the expansive room, not a single young man still seemed to live in the village. In my hands, my tea grew cold. I placed it on the table in front of me and balled my hands into the pockets of my cardigan.

"This war won't last forever, you know," Hugh said quietly. "Maybe it's time we start planning for what happens next."

I narrowed my eyes. *Next?* My stomach lurched. "What do you mean?"

"Dearest girl, I'm terribly fond of you."

"Fond?" Though my heart sped into a gallop at his use of *dearest girl*, I repeated the quintessential British phrasing, looking dubious.

"Forget fondness. I'm bloody tired of hiding my true feelings. I'm absolutely head over feet in love with you. How's that?"

My heart suddenly seemed to skid to a stop after its furious beating only seconds ago. I leaned forward, breathless. "Are you serious?"

"Why wouldn't I be?"

"Why didn't you say something sooner?"

"I thought you didn't return my affection. Or at least not in any sort of romantic way."

I groaned with the realization at how much time we'd wasted. One thing the war was teaching us was that nothing could be taken for granted—especially time. I shook my head, amazed. "We're fools. I thought you didn't love me."

"Where are those banged-up hands of yours?"

I giggled, removing them from my pockets. Underneath my gloves, bruises and burn scars covered my hands, evidence of my various mistakes in the workshop. They were not very ladylike.

Tenderly, he peeled off my gloves. "Marry me, Cora."

The feeling of his warm skin against my own, the soft way he caressed my battered fingers—the intimacy of his gesture knocked the breath right out of me. I was speechless. I'd always believed marrying would be the end of my art. But then again, I'd never imagined meeting someone like Hugh. After the last few dreary wartime years, I needed to seize happiness whenever it presented itself, for there was no telling what the future might bring.

I nodded. "Yes, of course. Let's get married."

"Yes?" he repeated as if not quite believing his ears.

"Yes, yes, yes, but we can't waste any more time. Let's get married as soon as we can."

He pushed away his empty plate and reached for his cane, but before he stood, a commotion around the room's entry caught our attention.

The duchess had entered the bazaar, making a show of unwrapping a silk scarf from around her hat before crossing the room with her usual vigorous stride, waving to the villagers as they called greetings. In a smartly cut, garnet-hued suit, she stood out, and she knew it. A broad smile stretched across her face as a cluster of little girls in plaid wool frocks encircled her. Once she moved away, blowing kisses, she headed toward us.

"What a perfect day for this bazaar," she called. "It's good you two managed to pry yourselves away from the dollhouse for a bit of cheer."

Her gaze settled on me and then darted to Hugh before returning to me. "Am I interrupting something?"

I reached for Hugh's hand, lacing my fingers through his. "We've just decided to marry. You're the first to know."

For once, the duchess appeared flabbergasted, but as she spotted our clasped hands, she clutched her own chest. "You sly little fox! I had no idea you and Havilland had a romance blooming right underneath my nose. Good for you. Now doesn't our dashing corporal head out soon? That doesn't give us much time to plan a wedding."

"We don't need much. We just want to make it official before he leaves."

The duchess nodded. "The duke and I made headlines for the speediness of our courtship, but you two make us look as slow as snails. All right then, let's head to the vicarage to see what we can put together."

Hugh and I exchanged amused glances. The duchess marched out of the school, but when she realized we were moving more slowly because of Hugh, she adjusted her pace to match ours and I saw her surreptitiously studying him. "So tell me, Corporal Havilland, do you have any idea where you're heading? Are they sending you to the front or to a training school?"

"Your Grace, I'm sorry, but I'm unable to share any information with you. My work's considered classified."

Hugh looked mortified to put her off, but the duchess's eyes widened and she nodded, clearly impressed. As we approached the church's office door, I hurried ahead to open it for her, and after she swept in, we followed.

THANKS TO the duchess, in less than an hour, I stood on the town chapel's front steps, smoothing down my freshly combed hair and steeling myself to enter.

By marrying Hugh, I was taking a risk. Despite his assurances, there were no guarantees he'd make it home alive from this war. And assuming he did return safely, then what? In front of that church, I had a dizzying moment. Did I really want to marry? Was I ready to surrender my vision of the future for a new one, a future I couldn't picture? A future that felt risky and unknown?

I took a deep breath. Yes, I was taking a risk, but there was no better risk than falling in love. I'd always been an optimist. To create art is, at its very core, a hopeful act. In a world that was all too filled with heartbreak and sorrow, I needed to choose hope. I needed to choose love.

As I climbed the stairs, my eyes adjusted from the pale January sunshine to the cool interior of the church. The opening notes of an organ played Mendelssohn's wedding march and a sea of faces, a mix of Roughmore Park's inhabitants and villagers, turned to look at me. I barely remember what happened during that brief ceremony, but as soon as we emerged outside, dried rose petals sprinkling over us like a light rain, an impromptu wedding parade began. Was it the children who started it? The nurses? I'll never know. Hugh and I were placed on the back of a wagon and we circled the village green with almost everyone from the bazaar joining us, marching, laughing, and singing. When we reached the Owl and Thistle, full foamy pints materialized in everyone's hands. Slices of Victoria sponge circulated. The mood felt ebullient and soon turned raucous as a group of men, both old-timers and patients, started a round of Morris dancing.

At some point, Hugh pulled me away from the wedding festivities; our presence was no longer needed to keep the momentum going. He led me to the duchess's sporty pearly white Vauxhall and I stared at him as he opened its driver's door. "What are you doing?" I asked.

"The duchess told me to take you back to the cottage before anyone noticed."

"In this?"

"How about it, eh? Good thing she taught you to drive." He gestured at me to slide behind the steering wheel, which I did, and he moved to the passenger's side, tossed his cane into the back seat, and nestled beside me. "Ready, my love?"

For ten months, I lived at Roughmore Park without Hugh while he was deployed by the military. His letters contained more black stripes than you'd find on a zebra—the censors had been busy. I had no idea where he was or the nature of his service. Was he on the front lines? Behind a desk somewhere? Not a minute passed when I wasn't fretting about him. If not for the dollhouse and men in the workshop, I would have gone mad with anxiety. Fortunately by mid-October it was becoming increasingly clear the war would be over very soon. Maybe by Christmas. Certainly by Easter. The men and I put in a final push to finish the dollhouse.

Finally, one morning in early November, we received word. The duchess and Dr. Tabor bestowed a surprise visit upon us. When they entered the workshop, a gust of misty air encircled them, but despite the dreary weather, the duchess positively glowed with goodwill. "I just received a telegram from the duke in London. The Armistice was signed last night!"

As I lay my hand across my heart, I heard the men behind me let out cries of surprise.

"I'll plan a champagne toast for tonight after dinner. Everyone is welcome to attend," she told the men, stepping forward to shake their hands and clasp their shoulders gently. Everyone broke into cheers. I told them to take the day off and return to the great house to prepare messages to their families. The duchess remained behind.

"The duke also noted that Hugh will be back here within the next few days."

My heart soared with this news, but before I had time to fully absorb it, the duchess slid an envelope from her skirt pocket.

"Oh, and another thing. I received a letter from Winny. Apparently the comte LeFarge is dead."

My relief at knowing Hugh was on his way home stuttered with this shocking development. "How did he die?"

"A train accident, nothing related to the war. A mechanical malfunction. Winny says Belva wasted no time packing up the Hôtel LeFarge. She and Jack are heading to California and already boarded a ship bound for New York City."

"And what's Winny doing now?"

"She'll remain in Paris to continue overseeing Curtis House."

I nodded calmly, but my thoughts careened wildly like a downed airplane. If I hadn't married Hugh, would I have immediately gone in search of Belva? Did a part of me still long for her? I pushed those questions from my mind. I loved Hugh. I'd chosen him and had no regrets.

I steadied myself by leaning against my workbench and smiling at the duchess.

"Your Grace, the dollhouse is ready to be moved to Roughmore Park."

A WEEK after the war ended, when low fog crept across the estate's acreage, obscuring the sun and shrouding the countryside in a gloomy darkness, we moved the dollhouse into Roughmore Park's Morning Room, where it would remain on display.

The day after its transport, I was in the great house, making small repairs that arose during the dollhouse's move, when I heard a familiar voice.

"Cora, are you ever going to finish that thing?"

When I turned, Hugh stood in the doorway. Though he looked a little thinner, nothing else appeared to have changed. His smile conveyed the same mischievous quirk, his eyes gleamed with intelligence, but more than anything, his whole being radiated relief at returning home. But in this case, home wasn't Roughmore Park. The way he looked at me communicated everything. Longing, excitement, and happiness—*I* was his home.

I dropped everything and hurled myself straight into his arms.

"Tell me, where were you?" I asked.

"Paris."

"Not a bad post."

"They had me building the ultimate magic trick."

"What do you mean?"

"I was put on a team creating an illusion to fool German bombers. In the northeast corner of the city, we built a replica of Paris out of wood, silk, and canvas. Even a fake train system was constructed, using moving lights to make it appear realistic."

His explanation sounded crazy.

"Why?" I asked.

"We hoped to trick German Gotha bombers and spare the real city."

"You're kidding."

"Far from it. From the air, our fake Paris looked incredibly authentic."

I shook my head in disbelief.

"Don't get me wrong, I'm so glad the war's over, but I must confess, I was rather eager to see if our little ploy would work."

"Well, I've just wanted you back."

"And here I am."

"Good. Let's get out of here." I lowered my voice and gave him a knowing look. "Because of the censors, I couldn't write about everything I've missed about you."

Hugh threw back his head, laughing loudly. "God, I've missed you, Cora."

Later, as we lay in bed together in my cottage, Hugh propped himself up on his elbow. "Some of the lads who worked with me on Fake Paris have designed theater sets in New York. I reckon if I can build a fake city, surely I can manage to fill a stage successfully. What do you think? Shall we move to America?"

I must have looked stricken because he embraced me, squeezing me so tightly I could barely breathe.

"Surely the duchess has a friend or two in New York City who wants a dollhouse."

"I'm sure you're right," I said faintly.

I should have confessed to Hugh what had happened when I was seventeen. Why I'd left. It would have saved me so much grief, if I'd just been honest. But something stopped me. I was ashamed of what I'd done and feared admitting my crime to Hugh. Yes, *crime*.

So I said nothing. New York was a big place, full of people, even back then. I hoped I could return, keep a low profile. For too long I'd been an exile. I'd paid my penance and been humbled. I'd be returning to the United States a different woman from the girl who'd fled a decade earlier. I couldn't run from my past forever.

Hugh and I settled into a boardinghouse not far from the Theater District of Manhattan. On my second day back in the United States, after Hugh left for a theater job he'd lined up, I hastened outside the hotel lobby and ducked into a taxi heading uptown. As my vehicle approached Central Park, my heart beat in my throat with a fury I'd never known before.

The taxicab halted and I got out, shivering in the cold wind howling down Fifth Avenue. Before me, a huge Beaux-Arts building blocked the sun. I climbed its stairs and proceeded inside. After nearly twenty minutes of searching, across a room, I spotted my own likeness, albeit younger. I'd finally returned to her. A young women with my same features, sat patiently, as people passed between us. I took a step closer and then another, waiting to be recognized.

22
Tildy

2024

On her last full day in New Hampshire, Tildy left the guest cottage and trudged toward the workshop, inhaling the metallic smell of snow and hoping the bleak, pewter-colored sky didn't presage another futile day of searching.

For two hours she sifted through Ben's family's knickknacks and was nearly convinced she'd never find anything worthwhile, when she opened a cardboard box and froze.

A stack of old black notebooks.

She lifted one, brushing a fine scrim of dust off the top, and then opened the cover, flinching as the spine cracked.

Inside the notebook's cover was a date: 1911. In elegant, swooping script below the date: *Cora Hale*. Architectural sketches drawn in pencil filled the rest of the pages.

Tildy didn't dare blink, almost didn't dare breathe for fear the notebook would vanish into thin air.

Suddenly she no longer felt stiff with cold.

Slowly she turned page after page, recognizing the Hôtel LeFarge in the sketches. As she made her way through the notebook, different images of the dollhouse's exterior and interior, measurements, and notes came into view.

Tildy sat back on her heels, nearly limp with relief.

"Zelly, we're in business!" she called out, startling the old dog. Already she could envision how these pages could be reproduced and enlarged for the Bel's exhibit.

Heart pounding, Tildy placed the notebook on a nearby box and fished around in the back pocket of her jeans, searching for her archivist gloves. Once she'd slid her trembling fingers into them, she reached back into the box, riffling through the collection of sketchbooks.

Delicately, as if the box was filled with explosives, Tildy carried it to the door, placed it on the ground, and then returned to open the second box below. When she folded back the cardboard tabs, a mishmash of old sepia and black-and-white photographs appeared.

Tildy lifted one of them. A group of men in military uniforms surrounded a familiar large dollhouse. The image's caption confirmed Tildy's suspicion: Roughmore Park, 1918. From its Wikipedia page, she remembered the great house had been used as a convalescent home during World War I and a close look at the picture revealed several of the men held crutches and a few had missing arms, slings, and bandaged heads and legs. In the center of the men, alongside the dollhouse, stood a young woman. Tildy's breath caught. Was this Cora, posing with her dollhouse?

In another shot, two women sat on a porch. She held the photo to catch the light better and recognized Joy Wolfe's familiar face. Though the hairdo and style of clothing had changed, Tildy recognized the second woman from the Roughmore Park photo: Cora Hale. It had to be.

Excited, Tildy flipped through more.

In each photo, Cora's face appeared slightly out of focus, like she'd been caught looking away from the camera, but there was no mistaking her elegant nose, the proud set of her shoulders. Tildy recognized her features from the photos she'd found at the Bel.

Zelly, sensing Tildy's excitement, lumbered over, wagging her tail.

Beneath the photos, Tildy found a small canvas rolled up. She untied it. Files and tweezers of varying sizes, a magnifying glass, and other smallish tools appeared. Tildy removed one of the files and rubbed its rough surface against the pad of her left index finger. *Cora Hale had once held this very object in her hands!* Happy tears of disbelief welled in Tildy's eyes. She'd finally found Cora Hale's treasure trove.

There were six boxes, and they were filled with sketchbooks, letters, photographs, and tools of varying sizes. From one box, Tildy lifted out a miniature wooden train filled with circus animals. The piece lacked the detail of Cora's other miniatures and Tildy inspected the chipped paint. On the wooden elephant, what looked like a half moon of tiny teeth marks marred the creature's back. A child's toy. It must have belonged to Ben's grandfather. Tildy set it down delicately.

Below the toy, more paper, and a large manila envelope with a name written in careful block letters:

FOR MEG LEIGH

Tildy's breath hitched. *Her mother.* Cora Hale had written a message to Tildy's *mother.* Tildy squeezed the envelope to her chest, praying whatever lay within would finally reveal the information she hoped to learn.

This was why she'd flown across the country.

This was what she had been waiting for.

It had been so long since she'd felt clearheaded. Finally, with these artifacts, Cora would come into focus. Tildy would understand the messages in the dollhouses. Most important, she'd learn the truth about her mother and the connection between her mother, Cora, and Belva would become clear—she felt sure of it. She sat back on her heels, beaming, but holding herself carefully, scarcely daring to breathe. She feared if she fully settled into the moment and allowed herself a deep exhalation, everything would crumble. The workshop, the notebooks, the photos—all of it would turn to sand.

With surprisingly steady hands, she opened the envelope and slid out a stack of loose typewritten pages. But when Tildy saw the heading, her relief wobbled toward doubt. Her vision tunneled, blocking out everything but the words printed across the page.

`The Confession of Cora Hale`

23
Cora

1919

It had taken almost a decade and I'd traveled thousands of miles, hoping to forget, but now that I was back in New York City there was no more escaping my past.

Slowly, I crossed the room toward the face that looked just like mine.

Art students gathered around the portrait, sitting on stools, making studies of the painting. As I neared the group, a docent stepped into my path. Half a dozen museum visitors trailed her like a brood of ducklings.

"And here is one of the Met's most popular paintings," the docent said. "Does anyone know the title of this portrait?"

An older woman in a jade-colored peplum jacket raised her gloved hand.

"It's *Young Woman in Hat* by Gustave Blanchet."

The docent smiled. "Correct."

But I felt as though the wind had been knocked from me. How could no one see it was *my* face in the portrait? It took all my restraint not to step forward and tell the truth: *That's actually wrong. It's my own self-portrait. My name's Cora Hale, and I'm the young woman in the hat.*

IT'S TRUE. Let me explain.

During the summer of 1910, I became a criminal.

One morning while working in his workshop, my father collapsed from a heart attack. I was at art school when it happened, and upon returning home that evening, I found our family doctor and my father's employees waiting to give me the news that at seventeen years old, I was alone in the world. Orphaned.

It was unsuitable for a young unmarried woman from a respectable background to live on her own, and since no other family existed to take me in, one of my father's clients, Mr. Transome, a board member for New York's Metropolitan Museum of Art, took pity on me. Not only did he invite me to spend the final two months of school living with his family, Transome also offered me my first job: I was to paint a portrait of his only daughter, Rose. This proposal spared me some anxiety concerning income while my father's estate was settled.

Numb with grief, I moved into the Transomes' lovely townhome, only a few blocks away from Central Park. I would share a room with my host's daughter, Rose. I didn't own much: a steamer trunk filled with clothes, a clunky valise in which I stored several books and art supplies, and two crates filled with the woodworking tools left to me by my father. These crates were stowed in the Transomes' basement since I possessed no immediate need for them. All in all, I took up little space. Rose, nearly five years older than me, practically oozed confidence and sophistication. She was engaged to be married in the fall to a handsome young man of promising stature. Despite the grief that clung to me as reliably as my shadow, I wanted to impress her.

On the afternoon that I arrived at the Transome house, while I unpacked my clothing, Rose sat on her bed watching me, her legs tucked underneath her skirt. I still remember that cornflower-blue linen fantail skirt, with its sewn-down pleats, because I admired the way it swished from side to side gracefully when she walked. I made a note to design a similar one for myself someday. Rose had a lovely figure. I envied her curves. If I'd had a bust and hips like hers, I told myself, clothes would look infinitely better on me.

Isn't that a remarkable thing about being young? One minute you're crushed with dark moods, and the next you're preoccupied with what to wear. In my harsher moments, I look back and curse my vapidity; in my more generous, I recognize my grief. In the days after my father's death, I sought help the way a drowning person grabs for flotsam to survive a shipwreck. Back in that bedroom, I didn't realize how desperately I was reaching for someone.

That someone would be Rose.

A week later, we were in our shared room, her leaning against her twin bed's walnut headboard, discussing her upcoming wedding plans while I sat cross-legged facing her, sketchpad on my lap, drafting pastel portrait studies.

"Have you ever been kissed?" she suddenly asked.

I tried to hide my surprise by looking down at my pastels. My mind whirled into gear as I contemplated my answer. What could I say without looking too fast, but also not coming off as a complete innocent? Instead of coming up with something clever, I hedged my bets. "A little."

"A little?" Rose giggled. "How have you been kissed *a little*?"

Silently, I cursed my stupidity, but before I could answer, she beckoned me to move closer.

"Is there anyone you'd like to marry?" she asked.

I shook my head, sensing this was an opportunity to show off a little. I shimmied into place beside her, and our bodies pressed together. "I'm *never* getting married."

"You never want to marry? How singular!"

"I plan to be the most sought-after portraitist in New York City."

"Daddy says you'll be exactly that. He says you have extraordinary promise, even for a girl."

The *even for a girl* bit made me flinch, but I knew there was something to it.

On that afternoon in the warm intimacy of her bedroom, when Rose leaned forward, bringing our faces very close together, I stopped thinking about art school and painting portraits. I was lost, admiring the brightness of her irises. They were so blue, as blue as the clear April sky outside.

"Even if you don't plan to marry, surely you want to kiss someone. Would you like to practice kissing with me?" she whispered.

Her question overwhelmed the internal operations of my brain and, like a fuse box, my system exploded. I simply stared at her.

Fortunately for me, Rose took charge. She tilted her head, closing the small gap between our noses, and placed her lips gently on my own. And as she pressed harder against me, the circuitry of my insides reconnected. Sparks flew. The wires running through me suddenly came back to life. First, with a sizzle, then a roar. Electricity coursed through every inch of my body, parts that had felt numb since the news of my father's accident. Finally, after being consumed with death, I felt *alive*.

She plucked a ringlet of my hair from where it had come loose from my pins and twirled it around her index finger. "I love your red hair," she breathed before sliding my earlobe between her teeth playfully.

That afternoon Rose fulfilled the promise of her name. Not only did she exude that sugary, slightly damp smell of roses, but she tasted sweet, and her skin was smooth and velvety soft, just like a petal. To my seventeen-year-old eyes, she was perfect. I couldn't get enough of her.

OVER THE next couple of months, whenever we were supposed to be working on Rose's portrait, we were practicing our kissing.

"Shouldn't I pose for you?" she asked one day as we stretched out on her bed. "Don't you need to start my portrait?"

But it felt like I'd been doing nothing but work my whole life, so I waved off her concerns.

"We can start next week," I said, grabbing her arms and pinning her below me as she laughed.

If such a Sapphic relationship sounds rather advanced, you might be surprised to learn our sudden intimacy didn't raise any eyebrows. For two young single women of our era, chumminess easily entailed holding hands, even exchanging a few kisses on the cheek. But behind closed doors, our explorations grew more sophisticated. Still, we never spoke of her upcoming marriage. I had no idea what Rose thought about our relationship. If I'm honest, I never bothered to consider what Rose was thinking about anything—I thought only of myself. All I wanted was to ease my own pain. To stop thinking. Our affair existed as little more than a breathless secret, an experiment. The entire dalliance was foolish in so many ways, but it soothed the parts of me that ached. When you're seventeen years old, alone, and grieving, you do many foolish things—or at least I certainly did.

Our final meeting, the one that would change everything, took place on a June evening in her father's office a few blocks west of Central Park.

"We'll have the place to ourselves?" I asked as we swanned along Fifth Avenue, arm in arm. "Where's your father?"

"Boston, I think. Or maybe Providence. He's somewhere north, meeting with a collector or an agent. Maybe an artist." Rose shrugged. She never had a head for details, and I'd come to enjoy her easy, careless approach to life.

When Rose unlocked the door to his office with her pilfered key and led me through the antechamber and into the main room, I recognized my father's work in the shelving and cabinetry lining the walls of the office. Most people would have admired the pottery, small sculptures, books, and paintings filling the space, but I noticed the vertical grain of the oak and the detail and precision of the angled corners on the room's crown molding, the framing beads, and panels. Faced with the fine craftsmanship of my father's work, a momentary pang of uncertainty struck through me. Why was I messing around with this girl? Where was my usual focus? Why wasn't I working? But then, unexpectedly, anger filled me. My father had left me, and worse—he left me *alone*. He had spent his life *too* focused on work. We had no friends, no family to speak of. By burying his grief under work, he'd isolated me from putting down roots.

I reached for Rose and pulled her toward me. I refused to be lonely anymore. First, I slid my hairpins out and let my long red tresses tumble down my arms and back, just the way Rose liked. While she twined my long ringlets around her own hands, I ran my lips along the tender part of her neck below her earlobe and my fingers toyed with the feathery lacy jabot fluttering at her neck like a dove's wing. One by one my fingers unfastened the buttons running up her chest until I could peel that pale pink blouse from her shoulders and let it fall to the ground, taking in the loveliness of her perfectly creamy skin.

I guided Rose to one of the office's damask couches and using the same single-mindedness that made me a great portraitist, I made her forget everything—her first name, the city we were in, the year—everything except that she wanted more of me.

We missed the signs of trouble. Passion obliterated our attention to our surroundings—oh, to be young and careless! Somehow I didn't hear the turn of the key in the lock. I missed the sound of the door opening, the footsteps, the creak of the threshold bearing Mr. Transome's weight.

Not until he bellowed "Stop!" did I realize we were no longer alone.

Rose was far quicker to react than I. In an instant, she scrambled to her feet, collecting and clutching her chemise, stockings, skirts, and blouse, and then skittered past her father, moving faster than a summer rainstorm while I remained rooted, kneeling on the floor beside the couch, locked in place.

Next thing I knew, I was alone with Transome. A shocked silence stretched between us. Slowly, I rose to face him.

"Christ, get dressed," he snarled, bending over to gather my belongings strewn across the floor. He hurled the bundle at me. Apparently my reflexes still worked because I caught the mess and began dressing. He watched me climb back into my clothes, his expression murderous, but also fascinated. Fear slithered through my belly. For the briefest of moments, I wondered if my best chance at survival lay in remaining undressed and offering myself to him, but below the thicket of his dark brows knitting together, I recognized not lust or conquest in his fiery eyes, but calculation.

When I was dressed, Mr. Transome finally spoke.

"You know, I could ruin you. If I let word of this get out, no one will ever hire you in this town." I started to protest, but he stretched out one of his pawlike hands to stop me.

"Don't say a word. Here's why: You broke into my office. You're a thief."

I blinked, realizing my shortsightedness. Of course. Why would Transome leak word of his own daughter's malfeasance? If anything, he'd be calling on her fiancé first thing in the morning to move up the wedding date. No, if he wanted to punish me, he'd take aim at my professionalism. No one would hire a portraitist they didn't trust. If I ever wanted to have clients of my own, trustworthiness ranked more highly than talent. Clients need to be able to depend on you. They certainly don't want to invite known thieves into their homes. By sneaking into Transome's office, I'd set myself up as a fool.

I thanked God my father had not lived to see this happen. It wasn't my affair with Rose that would have disappointed him beyond measure—no, it was the careless way I'd behaved on my first job. In his eyes, unprofessionalism was one of the worst types of sin.

My throat felt as if it was full of nails. "What do you want?" I managed, lacing my fingers together to hide how they shook.

"I'm willing to overlook the way you've abused my trust, if you'll do something for me." He went on to explain how his most recent acquisitions trip had gone poorly, so poorly he was home unexpectedly early with no paintings in hand for the Met. And also—more important—no funds. Had he lost the Met's money on a bad bet? In a tryst gone wrong? He confessed nothing. The details were sparse, but the gist was this: he was home empty-handed, but the Met expected something significant.

It was beginning to dawn on me: I wasn't the only one in trouble here.

The truth was, Mr. Transome's own reputation was far more valuable than mine. He was an established figure. His good family name was on the line. He could lose his job. His professional reputation. Everything.

It was then, with a flush of youthful arrogance, that I realized my power. I knew what he wanted from me.

Like any artist of that era, I knew how to re-create older works. We all did. Painting imitations was not only a staple of our training process, but it offered a path to income for a painter of even middling ability. Every artist in Boston, New York, Philadelphia, London, Paris, and beyond re-created famous paintings and sold them for a few dollars here and there. These imitations dotted the walls of houses throughout North America and Europe, but there was never any doubt of their true provenance. Everyone understood them to be duplicates.

"Yes, I'll paint for you," I said in a rush. "An original composition in the style of a master. No one will question its authenticity."

Mr. Transome stopped his pacing and pushed his spectacles up where they'd slid down his long nose. "Which painter?"

I sifted through my expertise. Of all the artists I'd imitated, no one had quite captivated me like Blanchet. I'd spent hours copying and recopying his masterpiece that hung in the Met. "I've painted more Blanchet studies than I care to count. I have notebooks full of his work. He's my favorite. When I'm done creating my painting, everyone will believe it's a real Blanchet."

Transome looked out the nearby window into the inky darkness. "I can get the paperwork forged. How long would you need?" he asked.

"Two months. No one will ever figure it out." The promises fell from my mouth with the ease of coins slipping through a hole in the bottom of a pocket.

He turned to me, his expression more sad than angry. "The truth always comes out eventually. But we'll do everything we can to hide it. You must tell no one of this."

I nodded.

"I'll tell the board I acquired a little-known Blanchet and am having it cleaned up. When you're done with it, you'll leave New York and never return."

When he said those words aloud, the significance of the plan hit me. Immediately, I began to doubt myself. I was not re-creating a masterpiece for casual decoration—it would be on a wall at the Metropolitan Museum of Art next to one of the master's originals. Wouldn't people take one look at my forgery and see that it was a pale imitation? Just as I was about to retract my offer, he smacked his hands together decisively.

Right then, I wished he had driven me to the East River and tossed me into its darkest, deepest waters. If I forged Blanchet, my life as I knew it was over. I'd be throwing away my dream of becoming a famous painter. For the rest of my life, if I wanted to avoid trouble, I'd have to remain obscure, cut all ties to my past. Without my reputation as a prodigy, how could I have a future?

I wrapped my arms across my chest, shivering uncontrollably.

Art forgery was against the law. A felony. I closed my eyes and let the harsh reality of my situation sink in. As soon as I picked up a paintbrush with the intent to deceive, I'd be breaking the law. I'd become a criminal. And the worst part? I had no one to blame but myself.

24
Tildy

2024

Tildy was holding her breath as she read. She exhaled, lowering the typewritten pages of the confession. She'd gotten so many things wrong. Very wrong.

Cora had painted *Young Woman in Hat.*

And Belva hadn't been in a happy marriage, far from it. She'd loved Cora—but how and when had they reunited? And did Belva know the truth about *Young Woman in Hat*?

With trembling fingers, Tildy called Emiko, quickly gauging how much to reveal.

"What's up?" Emiko asked after greeting her.

"Ohhh, not much, just wrapping things up here in New Hampshire."

"Have you found anything?"

"Uh, yeah. I did. Some sketches, photos."

Tildy winced, knowing she was fumbling her answer. She hated to not tell the truth, but Emiko didn't seem to notice the uncertainty in her voice. "That's great!"

Tildy did not feel great. "Yeah. How's everything going at the Bel?"

"Things have been uneventful here. Let's see . . . the dollhouse conservation team is terrific. No issues there. And the ceiling inspection team's arriving any minute, so we should have an update on that situation within the next few hours."

"Perfect, thanks. Do you have a sec to help me with something?"

"Sure. What?"

"Could you please text me a photo of the miniature portrait of Belva from her dollhouse?"

"You bet. Just give me a few minutes, okay?"

"Of course." Tildy thanked her and ended the call.

As she waited for a response, she shivered and stamped her feet, hoping to get her circulation going. Her phone pinged. Two photos of the miniature portrait appeared on her screen. The similarities between *Young Woman in Hat* and the miniature portrait of Cora were obvious—Tildy had recognized the connection when she first spotted the miniature in Belva's dollhouse and assumed the miniaturist had simply been copying the style of the famous painting. Tildy would never have assumed it was a clue to a forgery.

She hurried back to where she'd left Cora's confession resting atop a box. Tildy riffled through the pages to the section where Cora described losing her father. Tildy squeezed her eyes shut, picturing a stunned young woman surrounded by unfamiliar men. Until a few minutes ago, this woman had existed merely as a name and blurry face, but now Tildy understood a critical piece of this mysterious Cora Hale. A century may have passed between Tildy's losses and Cora's, and many aspects of life had changed, but grief remained the same. It hurt. It hurt enough to cause a person not to think straight. To make foolish, reckless decisions. To engage in dangerous activities.

And Cora had been only seventeen. Armed with extraordinary talent, but also alone and vulnerable.

Tildy opened her eyes, dropped to the floor, and continued reading.

25
Cora

1910 and 1919

I never saw Rose again. By the time I returned to the Transomes' house in the morning, she was packed, ticketed, and sent away.

Fearing I'd flee New York City at the first opportunity, Mr. Transome forced me to stay at his house until I finished the painting, but I wasn't planning to run. Where would I go? My entire life had been rooted in Greenwich Village, and now with my father gone, I had no one. I was confused, afraid, and alone. As far as I knew, no other family of mine existed, and I'd never been particularly close to my art school classmates. Painting was all I knew, all I had left.

When I was working, I felt anchored. My training took over. Ideas had been swirling around my mind for months as I'd contemplated creating a portrait of Rose. Although I was no longer painting her, I could use parts of my original vision while also incorporating aspects of Blanchet's style that I admired. On my first morning at work, Transome appeared in the doorway of the bedroom that doubled as my studio, clutching a large, colorful confection of a wide-brimmed hat bedecked with frilly flowers and ostrich feathers.

"What on earth is that ostentation?" I asked, wrinkling my nose.

"You'll be your own model. God knows, it's that hair of yours that makes you memorable. Change the color, cover it up with this, and no one will recognize you."

Reluctantly, I took the hat. Did no one really notice me beyond my red hair? The question was a vexing one. I decided this portrait would represent an experiment, not just with style, but with human behavior. If I took away my most defining feature, would people still recognize me? I refused to believe Transome was correct.

I used Blanchet's vivid palette of unmixed paints. But from there, I made changes. Visit any museum, and you'll see that nude women are a dime a dozen. The Greeks, Romans, Renaissance Italians, Dutch—those fellows loved to sculpt and paint women wearing nothing. Little had changed over the centuries. One of Blanchet's novelties, a device that made his work scandalous in the 1860s, was how he'd place a nude woman in an urban setting and surround her with clothed people going about their everyday activities. The park. The theater. Cafés and restaurants. I'd always admired the tension his paintings elicited, but I wanted a more original composition, something that would prompt my viewers to think. I decided to set up a more sly version of Blanchet's usual style: the clothed state of my subject would be ambiguous. My portrait would focus on my young woman's face, her bare shoulders and décolletage. The hat would be visible, but its size and elaborate design would draw attention to the fact that nothing else adorned the woman, at least not within view.

Using myself as a model, I got to work. As Transome insisted, I depicted my hair as raven's black, but aside from that, it was unmistakably my face that I painted, my own small act of subversion. Blanchet always used great variety in his brushwork, so I emulated his style, using swift, sketchy strokes for the hat and its flowers and feathers, but getting more detailed as I began work on the skin of my face and neck. By applying layer after layer of thin paint, a technique used by the Dutch masters, I created a complexion that appeared real and glowing. When I was done, my painted eyes appeared even more lifelike than I'd anticipated. Within the portrait, my penetrating gaze seemed to follow me through the room, asking *What are you doing*?

Indeed, what *was* I doing?

I created elaborate excuses. No one would be hurt by my forgery, I told myself. I hadn't murdered anyone. I was creating a painting for people to enjoy—how could this be a bad thing? Using this logic, my crime didn't feel all that awful, but as you can imagine, it didn't feel particularly satisfying either. Not wanting to dwell on the sordid reasons for painting the portrait, I worked as quickly as I could.

After I deemed the painting finished, Mr. Transome steepled his hands and stared at it for a long time, moving forward and backward and tilting his head from side to side. Jittery, I awaited his verdict, my foot tapping with pent-up energy. If someone had opened the door, I could have run straight to Saint Louis without stopping.

Finally he faced me. "It's perfect."

Tears blurred my vision. Like the swing from one end of a pendulum to the other, my impatient energy vanished. Exhaustion flooded me. The past two months had left me an anxious mess. I slumped into my chair. Relieved to finally be done, I said, "Even with the color of my hair changed, it's obviously me."

"No one will recognize you."

I must have looked shocked because he laughed.

"Come on, who will be looking for you in this painting?"

I moved in front of the portrait. "Do you think it will work? Will people really believe this is a Blanchet?"

"Of course they will. Remember, people see what they expect. Now stop looking so sorry for yourself. Even if no one knows it, you'll have a painting displayed at the Met," he snapped.

"What now?"

"You leave. Where do you want to go?"

I'd been pondering this question since starting the forgery. If I went to Paris, I could find work as a painting instructor, yet remain close enough to home that I'd hear if my crime was discovered. After a year of working and saving money, maybe I'd leave France and go somewhere farther away, more obscure. Constantinople. Johannesburg. Hong Kong.

After I said *Paris*, he nodded. "By tomorrow I'll have everything you need for your trip."

"I should begin packing."

"Of course," he said, moving to carry away the painting.

"Wait," I said. "Can you leave her? Just for one more night."

He almost protested, but changed his mind.

"The painting's good, you know. It's really very beautiful," he said before shutting the door behind him without the usual slam.

Despite the resentment Mr. Transome had stoked inside me, I felt surprisingly touched by his compliment. I knew the painting to be my finest work yet. I stared at my own face, studying the intimacy of our shared sad smiles. In the late-afternoon light, my skin in the painting glowed with the pearly luminescence of a full moon on a clear night.

Keeping my gaze on the portrait, I slid down the wall across from it, huddled into a ball, and wept. My back and hands hurt from the constant painting. Even my head and eyes ached from the strain. But I wept for what I was losing. My dreams for the future. My past. And my true love—painting. If I wasn't creating art, who was I?

NOW, NEARLY a decade had passed. I stood in the Met in front of *Young Woman in Hat*, still vividly remembering my desperation to leave New York City, to escape the pain of creating this portrait.

Around me, people wandered through the gallery. The tour group moved on. The art students continued their reproductions of *Young Woman in Hat*. No one glanced twice at me. No one stopped and asked, "Excuse me, isn't that you?"

I was invisible.

I'd made a forgery so successful that I'd erased myself.

While it should have relieved me to know my crime was undiscovered, there's an awful loneliness in keeping a shameful secret.

Any debate I'd harbored about telling Hugh the truth had vanished. I couldn't burden him with my own folly. Not only was the truth unbelievable, but it put us in danger. I'd be in terrible trouble if the truth of my forgery ever became public, and now that Hugh was such an important part of my life, I needed to protect him from my past.

I took a final look at my young face on the wall, said a silent goodbye, and walked away, determined to leave New York.

26
Tildy

2024

At the distant rumble of a car's arrival, Tildy looked out the nearest window, realizing daylight had faded into evening.

Ben was home.

She moved toward the door, eager to tell him about her discoveries, but then froze. Did she really want to jump right into showing Ben his great-grandmother's confession? Cora Hale was guilty of being an art forger. How would Ben react to learning his great-grandmother had been a criminal?

And then a more startling realization hit her: if news got out that *Young Woman in Hat* was a forgery, the consequences for the Bel could be catastrophic.

Tildy didn't have time to ponder how Ben would process any of this. Panicked, she jammed the typewritten pages under her shirt and tucked them into the waistband of her leggings at the same time the workshop's door groaned open and Ben appeared. Zelly roused herself from napping with a bark.

"Hey, guys, what's up?" A hopeful smile dawned across his face as he took in the stack of boxes by the door. "Did you find something?"

Tildy blinked, dazed by the audacity of what she'd just done. Regret reared up in her instantly, but what was she supposed to do: pull the pages out from underneath her shirt sheepishly? Her face heated with guilt. She nodded.

"Well? What did you find?"

"A . . . a bunch of stuff—sketches, dollhouse plans . . ."

Ben dropped his duffel bag next to the doorway and knocked his running shoes together to loosen the dirty snow clinging to his feet. "No kidding! That's great."

Tildy crossed her arms, feeling the papers against her skin. She didn't trust herself to speak, didn't know what to say. She had no idea how to explain everything to Ben. He had been nothing but generous and kind, and now she was lying to him. She was acting recklessly, irresponsibly.

"You don't seem quite as thrilled as I would have expected," he said, his smile faltering as he took in her crestfallen expression.

Tildy puffed out her cheeks. "I'm just . . . surprised. It's been a lot to take in."

"Well, I don't know about you, but I think tonight deserves some celebration, especially because it's your last night here. Let's go out!"

Tildy hesitated. There was no way she could keep up with this lie, not sitting across from Ben at dinner. And she needed to call Dale with an update, or at least text. But what exactly would she tell her boss? She had no idea how to break the news that the Bel's most beloved and valuable painting, the one that could possibly save them from closing, was a fake. Her phone, lying on the nearby table, reminded her that everything was falling apart. She swallowed and jammed it into her back pocket. Out of sight, out of mind.

Ben jangled his car keys out in front of him. "So what do you think? I'll drive."

Tildy laced her hands together. Now was the time to come clean, to tell him everything. That would be the right thing to do. But she didn't even know where to start. Maybe if she went to dinner with Ben she could buy some time while she figured out what to do next, how to handle the forgery and the Bel.

"You've been cooped up here for days," he said. "Time for a break, right?"

Still holding his car keys, Ben stretched his arms overhead, and for a moment, his flannel shirt traveled upward, revealing a peek of skin above the waist of his jeans.

Tildy's breath caught at the sight of his firm, muscled stomach. When had such a cute guy ever invited her out for dinner? Never. Technically this dinner was part of her job, so yes, she'd go out with him. Eventually she'd tell him the full story. The fact that Tildy felt a magnetic pull to Ben was completely beside the point. The fact that he was handsome, smart, and funny was not the point either.

She nodded. "Let me grab my purse from the guesthouse."

"Sure thing. I'll feed Zel and we can go. Meet at the car in five."

Tildy was already outdoors and halfway to the guesthouse by the time Ben and Zelly had shut the door to the workshop. She dashed inside the cottage, removing the hidden typewritten pages with shaking hands as she entered the bedroom. From her suitcase, she grabbed a T-shirt and wrapped the contraband inside, hating herself for hiding it. This document belonged to Ben. This was *his* history and she had taken it. *Stolen it.* Like Cora, Tildy was currently engaged in a criminal act, she realized. But the implications of the portrait's forgery affected the Bel and everyone who worked there too. If the painting's value plummeted, the Bel had no financial support. The place would close. Everyone would lose their jobs.

Tildy turned to look in the mirror and saw her own wild expression staring back at her. She closed her eyes, inhaled deeply, and counted to five slowly. She needed time to think, but from outside, a quick tap on the horn jolted her back to reality. Ben was waiting for her.

FIFTEEN MINUTES later, Tildy and Ben walked into the Mill, the town's one restaurant and pub. Heads turned to look at them, giving Tildy the distinct sense this place didn't get a regular infusion of new faces. The pine-paneled pub was far from packed, but turnout was pretty good for a weekday night. Though she'd been cold all day sitting in the workshop, now with eyes on her, the blood in her veins ran hot with guilt and embarrassment. She felt sure everyone could see *LIAR* stamped across her forehead in burning red-hot letters.

A hostess led them to a two-top next to a large window. Outside, beyond the building's old waterwheel, now stationary, a fast-running river shimmered in the moonlight. When Tildy sat across from Ben, the man she was lying to—betraying even—it felt like an out-of-body experience. She didn't recognize herself anymore. When she glanced at the menu, the letters appeared indecipherable. Overwhelmed by the unfamiliar choice of beers, she ordered a Sam Adams and a burger, while Ben asked for a black bean burger. When their waitress sashayed toward the bar, Tildy leaned back in her seat, trying to get a grip on herself.

Slowly, she slid out of the parka she'd borrowed from Ben's mudroom and hung it on the back of her chair. When she looked at Ben, he was watching her, a sly smile brightening his face. "You picked that beer because it's named for a historical figure, didn't you?"

She nodded and Ben laughed. "I figured," he said. "That's cute."

Cute, Tildy noted, pleased. No one had called her cute in a long time. But was he calling her cute? Or was the fact that she knew nothing about beer somehow cute? Suddenly she felt exhausted, but before she could come up with anything to say, their waitress returned carrying a big, frosty glass pitcher of beer and two empty pint glasses that she plunked on the table and proceeded to fill.

"Sorry, we didn't order a pitcher," Ben said.

"Those guys sent it over," the server said, jutting her chin toward a nearby booth.

A group of men raised their beers toward Ben, wishing him luck for that Friday night's high school basketball game.

Tildy reached for her pint glass and gulped a long pull. God, it tasted good. Cold and bubbly, it went down easily. Tildy rarely drank beer and now she wondered why. As she placed her glass back on the table, she realized half its contents had vanished.

Her attention was drawn to the arrival of two new people entering the pub. A couple. A striking dark-haired woman and a tall, handsome blond man.

Across the table, Tildy clocked how Ben suddenly looked stricken.

The woman caught sight of Ben, raised a hand in greeting, and headed straight toward him, smiling widely. "Bennnnn, I'm sooooo glad to run into you."

"Um, what are you doing here?" he asked.

"Well." The woman exchanged a pleased glance with her date. "I'm visiting my family to introduce them to my fiancé, Axel." She then proceeded to thrust out her left hand, nearly blinding Tildy with the flash of a brilliant diamond. Three carats? Five? Tildy knew little about jewelry, but that rock was huge.

"We met during our PhD program at Oxford and have both landed jobs at the University of Stockholm, which is where Axel's from."

Uh-oh. Tildy's eyes widened. This was the infamous June, the woman who had dumped Ben.

Next to the Viking, Ben suddenly looked extraordinarily pale, and Tildy felt a surprising defensiveness rise within her. Before she could think, she nudged her chair around the two-top and pressed against his side.

"Hi, I'm Tildy, Ben's girlfriend," she said brightly. "Sorry, I didn't catch your name. Who are you?"

The woman squared her shoulders, obviously miffed at having to explain herself. "I'm June." Warily, she eyed how Tildy casually draped an arm around the back of Ben's chair. "You live around here?"

Tildy remembered that June had once called Ben *unadventurous* so her mind raced as she conjured the most glamorous, adventurous persona she could possibly imagine. "No, I live in Napa Valley. I run a vineyard. I met Ben a few months ago at my local airfield, where I was tending to my plane. He had flown in for a quick weekend of wine tasting, and what do you know, sparks just flew, didn't they, babe?"

Somehow the charade just poured out of her. She turned to Ben, expecting him to look horrified by her ruse, but his color had revived. His eyes were back to twinkling. He reached for Tildy's hand and clasped it tightly, pulling her close. "They sure did."

And then Tildy did something very unexpected. Without thinking, she leaned forward, wrapped her hands around the back of Ben's neck, and kissed him. As soon as their lips made contact, Tildy realized the insanity of what she was doing and almost stopped, but . . . it felt nice. Better than nice. It was great! She lingered, leaned into the kiss more, and when she pulled away, she gasped and then giggled, two reactions she didn't have to fake at all, given that her brain was completely scrambled. A giddy feeling of amazement filled her. *What the hell was she doing*?

By this point, June was glaring at them both with a Siberian tundra-grade coldness, and Tildy knew she had to really stick the landing, so she turned back to Ben, cupped his chin, and winked at him. "Sorry, I just can't help myself. This whole long-distance thing just makes me so *wild* sometimes."

Tildy's gaze locked with Ben's for a moment and she felt her cheeks flush. How much had she been faking that kiss?

"Okay," June said loudly, folding her arms across her chest. "This place looks a lot more crowded than I expected. I think we'll head out. Ben, maybe we can meet for lunch before I leave town?"

He squeezed Tildy tighter to his side. "I'm pretty tied up these days."

June nudged Axel, but he remained rooted, seemingly intrigued by the spectacle playing out in front of him. After a harder shoulder bump, he finally got the message, and just like that, they departed, leaving Tildy and Ben snorting with laughter over their beers.

Ben wiped at his tearing eyes. "I can't believe you just did that, Til."

Til. He said it so easily, so intimately. She'd never liked the sound of her own name so much. Her face felt like it might crack open from smiling so widely. So enthusiastically.

"That was an Oscar-worthy performance! Where did you come up with all that? The vineyard? The airplanes?" he asked.

The anxiety that had practically paralyzed her when they arrived at the Mill had long ago broken apart into a gloriously loose feeling of freedom. *Where had those ideas come from?* She had no idea. Her far-fetched story about Napa and the planes felt nuts, but the kiss? Well, that felt completely natural. *Had* she been acting? Suddenly she wasn't sure. She searched his face. Was she mistaken, or had he really enjoyed it too?

"It's not like kissing you was such a hardship."

No sooner were the words out of Tildy's mouth than she regretted them. Ben opened his mouth to say something, but he appeared speechless.

Tildy straightened, mortified, and scooted her chair away from Ben.

He stared as she resumed her original spot across the table, his expression quizzical.

"Hey, guys, food's up." Their waitress appeared at the side of their table, holding two plates overflowing with food. She thrust the burger toward Tildy. "This one's yours, right, hon?"

Tildy nodded and accepted the plate, relieved for the interruption. Once the waitress unloaded Ben's meal from her arms and left, Ben smiled, lifted a fry from his plate, and held it out toward her. "Cheers. I guess all that . . . uh . . . drama really worked up my appetite."

Tildy, happy to see a return to normalcy, raised a fry of her own, and tapped it against his. "To Oscar-worthy performances."

They laughed and Tildy popped the fry into her mouth. The tight lid she usually kept on herself had loosened. It felt good. Not just because her whole body still tingled from the intensity of the spontaneous makeout session, and not just because she felt a little buzzed, she told herself. Their prank had been so satisfying. For one thing, Ben's twinkling eyes had reached supernova intensity. She couldn't get enough of how he was looking at her now. Like she was funny. Like she was pretty, even beautiful.

They continued eating and chatting and laughing. Tildy felt herself enveloped in a warm glow of goodwill. She had really needed to unwind. How satisfying to be far away from the stress of the Bel! She should have been thinking about Cora, the forgery, the dollhouses, and her mother but she just couldn't. At least, not now. She'd been working and worrying so much. Everything outside the pub faded. For the first time in ages, Tildy wasn't thinking about a million things at once, she wasn't worrying about work, and she wasn't trying to push away sad memories. She was just a girl drinking beers with a handsome, smart guy.

And then the buzz of an incoming call sounded nearby.

At first, Tildy ignored it. She was holding her breath, waiting to see what Ben would say next, but the sound came from the jacket on the back of Tildy's chair, muffled but insistent.

Buzz. Buzz. Buzz. Buzz.

"Should you get that?" Ben asked.

Reluctantly, Tildy nodded, fishing around in her jacket pocket.

When she extracted her phone and looked at it, Dale's name flashed on the lit-up screen. She swiped to answer.

"Tildy?"

Tildy licked the salt still lingering on her lips, trying to get a grip on herself. She squeezed her eyes shut. Back to work. "Yeah?"

"Tildy, we've got a problem, a *big* problem."

She leaned forward in her chair. At the sound of Dale's voice, Ben's brow furrowed in concern.

"The engineering firm is here to investigate the crack in the Main Reading Room's ceiling. It's bad. Really bad. We had to close early today and the Bel's been ordered to remain closed. The crack . . . it might be catastrophic. I need you back here."

His words were like a sudden wave of cold water crashing over her.

The library was closed. She needed to go home.

"I'll be there soon. My flight is tomorrow morning."

"Good. When you land, come directly to the library to grab whatever you need to work from home."

"Okay, where are the dollhouses?"

"The SFMOMA already picked them up today to store for us, along with *Young Woman in Hat* and the other major art pieces from our collection. Stanford and Cal are going to house the books and documents in their archives for us temporarily. Everything's being moved out now."

"That was fast."

"Things . . . things look pretty bad, Tildy." His voice sounded scratchy. Tildy realized with shock that Dale was choking back tears.

"Don't worry, we'll make a plan," she said softly. "It'll be okay."

Tildy ended the call, trying to believe things truly would be okay. But she was dazed. *Catastrophic. Closure.* The words pinged around her head. Closing their doors during the darkest days of the pandemic had been bad enough. Another closure could finish off the Bel once and for all. Would she still even have a job?

In a blur, Ben paid the check, stood, and reached out his hand to help her to her feet. He'd heard enough of the conversation to understand the situation was dire. His grip was warm and strong. For a moment, she considered confessing her mistakes. Her lies. She wanted to return Cora's papers. She didn't want to be a thief. If there was ever a moment to tell him the truth, this was it. Face-to-face.

"What?" His eyes crinkled around the edges. He was so kind. So generous.

The prospect of disappointing him horrified her.

"Nothing," she said, sliding her hands from his.

27
Tildy

2024

At the San Francisco airport, Tildy loaded her luggage into the trunk of an Uber, then slid into the back seat, collapsing against the cracked leather upholstery. Under a fine drizzle, the highway pavement gleamed like patent leather while tufts of fog slunk around the hills of South San Francisco.

Back in New Hampshire the night before, after Tildy hung up with Dale, she and Ben had driven home, parked, and headed to the workshop. There, they surveyed the six boxes of Cora's belongings. Ben nudged one with his toe. "Take all this back to California with you. You'll need it for the exhibit."

"I don't think there's an exhibit anymore. And I can't take your family's history all the way across the country."

"Why not? This is what you came for. Consider it a loan."

That last bit almost broke Tildy in two. She thought of Cora's confession hidden—stolen!—in her bags. She'd betrayed Ben. His faith in her was too much. She balked. "I can't check this stuff onto the plane. I wouldn't want to let any of it out of my sight."

"Let's consolidate the sketchbooks and artifacts down to a couple of bags, and we'll get you a second seat to accommodate the extra cargo. You won't have to check a thing."

Early the next morning when she'd said goodbye to Ben, he'd hugged her tightly and promised to keep in touch, but Tildy didn't see how that was possible after the lies she'd told him. And she had stolen from him.

Tildy still couldn't bring herself to tell him about Cora's confession, and on the cross-country flight with Ben's family's relics tucked safely beside her, Tildy had finished reading the diary. Everything Tildy thought she knew was wrong. She'd underestimated Cora and her clients. Those realizations swirled around her with dizzying, almost sickening speed.

Tildy was a stranger to herself. A thief. The thought of smuggling Ben's family papers away made her feel sick, but she felt trapped. For the Bel to survive, no one could know about the Blanchet. She needed to keep Cora's secret. Everyone at the library depended on her, especially now given the current closure.

And then there was Daisy Hart. Reading about Tildy's mother had been overwhelming, so overwhelming, in fact, that Tildy couldn't allow herself to fully sink into thinking about her. Not yet. Difficult as it was, she needed to put all thoughts of her mother aside. Tildy needed to focus on the most immediate problem at hand: the Bel's closure.

When her driver pulled alongside the curb outside the Bel, a steady stream of men in coveralls poured from the library's front doors. Tildy couldn't be sure if they were movers or engineers at work on the ceiling. She asked the driver to wait. She ran inside.

As she stepped inside the library's foyer, she saw the entrance to the Main Reading Room was blocked by a heavy plastic tarp, which Dale stood in front of, huddled over a clipboard with two research librarians. When he saw Tildy, he handed the paperwork off and hurried toward her.

"You're here." Dale's eyes were bloodshot, and he'd abandoned his suit jacket, leaving him in rumpled trousers and a buttoned-up shirt smeared with dirt and dust. Tildy knew he was somewhere in his early sixties, and he suddenly looked every day of his age.

"What happens now?" she asked, patting his shoulder.

"We wait to hear back from the engineers. Maybe we move. Become something new. Rebuild."

"Really? How?"

"The board and I have decided to sell the Blanchet. It's our most valuable piece by far."

"But—"

"No one wants to do this, but selling the painting will help us buy us some time. We'll figure out our options. Our lawyers are working out a way to make it happen."

Suddenly Tildy couldn't breathe. Selling *Young Woman in Hat* would bring it under intense scrutiny. She racked her brain, considering the likelihood the portrait could be discovered as a fake, but its provenance papers were solid. Of course, there was always the chance some testing could reveal a difference in dating its materials, but at the moment, no one had any reason to suspect the portrait wasn't a Blanchet, so there was no reason to test it.

The only person who knew the truth about the portrait was Tildy.

If she kept her mouth shut about Cora's confession, the Bel could survive. Wouldn't Belva and Cora have been willing to make that compromise?

In Tildy's mind's eye, the Bel loomed in front of her, seemingly defying gravity as it teetered on its ridge overlooking Cow Hollow and the Marina, like an heirloom teacup placed close to the edge of a shelf. If its building had to be abandoned or destroyed and the library moved, was it still the Bel? Tildy tried to imagine Belva's collection living in a new space. She couldn't picture it, but maybe she was being too narrow-minded. Wasn't Belva's vision more than a building? If the Bel could continue its mission of creating space for the past, wasn't that the most important thing? Sure, it would be sad to lose this old building filled with so much history, but with a new library, new history would be created. One of Belva's primary goals had been to build a community. She'd wanted people to come together to learn and reflect, to find joy in art and celebrate that joy with others. That could happen in many different places.

Tildy could understand how a new future was possible, but if she had to keep *Young Woman in Hat*'s secret, she wanted the truth about Cora's dollhouses to come to light. Cora needed recognition for her beautiful creations.

"What about the dollhouses? Can we still do the show?"

Dale let out a gusty sigh. "A dollhouse show just isn't in the cards. We're going to sell the miniature of Roughmore Park and maybe Hôtel LeFarge too."

"Sell them?" she echoed, shocked.

"Yeah, there's a surprising amount of interest. We're already fielding inquiries from buyers with deep pockets. Sorry, but the exhibit's off."

Tildy shook her head. *No, no, no*. People had to learn about the dollhouses.

"Dale, listen: there was no time to tell you yesterday, but I found a bunch of the dollhouse maker's old photos, tools, sketchbooks, and papers. Most important, I found her diary. Her dollhouses tell hidden histories of the women who owned them. Cora was helping her clients hide important truths about themselves. Even if we can't host an exhibit, the public must find out about them somehow."

Dale frowned skeptically.

Tildy rushed on. "Meet me at the SFMOMA's Collection Center in South San Francisco tomorrow at ten o'clock so I can update you on what the dollhouses really represent."

"Fine, but I won't have long."

"This will be worth your time. I promise."

He nodded and headed to a group of movers who were flagging

him down. Tildy looked at her vibrating phone and saw a text had come through.

> **Phyllis:** Judy and I arrived early. We're at the Fairmont. When can we meet?

Tildy slapped her forehead. Over the last twenty-four hours she'd been so distracted. She'd forgotten Phyllis Wolfe Mason was scheduled to arrive in San Francisco with her mother's dollhouse. When Tildy thought about Cora's confession about Sawhill, her stomach lurched. The Wolfes had been hiding a *big* secret. Their entire story was a lie. No wonder Phyllis didn't want to let the miniature Sawhill out of her sight, but was the old woman *really* ready to change the narrative about her beloved mother's legacy? Tildy texted Phyllis instructing her to meet the following day at the SFMOMA's Collection Center in South San Francisco.

28
Cora

1919–1939

Hugh and I bought a house and established my miniatures-making business in New Hampshire. Hugh would travel occasionally to New York City for theater jobs. Letters arrived for me from all over the country, inquiring about my services. I suspected Belva and the duchess had spread word about my dollhouses. I had no idea so many women hid secrets. My new clients were often of humble origins, but that didn't make their hidden lives any less interesting.

We settled into our new home, hiring a kind older couple, Lorraine and Harvey Benton, who helped us cook and clean and tend to the house and its grounds. In 1924 I gave birth to our son, Tommy. Not only were we smitten with our baby, but the Bentons bonded with him as if they were his grandparents.

During the hard times of the 1930s, Hugh and I were lucky. We hadn't invested in the stock market and continued to receive job offers, even during the bleakest years of the Great Depression. Americans still craved entertainment. People needed it. Everyone sought escape from the gloominess of everyday life. Sports, the movies, theater—people were still willing to spend their hard-earned pennies on entertainment.

Along with most Americans, I followed the adventures of Joy and Charlie Wolfe with great interest. Some might have even called it obsession. The Wolfes had grown famous for documenting their globetrotting through film and photo. Though Charlie had been notable for circumnavigating the globe by boat with the illustrious naturalist Edmund Paris, it wasn't until he met and married his young, plucky bride, Joy, that the two truly became national figures, flying all over the world in *The Ray*, their trusty Sikorsky S-39. He served as pilot and she documented their travels with a vast collection of cameras and notebooks. The good-looking twosome explored the African savannah, the jungles of Borneo, the snowy hinterlands of the Arctic Circle, and as soon as *Life* or *Photoplay* hit newsstands carrying the latest stories of their exploits, Tommy and I pored over the photo spreads of the Wolfes with the same type of intensity a surgeon brings to the operating table. I also drank up every word of Joy's columns for *Good Housekeeping* and *Collier's*. Whenever the Wolfes released a new film, Hugh, Tommy, and I could be counted upon to arrive first in line at the cinema.

All of this was to say that when I received a summons in 1935 from Joy Wolfe inquiring about a dollhouse commission, I was elated, not to mention completely starstruck. Hugh and I scrambled to pack up our car and drove to Massachusetts with the windows down. We sat back in our seats, enjoying the breeze as the lush, leafy wooded countryside zipped past us.

When we turned off the main road and neared the white Stick-style house with forest green trim, I studied Sawhill closely. Of course, I'd seen pictures of it, but there was something about seeing the size in person that provided a far more accurate sense of scope. Just replicating the exterior in miniature would keep me busy for quite some time. A close relation to Victorian architecture, Stick-style buildings utilized fairly basic forms, made more interesting with asymmetrical composition, steeply pitched gables, and verticality; they were further enhanced by decorative flourishes and trim, such as intricately patterned wooden shingles.

Sawhill rose from its sweeping lawns as a three-and-a-half-story wooden-frame house with a tower, adding both whimsy and an extra story to the home's left side. Elaborate wooden ornamentation resembling wishbones encircled the house's first floor wraparound porch.

On the porch steps stood Phyllis Wolfe, Joy and Charlie's eight-year-old daughter, her arms akimbo, studying the sky before lowering her gaze to us matter-of-factly.

"Hello, I'm Filly. Good thing you arrived when you did. See those cumulonimbus clouds?" She pointed upward. "They look quite serious. A storm's on the way."

When Hugh and I looked overhead, we could see she was right. Mountainous thunderheads bruised the sky.

A dark-haired woman I recognized instantly as Joy arrived on the porch to greet us alongside her daughter. In her pristine white button-down blouse, double string of pearls around her neck, and high-waisted khaki-colored trousers, Joy looked equally ready to host a cocktail party or follow a herd of elephants through the West African bush.

"Hello! Welcome to Sawhill." She shook our hands and made to usher us inside. "Please, come on in. I promise the house is cooler than it is out here."

"Mother, a storm's coming," Filly said. "They should unload their luggage now."

Joy shaded her eyes and looked upward. "Oh, Filly, as always, you're right. Shall we?" Not missing a beat, she ran, laughing, down the porch steps, the three of us trailing her. Only then did I notice she was barefoot. Hugh threw open the trunk of the car and we loaded our arms with suitcases and then sprinted back to the house just as the first fat raindrops began to land on us.

Once inside the high-ceilinged entry hall, my pace slowed to a stop as I admired the model of the Wolfes' legendary plane, *The Ray*, hanging overhead, shiny and yellow, even in the gloom brought on by the late-afternoon summer storm outside. Charlie Wolfe and a second woman appeared at the top of the stairs and descended toward us, both beaming. He was bowlegged, of medium height, and deeply tanned, giving him a weathered, older look that belied his forty-four years.

"Glad you could make it. Thanks for coming down for a visit." When Charlie shook my hand, I nearly winced at the strength of his grip. "This is Beryl, Joy's assistant."

"Pleasure to meet you," Beryl said, holding out her hand. Her short blond hair reminded me of Amelia Earhart's.

"Let's head into my office for a chat," Charlie said. "Fil, bring us some refreshments?"

Filly bounded off as Charlie, Joy, and Beryl led the way into a cherrywood-paneled room. Rain slashed against the windows, but I felt safe surrounded by the maps, shelves of books, and framed photographs. A whole world existed within Charlie's office, and I was intrigued. Behind his desk sat an aquarium filled with fish gleaming like silver dollars. More glass tanks filled the room. Hugh and I rotated, marveling at the treasures from their travels.

When my gaze fell upon a pile of shiny black-and-copper-colored scales coiled into a ball in one of the nearby terrariums, Charlie ran a hand over the glass affectionately. "This is Petunia, my python. Don't believe everything you read about serpents. She's a doll. Loves to curl up around my shoulders and stay warm."

Hugh studied the skeleton of some sort of winged creature displayed within a case in the corner of the room. "What's this?"

"A stingray." Charlie pointed to the long fringe framing the bristly skeleton at the center. "Those aren't bones, it's cartilage. Fascinating, eh?"

"It really is. Our son, Tommy, would be in heaven here," Hugh said, moving along the shelf to peer into a terrarium with a large speckled black-and-green frog.

Charlie lit a cigarette, took a long drag, and proceeded to blow a smoke ring. "Well, why don't you send for him? He and Fil will have a grand time together."

"He's at home with our housekeeper and her husband." I swallowed. "He's never taken the train on his own."

"How old is he?" Joy asked.

"Eleven."

"Why, he's more than capable of a trip on his own!" Charlie boomed. "At that age, I was working in a factory for eleven hours a day, six days a week. Get the boy down here. Let's make this visit a full family affair."

Hugh gave me an encouraging nod. In the couple of years since the Lindbergh baby had disappeared, I'd kept Tommy close. I knew I wasn't alone. Many mothers had. Still, I didn't object as Joy led me to the house's small phone booth outside the kitchen. I dialed our house number, and as I relayed the plan to Lorraine, I pictured the photos I'd seen of Filly standing at her mother's side in Africa, both holding rifles. During that trip, Filly couldn't have been more than eight. Tommy would be just fine, I told myself.

When I hung up, I slipped into the hallway and spotted Filly sitting at a table in the nearby breakfast room, outlining geometric forms, one after another, and surrounded by pages of similar sketches. "What are you drawing?" I asked, looking over her shoulder.

"Clouds. I'm simplifying them down to their most basic shape."

"Of course, now I see them. How clever of you."

The girl stopped drawing and studied the view beyond the window carefully. "Look, it's brightening. Already the clouds are taking on more of the honeycomb type of stratocumulus clouds. The weather should be more promising tomorrow, at least in the morning. Is your son coming to visit?"

"He'll be here around midday."

Filly nodded with a grave approval I found endearing. "I hope he gets a window seat on the train. Does he know the ten basic types of clouds?"

"I don't think he does."

"I'll tell him all about them. There can be surprising variety within the ten categories, but once you understand basic patterns, it helps with forecasting the weather. No matter where you are in the world, clouds are the same."

When Tommy arrived in time for lunch the next day, I smothered him in my arms, but he quickly wriggled free, eager to pull an empty Wheaties box featuring Charlie and Joy on its front.

"Sir, would you please sign this?" he asked Charlie, pointing to where *Champions of Aventure* stretched across the box in bold white lettering.

"You're a good sport, Tommy," Charlie said, scribbling his name. "Next time I need a first mate on an expedition, I'm calling you up for active duty."

Tommy looked pleased by Charlie's words, but when Joy signed her name and winked at him, my son turned pink all the way up to the tips of his ears.

Hugh, Tommy, and I spent the next three years traveling back and forth from our house in New Hampshire to Sawhill so I could work on the dollhouse. Every time we visited, I never failed to be enchanted by the Wolfes' big personalities. Theirs was a noisy household often filled with guests and laughter, storytelling and adventure. Tommy and Filly hiked, fished, rode horses, drew maps, and grew into fast friends. During one time we stayed with them, Petunia escaped her tank and everyone tore the house apart, searching for the python. It was Filly who finally found her that evening, curled up under the covers of her bed.

"I should have checked where we bunk first," Charlie said with a laugh. "Petunia likes to stay warm."

Needless to say, after that I always threw back my covers completely and inspected the linens before climbing into bed at Sawhill.

While I loved each dollhouse I created, Sawhill was secretly my favorite. Hugh wired it with electricity so the aquariums and many of the display cases lit up. I refined my metalworking abilities so I could construct a miniature of *The Ray* to hang in the dollhouse's foyer. I built skeletons out of all kinds of unconventional materials from real animal bones to clay to thread and fabric. I particularly enjoyed making the birds and animals, both the Wolfes' pets and taxidermy specimens, which I constructed out of felted wool, wire, paint, and modeling clay.

In 1939, Joy came to visit me at my workshop in New Hampshire. Tommy had just started his first year boarding at Phillips Exeter Academy near the coast, and Hugh was in New York City, designing a set for a show. Joy's warmth provided a good dose of energy to my quiet house. When she came out to the workshop, she circled the dollhouse, clicking her tongue. "My goodness, Cora, I know Hugh's the one with the background in magic, but you have a sorcery all your own. This is magnificent."

"Thank you."

"Charlie and I are heading off to the South Pacific in two weeks."

"Right, I nearly forgot. Just the two of you?"

"Yes, we're traveling light, so we won't have to be gone for long. Charlie and I will be living out of *The Ray* while we visit the more remote stops on our itinerary. I'll be working the camera and doing all the documenting—no crew. Phyllis will stay behind at Sawhill with Beryl."

"She'll miss you, I'll bet."

Joy tilted her head from side to side, considering. "Honestly, I'm not sure she minds. She doesn't really love to travel the way we do." She leaned down on my worktable, resting on her elbows to look inside the dollhouse. "How much longer do you need for this, do you think?"

"Another six to eight months is my bet. I've completed most of the hard stuff already, so it's really just tables, chairs, and basic furniture for the rest. Pretty straightforward."

She nodded. "Before I go, I need to ask you something."

"Of course. Anything."

Joy withdrew a stack of photos from her trouser pocket and placed them on the table between us. "Can you work these into Sawhill somehow?"

Intrigued, I lifted one, studied it, and spread the others in front of us to get a better view. Based on what I was seeing, I didn't need to ask any questions. Beryl was in every photo, nestled close to Joy.

For as long as I'd known Joy, I'd waited, wondering if she planned to hide any secrets in her dollhouse. I finally had an answer.

29
Tildy

2024

As Tildy walked into the SFMOMA's storage facility on Saturday morning, she finished off the coffee she desperately needed after a long night of little sleep. She'd spent hours rereading Cora's confession, figuring out what to say to the group this morning—and what to leave out. As Dale and Emiko approached, Tildy threw away her coffee cup and then clamped her arm over her bag protectively. She squared her shoulders. If the group was going to buy Tildy's version of Cora's story, she needed to stay sharp.

Tildy was greeting Dale and Emiko as a silver minivan pulled up outside the storage facility. Two older women emerged from the vehicle. Tildy pushed open the building's glass door and stepped outside. "Phyllis?"

"My dear, aren't you a sight for sore eyes!" Phyllis called to her. The white-haired woman was tiny. In her forest-green cardigan and tweedy wool trousers she looked like an elf. She rushed toward Tildy, her white orthopedic shoes a blur of movement.

The other woman, this one with a gray hairdo reminiscent of Dorothy Hamill, arrived at her mother's side slightly out of breath. "Sorry we're late. I'm Judy. We had mai tais at the Tonga Room last night and, boy, were they potent!"

Tildy shook hands with both women and introduced them to Dale and Emiko while a crew descended upon the minivan to unload the dollhouse and bring it inside.

"Why are we meeting here instead of the library?" Phyllis asked.

Dale explained the situation and then held out his arm gallantly. "Shall we head inside? I'm eager to see Sawhill."

Judy cast a worried look at her mother, but Phyllis nodded decisively. "Lead the way."

Once inside the Bel's storage space, everyone moved toward where the Hôtel LeFarge and Roughmore Park were set on individual tables under bright lights. A few feet away, Sawhill was being unpacked onto a table of its own. Tildy peeled off from the group to where *Young Woman in Hat* hung on a steel mesh storage rack.

So, this is you, Tildy thought to herself, staring into Cora's lifelike eyes.

None of the blurry photos of Cora Hale did her justice.

A sense of awe overwhelmed Tildy. Despite the fact that the canvas was relatively small—a little over three by four feet—Cora had created a sense of vast mystery, intimacy, and beauty. How had she managed to infuse so much life into one woman's face with just paint? Of course Tildy had been trained to analyze the technical components of the portrait and formulate an answer to this question, but the truth lay so much deeper than any description of color, line, form, shape, and space. Cora had achieved what few other painters could. She'd created a portrait that stopped you dead in your tracks, knocked the breath out of you, and filled you with wonder.

"Tildy? You've got to come see this," Dale called.

For a beat, Tildy remained glued in place, her gaze locked with the painting. "Sorry," she whispered before hurrying away to rejoin the group.

TILDY WOULD never have imagined that Sawhill could exceed her expectations, but it did. More than the stately re-creations of Hôtel LeFarge and Roughmore Park, the best word to describe Sawhill was "whimsical." Its Stick-style architecture, a combination of Victorian and Queen Anne influences, was quirky and interesting, charming and unique, but most of all: fun. From its steeply gabled roof, a tower added the third floor to the miniature's left side, making it the type of house that occupies every imaginative child's fantasy of where they'd want to live. The dollhouse's exterior was white with forest-green trim, but as soon as Tildy saw the interior, she knew this was her favorite of the dollhouses.

From top to bottom, wonderful details filled the house. There were too many exhibit cases the size of domino tiles to count. Seashells, butterflies, and flowers filled them—how had Cora made such minute creations? Tribal masks and taxidermied creatures decorated the walls. Flora and fauna specimens covered every surface of furniture. Miniature maps and botanical illustrations were everywhere. From the ceiling in its main foyer dangled a small canary-yellow airplane. The precision of the artistry was staggering.

"It's incredible," she said, prying her gaze away from the dollhouse to look at Phyllis.

Emiko circled the dollhouse, shaking her head. "Why in the world have you kept this hidden for so long? I've never seen anything like it."

Phyllis's expression was grave. "My mother commissioned this dollhouse from Cora Hale, because she wanted a way to document the truth about her life."

Dale and Emiko glanced at the dollhouse, confused.

"In the thirties, my parents were legendary for their adventurous, globe-trotting, romantic lives. If you're a fan of *It's a Beautiful World*, you know the story of its success: my mother had been writing her memoir, but after my parents disappeared in the South Pacific in 1939, my mother's assistant, Beryl, who became my guardian, oversaw publication of the book. She hoped the memoir would generate enough income to support us, and of course, it exceeded our wildest expectations. The musical and then Oscar-winning film didn't hurt either."

"I just read somewhere that 'Love Is the Greatest Adventure' is the most commonly played song for couples walking down the aisle." Emiko began humming the musical's well-known tune.

"Exactly. My parents became immortalized as this young beautiful couple with the world at their feet, but unfortunately the truth was far more complicated." Phyllis reached into the dollhouse and withdrew a wardrobe from the bedroom. When she turned the piece of furniture around, she revealed a black-and-white image decoupaged to its back. Emiko, Tildy, and Dale leaned forward to study the photo of a young Joy Wolfe with a woman, both draped across an outdoor chaise longue on a porch, arms wrapped around each other, their long legs entwined. Joy was closest to the camera, laughing and wearing a high-necked floral bathing suit. The unknown woman also wore a bathing suit, this one a dark solid color. Joy looked straight into the lens as the other woman, her face in profile, kissed a spot just next to Joy's lips.

No one said a word.

"This is my mother with Beryl, her assistant. They were in love."

"But . . . but that can't be right," Emiko stammered. "*It's a Beautiful World* is all about the great romance between Joy and Charlie."

Phyllis nodded sadly. Her shoulders slumped. She wobbled, but before she could topple over, Dale caught her. Tildy grabbed the closest chair and rushed it to Phyllis.

Judy pulled a water bottle from her backpack and helped her mother take a long sip.

When no one said a word, Tildy stepped in. "When I was in New Hampshire, I found Cora Hale's diary and she describes everything. Joy and Charlie did love each other . . . but as friends. From the first moment they met in Kansas during an air show, they recognized the potential for an extraordinary partnership with each other, but they were never actually in love."

Tildy reached into the dollhouse to remove the furniture Cora had described in her confession. A dresser, Joy's bed, Joy's desk. One by one, she handed the pieces to show Dale and Emiko, who pored over each one, studying the photos decoupaged onto them. The images all showed Joy and Beryl together. Their affection for each other was unmistakable.

"May I have a copy of Cora's diary?" Phyllis asked Tildy. "I'd love to read what she wrote about my parents. What an amazing stroke of luck that you found it."

"Yes, of course," Tildy said, feeling anything but lucky. "I'll make copies for everyone." As soon as the words came out of her mouth, Tildy regretted them. By highlighting this so-called *diary* of Cora's, Tildy was walking a fine line. If she had to start making copies of it, she feared people might figure out some parts were strategically missing. The diary and Cora's connections to Transome and her oblique references to her misdeeds in New York City could lead people to figuring out a problem existed with *Young Woman in Hat*. Tildy's stomach flipped sickeningly. All she wanted to do was to stop telling lies, go home, climb into bed, and pull the covers over her head.

"I've been trapped in this secret for almost as long as I can remember," Phyllis said, interrupting Tildy's thoughts. "But I lost so much. In the space of one year, my parents died and then our beloved home burned to the ground. Beryl could never reveal the truth about her relationship with my mother, because obviously I would have been taken away from her. She tried to secure my future with *It's a Beautiful World*, but the book built a whole mythology that's gotten away from us." Her voice trailed off weakly.

Gathered around Sawhill, everyone remained silent, trying to reconcile Joy's story with reality. Even Tildy, who'd had more time to digest this information, was still processing it.

After a few minutes, Phyllis cleared her throat. "My mother, father, Beryl—they all had to work so hard to hide who they really were. They felt such shame and fear. It's tragic, but the truth has remained hidden for far too long. Judy and I have decided it's time to set the record straight. People love the story of my parents and *It's a Beautiful World*." She glanced at Judy. "We hope that when people learn the truth, maybe it will encourage everyone to approach others with bigger hearts, more understanding and compassion. Don't you think we all need more of that right now?"

"I do. And this is a beautiful idea," Dale said. "But the responses won't all be positive. People will level all kinds of awful accusations toward your parents. Are you really ready to put your family into the spotlight like this?"

With Judy's help, Phyllis rose to her feet and stood in front of Sawhill, facing the rest of the group. "The truth is long overdue. People shouldn't have to live a lie to survive, right?"

Judy held her mother's hand up like she was a winning prizefighter. "I'm right there with you, Mom. We can handle the haters."

"The Bel will stand by you too. We'll do whatever you need," Tildy said, taking Phyllis's small bony hand in her own. "Your parents weren't alone. Sawhill isn't the only dollhouse to tell a hidden story about its former owner. Cora's others did too."

Tildy pointed at the Hôtel LeFarge and started her story about Belva and Cora meeting in Paris. She explained how Cora had erased the comte's presence from the dollhouse, but she said nothing about the miniature portrait of Belva nestled in the dollhouse or the tiny sketch of Tildy's mother. She also said nothing about Cora's banishment from New York, nothing that would lead anyone to connect *Young Woman in Hat* to Cora.

While she spoke, Tildy feared her story would start to unravel. But then she remembered Cora quoting Transome in her confession: *People only see what they expect.* In this case, Tildy hoped he was right. No one had any reason to question *Young Woman in Hat.*

As everyone studied Hôtel LeFarge with new understanding shining in their eyes, Tildy thought about the script she always followed when leading tour groups: *Belva's life was just like a fairy tale.* Except whose life was ever truly a fairy tale? Rationally, of course, she knew this, so why had she spouted that stupid line over and over? Because she wanted to believe it. It was a lot easier to simply believe a happy, uncomplicated story than to ask questions and actually do the hard work of figuring out the answers . . . answers that might bring up more difficult truths than the uncomplicated stories did. She'd taken the course of least resistance with her mother too. Tildy, always eager to please her mother, never asked questions. It was easier to simply stay quiet and maintain the peace.

"Each of the dollhouses in the Bel's possession is here because their owner wanted their true stories to be told someday," Tildy said.

When she finished describing the relationship between Belva and Cora, she studied everyone's faces for a jolt of understanding. But no one so much as glanced at *Young Woman in Hat.* Tildy was relieved, but also disappointed. An unexpected impulse to shake everyone and explain the truth about Cora came over her, but for her plan to work, she needed people to believe what she was telling them. Lying felt terrible.

Emiko sidled over to Roughmore Park. "So, Tildy, what secret was the duchess hiding?"

30
Cora

1941–1966

Thirty years had passed since I painted *Young Woman in Hat* and signed it as Blanchet. As far as I knew, no one suspected it to be a fake. Not a single soul. During the intervening years, the threat of discovery had eased and I was no longer always checking over my shoulder, searching for signs of trouble.

Young Woman in Hat had developed a life of its own. My forgery's popularity grew. Though I avoided going into New York City, on the rare trips I made, reproductions of *Young Woman in Hat* brightened many a shop window. The museum used it on marketing posters. That young woman's face, *my* face, was everywhere in New York City. No one made the connection to me, and why would they? If anyone ever noticed a resemblance, it would simply be a coincidence. I was a nobody. Although this anonymity ensured a comforting measure of safety, it also frustrated me. I'd created a beloved painting, one people couldn't get enough of, yet I couldn't take credit for it. I tried to tell myself it didn't matter, that I was an artist because I loved the act of creating art, not for recognition or adulation, yet a part of me—a part I felt ashamed of—stung painfully at how I longed for acknowledgment. The price of my duplicity seemed to consist of watching the portrait's success with the public. As a result, I tried not to think about it. To agonize over *Young Woman in Hat* would only bring heartbreak. Even if I did try to claim the painting as my own, no one would have believed me to be capable of producing such a masterpiece, and that hurt worst of all.

In December of 1941, as I sat upstairs in front of the fireplace in our bedroom, reading a recent *New York Times* that Hugh had brought back from a trip to the city, I noticed an obituary: Mr. Transome's. I lowered the newspaper to my lap and looked through the window at the rolling mountains in the distance. I admit, I felt relief knowing he could no longer hurt me. But his passing also elicited a new emotion in me: resentment. Because of that man, I'd lived in fear for decades. I'd made myself small, so he could remain big. That realization summoned an unexpected anger in me. Most of all, I hated my cowardice. I feared admitting the truth to Hugh. All this time I'd been telling myself I withheld the information to keep him safe. As if my lying was a form of self-sacrifice, of bravery. In truth, I didn't tell him because I didn't want to witness his disappointment in me.

From downstairs, I heard the kitchen door slam. Hugh had arrived home from his daily constitutional. I rose from my chair, determined to finally set the record straight.

When I reached the living room, I heard the crackling of a man's voice on the radio saying, "There has been serious fighting in the air and on the sea."

Only a few feet away from me, Hugh stood in front of the radio, his face tense and grave. Within his white-knuckled grip, he clutched his cane.

Alarm tightened my stomach.

I gestured at the radio. "What's happening?"

Hugh's face had gone gray. "The Japanese have attacked Hawaii. I think we're a nation at war."

Not again, I thought. *Please, not again.*

As Hugh and I held each other for comfort, I pushed my secret to the back of my mind.

Overnight, the war changed everything.

While most Americans spent the 1930s ignoring events on the

other side of the Atlantic, Hugh had been tracking Hitler's march through Europe with growing alarm, reading the newspapers and watching newsreels. After Neville Chamberlain declared war on Germany in 1939, Hugh debated returning to England to help, but Tommy and I talked him out of it. So when the US Army approached him early in the war, he couldn't answer the call quickly enough. His role in creating Fake Paris and ensuing theater experience gave him unusual skills the army wanted to put to practical use. Hugh was whisked away, sent mostly to destinations on the West Coast, where fears of Japanese spying ran high. He said very little about his projects, but from the few details he dropped, I figured out he was building large-scale illusions to camouflage factories producing war material.

At the start of 1943, Hugh called one evening to tell me he was done with an assignment in Seattle, a city best known at that time for its airplane manufacturer, Boeing. Since the war began the men and women of the Pacific Northwest had been busy cranking out the nation's new warhorse, the B-17 bomber. Many years later, I learned Hugh had been part of a team designing and constructing Wonderland, an illusion of a town constructed from painted canvas, wire mesh, burlap, and wood to hide Boeing's factories from aerial view.

"What's your game plan for your final evening in Seattle?"

"We're heading to a place called Pioneer Square," he said cheerfully. "I've been guaranteed lovely lasses, stiff drinks, and bloody steaks."

I laughed. "When do you come home?"

"I fly to Chicago tomorrow and then onward a day or so after that. I should be in New Hampshire by the end of the week."

The following day as I was sitting down for lunch with our housekeeper Lorraine, a knock at the front door interrupted us. Not until I faced two army officers wearing somber expressions did it occur to me to be afraid.

"Mrs. Havilland?" one asked, tucking his hat below his elbow.

No one who knew me used that name. I suddenly wanted to tell them to shut up, to keep my husband's beautiful name off their lips. My knees began to shake. I seemed to melt. Next thing I knew I was sitting on the floor, blinded by the bright stripe of daylight glowing between the men's dark uniforms.

Somewhere above Idaho's mountains, they told me, Hugh's plane had gotten lost in fog and crashed.

Hugh was dead.

I couldn't believe my dashing, clever, kind Hugh had died in an accident. He'd survived one war, only to perish on the periphery of another. The cruelty of it left me shattered.

Without Hugh, I was rudderless. For nearly thirty years, not only had he served as my right-hand man, but he was my love and best friend and a wonderful father to Tommy. I'd spent more of my life with Hugh than without him.

THE GOVERNMENT sent Hugh's body home to New Hampshire, where Tommy and I buried him.

For months I stayed out of the workshop. Tommy was at boarding school, and Lorraine and Harvey Benton hovered nearby, offering meals and company, but I withdrew into myself. During my early days in Paris when I grieved the loss of my father and my painting career, I'd taken to long walks throughout the city. I resumed those, but instead of Paris's streets, I trod the wooded paths and country roads of New Hampshire. I'd disappear for hours.

I regretted never telling Hugh about the portrait that changed the course of my life. Once he was gone, I realized what a fool I'd been to hide the truth from him. He wouldn't have cared about the dalliance with Rose Transome. If anything, Hugh would have hunted down Mr. Transome and demanded my vindication. Why had I doubted Hugh's faith in me? He would have believed me.

He believed I was capable of anything. His love was limitless. He would have been upset only because I hadn't trusted him enough to tell the truth. And now, I'd lost my opportunity. He'd been taken from me too soon. If it hadn't been for Tommy still needing me, I think I would have been completely lost.

ONCE AGAIN, art saved me. I received a letter from a woman in Virginia that intrigued me and before I knew it, I returned to making dollhouses. Throughout my career as a dollhouse maker, I'd figured out many ways to hide secrets, but my new client offered a novel challenge. She'd served the war effort in the early '40s as a codebreaker in a special division of Black women cryptologists. Invisible to everyone, she helped end the war, and my gratitude to her was boundless. In my opinion, a monument dedicated to her belonged in every town square across the country.

Then, in 1950, my life took another turn. One evening, the phone in my workshop rang, and when I answered it, I thought I'd misheard the woman on the other end of the line. I held the receiver away from my ear, staring at it, confused.

"Mrs. Hale? Mrs. Hale? Are you still there?"

I pulled myself together. "Yes, I'm here."

"I'm calling on behalf of Mr. Disney. He'd like to invite you out to California for a visit."

A MONTH later, I was in Los Angeles. From the back seat of a Chevy Bel-Air, I caught only glimpses of houses flashing through the stucco walls and hedges running along the road of Holmby Hills.

Years earlier in New Hampshire, Hugh, Tommy, and I had bundled into coats, mittens, hats, and snow boots and driven half an hour away to Manchester to see Walt Disney's *Snow White and the Seven Dwarfs*. The film had thoroughly captivated us. I still remember my amazement when *The End* appeared on-screen, the houselights came up, and I inhaled the smell of damp wool, cigarette smoke, and popped corn, as my brain adjusted from the world of the movie to the realization that we were in a crowded theater. That movie was a feat like nothing I'd ever seen before. To be mesmerized by animated figures, to believe the voices that came from these drawings and not humans, and not just to believe them, but to *feel* them—this felt revelatory. It was magic.

I went to California to meet Mr. Disney and hear what he had to say, because I needed a change. I was in search of magic again.

When my driver pulled the car up to Mr. Disney's address, a large gate slowly swung open. Moments later, I emerged from the car in front of the sprawling split-level modern house, feeling a slight pang of disappointment. If Mr. Disney wanted a dollhouse, his home didn't hold the architectural appeal that the rest of my work did.

Before I reached the front door, a train's horn blasted. Surprised, I turned, shading my eyes against the low slant of sunshine suffusing the ridge in the buttery glow I'd come to associate with Southern California, a hue that conjured the feeling of warm sand on the beach, the clink of ice cubes in a gin and tonic, and the dry scratch of palm fronds rustling in the Santa Ana winds.

A man sitting atop a small, shiny crimson locomotive train came into view about fifty yards away, heading toward me. Next to him, a large standard poodle galloped alongside the train tracks, barking wildly and wagging her tail.

"Hello!" called the man I assumed to be Mr. Disney. He waved and hopped off the locomotive. As he strode toward me, the poodle bounded in front of him. "Whoa, there. Easy girl," Disney called out, laughing, and the poodle skittered to a halt in front of me and sat, her rump swinging back and forth with the enthusiastic wagging of her tail. When I held out my hand, she placed her snout under it, eager to be patted.

A broad smile stretched beneath Mr. Disney's thick neatly trimmed gray mustache. His wasn't a handsome face per se, but it exuded friendliness and exuberance. Though he appeared to be my age, maybe even slightly younger, he radiated a boyish excitement.

"My secretary said you sounded skeptical on the phone, but here you are. Thanks for coming." He grabbed my hand, pumping it up and down. "Call me Walt. May I call you Cora?"

"Yes, of course," I said. Then I pointed at the train. "And please, tell me about this."

He pushed back a light-blue-and-white-striped train conductor's cap from his forehead and scratched at his hairline, beaming broadly. "This is the Carolwood Pacific Express."

"What scale is it?"

Walt's eyes twinkled with delight. "I knew you of all people would appreciate it! It's one-eighth scale. Fully operational." He then waved his hands around, drawing my attention to another large outbuilding and a red barn in the distance. "The tracks encircle the property. My girls are teenagers now, but on a good day, I can still entice them to join me for a ride or two."

"Amazing."

"You must be wondering why I called you here. The Disney campus would be one thing, but inviting you to my house? Well, I can see why you thought my secretary might have been pulling your leg."

"I confess, I've been curious."

He slapped the side of his thigh, guffawing, and then tossed the dog a treat before tugging a handkerchief from his breast pocket to dab at the perspiration beading on his forehead. "Please, follow me."

We set off for a barn in the distance, passing a large swimming pool and four-car garage.

"I first heard about you in 1939 at the Golden Gate International Exposition," Walt explained. "I've met Mrs. LeFarge and have seen your Petite Hôtel LeFarge. It's marvelous."

"Thank you," I said, aware that my pulse quickened at the mention of Belva. "I suppose for those of us interested in miniatures, it's a rather small world, isn't it?"

"Yes, indeed," he said, slowing his pace, rubbing his chin deep in thought. Though twilight was creeping across the yard, the heat of the stone walkway still radiated through the soles of my ballet flats. Inside the main house, lights blinked on. I inhaled the sweet scent of Mrs. Disney's rose garden.

Walt's attention snapped back to refocus on me. "I've developed a miniatures obsession. I've always loved trains, so I've been collecting different models of them, but I'm also intrigued by the idea of creating whole miniature worlds of my imagination."

He held open one of his barn's doors to reveal a workshop. When I stepped inside, I saw it contained every tool he might have needed, plus several I'd never seen before, but what really captivated me were the display cabinets filled with miniatures lining his workroom. I spotted a collection of cars filling the shelves—an early Ford Model T, a Rolls-Royce, a Cadillac. I smiled, thinking of the collection of motorcars we once built for Roughmore Park. Walt owned ships too: a steamboat and a destroyer. He also collected miniature instruments: banjos, a guitar, and an organ.

When we reached the final cabinet, Walt turned to me, cheeks glowing and eyes sparkling with intensity. "Cora, the reason I invited you here is because I want to build a world I've been calling Disneylandia, and I need your help."

I DIDN'T return to New Hampshire that winter. After forty years of making dollhouses, I was ready for a change. I rented a bungalow for myself in Los Feliz, not far from the Disney campus in Burbank, where Walt had set me up with an office. He put me on the planning team for his traveling show of miniatures, Disneylandia.

Walt had long used miniatures to help his animators develop

several iconic characters, like Pinocchio and Bambi. A model shop was built expressly for this purpose. Later, miniatures were created to help plan and design the sets and special effects for movies like *Mary Poppins* and *Twenty Thousand Leagues Under the Sea*, but I was tasked with something slightly different.

I built models to help Walt develop his plan for Disneylandia, an idea that kept growing bigger. His vision for miniature scenes of Americana evolved into a garden with trains, both big and small, and then that plan turned into an amusement park featuring a village of miniatures called Lilliputian Land, which eventually morphed into what we now know as Disneyland, an amusement park centered around his nostalgia for his childhood home in Marceline, Missouri. Disneyland expanded to include a village square, shops, restaurants, a movie theater, amusement park rides, a river paddleboat, a Wild West saloon, spaceships, and Sleeping Beauty's Castle. And I'll bet you've already guessed what would circumnavigate the entire property. Yes, one of his beloved trains.

Though the idea for Disneyland evolved over the years, I never lost the sense of adventure I'd experienced when I first met Walt at his house in the Holmby Hills. As I worked on creating a series of miniatures, each a feature of the park, Walt would move the pieces around, honing his vision.

Men who ran various amusement parks throughout the country came to offer expert advice and each one predicted that Disneyland would fail, but Walt remained undeterred. Defiantly, he clung to his concept. As far as he was concerned, he wasn't building something as mundane as an amusement park. He was building a whole new world, one of imagination and happiness. His commitment to his vision impressed me. For so long, I'd lived in obscurity, never drawing attention to my work, even hiding most of it, but Walt was willing to risk everything for his dream. And not only that, he put his name all over it. I envied his bold confidence. There was nothing to hide in Walt's work, no secrets. He did whatever he wanted.

As I saw it, this work for Disneyland brought me full circle to those miniature stage sets I'd first seen in Paris. Disneyland took me back to the hallway at the Palais Garnier, where each scene provided a glimpse into a different world. Disneyland also offered a series of stages to be designed: Main Street, Frontierland, Adventureland, Tomorrowland; these were the miniature sets I created—the buildings, the amusement park rides, the landscaping. I immersed myself in getting the details correct. The lighting, the architecture, the color palette, even the plants helped us set the stage. Along with several other designers, I created miniature models of the focal points for our early planning: Sleeping Beauty's Castle, the Town Square, and the Opera House. When Walt would crouch down to eye level to observe the miniatures, I'd see the same excited glimmer in his eyes from when we'd first met. His appetite for creativity was freeing and contagious and it reminded me of Hugh. Though I'd just turned sixty at that point, I felt motivated and inspired.

The camaraderie of working for Disney also reminded me of my workshop back at Roughmore Park, although now I was surrounded by young, energetic men and women with big plans for the future, instead of shaky war veterans who were grateful for a quiet place to immerse themselves in forgetting the past.

One morning in 1954, I stopped by the Burbank campus's main canteen to pick up a doughnut. There, I overhead a group of women from Ink and Paint chatting. One of them held a newspaper and was regaling the rest of the table with a story.

"Listen here, gals, it says a painting just sold for over fifty-five thousand bucks!"

"Fifty-five thousand? Knock it off, you've got to be kidding."

"I'm not! It says right here that fifty-five thousand bucks is the most that's ever been spent on a painting." The woman traced her index finger along the paper and, affecting a news reporter's twang, she proceeded to read aloud: "Blanchet's *Young Woman in Hat* just sold to San Francisco heiress Belva Curtis LeFarge. Mrs. LeFarge bought the masterpiece from the Met and will display it in the library named after her in Pacific Heights."

"Well, *la-di-da*," giggled one the others at the table. "Tell you what, if I had a fortune like that, I sure can think of other ways to spend it."

"Must be nice to be rolling in cash," another woman said, shrugging.

The women kept talking, but I stopped listening. Belva had bought *Young Woman in Hat*? I swallowed hard, reeling from that number: *fifty-five thousand dollars*. Shaken, I exited the canteen and paused on the perfectly manicured pathway across the lawn. Even in January the endless parade of beautiful Southern California weather marched along with a cloudless, pale blue sky. I blinked against its brightness, trying to make sense of what I'd just overheard.

If there was one thing I'd learned from Walt Disney, it was to believe in your work. I scurried to my office and, with trembling fingers, dialed the operator to ask for the Belva Curtis LeFarge Library in San Francisco. When I was connected, a young woman's voice came on the line and I asked to speak to Belva, but instead of my call being put on hold, there was a fumbling sound, and then, "Hello?"

My breath caught in my throat. It was her. Almost forty-five years had passed, but she sounded the same. "Belva?"

"Yes, who's this?"

"It's me, Cora."

Not a single sound traveled over the telephone line and for a second, I feared we'd been disconnected. "Cora? Is that really you?" Belva asked faintly.

"It is. Can you talk?"

Belva hesitated and then burst into overwhelmed-sounding laughter. "I've been waiting to talk to you for decades."

ONCE BELVA and I recovered from the shock of hearing each other's voices again after all those years, it was like a spigot had been turned on. Over the phone, we swiftly arranged the logistics of my visit to San Francisco. I said nothing about *Young Woman in Hat*. Minutes after our call ended, I was packing my belongings and leaving Burbank to head her way.

As I drove north, my shock over the painting was replaced by a new realization: I was *finally* going to see Belva again. My fingers tightened on the steering wheel. Over the years, whenever a memory of her had come to me, I'd pushed it away. Thinking about Belva was like turning on a light, realizing the bulb was too bright, and turning it off. But now, I left the switch on. Had she found a new love? Was she remarried? I had no idea. Of course, I should have wished her nothing but happiness, but I was shocked to find myself hoping she was alone. Did that mean I still had feelings for her? I brushed that question aside, tried focusing on the road, but couldn't stop myself from thinking about our time together in Paris. How she'd been so good at dramatizing voices when she read aloud. How she'd quieted unexpectedly when I'd told her she was beautiful. How she'd kissed me under the moon on the night of her party.

When I arrived at the Belva Curtis LeFarge Library, it was evening. I parked but didn't leave the car immediately. Since returning to the United States I had scoured the newspapers, searching for any information about Belva, but all I'd been able to find was that she'd built the library and Jack, her son, had died in the Pacific during the war.

I needed this visit to result in more than simply getting answers about my old painting. I needed to know why she'd sent me away. Had she really never loved me? I squeezed my eyes shut. I wasn't praying exactly—just hoping very, *very* hard. I wanted to believe a spark still existed between us.

When I opened my eyes, I found Belva striding across the courtyard toward my car. Beneath the trappings of the major style changes that had transpired since we last saw each other in 1914—short hairstyles and higher hemlines, to name just a few—Belva was every inch as radiant and energetic as ever. When we embraced, her cheek felt like velvet against mine. Aquanet and expensive perfume wafted around us. It took all my resolve to let her pull away.

"Belva, you look exactly the same," I managed to say.

"My dear, you are an exceptionally skilled liar. Thank you. Can you believe we're finally back together after all this time? For a woman in her early sixties, your hair is still gorgeously red." She let her hand rest on my upper arm. "I'm nearing seventy, but most of the time I still feel like that woman who used to read aloud in your workshop behind Curtis House."

"Most of the time?"

"Well, maybe not first thing in the morning, especially if I've stayed up too late reading a good book or drinking a dry martini." She cupped my elbow and led me toward the library. "My goodness, time's just slipped away from us, hasn't it?"

Her voice sounded high and fast, maybe even a little guilty, like she was a child making an excuse for why a cookie had suddenly disappeared from an unsupervised dessert plate. Yes, Belva was right, the years had slipped away, but I'd never stopped thinking about her. More than once I'd considered writing to her, but I never knew what to say. What excuse was I supposed to use to contact her? How would I explain myself? It never occurred to me I could have written something as simple as *Belva, I've missed you*. I placed my hand over where hers gripped my arm and held it tightly. She smiled at me and leaned her weight into mine, nudging us forward.

As we approached the library's door, I admired the limestone building. And there, carved into the stone above the front door: The Belva Curtis LeFarge Library. Here was another person willing to stamp their name on their dreams. I cleared my throat. "You've certainly been busy. What a beautiful spot. What gave you the idea to build it?"

"Believe it or not, our dollhouse did. It showed me how much I loved collecting and curating. I figured if I could do it on a small scale, why not try a large one too? My plan was always for the library to serve the public, and I got lucky with my timing. We opened in 1926. When the Depression hit only a few years later, we ended up offering classes, medical clinics, and all kinds of other services at that time, and the library really became woven into the fabric of the community. Since then, along with classes, we host concerts, lectures, a few exhibits—we've tried it all."

Walking along the flagstone path toward the library's entrance, I took a deep breath. "Tell me, did you ever remarry?"

"No. For many years, it was just Jack and me. And then I lost him."

"I heard. I'm so sorry."

She flinched, but nodded. "I've spent most of my time in San Francisco, although there's been travel. I'm always on the hunt to find interesting things for the library. My life has been dedicated to building this place and filling it with wonders. And I suppose I don't just mean books and art, but also a community of people who appreciate such things. And you? Have you built any more dollhouses?"

"In fact, I have. Many of them."

She stopped, her mouth open in surprise. "Really?"

I nodded, and there, as purple twilight fell upon us in the courtyard and lights winked on in the houses surrounding us, I told her that I'd discovered more women who needed my special dollhouses. And men too. I described my beloved band of helpers at Roughmore Park. I spoke about Hugh. About Tommy.

"I knew I was right to take a chance on you in Curtis House. Winny was about to throw you out on the sidewalk, but I *knew* you were someone destined for wonderful things."

For a moment, I saw my opening. I wanted to ask her what she'd *really* seen in me, but I faltered and instead inquired after our old friend. "Whatever happened to Winny?" I asked.

"She retired to Kentucky, of all places. I never fully appreciated her fascination with horse racing when we were in Paris, but apparently over the years she built a little nest egg from her winnings and bought a lovely old place right outside of Louisville. From what I understand, she was a regular at Churchill Downs. Now, let's go inside."

Belva opened one of the doors, and she led me into the marble foyer. "We have the place to ourselves at this hour. No need to lower your voice."

Not until I entered the building did I finally understand Belva's living arrangement—she truly lived *inside* her library. Every night she went to sleep in her bedroom on the top floor of the library and every morning she awoke, dressed, and then strolled downstairs to her office on the first floor where she ate breakfast overlooking the Bay.

She waved at me to follow her up a set of stairs. "We're going to start with the top."

In her private apartment, we stood in front of the enormous windows admiring the nighttime view. The city's lights reflected on the smooth surface of the Bay, glittering like beads on black silk. In the distance, the dark violet hills of Marin County appeared remarkably uninhabited compared to San Francisco's endless spread of rooftops. As we turned to leave, I noticed a white Jenny Lind–style crib set in the corner of Belva's bedroom.

"Who's that for?" I asked, pointing at it.

"Oh, the library's resident baby. You'll meet her soon."

"You have a baby?"

"Goodness, no. She's not mine, but I adore her."

I laughed. The Bel was certainly a library like none other. But then again, Belva was a woman like none other.

Everywhere I looked, not only did I spot paintings and books from Hôtel LeFarge, but also from my beloved Curtis House. The Paris boardinghouse had closed its doors once and for all in the days before the Nazis invaded France. On a nearby wall, I glimpsed a Corot seascape that had once hung in the Curtis House parlor. "I always admired the moodiness of that painting."

"Well, I just acquired a piece that you're going to love." She bit her lip, beckoning me to follow her out of the room and back downstairs. "It's the most I've ever spent on a painting, but when I saw it, I just knew I had to have it."

Slowly I followed her down three flights of stairs to the Main Reading Room. Despite the grandeur of the space, I felt nothing but dread as I came face-to-face with a portrait I hadn't seen in thirty-five years.

There hung *Young Woman in Hat*.

"Amazing, isn't it?" As she described how she'd acquired it, I felt her watching me carefully, but I simply stared at the painting. I'd left my own body and finally knew how it felt to die suddenly. There was no pain, no emotion, no anything. Just shock.

From somewhere far away, I heard Belva's voice faintly but couldn't make out the words. It was like being submerged underwater. I was holding my breath. Distant sounds reached me, but nothing identifiable.

And then the words took shape. "Cora?"

A nudge on my arm.

"Yes, yes, I'm here," I stammered.

"Oh no, what have I done?" Belva stood in front of me, blocking my view of the painting. Her face crumpled in concern.

"I'm fine. I just . . . I feel light-headed. I need to sit."

"Of course, come over here." Belva guided me closer to the painting and parked me in one of the room's study desk chairs.

Of all the pieces of art for Belva to acquire, why did it have to be this one? But then I stared at the painting again.

Of course, it had to be this one.

My stomach pitched dangerously.

I was so close to the portrait, I swear my own likeness seemed to be whispering to me—*coward, coward, coward*. For years I'd lived in fear of this painting. I'd kept myself quiet because of it. And for what? So that almost half a century later I could be reunited with Belva, one of my great loves, and forced into another lie?

I'd spent most of my life helping other women reveal the great truth of their lives and the time had come for me to reveal my own. I couldn't keep this secret any longer. I regretted never confessing to Hugh. After all these years, I'd found my beloved Belva. I wouldn't make the same mistake twice.

"I painted that portrait," I mumbled as if testing how the words sounded.

Belva turned to me but said nothing.

On wobbly legs, I stood. "I painted that self-portrait when I was seventeen years old. I covered up my red hair, but it's me," I said, louder, walking toward *Young Woman in Hat*. I kept talking. I told her everything. My father's death. Rose Transome, Mr. Transome. My forgery. Every single vile detail.

As I spoke, Belva's eyes shimmered with tears. Those freckles she hid under a layer of powder blazed in sharp relief against the paleness of her skin. I braced myself, knowing that at least if I was going to lose Belva again, it wouldn't be because of a misunderstanding. I wouldn't be left wondering about anything.

"So all this time you've been afraid of being revealed?" she asked, her voice low.

I nodded, my eyes downcast.

From her skirt's pocket, Belva removed a small black velvet square. She turned it upside down. Out slid the tiny portrait I'd painted of her for the Petite Hôtel LeFarge, glimmering on her palm like a jeweled brooch.

"I've always loved this miniature. You painted my face so realistically in such tiny scale, and then there's the daring composition and the swirl of ostrich feathers on the hat—it's extraordinary. Whenever I look at it, I feel bold and brave. And then when I saw your face looking out at me from *Young Woman in Hat* at the Met, I just knew. I felt that it was your painting, although I couldn't understand how. I remembered that when you arrived at Curtis House, you had a high recommendation from one of the Met's board members. And I began to wonder if you'd somehow managed to pull off a great feat of forgery. Now everything makes sense. Your solitariness. You were always so determined to keep your distance from everyone." She looked back to the portrait. "Good grief, you really could paint! I can't believe you were only seventeen when you made this."

"Honestly, neither can I."

Still looking at the painting, Belva took my hand in hers and I felt ready to collapse with relief. I couldn't believe I'd kept this secret for so long.

"So it really is you," she said quietly.

"No one's ever noticed before."

"How could they not?"

"Transome insisted it's because people see what they want to see."

"That explains why I spotted your resemblance." When she turned away from the portrait to face me, I got the sense she was trying to peel away time, to see me exactly as I'd been in Paris so many years ago. "All this time, I've wanted to see you again."

"But why did you really send me away in the first place?" I knew the easy answer: Jack. And because I now had Tommy, I understood this. She hadn't wanted to lose her child. And who could blame her for that? Certainly not me. But underneath this obvious response, I wanted to hear her say something different. I needed the truth. She nodded, seeming to understand this, though now it was she who was flustered.

"I . . . I wasn't strong enough to claim you as my own, Cora. And I'm sorry for that. You've always been brave, but it took me longer to get there."

"Me? Brave? But I've been hiding from this painting for decades."

"Nonsense. You hid this to survive, not because you were cowardly. Tiny piece by tiny piece, you've built a big life, Cora. You should be proud of that."

I swallowed nervously, pointing back to the painting on the wall. "But are you upset it's not a Blanchet? You just spent a fortune on a fake!"

"There's nothing fake about it. That portrait's worth every penny and even more. And now that I know you really painted this, I love it far more than I did ten minutes ago. You painted a masterpiece. And it brought you back to me." She gave me a sly look.

"I'm not sure I understand," I said quietly.

"I made a big fuss to the newspapers about buying this piece, hoping word would reach you. I didn't know how to find you, and I hoped that maybe if you heard what I'd done, you'd come find me."

She wrapped an arm around my shoulder and squeezed. "And my plan worked."

I DECIDED to stay in San Francisco. I called Walt and told him I was ready to slow down, that while I loved my work as a miniaturist, my heart was elsewhere. He was surprised and disappointed, but we promised to stay in touch. Then I wasted no time packing up my life in Los Angeles and moving into the library with Belva.

Most people saw us together and thought it sweet to see two old friends reunited. Of course, she was more than a friend to me. Those who understood the truth didn't want to stir up trouble so they gave us our privacy. By that time, as two older women, we possessed an aura of invisibility and we used it to our advantage. Finally we enjoyed the freedom to do whatever we wanted, right under everyone's noses.

Belva and I told no one about my creation of *Young Woman in Hat*. Aside from my reputation, the Met would have come off badly, and damaging a prominent art museum held little appeal for Belva. She suggested moving it upstairs to her private apartment, where few would see it, but I insisted on leaving it in the Main Reading Room. I wanted someone to notice me in the portrait. I hoped someone might finally ask questions about my resemblance to the woman in the painting, but no one ever did. My crime remained hidden in plain view.

For the first time in decades, I produced art in regular scale, along with my dollhouses. Belva asked me to design art for the library and insisted on converting her son's old room into an artist's workshop for me, saying it was the best way to honor the loss of her darling Jack.

While pondering what to make for the Bel, I thought back over my career, reviewing my favorite creations, and the answer popped right out at me. Of all my dollhouses, the one I built for Joy Wolfe,

Sawhill, held a special place in my heart because its menagerie of creatures had a hold on me. I'd loved creating miniature animals for the Wolfes and decided my new home could use this same element of creativity.

Libraries are viewed as such solemn places—but why? Reading is magic. Think of the imagination and sense of adventure that readers employ every time they crack open a book. There are few places filled with more magic than libraries, no doubt about it. And obviously, there was no more magical and inspiring place to live than the Bel, so first, I set myself loose on the Children's Room. Mice, cats, rabbits, an elephant, ducks—I filled the space with statues of animals, but then decided not to limit the fun to children. Next, I cast a life-size bronze of Belva's beloved Gruffwood for the library's foyer, and then I made the owl perched by the circulation desk in the Main Reading Room.

MEG, DURING this period, I spent a great deal of time with you. You were the library's resident baby that Belva was referring to when I'd first arrived. Of course, back then everyone called you Daisy. The morning after my arrival at the Bel, your father carried you through the library's front door and as soon as I saw your large, curious eyes looking out at me over the round apples of your cheeks, I felt an unmistakable bond. You were almost two and I was almost sixty-two, but we were a pair of motherless daughters and that made us kindred spirits.

When your father first held out his hand to greet me, I understood why Belva adored him. Eddie Hart was the type of man you needed to keep away from busy streets because his big bright smile could cause a seven-car pileup in no time. He was friendly and warm, but in his light brown, almost golden, eyes, I could see a deep sadness lingered. Not surprising, after all the man endured.

According to Belva, a twenty-two-year-old Eddie Hart had

showed up at the Bel after the war ended, clutching Jack LeFarge's dog tags in his tanned, calloused hands. Belva never described that first encounter to me in detail, but Eddie Hart was one of eleven men pulled from shark-infested waters nearly two weeks after the USS *Juneau* had been torpedoed and sunk by the Japanese in the South Pacific near Guadalcanal. For five nights, Eddie and Jack clung to a doughnut raft together until Belva's son died from exposure. Before Eddie walked out of the library that day in 1945, Belva offered him a job as the facility's head caretaker, and within the week, he'd moved into the small cottage behind the library. Three months later, in a ceremony Belva insisted take place in the Main Reading Room, Eddie married Belva's favorite librarian, a young woman named Paige Leigh.

Belva didn't subscribe to the idea that married women shouldn't be employed, so Paige continued her librarian duties, and Belva doted on the young couple, treating them as if Eddie was her son, Paige her beloved daughter-in-law. After eight years of hoping for a baby, Paige finally discovered herself pregnant. On January sixth, you were born, and on the evening of your arrival, Belva threw a party in the Main Reading Room with pink champagne and pink balloons. Somewhere, there's a great photo of Belva and Eddie posed in front of the Bel, smoking cigars, and looking awfully pleased with themselves.

But everyone's joy was short-lived. Tragically, Paige passed away from a fever less than a week after your birth.

Bereft, Eddie considered returning home to his parents in Illinois, but Belva wouldn't hear of it. She hired a nurse and announced she would care for you while Eddie worked.

According to library lore, Eddie protested Belva's plan, saying, "It's swell of you to offer, but come on, a library's no place for a baby."

But Belva swept her arms toward the bookshelves surrounding

them and said, "Nonsense. Libraries are the perfect place to grow up. Just think how smart she'll be."

"But what will we do when she's actually moving around? She'll get into all the books, make messes, and will be nothing but trouble in here."

Don't forget, this was the 1950s, the age of McCarthyism, and any whiff of censorship made Belva very cross.

"Any trouble a young person can find in a library is the best kind of trouble," she said with a sniff.

So that settled it. You were raised in the library, and despite your father's reservations, you thrived. Though your parents bestowed the classically lovely name of Margaret upon you, soon everyone adopted the nickname Daisy, and it suited you perfectly. Within the library, you were our little flower. There was always someone eager to play with you or take you for a walk. And whenever your father had a spare moment, he spent it with you.

MEG, I'M not sure you remember this, but you were a first grader when your father met Annabelle. She'd started coming to the library to teach a weekly accounting class. Before long they were married and she moved into the cottage behind the Bel, where you and Eddie were living. While your mother, Paige, had always been confident and outgoing, Annabelle was shy and anxious, even insecure. Belva and I could see she competed with you for your father's attention.

When Eddie married Annabelle, it was clear he didn't consider her the great love of his life, not by a long shot. He wanted peace and stability, and a motherly figure for you. No one could blame him for that, but it was hard on Annabelle. She knew she was second fiddle to you and the memory of your mother.

In the face of Annabelle's increasing bitterness, your father's adoration of you never wavered, but he too could see the problem, and like most men are wont to do, he tried to keep you both happy, hoping everything would blow over. But it didn't. The arrival of your half sister, Edith, did little to ease Annabelle's difficulties. Your stepmother grew more territorial than ever, her criticism of you more relentless. Unsurprisingly, you turned uncharacteristically defiant.

That summer after you turned seven, Belva and I decided to bring you with us on our annual summer trip to my old house in New Hampshire. You loved everything about that vacation—exploring the small town of Hopkins, swimming in the pond, learning basic woodworking in my shop—but most of all, with an entire country separating you from your stepmother, Belva and I could see how you finally unfurled from the tense, guarded shell you'd taken refuge within. We vowed to do everything in our power to keep you protected from more strife, but I'm all too aware we failed.

DURING THE summer of 1960, I received a phone call from the old Duke of Lennox. His wife, Ursuline, the duchess, had died. In her will, she left her dollhouse to me.

The best way I could honor my friend was to exhibit her dollhouse. "Could you please ship it to me at the Belva Curtis LeFarge Library in San Francisco? People will get a real kick out of seeing Roughmore Park's grandeur."

But the duke cleared his throat, and I sensed a problem.

"I must ask a favor," he said.

"Of course, what?"

"The dollhouse mustn't be shown to anyone. At least, not for a long time."

"Why? This isn't about the driving school, is it? After all these years, surely that can't be considered controversial anymore."

"The old driving school isn't exactly the issue. During the '40s, the hunting lodge was used again for classified wartime purposes."

I remembered the subversive delight the duchess had taken in training women drivers. What unconventional roles for women had she cooked up for the last war? I then thought of another client of mine, a woman who revealed she'd been a codebreaker during the Second World War for the US government. Though no one wanted to discuss the topic, it was clear the fairer sex had played a far more involved role in the war than officials wanted us to believe. "Tell me, were women involved in whatever covert activities were happening at Roughmore Park?"

"Yes."

"And did the duchess oversee the operation?"

From the other end of the line, the old duke wheezed a gusty, exasperated sigh. "My dear, I really can't say anything more on the subject, but apparently in the late '40s, my wife tracked down several of the old chaps who'd worked with you originally and commissioned them to update the dollhouse's hidden compartment to reflect the hunting lodge's more recent activities."

I couldn't resist smiling. "Did she?"

"Unfortunately, yes. Bloody foolish risk, it was. If I'd been aware of what she was up to, I'd have sent those men straight home."

"What did you think they were doing?"

"Making repairs on the dollhouse, that kind of thing. Not until I read my wife's will did I find out about what they'd added. Anyway, please refrain from exhibiting the dollhouse until the year 2000, at the very earliest."

"But that's forty years from now! Practically an eternity."

"Exactly. By design. We cannot have any questions being asked about the role my wife and I played in the war. It's a subject best left alone. Do you understand?"

Reluctantly, I agreed to his conditions.

After the duke and I worked out the logistics over the phone and planned the dollhouse's trip to the United States, I found Belva sitting in an Adirondack chair, watching you, Tommy, and his two boys swim in the pond. "Did I just hear the telephone ring?" she asked, accepting the sweating glass of lemonade I pressed into her hand.

I took a seat in the empty chair beside her and told her the reason for the Duke of Lennox's call.

"I'm sorry to hear Ursuline's gone." She sipped her lemonade, lost in thought. "Ship the dollhouse to the library and we'll put it on display. It'll be a hit, I'm sure."

"He explicitly said I'm not to exhibit it. Not for ages. Years."

"That's absurd. Why?"

"Apparently it holds classified wartime secrets from the '40s."

"You're kidding."

"I'm not."

"Oh, for crying out loud."

"Far be it from me to reveal England's state secrets," I grumbled, leaning my head against the chair, staring out at the pond's rippled surface. "Sometimes I envy you for the way your library bears your name. I admire this about Walt too. There's no hiding what you both do."

"It's a bit egotistical of me, I suppose."

"You egotistical? Never!"

We laughed and then Belva took a long sip of lemonade before saying, "It must feel rewarding to have helped so many women tell their real stories."

"It has."

"But . . ." She looked at me pointedly.

"But what?"

"Well, it must also be frustrating to remain invisible. Isn't it?"

"The work speaks for itself. The dollhouses aren't about me."

"But . . ." I could tell it was taking all of Belva's restraint not to say more. She *always* had more to say.

“Not all of us want buildings named for ourselves,” I huffed.

“Perhaps not. But we don’t want to vanish either.”

I closed my eyes for a moment, letting the sun-warmed wood of the chair soak into my back. “I’ve never fussed over vanishing,” I finally admitted. “But now I’m not so sure. Is that selfish of me? Vain?”

“Women vanish far too easily. Your work shouldn’t be hidden. Art’s not meant to be locked away, my dear.” Belva rattled the ice in her glass. “It’s meant to connect us, to make us cry and laugh, to make us feel less alone.”

“But my art contains secrets belonging to other people.”

“I understand that. But eventually those secrets can be revealed. These women will get their day in the sun. And someday your work can be appreciated.”

After that conversation, I built a secret room in the Bel, where Belva and I stored her dollhouse and Roughmore Park. You, your father, Belva, and I were the only people who knew about that room. Of course, at that point, we thought we still had plenty of time together.

31
Tildy

2024

When Tildy steered Phyllis, Judy, Dale, and Emiko over to Roughmore House, she hoped to find its hidden compartment exactly where Cora had described it in her confession.

Before Tildy had gone to bed the previous night, she'd emailed one of her grad school friends, an archivist at the Imperial War Museum in London, to ask if she had any information about Roughmore Park's wartime role during the '40s. When Tildy awoke that morning, her friend had responded, confirming what Tildy had suspected.

Now Tildy circled to the rear side of the dollhouse, running her fingers along the base's simple panel below where the kitchen, pastry room, and other servant work areas were visible. Intermittently, she applied pressure, searching for an invisible spot where she hoped she'd feel some give, a release. And then, right in the middle, she felt it—a latch. She pushed the panel and it popped open.

Tildy squatted for a better view. Behind her, everyone else craned their heads to see better.

There, below the grand formal rooms of Roughmore House, a less grand space came into view. A cement floor covered in oil spills. A fully stocked tool rack, a stack of tires, an air compressor, a car jack, and other machinery filled the largest room. Charts diagramming engines and cars hung on the walls, alongside pegs filled with coveralls. Tildy sighed with relief to see the miniature driving school really existed. She could practically smell the gasoline, grease, and sweat. In the kitchen off to the side of the main garage, more domestic details appeared. On the small round dining table, a Battenberg cake was displayed on a plate with one slice removed to reveal its raspberry and lemon filling. A potted red geranium was visible on the kitchen's small window sill. The bunk room also showed several feminine touches. A pink bathrobe lay across one of the cots. A box of hair rollers was set on a card table. These finely observed details always marked Cora's work.

Tildy slid out a panel lined with cars, trucks, and motorcycles, held it aloft. "During the war, the Duke and Duchess of Lennox operated a driving school for women to train them to serve on the front as couriers, and drivers of ambulances and trucks."

Everyone gathered around the collection of tiny vehicles, marveling over them as Tildy continued to describe the driving school.

"But why did Cora need to keep this hidden for so long? Hasn't it been ages since anyone would consider a driving school controversial?" Phyllis asked.

Tildy explained what her archivist friend had shared in her email. "In 1940, Churchill established the Special Operations Executive, the SOE, an organization that launched an underground army of agents tasked with sabotage and resistance against the Nazis," Tildy explained. "The old hunting lodge where the duchess once housed her driving school was enlisted as a secret training ground for these agents."

"And let me guess," said Phyllis. "Some of those agents were women."

"Exactly. This room was added by the duchess in the late '40s." Tildy pointed to a cramped room off the garage, where four chairs surrounded a table. She pulled a magnifying glass from her pocket and held it up to study the maps dotted with tiny pinheads hanging on the walls. "See these? Agents used them to plan operations in

France, Belgium, and the Netherlands." She then removed a pair of tweezers from her pocket and reached into the room to lift a tiny one-piece canvas suit and backpack from one of the cubbies and placed them carefully on the palm of her hand.

"This was what agents wore when they parachuted into occupied France."

Next, Tildy removed a silk scarf no bigger than a square inch and a half from inside the backpack. "Agents wore these silk scarves because maps were printed on them. Look closely." Using the points of the tweezers, Tildy followed the faint lines printed on the scarf. "This one appears to be a map of France, Germany, and Italy, I think."

"Whoa," Emiko said. "Look at that tiny pistol on the table."

"Incredible, right? When the duchess died in 1960, very few people knew about the role women played in organizations like England's SOE or the US's Office of Strategic Services, the OSS. It wasn't until many of these agents started dying in the 1980s or thereabouts that their wartime contributions became public."

"Do you know who exactly trained at Roughmore Park?" Dale asked.

Tildy shook her head. "Not yet, but my friend at London's Imperial War Museum is working on it."

"Incredible." Dale rubbed his hands together eagerly, his eyes bright.

"If we go public with these discoveries, the Bel will be providing a new view into several historical figures everyone believed they knew," Tildy said. "This could be huge for the Bel's reputation. We'll be seen as groundbreaking, rewriting history, even. Perhaps this could attract a sponsor."

"Should I get to work on a press release about these findings?" Emiko asked Dale.

"Definitely," he said. "The sooner we can get the word out about the dollhouses, the better."

"Phyllis, what do you think, are you are really up for talking to the press about what your mom's dollhouse reveals?" Emiko asked.

As the group discussed logistics, Tildy rubbed her temples. Her plan seemed to be working. By next week, news of the Bel's discoveries would be out. People would finally learn about Cora and her dollhouses, even if there was no exhibit. Tildy chewed her lip. Why didn't she feel happier? She glanced at *Young Woman in Hat* and knew exactly why she felt miserable.

AN HOUR later, Tildy returned to her apartment and collapsed onto the white twill couch in her living room. After a foggy morning, a storm had moved in. Rain pounded the glass of the window behind her. Wind rattled its panes. When she checked her phone, several texts from Ben appeared. She tossed the phone onto the cushion beside her, unable to bring herself to answer. She had too much to hide from him.

Tildy pulled her knees to her chest and shivered. In the gloom, her white walls, white rug, and white IKEA coffee table and bookshelves all appeared the color of dingy dishwater. If Tildy were to make a dollhouse version of her apartment, it would be a sad little thing. Boring. Basic. Uninspired. Nothing communicated style, permanence, or personality.

But then Tildy hopped up and jogged to her bedroom, where she pulled down a box from the top shelf of her closet and rummaged through it. When she found what she wanted, her heart beat faster. She hugged the blanket to her chest, picturing her mother knitting it. One summer when Tildy had been little, she'd taken swim lessons at an outdoor pool near their house. While Tildy learned how to float on her back, hold her breath, kick and pull, her mother had worked on the blanket. It took all summer, but she'd finished it. For years Tildy kept the colorful blanket on her bed. First at home and then in her college dorm room, but when her mother died, Tildy had packed it away, not wanting the constant reminder of how much she'd lost. Now she burrowed her nose into the wool, breathing in the faint smell of coffee that always reminded her of her mother. Tildy returned to the living room and spread the blanket along the back of the couch. Its brightening effect was immediate. With its chunky stripes of lemon yellow, hot pink, and turquoise, its colors popped, bold and vibrant, two qualities Tildy normally shied away from. No more. The blanket and its bright colors were staying put. Tildy dropped back down on the couch, nestling up to it.

She pulled the knit blanket closer to her chin, thinking more about her mother. For as long as Tildy could remember, Meg Barrows had carried a tension. Even as a girl, Tildy had picked up on this and believed she didn't quite measure up to her mother's high standards. She interpreted her mother's unease as dissatisfaction. Tildy had tried so hard to please her. The good grades, exemplary behavior, her staying close to home—all of this had been done to satisfy her mother. But now Tildy understood the problem wasn't her. Her mother had been weighed down by her own problem: the guilt of a terrible secret.

32
Cora

1966–1974

Meg, I don't think it was possible to predict the trouble brewing in your stepmother, Annabelle, but pondering this has kept me awake many a night.

When your half sister, Edith, was a baby, her colic exacerbated Annabelle's brittle moods. Annabelle then suffered a series of miscarriages, each one chipping away at her temperament, making her more and more severe and demanding, especially when it came to you. The pattern of animosity between you two grew too deep to change.

Shortly after Annabelle successfully gave birth to your half brother, Henry, we learned of Belva's cancer. She had less than half a year to live, and one of the final items of business she wanted to settle was your future, Meg. By that point, it was winter of 1967. You were fourteen and the library's cottage was not big enough for you and Annabelle. In fact, all of San Francisco wasn't big enough for the two of you. As much as it pained your father to admit, he agreed: you needed a fresh start, somewhere far away from your stepmother, so Belva arranged for you to attend a boarding school in New Hampshire the following fall. We knew Belva would be gone by then. The plan was for me to deliver you there, help you settle in, and I'd live nearby in my house by the pond.

What we didn't expect was the Bel's fire.

It started late one April evening in the cottage. Your father and little Henry were asleep in the upstairs bedroom, while you and your half sister were in your beds downstairs in the small back room you shared. Annabelle had dozed off reading in the living room, alone.

The conflagration started in the kitchen. At blame, the toaster.

For some reason, you awoke, saw the smoke, and climbed out a nearby ground-floor window with Edith. Your cries for help from the library's front courtyard alerted the neighbors, who called the fire department. When help arrived, the firemen rescued your stepmother, but your father and Henry could not be saved in time.

Upon hearing the tragic news of your father and the baby, Annabelle grew hysterical. She raged that you had started the fire. None of the firemen took her accusations seriously—the official investigation later confirmed your innocence—but the reporters on the scene pounced on Annabelle's salacious story. Quickly, your stepmother was taken to the hospital for minor burns and sedation, but already the damage had been done and rumors of your guilt spread faster than the fire's flames. I took you and your stepsister to a nearby friend's house, where the three of us spent several days, hiding from the reporters, who were having a field day with the idea of a young arsonist igniting family drama. The shock and the enormity of the loss rendered you both mute for at least a week, maybe even a little longer. It was a difficult time, further complicated by Belva's imminent death, an event we were all dreading.

Your stepmother's fragile mental state didn't recover right away and she was moved to a nearby facility for a longer, more restful stay. Edith was sent to live with one of Annabelle's sisters. You and I moved into the Fairmont and spent our days tending to Belva, knowing her remaining time with us was limited. As Belva grew increasingly weak, it became clear we were counting down the hours, not days.

Out of respect for Belva's deep roots to the community, many of the reporters who had initially picked up the story of the fire stopped covering it. The news trailed away, especially under pressure from the fire department, another organization with loyal ties to Belva. But still, the damage was done. We were shaken by how quickly fortunes can change, how far too easily people can believe the worst in one another.

Do you remember that on the day Belva left us, you read *Jane Eyre* to her? Despite the pain we knew she was in, a faint smile played at her thin, dry lips as you read about Jane and Mr. Rochester. Everything about Belva's life had always been vivid and big, so I think she was relieved to go. She was never a woman who liked to lie down and rest.

In retrospect, I understand we asked too much of you. You survived the traumatic experiences with the fire, the loss of your father and half brother, and your stepmother's breakdown, only to be expected to endure another—and all at the tender age of fourteen. I've often wondered if it was a mistake to encourage you to go from Daisy to Meg and to take on your mother's maiden name—Leigh—when you left San Francisco. I thought a new name would offer you a fresh start, but now I realize the change implied shame and guilt, that you had a history to hide, despite your innocence of any wrongdoing. After a few months in New Hampshire, you appeared to be flourishing. You developed friends and excelled as a student, but I could always see you held everyone at an arm's distance. I recognized that quality in you because I've also spent a lifetime guarding myself too. It's exhausting.

I often think back to the first day I met Hugh, when he asked me if we all have one great love out there waiting for us. My life has been filled with mistakes, but I've always been correct about at least one thing: somehow our imperfect bodies hold endless reserves of love. The heart and its ability to expand is a truly mystifying phenomenon no doctor or scientist has ever properly explained. Though I'd loved Hugh completely, I'd found Belva and loved her too. And then, along with the endless pride and love I experienced with my son, Tommy, I found a daughter in you. How lucky I've been.

Over three weeks have passed since I commenced writing down these details of my life. I visited Dr. Haynes yesterday and he warned me I'm living on borrowed time. These recent episodes with my heart apparently constitute rehearsals for the big show that's sure to come soon. I know you think I'm morbid when I speak like this, but at my age, there's no time to mince words.

Meg, I've written this story to show you the mistakes I've made and urge you to let go of your own feelings of blame and shame over the fire and the breakdown of your family. None of it was your fault. I've spent the majority of my life nursing a similar guilt and carrying secrets and, trust me, no good comes from perpetuating these burdens. Now that this stack of typed pages reveals those secrets, I feel lighter, freer. Not bad for an orphan who once believed her life was over before it really began.

After you read this, please retrieve the dollhouses from their hiding place in the Bel. I hope once the stories behind Petite Hôtel LaFarge and Roughmore Park come to light, others will feel more confident to come forward with their dollhouses. Much can be learned from those women and their courageous stories.

And finally, Meg, don't hold on to your secrets until they've eaten you alive. Trust those you love to stand by you no matter what.

Signed,
Cora Hale Havilland
Hopkins, New Hampshire
August 25, 1974

33
Tildy

2024

It broke Tildy's heart to think of the shame her mother carried until the day she died. Meg Barrows's life had been indelibly marked by the guilt and sadness of a tragic misunderstanding. If Cora had actually sent the letter and Meg had read it, would she have heeded her advice? Would Tildy's mother have unburdened herself of her secrets? Tildy hoped so.

Sadly the arrival of this knowledge was too late.

Or was it?

Too many secrets were eating away at Tildy. She didn't like the person she'd become.

Overnight she'd turned into a liar. A thief.

Worst of all, she was betraying a friend.

Wrapped in her mother's handknit blanket, Tildy finally knew what she needed to do. Her mother may not have been able to read Cora's letter and learn from it, but Tildy could.

She picked up her phone, wincing at the sight of the unanswered text messages from Ben. Tildy couldn't hide from the truth forever. She called him. A moment later, Ben's face appeared on her phone's screen. His initial smile faded as he looked at her. "Are you okay?"

"I need to tell you something."

Tildy described finding his great-grandmother's confession. She explained how she hid the confession from Ben and stole the papers; and then, she recounted everything that had happened since she returned to San Francisco. The words were falling from her mouth and she couldn't stop them. She wasn't even sure she was making sense. Finally, she ended by saying, "I'm really sorry I lied to you and stole your great-grandmother's papers."

"Oh."

That was all he said. Tildy squinted at her phone's screen, trying to get a better look at Ben's face. Even in that one small word—*oh*—he sounded so bewildered, stunned. Anger, she could handle. She'd prepared for that. But disappointment? She felt gutted.

"I should have told you everything."

"Yeah." He frowned in confusion and refocused his gaze away from the phone screen. "I'm just so surprised. I thought we really hit it off."

"We did."

"Well . . . did we? I mean, you withheld something pretty major. You lied to me."

Tildy's heart felt like it cleaved in two. He was right. She should have just told him the truth from the beginning. "That was really stupid of me. I never should have done that."

"I . . ." He raked his hand through his hair. "I just don't know what to think. I really liked you."

Tildy nodded hopefully, not daring to breathe.

"But I need time to think about this. I don't know how we can be friends anymore if I can't trust you."

Tildy felt the sting of tears, but she blinked them back. "I understand. I'm so sorry."

"Well, I'm glad you finally told me," he said, sighing. "I wish things had worked out differently for us, but I hope the Bel survives."

Tildy shook her head, frustrated. She hadn't only called to apologize for lying about Cora. "Wait, before you go, let me just say one more thing: the best part of my trip to New Hampshire had nothing to do with finding stuff for the exhibit. It was meeting you."

Her stomach dropped. She'd never spoken so vulnerably. "I know you probably hate me now and want nothing to do with me, and I completely understand why you feel that way, but I really loved spending time with you. It's been a long time since I've laughed so much and had fun. Thank you for being so kind and generous to me. I just wish I hadn't messed everything up at the end."

He nodded sadly. "Listen, I should go. Good luck with the Bel. Keep whatever you need for the exhibit. My family can get it all back eventually."

Tildy didn't know what else she could add. "Thanks," she said weakly, but already Ben had ended the FaceTime call, leaving her staring at her phone screen.

Was that really the end? Tildy dropped her phone to the sofa cushion and buried her face in her hands, miserable. Why hadn't she just been honest with him? It was so unlike her to lie. She had been trying to do her job of protecting the Bel and its staff. She hoped he understood that—that she *was* someone who could be trusted.

Moments later, her phone rang with another FaceTime call. She pounced on it and answered. "Ben?" She was breathless as his face came into view again.

Outside, the sky had brightened, and the glare on Tildy's phone suddenly made it hard for her to see his expression.

"Sorry I hung up on you so quickly."

"Don't worry, I get it. I dropped a lot on you."

"You did. But I was thinking . . . your mom knew my great-grandmother?"

"She did. Cora was a big help to her. They were friends for a long time."

"Well then, it feels wrong that we shouldn't be friends anymore."

Tildy smiled, tilting her screen in a few different angles, trying to catch a glimpse of him through the glare. Her heart soared. She tried to sound calm. "I agree."

"But if we're only going to be friends, I guess that means no more kissing."

"Oh, right. Well, I . . ." Finally, she found the right spot to look at her phone without any glare. When she saw Ben's face, he was smiling.

"I'm just messing with you. You're such an open book. How did you ever hold back all that stuff about the forgery?"

"I have no idea. It was so stupid of me to think I could handle it by myself."

"You made some mistakes, but that's life. We've all been there."

Tildy blinked back tears. "I can't believe I lied to you like that."

"Wait a sec, don't start crying on me." Ben chuckled. "When you left, I knew something wasn't right."

"I felt terrible, but had no idea what to do."

He nodded. "So? What happens now?"

Tildy took a deep breath and made a decision. "I'm going to tell my bosses the truth. I have to."

"But won't that be the end of the Bel?"

"The truth needs to come out."

Ben nodded, but he looked worried. "I don't envy you."

"These secrets are killing me. You're sure you don't mind people finding out about Cora's forgery?"

"No, I'm not worried about being run out of town because my great-grandmother created a painting that everyone thinks is amazing. If anything, it's pretty messed up that Blanchet gets credit for *her* work."

Tildy nodded, thinking. "You're exactly right. Time to set the record straight."

34
Tildy

2024

Tildy sat at a sleek blond-wood table across from Lauren Kitterell and Dale Anderson on the thirty-fifth floor of a high-rise in San Francisco's financial district. They all held copies of Cora's confession.

Tildy had explained everything to Lauren and Dale: Cora Hale, the real artist behind *Young Woman in Hat*, Tildy's personal connection with the Bel, her mother's secrets, and how Tildy had covered it all up. Sheer terror gripped her. Her recent lies and mistakes went against a lifetime of following rules, of trying to please people. The idea of Lauren and Dale being mad at her was almost too much to bear.

From a folder in front of her, Tildy removed her resignation letter and pushed it toward the center of the table.

"I'm resigning because when I hid my findings about Cora Hale and her connection to my family, I took advantage of not only your trust in me, but the trust of everyone else who works at the Bel. I should have been completely honest."

When she stopped talking, the only sound in the room came from the slight hum of traffic, thirty-five floors below. Tildy's mouth felt so dry that her tongue seemed glued to the roof of her mouth.

A week ago, resigning from the Bel would have been inconceivable to Tildy. She loved the Bel, but now she was starting to see how she'd blurred the boundaries between her own life and the library.

In her mind, she'd made a grievous error in judgment and needed to be held accountable. It was the right thing to do. End of story.

What Tildy didn't tell Dale and Lauren was that when she'd signed her resignation letter earlier that morning, a surprising amount of relief had flooded her. Since her mother died Tildy had been working, working, working. First, to finish college; then, to care for her dad while juggling graduate school; and most recently, to keep the Bel afloat. The stress of it all had been taxing her more than she realized. She needed a break.

It was Dale who first lowered the photocopied pages of Cora's confession, his expression morose. "You know this jeopardizes everything we've worked for, don't you? If *Young Woman in Hat* really wasn't painted by Blanchet, there goes our one shot at survival."

Tildy took a deep breath. "That's what I thought initially too, but I had it all wrong. This is an amazing opportunity for the Bel to reveal that a masterpiece long believed to have been created by one of the widely accepted greats was actually painted by a largely unknown woman, Cora Hale, when she was seventeen year old. And then there are her dollhouses, which set the record straight in several important areas. Her body of work represents a major discovery. This is a big moment for the Bel to rewrite history. You were excited about Cora Hale and the dollhouses earlier. What changed?"

Dale ran a hand across his brow. "Gustave Blanchet's work commands enough market value to save the Bel; Cora Hale's doesn't. If he didn't paint *Young Woman in Hat*, we're in trouble. Tildy, who else knows about this?"

"No one," Tildy said, quickly deciding to leave Ben Havilland out of this discussion.

"I propose we keep it that way, at least for a little bit longer," Dale said.

Lauren removed her glasses to glare at him. “Are you suggesting we continue the fiction that Blanchet painted *Young Woman in Hat* while we sell it?”

“I’m suggesting we don’t go public with any of this until we’ve thoroughly investigated these claims. I mean, be reasonable. This whole thing sounds crazy.” He held up the photocopied pages with a bewildered expression. “Let’s just review where we are right now: for the last century, there’s never been a single doubt about the provenance of this portrait, but now, all of a sudden, we’re going to believe some story by an unknown woman claiming to be the artist behind this masterpiece?”

“But Belva wouldn’t have wanted it any other way,” Tildy said.

“I agree with Tildy. Why are we so committed to this being a Blanchet?” Lauren asked. “The revelation that Cora Hale’s extraordinary work has been found after being hidden all this time is very exciting. This could be exactly the type of story the Bel needs right now.”

“With all due respect, Lauren, you know how the art world works,” Dale said.

Lauren stacked Tildy’s resignation letter on top of her copy of Cora’s confession. “Let’s take a beat. Dale and I need to meet with the board to discuss what comes next. Tildy, we’ll be in touch with the details of your resignation.”

Tildy rose slowly on shaking legs, forcing herself to swallow. She couldn’t believe she’d quit. She had no idea what to do next. She couldn’t remember the last time she’d taken a break from working. Looking over their heads, she studied the clock on the Ferry Building. Beyond that, the Bay Bridge stretched out toward Oakland. A whole world existed beyond San Francisco.

35
Tildy

2024

Tildy was knitting a scarf and unraveling a big knot of yarn when Lauren Kitterell's name appeared on her phone screen. Two weeks had passed since Tildy resigned and although it was weird to adjust to days of unstructured time, she was getting the hang of it.

Tildy answered the call, and an hour later, she walked into Sacred Grounds in Cow Hollow to find Lauren stirring raw cane sugar into a latte. After they greeted each other, Lauren pushed a *People* magazine across their small table. "Have you seen this yet? I just snagged my copy and got you one too."

From the magazine's cover, ninety-seven-year-old Phyllis Mason beamed into the camera with the high wattage of a newly crowned beauty pageant queen. In one hand she held up a black-and-white photo of her parents, in the other, she clutched a copy of her mother's memoir *It's a Beautiful World* with its memorable vintage chocolate-and-beige zebra-stripe-patterned dust jacket. Splashed across the magazine's cover *The Truth About My Parents* was written in bright red letters.

"This is perfect," Tildy said, opening the magazine to the full spread of Phyllis and the miniature of Sawhill. "I saw her on *60 Minutes* last night too."

"She's very inspiring, isn't she? People are responding really well to her story." Lauren took a sip of her latte. "So, Tildy, I asked you to meet me because I have a number of things to discuss with you.

First, some good news: the engineering team that's been inspecting the stained-glass ceiling has found the damage isn't as bad as initially feared."

Tildy raised her hand to her chest, relieved. "No way. That's wonderful."

Lauren placed her mug back on the table, nodding. "Unfortunately the stained glass needs extensive repair and cleaning, but we'll have it back within eighteen months. In the meantime, a temporary skylight's being put in place to maintain the space's temperature and security. Sadly it lacks any of the artistry of the original, but it's better than nothing, right? It means the Bel can reopen in three days."

"Wow, that's great news."

"It is. And even better: our Cora Hale retrospective will take place at the Bel and will include all her work. *Young Woman in Hat* and the dollhouses."

"So the painting isn't being sold?"

"No, not anymore. An organization has stepped forward, eager to support our future work. When I first got the call, the CEO told me how they've been following the news about our dollhouse discoveries with great interest, but it was the revelation that Cora Hale was the artist behind *Young Woman in Hat* that really sealed the deal for them. Let's just say our new partner isn't afraid of surprises."

Tildy's mouth had fallen open and Lauren laughed. "Oh, and you'll be happy to know the CEO isn't Sean Finneman. You're really going to like her."

Her. Tildy nodded, pleased.

"The Cora Hale exhibit is getting us a lot of great attention." Lauren looked around the small coffee shop before leaning toward Tildy and lowering her voice. "Val Frederick's people have reached out to us."

Tildy pursed her lips. "Um, who's that?"

"What? You've never seen her? She's one of the most popular people on TV!"

"Sorry, I don't watch much TV."

"But haven't you seen a city bus lately?"

Tildy thought about the brightly colored ads covering the Muni buses clattering along the city's streets and the glamorous Black woman whose face smiled widely from their sides.

"Oh, right, are you talking about the lady with that show . . . is it *Open House*?"

"Bingo. *Open House* is a top-rated show right now. You've got to give it a try. I've been totally bingeing it. In each episode Val interviews a celebrity in their own home, so it's a part interview, part house tour. She's done a few episodes focused on historical figures, and apparently Val wants to do a special on the Bel with a focus on Belva, Cora Hale, and the dollhouses."

As each piece of Lauren's good news sank in, relief filled Tildy. The Bel would live on. That had been Tildy's goal all along and it was happening. The fact that the Cora Hale retrospective would open at the Bel and get a boost from all this publicity was even better news. As tears suddenly blurred her vision, Tildy realized that she wasn't just happy—she was also sad.

The Bel was moving on without her.

Although she'd been growing increasingly excited about making friends, traveling, picking up new hobbies like knitting, and eventually finding a new job, she would never get over leaving the Bel.

From the first time she'd walked into the library as a fifth grader, she'd experienced a comforting connection, one that struck deep down into her core. It was strange, this connection. She'd never fully been able to explain it until the discovery that her mother had spent her most formative years in the library. Once she'd learned about Meg's history at the Bel, it validated why the place resonated so strongly with Tildy. It was home. And home was so much more than a place. It was where her happiest and most challenging memories existed side by side, a reminder that she had survived grief and uncertainty and was strong enough to handle whatever lay ahead, even if that meant letting go of the very place she'd once thought she couldn't live without.

"That's amazing. Congratulations. I can't wait to see what comes next for all of you at the Bel," Tildy said, and she was surprised to realize that she meant it. "And you know, in my haste to resign, I never followed up on an interesting lead. In Cora's letter to my mother, she mentions creating more dollhouses than the three being prepared for the exhibit."

"Could you look into finding them?"

"Me?"

"Yes, you." Lauren pulled a folder from her large purse and handed it to Tildy. "On behalf of the board, I'd like to offer you the position of executive director of the Bel. You've proven you understand the vision of this library, and we think you're the best person to steer this organization, especially with this upcoming exhibit. All the offer details are in that folder."

Tildy's mouth fell open. "But what about Dale?"

"He's decided to retire."

Tildy stared at Lauren, slack-jawed. "Really? You want me back?"

"We do."

Tildy bit her lip, her face reddening with embarrassment when she thought about how many mistakes she'd made after she found the Bel's secret room. "But I acted very unprofessionally. I covered up so much."

"That's true and the board and I have discussed that, but if there's one thing that defines the Bel, it's that everything's personal with us. This isn't just a library or museum, it was Belva's home . . . and your family's. We understand your motivations for doing what you did and we assume you've learned a valuable lesson."

"I did. I've actually learned a lot of valuable lessons in the last few weeks."

"Well, the Bel would be honored to have you return. The job is yours if you want it. If you need to think about it for a bit, take your time."

Tildy didn't like making quick decisions. She preferred to mull over her options. She wrote out pros and cons lists. She wasn't shy about asking for advice from people she trusted.

But in this case, she didn't need to think at all.

36
Tildy

2024

The day before the Bel's Cora Hale exhibit was to open, Emiko crashed into Tildy's office carrying a white cardboard box stamped with Saks in black letters. "Excuse me, but what's *this*?"

Tildy looked up from her laptop. "Oh, that must be the dress I ordered for tomorrow night."

When Tildy had returned to working at the Bel, the top item on her to-do list was celebrating the library and its survival. At her first staff meeting as executive director, Tildy had posed a question to the group: "How about we kick off the Cora Hale retrospective with a launch party?"

Although Tildy expected a positive response, nothing prepared her for the fervor that took hold of everyone at the prospect of celebrating. The vote was unanimous.

As soon as the Bel issued a press release about the event, Val Frederick's producer called wanting to include the celebration in the *Open House* episode, so before Tildy quite knew what was happening, the famous star had offered to emcee the party. Overnight, the launch party went from being a small community-building event for the Bel's staff and library members to an A-list event with San Francisco's most notable movers and shakers—politicians, business leaders, and even several famous actors, musicians, and directors—angling for invitations.

Finally, Cora Hale was getting the recognition she deserved and so were her clients. The Duchess of Lennox, Joy Wolfe, and of course, Belva—each woman's complete story was finally being told, and it wasn't just the famous dollhouse owners receiving attention.

On the day Tildy returned to the library after her brief resignation, she checked the Bel's email account dedicated to tips about the dollhouses and found hundreds of unread messages. In the chaos of the Bel's closure, the emails had been forgotten. When Tildy sifted out the junk messages, she found an email from a woman named Esther Arden, who, after reading *People*'s story about Phyllis and Cora Hale, had gone up to her attic to take a look at her grandmother's dollhouse. To Esther's astonishment, she'd found Cora's stamp on the old dusty six-room dollhouse. Esther inspected the dollhouse closely and discovered tiny letters and numbers that composed patterns in the miniature's wallpaper. Mystified, she emailed the Bel.

Tildy, remembering the World War II codebreaker mentioned briefly in Cora's confessional letter, had called Esther immediately. Research followed, and with Tildy's help, Esther learned her grandmother, Maude Arden, had written her life story in code that Cora had used to create the dollhouse's wallpaper designs. It was ingenious. According to the coded message, Maude had worked for the US government during World War II as a member of an elite group of Black women cryptologists, a group whose wartime heroism was still classified.

"But hopefully now that we've found this artifact documenting what my grandmother and her friends did, their work will be declassified soon," Esther said to Tildy over the phone.

"Are you sure you want to put the dollhouse in the exhibit?"

"Oh, yes! Let's put a little pressure on the government to do the right thing. It's time for my grandma Maude and her colleagues to have their stories told!"

"I couldn't agree with you more."

TILDY FOUND six more emails sent by people coming forward with dollhouses made by Cora Hale. Like Maude's, these other dollhouses were nowhere near as big and fancy as the Hôtel LeFarge, Roughmore Park, and Sawhill, but they were every bit as enchanting. They revealed stories of ordinary women who'd kept extraordinary secrets about themselves in their dollhouses. Hidden careers and relationships, family secrets—the dollhouses told many important truths.

Four of the families were willing to contribute their dollhouses to the exhibit, but the remaining two others chose not to put their family's history on display for everyone to see, at least not yet, a decision Tildy understood and respected.

Tildy had a feeling more of Cora Hale's dollhouses remained undiscovered and forgotten in people's attics and basements. During her upcoming *Open House* interview with Val Frederick, Tildy planned to emphasize her hopes that the exhibit would encourage more people to look at their old family artifacts closely. Who knew what other hidden secrets would be revealed?

SINCE TILDY was going to appear on national television, she wanted to look good. She took the Saks box from Emiko and set it primly on her desk. With a pair of scissors, she sliced at the tape, and explained, "I considered doing one of those couture rentals, but then I just went for it and bought my own outfit."

After a moment of sifting through the tissue paper, Tildy lifted out a full-length silk dress. Depending on the light, its color shifted from silvery pale pink to a darker rose hue.

At the sight of the gown's tags, Emiko placed her hands on her hips. "No way. You seriously ordered a Lanvin?"

It had cost more than Tildy wanted to think about, so she just laughed. There was an upside to having a boring life: she'd saved a lot of money.

"Well, what are you waiting for? Try it on."

Tildy shut her office door, while Emiko pulled a shoebox out of the package, squealing, "Shoes too? Can I see them?"

"Go ahead," Tildy said as she undressed. The cool, whisper-thin silk fell around her, making her feel like she'd plunged into a pool, a sensation enhanced no doubt by the rippling and iridescence of the fabric as it settled on her.

Emiko admired the pair of silver sandals she'd removed from the box. "You're going to need to practice wearing these heels before you bust them out tomorrow." When she turned and saw Tildy, she dropped the shoes and shrieked. "Gorgeous!"

Never before had Tildy worn something that fit so perfectly and made her feel so stunning, so statuesque. She twirled over to her office's closet, opened its door, and struck a pose in front of the full-length mirror fastened inside.

Emiko peered over Tildy's shoulder, admiring the dress too. Its neckline was high and grazed Tildy's collarbone, draping artfully over her breasts and then cinching at her waist before falling to the floor in tiny pleats. When Tildy moved, the pleats expanded, making the skirt billow and sway gracefully. Tildy turned, still studying her reflection in the mirror by looking over her shoulder. The gown was backless. Only a pair of tiny spaghetti straps crossed in a spot near her shoulder blades.

"Til, if you wear this, you have to go the full distance." Emiko pulled her phone from her pocket to scroll through her contacts.

"What are you doing?"

"Calling La Vie on Union to schedule you a cut and blowout." Emiko turned away from Tildy and started talking to the person at the other end of the line before reaching back to inspect one of

Tildy's hands. She wrinkled her nose. "Yikes, can you squeeze her in for a manicure too?" She glanced at Tildy's feet. "And pedicure."

Tildy fingered her ponytail, feeling the crackly and dry ends of her hair. She actually did need a trim.

Emiko ended the call. "Fortunately I've done a little side PR work for that salon so they owe me a favor and can squeeze you in last minute."

"But I really don't have time for this today. I have so much to do to get ready for tomorrow."

"Consider this an intervention. You really need to take better care of yourself, but be careful. If you keep buying designer dresses like this, you're going to lose your street cred as a legit library nerd."

"Never. I'll always be happiest curled up at home in my pajamas, reading a book."

Emiko shooed her away playfully. "Fine. Now, get back to work, but when's Ben Havilland arriving? He needs to do a brief interview with *Open House* when he gets here."

"Tomorrow morning."

"Did you even bother to book him a hotel room or will he be staying with you?"

"Of course he's got a hotel room. We're not like that."

"Sure. Got it." Emiko gave an exaggerated wink as she left Tildy's office. "Just friends."

The truth was Tildy didn't know how to describe her relationship with Ben. Their conversations were interesting and fun, and yes, there was definitely flirting, but he lived on the other side of the country, so little chance existed of their relationship turning into something more serious. Tildy told herself that was fine. Her new friends from the knitting club kept her busy and she was considering taking tennis lessons too. Between planning the exhibit, her new job as the Bel's executive director, and her frequent calls with Ben, her days were packed.

Just then, a text notification pinged.

Ben: See you tomorrow

She stared at the text, swallowed, and before she could chicken out, she tapped a response:

Excited to see you!

And feeling truly hedonistic, she added two more exclamation marks.

Though the excessive punctuation felt decadent and wild, Tildy's fingers migrated over the emoji keyboard for a moment, but cooler heads prevailed. She hadn't completely lost her mind. Before she could get too carried away, she hit send, a giddy smile plastered across her face.

37
Tildy

2024

Never before had the Bel been busier than on the morning of the Cora Hale Retrospective launch party.

Over the weeks leading up to this day, Tildy had binged *Open House*, sometimes even staying up past her bedtime, telling herself she just needed to squeeze in *one more*. Everyone had been right. It was a great show and Val Frederick shined as its host. *Open House* offered a creative and smart format, a clever update on the classic celebrity interview.

At six o'clock in the morning, Val and her *Open House* crew strode into the Main Reading Room. Awed, Tildy studied Val, realizing how different she looked in real life. *Us Weekly* has it all wrong, Tildy thought. Stars, they're *not* just like us. Not one bit. For one thing, Val was tall. Crazy tall. Her legs alone looked six feet long. She glowed with a luminosity that exceeded the scope of normal human radiance.

When Val interviewed Tildy later on camera, those minutes passed in a blur of equal parts excitement and terror.

"Great job," Emiko told her afterward. "You sounded like such a pro."

"Really? I don't remember a single word I said."

"Don't worry, you were awesome," Emiko said over her shoulder as she hustled off to manage party logistics. Between the caterers and *Open House* crew, the Bel bustled as if it was Grand Central Station at rush hour. Tildy had never seen the place so busy, so alive.

THAT EVENING Tildy stood on the threshold of the ballroom, wearing her glamorous Lanvin gown, surveying the exhibit. The ballroom's freshly waxed parquet floors gleamed. Outside the room's French doors, the sky purpled with twilight. *Young Woman in Hat* hung in a place of honor next to the exhibit's entrance, along with sketches from Cora's notebooks and photos, all enlarged. The dollhouses, scattered throughout the ballroom, looked perfect. Each had a display describing its owner and her life. Many of these displays also included large reproductions of Cora's building plans.

Tildy's chest tightened with emotion as she took it all in. For the evening's guests, she hoped the exhibit would prove revelatory. Important women's stories had been overlooked for too long. But the journey of uncovering all this information had been more than an important history lesson for Tildy. It offered a whole new homecoming. She belonged at the Bel. That morning in her office before her colleagues arrived, Tildy wrote a letter to her mother's half sister, Edith Hart, the woman Tildy believed to be her aunt. With the help of one of the library's genealogy databases, Tildy had located Edith, living in the Outer Sunset, not far from the beach, married with three grown children of her own. Rather than going down the rabbit hole of searching for these people on social media and trying to figure them out, Tildy wouldn't jump to conclusions. She'd wait and see how Edith reacted to her letter. Normally this type of uncertainty would have sent her into an anxious tailspin, but after writing the letter, Tildy had sealed it, placed it on a corner of her desk to be mailed, and felt surprisingly peaceful. She already had the family she needed.

"So how's everything looking?"

Tildy turned around now to see Emiko. "Amazing."

"Where's Ben?"

"He should have landed hours ago, but I haven't heard a peep."

Tildy checked her messages. No texts. Disappointment nagged at her. "Hopefully he's on his way."

"Keep me posted. When he arrives, I need him for the *Open House* crew." Emiko hurried away.

With a sigh, Tildy pictured Ben stuck at an airport in the middle of the country somewhere, rerouted and delayed.

With every passing minute, the party grew louder. People kept coming up to Tildy to congratulate her. Jazz played over the speakers, and the sound of conversations and laughter filled the air.

Cocktail shakers clacked with ice as the bartenders bounced them up and down. Nearby a row of martini glasses filled with pink liquid glowed; the evening's signature drink.

The Coratini

1.5 units Hendrick's Gin
1 unit St-Germain
2 units fresh pink grapefruit juice
Garnish with a fresh slice of grapefruit and a sprig of rosemary

Now Tildy searched the ballroom, hoping to spot Ben, but he was nowhere to be seen. Instead another familiar figure pushed her way through the crowd toward her.

"Yoo-hoo, Tildy," Phyllis said, waving.

When the old lady reached Tildy, she handed her a small jewelry box. "I made you something."

Tildy took it, her mouth a small O of surprise.

"Well, go ahead. Open it."

Tildy lifted the box's lid to reveal what looked like a small, single earring. Swirls of tiny strips of paper curled into the shape of clouds.

"It's one of my mobiles in miniature. I hope you can hang it in my mother's dollhouse. My eyesight's not what it once was, so this little stinker took me forever, but it was worth it. More than anyone, Cora encouraged my career as an artist. It would be one of the great honors of my life for my art to be displayed within the dollhouse she created for my mother."

"I can't think of a more fitting tribute to you, your mother, and to Cora. Thank you, it's wonderful." Tildy held up the mobile, admiring it. "I've been meaning to ask you something, Phyllis. Why do clouds interest you so much?"

"They've always represented a source of comfort for me. When I was a girl, I hated traveling. I could never figure out why I didn't share the same hunger for adventure that propelled my parents. In fact, I felt slightly ashamed, figuring it was cowardly of me. Anyway, wherever we went, no matter what strange foods surrounded me or uncomfortable hammock or cot I had to sleep upon, the clouds remained the same. Those ten shapes can be found all over the globe. I think I focused on them to feel safe. Later, after my parents died, I thought of them every time I looked at the sky."

Tildy leaned forward and gently hugged Phyllis.

"Is it true the exhibit's being extended?" Phyllis asked.

"Yes. Tickets for the next three months have already sold out." Tildy shook her head, amazed, thinking back to that day when a school bus broke down in front of the Bel. She could hardly believe how the library's fortunes had changed in the three months since she'd found the secret room.

A woman's voice suddenly boomed through the speakers, welcoming everyone to the party.

Tildy and Phyllis turned to the small platform next to the bar, where Val Frederick perched over her audience, looking resplendent in a form-fitting silvery, glittering dress. She held a microphone and waved.

"Thank you for joining us tonight to celebrate this remarkable exhibit. I think we can all agree it's long overdue," Val said before introducing Lauren Kitterell, who stepped up to join her on the dais.

As Lauren described the Bel's mission, Tildy snaked through the crowd. When she reached the small stage, she climbed up alongside them. After Lauren handed her the mic, Tildy squinted under the bright lights and thanked everyone for coming, hunting the faces in front of her for a glimpse of Ben.

He wasn't there.

Tildy refocused. "When I look at Cora Hale's work, I wonder how many other women's stories are out there, waiting to be uncovered? *Young Woman in Hat* and the dollhouses remind us how easy it is to disappear, but this exhibit is about claiming one's place in the world, not disappearing."

The room seemed to vibrate as people applauded.

"It's no understatement to say Cora Hale has saved the Bel," Tildy said. "We needed help, and an important partner arrived just when we needed them. It gives me great pleasure to introduce Dr. Nera Patel, the CEO of YourStory.com."

A woman in a full-length emerald-colored satin gown took to the dais with a gracefulness that belied the fact that she was wearing three-inch-high stilettos. "This exhibit represents our core beliefs at YourStory: we celebrate curiosity and creativity," Nera said, flashing a smile at Tildy, "and are willing to investigate our beliefs and histories, even if the results have the potential to make us uncomfortable and challenge us at first."

As Nera continued speaking, Tildy had the sense the woman could be trusted to deliver both good and bad news with an equal measure of calm confidence. She had the steadiness you wanted in a surgeon or airline pilot. The Bel was safe. Tildy's eyes swam with happy tears.

At that moment, Ben appeared in the front row. His gaze locked with Tildy's. With everyone focused on Nera, Tildy slipped off the platform and headed out of the ballroom.

When she stopped in a quiet spot in the Main Reading Room, Ben was right behind her. "There you are," he whispered into her ear. His warm breath on her neck made goose bumps rise on her flesh. "Don't you want to hear more about YourStory.com?" Ben asked.

Tildy shook her head. "I know all about it. The Bel will be fine now." She paused, admiring Ben's stylish dark blue suit. "I'm so glad you made it. You look great."

"My sister said nothing in my wardrobe was cutting it so she insisted I go to Boston to find something worthy of such a big occasion. But who cares how I look? Look at you! Perfect in pink."

Momentarily shy, they held each other's hands, smiling.

Tildy had feared that seeing Ben in person wouldn't quite live up to the hopes she had for their reunion. Sure, all their FaceTiming and texting had been great, but maybe their chemistry wouldn't be as good as she remembered. But as soon as Ben took ahold of her hand, she knew her concerns were silly. A shiver of anticipation traveled straight up her spine. She was tired of playing everything safe, of planning every minute of her day. Ben's twinkling eyes made her dizzy. This feeling, this electric tingling toes, belly-on-fire, heart-in-throat feeling—it could no longer be ignored. Spontaneity took hold in her, an impulse she'd been suppressing for far too long.

"I want you to stay longer. Do you really have to fly back to New Hampshire tomorrow?" Tildy asked, tugging him close enough to breathe in the scent of soap clinging to his neck.

"Actually, I don't. My school is closed for spring break so I've got a full week out here."

"Oh, that's great!"

"And you know, I've been thinking. When the school year ends, it could be a good time for me to leave New Hampshire and try something new."

"Really? Like what?"

"I've got a few possible plans, but I could see myself spending more time on the West Coast."

"Wow, that's—that's wonderful."

"So what's coming up on your schedule later this year?"

Tildy, who always knew exactly what she was doing every day, down to the minute, laughed and shrugged. "Hopefully spending more time with you."

"Really?" he asked, pulling her closer.

She nodded. For the first time in her life, Tildy didn't worry about what would happen next.

Author's Note

In late 2020, after emailing my editor the manuscript for my fourth novel, a story about the hardships and heartbreak of war, I cleaned my office of the detritus that always accompanies the final push of meeting a deadline—notecards, old photos, books, empty coffee mugs, and chocolate bar wrappings—and my gaze caught on the dollhouse that had been in my family for five generations. Since my daughters had outgrown it, the antique had been serving as a small bookshelf. I studied it, noting the chipped exterior paint and the faded, curling edges of wallpaper lining its interior, and thought back fondly to the hours I spent as a child, sitting in front of that dollhouse, lost in my imagination. The dollhouse had offered me a gateway into a world of creativity. It was my first foray into storytelling, and I learned to sew, knit, quilt, draw, and build miniature furnishings because of it. Over forty years later, as I considered the many ways that old family artifact had influenced my life, I realized my next book needed to be about dollhouses.

For the next few months I tinkered with different ideas, searching for my entry into this new story. I read about famous historic dollhouses and miniaturists, including the Rijksmuseum's collection from the seventeenth century, Queen Mary's Dolls' House, the silent film actress Colleen Moore and her fairy castle dollhouse, the Thorne Rooms, and Walt Disney, but what stuck with me most were several articles about a 2017 Smithsonian exhibit on Frances Glessner Lee (1878–1962). Lee, a Chicago heiress, combined her love of miniatures with her passion for forensic science (a weird pairing to be sure!) to create a collection of dioramas intended to help law enforcement agents solve crimes. These dioramas, known now as the Nutshells of Unexplained Death, each portray a miniaturized grisly crime scene and all the clues needed to answer the mystery of what happened. I had *zero* interest in writing a scary novel about crime scenes, but I *loved* the concept of a dollhouse containing clues about its previous owner's life. From this idea, I really let my imagination run wild. I wanted to immerse myself in a world where dollhouses solve mysteries, where art saves the day.

I pictured one of my favorite places—San Francisco—and an old library, a combination of the Isabella Stewart Gardner Museum and the JP Morgan Library, and wondered what would happen if a collection of mysterious dollhouses was found hidden inside it? And what would happen if these dollhouses, which had been owned by notable women of the early 1900s, revealed unknown aspects of their lives and rewrote history?

From those questions, a fictional story populated by characters inspired by real-life women took shape. Belva Curtis LeFarge was inspired by several real-life figures, but most notably Isabella Stewart Gardner (1840–1924) and her famous museum in Boston. Although Cora Hale is completely fictional, there's a parallel to be made to Carrie Stettheimer (1869–1944), a theater set designer who re-created her family home in miniature and commissioned several famous friends, including Marcel Duchamps, to create miniature art for her dollhouse. Two women—Dorothy Levitt (1882–1922) and Edith Vane-Tempest-Stewart, Marchioness of Londonderry (1878–1959)—served as the muse for my Ursuline Maine Newcomb, the Duchess of Lennox. The character of Joy Wolfe took shape based on Amelia Earhart (1897–1937) and Osa Johnson (1894–1953). My mysterious codebreaker was informed by Elizebeth Friedman (1882–1922) and a section of Liza Mundy's *Code Girls* in which she says the work of Black women codebreakers remains classified and, therefore, largely unrecognized.

There's a long, rich history of people turning to dollhouses and miniatures to escape their problems and find a measure of comfort and control during difficult and uncertain times, and 2020 was no different. During my research, I came across a recent *New York Times* article about how people were creating modern dollhouses and sharing their work on Instagram to stave off loneliness and build community, and once I began combing through social media posts, I was hooked. Soon I'd stripped our old family dollhouse down to its original wood and was remodeling it—as part of my research for this book, of course, but the truth is I was having fun. *A lot* of fun.

While I sanded and slathered the dollhouse in primer, ideas for this story came to me, and when I waited for glue and paint to dry, I'd turn to my laptop and slide down rabbit holes of research. Not only was I discovering fascinating historical figures, but I felt myself drawing closer to the women of my own family, especially my grandmother, who was very artistic and an avid collector and maker of miniatures. As I carried on her work by breathing new life into the pieces she left behind, I found joy. It's very satisfying to transform an old forgotten item and produce something new and beautiful. By making art and tapping into history, I found the perspective I needed to help me make sense of an uncertain and challenging world.

Acknowledgments

I could not have written this book without my extraordinary agents, Michelle Brower and Danya Kukafka. From the first moment I told them I wanted to write about dollhouses, they were all-in, and I'm grateful for their enthusiasm, expertise, and advocacy. I'm also indebted to the big heart and keen eyes of my editor, Liz Stein, who understood my vision and made it so much better. To Liate Stehlik and the incredible team at William Morrow and HarperCollins, thank you.

Each of my books has offered an adventure in research, but this one was unique with its hands-on learning experience. Thank you to Bill Robertson, who spent hours with me on the phone brainstorming ways to make this story come to life. His marvelous work as a miniaturist and tool historian can be admired at @wmrrobertsonminiatures. Another big thank-you goes to Becky Gannon, who first connected with me about her *Mad About Miniatures* podcast, but we developed a friendship that has endured well beyond the interview taping. She introduced me to the Instagram, YouTube, and Etsy worlds of miniaturists who have inspired and taught me so much. I also learned a ton from Steve Dando and my Sawdust Therapy classmates at Woodcraft of Seattle.

Though I complain about the Pacific Northwest's weather, my good fortune to live in a very bookish place cannot be emphasized enough. The first draft of this book came together during a retreat at the University of Washington's Whiteley Center on San Juan Island during the spring of 2021, a time when I was practically chewing through the walls of my house and ready to hide out somewhere different. More recently, I've found a wonderful place to work at the downtown Seattle Public Library's Eulalie and Carlo Scandiuzzi Writers' Room. And libraries aren't just places to write and read—I've had a blast leveling up my miniature-making skills with cool technology and fun people at the makerspaces in Bellevue Library and Federal Way Library, both part of the King County Library System. My friends at Humanities Washington have also provided a big boost by introducing me to new readers throughout the state—thank you. The Seattle area's amazing community of authors, booksellers, and librarians is truly unparalleled.

Endless love to Kate, Caroline, and Dave, my parents, extended family, and friends, who never tire (or at least disguise their fatigue well) of my constant talk about books, reading, and dollhouses.

Last but not least, if you're reading this, thank YOU! I know I'm biased, but readers really are the best people. I'm grateful for your support.

About the Author

A native New Englander, Elise Hooper spent several years writing for television and online news outlets before getting an MA and teaching high-school literature and history. Her debut novel, *The Other Alcott,* was a nominee for the 2017 Washington Book Award. All of her books—*Learning to See*, *Fast Girls*, *Angels of the Pacific*, and *The Library of Lost Dollhouses*—tell the stories of extraordinary but overlooked women. Elise lives in Seattle with her husband and two daughters.

Discover more from beloved author

ELISE HOOPER

ANGELS OF THE PACIFIC

"Absolutely riveting. A stay-up-all night read about two very different women who discover just how strong they can be—and just how much they'll dare—during the brutal Japanese occupation of the Philippines in World War II. This story of endurance and sisterhood will have you turning pages late into the night."

—**Lauren Willig**, *New York Times* bestselling author

FAST GIRLS

"Will hurl you down the track of American history and have you rooting for some of the toughest underdogs ever to aspire to Olympic gold. Three of the fastest girls in history finally get their day in the sun, and we get to bask in their glory. I couldn't put this one down."

—**Kerri Maher,** author of *The Kennedy Debutante* and *The Girl in White Gloves*

LEARNING TO SEE

"For photo buffs and others familiar with her vast body of work, reading the book will be like discovering the secret backstory of someone they thought they knew. . . . Seamlessly weaving together the time, places, and people in [Dorothea] Lange's life. . . . Hooper excels at humanizing giants."

—***Washington Post***

THE OTHER ALCOTT

"Elise Hooper's thoroughly modern debut gives a fresh take on one of literature's most beloved families. To read this book is to understand why the women behind *Little Women* continue to cast a long shadow on our imaginations and dreams. Hooper is a writer to watch!"

—**Elisabeth Egan,** author of *A Window Opens*

DISCOVER GREAT AUTHORS, EXCLUSIVE OFFERS, AND MORE AT HC.COM